02

31 JAN 23

CW00411583

17

To renew this book, phone 0845 1202811 or visit
our website at www.libcat.oxfordshire.gov.uk
You will need your library PIN number
(available from your library)

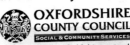

3303265608

'He said that
Shamil had
ordered Hadji
Murat to be taken
dead or alive.'

Leo Tolstoy
The Cossacks and Hadji Murat

Translated and with Notes by
David McDuff *and* Paul Foote

PENGUIN BOOKS

PENGUIN BOOKS

UK | USA | Canada | Ireland | Australia
India | New Zealand | South Africa

Penguin Books is part of the Penguin Random House group of companies
whose addresses can be found at global.penguinrandomhouse.com

 | Penguin
Random House

A CIP catalogue record for this book is available from the British Library

ISBN: 978-0-241-26189-7

www.greenpenguin.co.uk

MIX
Paper from
responsible sources
FSC
www.fsc.org   FSC® C018179

Penguin Random House is committed to a
sustainable future for our business, our readers
and our planet. This book is made from Forest
Stewardship Council® certified paper.

Leo Tolstoy

Born 1828, Yasnaya Polyana, Russia
Died 1910, Astapovo, Russia

The Cossacks was first published in 1863 in the Russian literary magazine *The Russian Messenger*. *Hadji Murat* was written in 1896–1904 and was published posthumously in 1912.

Contents

The Cossacks   1

Hadji Murat   229

Notes   389

The Cossacks

A Caucasus Tale of 1852

Everything has grown quiet in Moscow. At rare, rare intervals the squeak of wheels is heard somewhere along the winter street. There are no lights in the windows now, and the street lamps are extinguished. From the churches float bell sounds which, as they sway above the sleeping city, remember the morning in prayer. The streets are empty. At rare intervals somewhere a nocturnal cab driver kneads sand and snow with narrow runners and, reaching the next corner, falls asleep, waiting for a fare. An old woman passes on her way to church where already, reflected on the golden mountings, asymmetrically placed wax candles burn with a rare, red light. Working folk are already rising after the long winter night, and going to their labours.

For the gentlefolk, however, it is still evening.

In one of the windows of Chevalier's, light shines illegally from behind a closed shutter. At the entrance stand a carriage, a sleigh and cabs, their backs crowded close together. There is a post troika there, too. The yardkeeper, muffled up and shrinking from the cold, seems to be hiding round the corner of the house.

'What are they beating the air about now?' thinks the lackey who sits in the entrance hall with a pinched and sunken face. 'This always happens when I'm on duty!' From an adjacent brightly lit room come the voices of three young men who are having supper. They sit in the room at a table on which stand the remains of supper and wine. One of the men, small, rather neat, thin and not very good-looking, is watching his departing companion with tired, kindly eyes. Another, a tall man, lies beside the table that is strewn with empty bottles, toying with the key of his watch. A third, in a new-looking sheepskin jacket, is pacing about the room, stopping now and then to crack an almond in fingers that are rather thick and strong, but with clean nails, and keeps smiling at something; his eyes and face are burning. He speaks with warmth and gestures of the hands; but it is plain that he cannot find the words, and all the words that come to him seem inadequate to express everything that has welled up within his heart. He smiles all the time.

'Now I can say everything!' says the man who is leaving for the south. 'It's not that I'm trying to justify myself, but I should like you, at least, to understand me as I understand myself, and not in the way that vulgar opinion looks upon this matter. You say I am guilty in her regard,' he says to the other, who is looking at him with kindly eyes.

'Yes, you are,' replies the small, not very good-looking man, and even more kindliness and weariness seem to be reflected in his gaze.

'I know why you say that,' the man who is leaving goes on. 'You think that to be loved is as great a happiness as to love, and if a man once attains it, it will be enough to last him for the whole of his life.'

'Yes, quite enough, my dear fellow! More than enough,' continues the small, not very good-looking man, opening his eyes and closing them again.

'But why shouldn't one love, too?' says the man who is leaving, falls into reflection and looks at his friend almost with compassion. 'Why shouldn't one be the one who loves? Love doesn't come just like that. No, to be loved is a misfortune, it's a misfortune when one feels guilty because one isn't giving what one can't give. Oh my God!' He made a gesture with his arm. 'I mean, if only it could have happened reasonably, and not all topsy-turvy: it always seems to happen in a way that's somehow alien to us, and doesn't suit us. Why, it's as if I'd stolen that feeling of love. And you think the same; don't try to deny it, you can't help thinking so. But can you credit it: of all the stupid and vile things I've managed to do in my life, and there have been many, of this one thing alone I do not repent, and cannot repent. Neither at the beginning nor later on did I lie, either to myself or to her. It seemed to me that at last I had fallen in love, but then I saw it was an involuntary lie, that one cannot love like that, and I could go no further; and she went. Was I to blame because I couldn't go on? What was I to do?'

'Well, it's all over now!' said his friend, lighting a cigar in order to ward off sleep. 'There's just one thing: you haven't yet been in love, and you don't know what it means to be in love.'

The man in the sheepskin jacket was about to say something again, and he clutched his head. But what he wanted to say remained unsaid.

'Haven't been in love! No, it's true, I haven't. But on the other hand within me there's a desire to love, and nothing could be stronger than that desire! But then again, does such a love even exist? Something unfinished always remains at the end. Well, what can one say? I've made a mess, made a mess of my life. But now it's all over, you're right. And I feel that a new life is beginning.'

'Of which you will again make a mess,' said the man who was lying on the sofa toying with the key of his watch; but the man who was leaving did not hear him.

'I'm both sad and glad to be going,' he continued. 'Why sad? I don't know.'

And the man who was leaving began to talk only about himself, failing to notice that this did not interest the others as much as it did him. A man is never such an egoist as at the moment of emotional rapture. It seems to him that at that moment there is nothing more excellent and inter-esting than himself.

'Dmitry Andreich! The coachman won't wait any lon-ger!' said a young house serf, entering in a fur coat, a scarf tied round his head. 'The horses have been there since twelve, and it's four now!'

Dmitry Andreich cast a glance at his servant Vanyusha. In Vanyusha's scarf, in his felt boots, in his sleepy face, he heard the voice of a different life that summoned him – a life of toil, privations and activity.

'Indeed it is! Farewell!' he said, feeling for the undone fastener on his coat.

In spite of advice to give the coachman another tip, he put on his cap and stood in the middle of the room. The friends exchanged kisses once, twice, paused and then kissed for a third time. The man in the sheepskin jacket went over to the table, drank the glass of champagne that stood on it, took the small, not very good-looking man's hand, and blushed.

'No, I'll say it all the same . . . I must and can be frank with you, because I love you. I mean, you love her, don't you? I've always thought so – yes?'

'Yes,' replied his friend, smiling even more gently.

'And perhaps . . .'

'If you please, sir, I've been told to put out the candles,' said the sleepy lackey, who had listened to the last part of the conversation and wondered why the gentlefolk always talked about the same thing. 'Whom shall I make the bill out to, sir? Yourself, sir?' he added, turning to the tall man, and knowing in advance whom to turn to.

'Yes, to me,' said the tall man. 'How much?'

'Twenty-six roubles.'

The tall man thought for a moment, but said nothing and put the bill in his pocket.

Meanwhile the other two went on with their own conversation.

'Goodbye, you're an excellent fellow!' said the small and not very good-looking gentleman with the mild eyes.

Tears came to the eyes of both. They emerged on to the front steps.

'Oh, by the way,' said the man who was leaving, turning to the tall man and blushing as he did so. 'Please settle Chevalier's bill and then write to me.'

'Very well, very well,' said the tall man, putting on his gloves. 'How I envy you!' he added quite unexpectedly, when they were out on the front steps.

The man who was leaving got into the sleigh, wrapped his fur coat about him and said: 'Well, come on then! Let's be off . . .', and even moved over in the sleigh a bit in order to make room for the man who had said he envied him; his voice trembled.

The tall man said: 'Goodbye, Mitya, may God help you to . . .' All he wanted was for the other man to leave quickly, and so could not say what he wanted.

They were silent for a moment. Again someone said: 'Goodbye.' Someone said: 'Ready!' And the coachman set the horses in motion.

'Get on with it then, Yelizar!' cried one of the farewell party.

The cabmen and the coachman began to stir, clicking their tongues and twitching the reins. The frozen carriage began to squeak across the snow.

'He's a splendid chap, that Olenin!' said one of the farewell party. 'But why on earth does he want to go to the Caucasus, and as a cadet, too? I wouldn't do it for anything . . . Will you be dining at the club tomorrow?'

'Yes, I will.'

And the farewell party dispersed.

The man who was leaving felt warm, even too hot in his fur coat. He sat down on the bottom of the sleigh and undid the coat, and the dishevelled team of three horses dragged itself from one dark street to the next past houses he had never seen before. Olenin felt that only people who were setting out on long journeys ever travelled through these streets. All around it was dark, silent and dreary, but inside he was so full of memories, love, regret and pleasantly choking tears . . .

'I love them! Love them dearly! They're splendid! First-rate!' he kept repeating, and felt like crying. But why did he feel like crying? Who was splendid? Whom did he love so dearly? He did not really know. Sometimes he studied some house and wondered why it was built so strangely; sometimes he wondered why the driver and Vanyusha, so alien to him, were so close to him, like him being shaken about and swaying with the movement of the horses as they stretched the frozen traces, and again said: 'They're splendid fellows, I love them!' Once he even said: 'How it takes one! Excellent!' and wondered why he had said it, asking himself: 'I say, I'm not drunk, am I?' He had, it was true, drunk his share, a couple of bottles of wine, but it was not the wine alone that was having this effect on him. He remembered all the sincere – so it had seemed to him – words of friendship that had been shyly, almost spontaneously uttered to him before his departure. He remembered the handshakes, the glances, the silences, the sound of a voice saying: 'Goodbye, Mitya!' – when he was already out in the sleigh. He remembered his own determined, frank sincerity. And it all had a touching significance for him. Before his departure not only friends and relatives, not only people who were indifferent to him but also those who were unsympathetic to him and did not wish him well – they all seemed to have agreed among themselves to love him more deeply, to forgive him, as before confession, or death. 'It may be that I am not to return from the Caucasus,' he thought. And he felt that he loved his friends, and that there was someone else he loved as well. And he felt sorry for himself. But it was not love for his friends that softened and exalted his heart to a point where he was unable to repress meaningless words that uttered themselves of their own accord, and it was not love for a woman (he had never yet been in love) that had put him into this state of mind. Love for himself, ardent, full of hope, a young love for all that was good in his soul (and now he felt that there was nothing but good in it), made him weep and mutter incoherent words.

Olenin was a young man who had never graduated, never served anywhere (apart from an obscure position in some office), squandered half his fortune, and reached the age of twenty-four without having chosen any career or ever having done anything much at all. He was what in Moscow society is called '*un jeune homme*'.

At the age of eighteen he was free, as only rich young men of the 1840s could be free, rich young men who had lost their parents at an early age. For him there were no fetters, neither physical nor moral; he could do anything he pleased, he lacked nothing and was bound by nothing. He had neither family, nor fatherland, nor faith, nor wants. He believed in nothing and acknowledged nothing. But, while acknowledging nothing, he was not a gloomy, blasé or argumentative young man, but was, on the contrary, forever in the grip of some new enthusiasm. He had decided that there was no such thing as love, yet the presence of a young and attractive woman never failed to root him to the spot. He had long known that honours and rank were nonsense, but felt an involuntary sense of satisfaction when Prince Sergiy came up to him at a ball and spoke to him kindly. But he yielded to all his enthusiasms only in so far as they did not bind him. As soon as he yielded to an aspiration and began to sense the approach of toil and struggle, the trivial struggle with life, he instinctively hurried to tear himself away from the emotion or the task, and restore his own freedom. It was thus that he embarked

upon society, the civil service, farming, music, to which
at one time he had planned to devote his life, and even the
love of women, in which he did not believe. He reflected
on where he should put all the strength of youth that is
only present in a man once in his life – into art, science,
the love of a woman or practical activity – not the strength
of intellect, emotion, education, but that unrepeatable
impulse, that power that is granted to a man only once to
make of himself anything he wants, and in the way that
catches his fancy, and of the whole world anything he likes.
There are, it is true, men who lack this impulse and who,
as soon as they embark upon life, shoulder the first yoke
that comes along and honestly labour beneath it for the
rest of their lives. But Olenin was too intensely conscious
of the presence within him of that omnipotent god of
youth, that ability to transform oneself into a single desire,
a single thought, the ability to will and do, the ability to 11
throw oneself headlong over a fathomless precipice, without knowing why or wherefore. He bore this realization
within himself, was proud of it and unconsciously happy
in it. Until now he had loved only himself and could not
but love himself, as he expected only good of himself and
had not yet had time to become self-disillusioned. As he
left Moscow, he was in that happy, youthful state of mind
in which, aware of past mistakes, a young man suddenly
says to himself that all that was not 'it' – that all that went
before was accidental and unimportant, that earlier he had
not really wanted to live *in earnest*, but that now, with his
departure from Moscow, a new life was beginning which
would contain no more of those mistakes, no remorse, and
probably nothing but happiness.

As is always the case on a long journey, for the first two
or three stops the mind remains in the place from which
one sets out, and then suddenly, with the first morning
encountered on the journey, is borne onward to the

journey's goal, already building there the castles of the future. So it was with Olenin.

Once he had left the city behind and surveyed the snowy fields, he felt glad to be alone among those fields, wrapped himself in his fur coat, lowered himself on to the bottom of the sleigh, settled down and began to doze. The goodbye party with his friends had moved him, and he began to remember the whole of the last winter he had spent in Moscow; and images of that past, mingled with vague thoughts and reproaches, began to rise unbidden in his mind.

He remembered his friend who had seen him off, and his relations with the girl they had talked about. The girl was rich. 'How could he love her, in spite of the fact that she loved me?' he thought, and unpleasant suspicions came into his head. 'There's a lot of dishonesty in people, when you think about it. But why have I never been in love, really?' The question presented itself to him. 'Everyone tells me that I haven't. Am I really a moral freak?' And he began to remember his infatuations. He remembered the early stages of his life in society and the sister of one of his friends, with whom he had spent evenings at a table with a lamp that illumined her delicate fingers at their needle-work and the lower part of her attractive, delicate face, and he remembered those conversations, which had dragged on for ever, and the general awkwardness, the constraint, and the constant sense of anger at all that stiffness. A voice had always said: 'this is not "it", this is not "it"', and true enough, it turned out not to be 'it'. Then he remembered a ball, and the mazurka he had danced with the beautiful D. 'How in love I was that night, and how happy I was! And how hurt and annoyed I was the next morning, when I woke up and felt that I was free! Why doesn't love come, why doesn't it bind me hand and foot?' he thought. 'No, love doesn't exist! The lady who lived next door and used to tell me, just as she told Dubrovin and the marshal of nobility, that she loved the stars, was also *not* "*it*".' And now he remembered his farming work in the country, and again there was nothing enjoyable to dwell on in those memories. 'I wonder how long they'll discuss my departure?' came into his head. But who were 'they'? He did not know, and after this a thought occurred to him that made him frown and utter incoherent sounds: it was the memory of his tailor, Monsieur Cappelet, and the six hundred and seventy-eight roubles he owed him – and he remembered the words with which he had begged the tailor to wait another year, and the expression of bewilderment and submission to fate that had appeared on the tailor's face. 'Oh, my God, my God!' he kept repeating, wincing, and trying to drive away the unbearable thought. 'Yet in spite of that, she loved me,' he thought about the girl who had been the subject of conversation at his farewell supper. 'Yes, if I'd married her, I wouldn't have any debts, and now I owe money to Vasilyev.' And he summoned up a mental picture of the last night of his card game with Mr Vasilyev at the club, where he had gone directly after leaving her, and remembered his humiliating requests for another game, and Vasilyev's cold refusal. 'A year of thrift, and it will all be paid, and the devil take them . . .' But in spite of this certainty, he again began to count up his remaining debts, their dates and proposed terms of repayment. 'And actually, I also owe money to Morel, and not only to Chevalier,' he remembered; and he saw before him again the whole of the night in which he had incurred such debts. It had been a drinking spree with gypsies organized by some visitors from St Petersburg: Sashka B—, an *aide-de-camp* to the Tsar, and Prince D—, and that pompous old man . . . 'And why are they so pleased with themselves, those gentlemen?' he thought, 'and on what basis do they form a special clique to which, in their opinion, other people find

13

it highly flattering to belong? Is it because they're
aides-de-camp? I mean, it's awful, the way they consider
other people to be fools and scoundrels! I would show
them that I, on the contrary, don't want to associate with
them in any way. However, I think Andrey the steward
would be very puzzled that I was on familiar terms with a
gentleman like Sashka B—, a colonel and an *aide-de-camp* . . .
And indeed, no one drank more than I did that evening; I
taught the gypsies a new song, and everyone listened.
Though I've done a lot of stupid things, I'm still a very, very
fine young man,' he thought.

Morning found Olenin at the third post station. He
drank tea, moved his bundles and trunks with Vanyusha's
help, and then settled down among them in a sensible and
straightforward manner, knowing exactly where all his
things were and how many there were – where his money
was, and how much it came to, where his passport was, and
his post horse order form, and his highway toll vouchers –
and it all seemed arranged in such a practical way that he
felt cheerful, and the long journey appeared to him in the
form of an extended outing.

Throughout the morning and the middle of the day he
was entirely immersed in arithmetical calculations: how
many *versts* he had gone, how many remained to the next
station, how many to the next town, to dinner, to evening
tea, to Stavropol, and what proportion of the whole journey was already completed. As he did so, he also worked
out how much money he had, how much would remain,
how much he would need to pay off all his debts and what
proportion of his whole income he would spend in a
month. Towards evening, after tea, he worked out that
there were still nine-elevenths of the whole journey left
before he got to Stavropol, that in order to pay his debts
he would need seven months of thrift and one-eighth of
his entire fortune – and, reassured, he wrapped himself

up, lowered himself into the sleigh, and again began to doze. His imagination was already in the future, in the Caucasus. All his dreams about the future were connected with images of Amalat-Beks,[1] Circassian[2] maids, mountains, precipices, fearsome torrents and dangers. All of this appeared dimly and vaguely; but glory, with its allure, and death, with its menace, constituted the interest of that future. At one moment, with extraordinary bravery and a strength that amazed everyone, he was killing and subduing a countless number of mountain dwellers; at another, he was himself one of the mountain dwellers, helping them to defend their independence against the Russians. As soon as he pictured the details, the old Moscow faces always figured in them. Sashka B— was there, either with the Russians or the mountain dwellers, fighting against him. For some unaccountable reason, even M. Cappelet took part in the conqueror's triumph. If, meanwhile, he did remember the old humiliations, weaknesses and mistakes, their memory was only a pleasant one. It was clear that there, among the mountains, the torrents, the Circassian maids and the dangers, those mistakes could not be repeated. For once he had confessed them to himself, that was the end of it. There was yet one other dream, the most precious one of all, which mingled with the young man's every thought about the future. It was the dream of a woman. And there, among the mountains, she appeared to his imagination in the guise of a Circassian slave girl, with a shapely figure, a long plait of hair and deep, submissive eyes. He saw an isolated hut in the mountains, and on the threshold there *she* was, waiting as, tired, covered in dust, blood and glory, he returned to her, and he imagined her kisses, her shoulders, her sweet voice, her submissiveness. She was lovely, but she was uneducated, wild, coarse. In the longer winter evenings he began to educate her. She was intelligent, quick on the uptake, gifted, and rapidly

absorbed all the necessary knowledge. Why not? She could very easily learn foreign languages, read works of French literature, understand them. *Notre-Dame de Paris*,[3] for example, would be bound to please her. She could also speak French. In a drawing-room she could possess more natural dignity than a lady of the very highest society. She could sing, simply, powerfully and passionately. 'Oh, what nonsense!' he said to himself. But now they had arrived at some post station, and he had to change sleighs and tip the drivers. But once again he began to search in his imagination for the nonsense he had left behind, and again he saw the Circassian maids, the glory, the return to Russia, the appointment to the position of *aide-de-camp* and the lovely wife. 'But there's no such thing as love,' he said to himself. 'Honours are nonsense. But what about the six hundred and seventy-eight roubles? . . . And the conquered terri-
16 tory that will give me more wealth than I'll need for a whole lifetime? As a matter of fact, though, it will not be right for me to avail myself of all that wealth on my own. I will have to share it. But with whom? Six hundred and seventy-eight roubles to Cappelet, and then we shall see . . .' And now the visions that clouded his thoughts were rather confused ones: only Vanyusha's voice and the sense of interrupted motion disturbed his healthy, youthful sleep – and, lost to the world, he clambered into another sleigh at the next station, and travelled on.

Next morning it was all just the same: the stations, the servings of tea, the horses' cruppers in motion, the brief conversations with Vanyusha, the vague dreams and drowsiness at evening, and the same tired, healthy, youthful sleep that lasted all night.

3

The further Olenin travelled from central Russia, the further all his memories seemed from him, and the nearer he drew to the Caucasus, the happier his mood became. 'I want to go away for good, and never go back, never show myself in society again,' he sometimes thought. 'And these people I see here are *not* people, none of them know me and none of them can ever be in Moscow, in the social circles I frequented, and find out about my past. And no one in those circles will ever find out what I have done by living among these people.' And a sensation of freedom, completely new to him, freedom from the whole of his past, seized him among those coarse beings whom he encountered along the road, and whom he did not consider to be *people* on a level with his Moscow acquaintances. The coarser the people, the fewer the signs of civilization, the freer he felt. Stavropol, through which he had to pass, upset him. The signboards – there were even signboards in French – the ladies in carriages, the cabs on the square, the boulevard, and a gentleman in a hat and overcoat, walking along the boulevard and surveying the passers-by – made a painful impression on him. 'Those people may possibly know some of my acquaintances,' – and again he remembered the club, the tailor, the cards, the *beau monde* . . . After Stavropol, however, everything was all right again – wild and also beautiful and warlike. And Olenin felt more and more cheerful. All the Cossacks, the drivers and stationmasters seemed to him simple creatures with whom he could simply joke and chat without considering what class of society they belonged to. They all belonged to the human race, which Olenin loved in spite of himself, and they all treated him in friendly fashion.

On their arrival in the province of the Don Cossacks,[4] the sleigh had been exchanged for a cart; and after Stavropol the weather became so warm that Olenin rode without his fur coat. It was already spring – an unexpected, cheerful spring for Olenin. Now they were not allowed to leave the Cossack settlements at night, and were told that it was even dangerous in the evening. Vanyusha began to grow anxious, and they carried a loaded rifle with them in the cart. Olenin became even more cheerful. At one stop, the stationmaster told them about a terrible murder that had recently taken place on the road. They began to encounter armed men. 'This is where it begins!' Olenin said to himself, constantly expecting the sight of the snowy mountains of which so much had been spoken.

18 Once, before evening, the Nogay[5] driver pointed with his whip to some mountains that rose out of thunderheads. Olenin began to study them eagerly, but the visibility was poor and the mountains were half covered by the clouds. Olenin could see something grey, white and fleecy, but no matter how hard he tried he could not find anything attractive in the spectacle of the mountains of which he had read and heard so much. He thought that the mountains and the clouds looked exactly the same and that the especial beauty of the snowy mountains, of which he had been told, was an invention of the same order as the music of Bach or the love of women, in which he did not believe – and he gave up waiting for the mountains. On the next day, however, he woke up early in his cart because of the crispness of the air and glanced indifferently to the right. The morning was perfectly clear. Suddenly, some twenty yards away, it seemed to him in that first moment, he saw the enormous, pure, white masses with their delicate contours, and the fantastic, distinct, aerial line of their summits and the

distant sky. And when he had grasped the whole extent of the distance between him and the mountains and the sky, the whole immensity of the mountains, and when the whole infinitude of that beauty had conveyed itself to his senses, he was afraid it was an apparition, a dream. He shook himself in order to wake up. The mountains were still the same.

'What's that? What is it?' he asked the driver.

'The mountains,' the Nogay driver replied indifferently.

'I've been looking at them for a long time, too,' said Vanyusha. 'It's wonderful! They'll never believe me at home.'

The rapid motion of the troika along the even road made the mountains seem to be running along the horizon, their pinkish summits gleaming in the rising sun. At first the mountains only astonished Olenin, and then they gladdened him; but then, as more and more intently he studied this chain of snowy mountains that rose, not from other black peaks, but straight from the steppe, growing aloft and fleeting away, he gradually began to penetrate this beauty, and to *feel* the mountains with his senses. From that moment all that he saw, all that he thought, and all that he felt, acquired for him the new, majestic character of mountains. All his Moscow memories, his shame and remorse, all his trite and vulgar dreams about the Caucasus, all of them vanished and did not return. 'Now it has begun,' a solemn voice seemed to say to him. The road, and the Line of the Terek,[6] now visible in the distance, the settlements and the people – all this now seemed to him a joke no longer. If he looked up at the sky – he remembered the mountains. If he looked at himself, at Vanyusha – again it was the mountains he saw. There two Cossacks were riding by, the rifles in their cases slapping regularly against their backs, and the bay and grey legs of their horses mingling together; and the mountains . . . On the other side of the Terek he could see the smoke of an *aul*; and the mountains ... The sun was rising and glittering on the Terek, now visible behind the reeds; and the mountains ... An ox cart was leaving the settlement, beautiful women were walking along, young women; and the mountains ... 'There are Abreks[7] roaming about the steppe, I'm not afraid of them, I have a rifle, and strength, and youth; and the mountains ...'

4

The whole sector of the Terek Line – about eighty *versts* in length – on which the settlements of the Grebensk Cossacks are situated displays a uniform character with regard to both landscape and inhabitants. The Terek, which separates the Cossacks from the mountain dwellers, flows muddy and swift, though already broad and smooth, constantly depositing greyish sand on its low, reed-grown right bank, and eroding the steep, though not high, left bank with its roots of centenarian oaks, its rotting plane trees and young brushwood. Along the right bank are situated the *auls,* pacified[8] but still restless; along the left bank, half a *verst* from the river, at a distance of seven or eight *versts* one **21** from the other, are the settlements. In olden times, most of these settlements were situated right on the edge of the bank; but the Terek, deviating to the north from the mountains each year, washed them away, and now all one can see is sprawling old overgrown ruins, with gardens of pear trees, plum trees and poplars, tangled with blackberry and wild vines. No one lives there now, and all one can see is the tracks in the sand of deer, *biryuki,** hares and pheasants, who have come to love these places. A road passes from settlement to settlement, cut through the forest as by a cannon shot. Along the road there are cordons, with watch posts in which Cossacks stand; between the cordons there are watchtowers with sentries. Only a narrow strip of fertile wooded land, some three hundred *sazhens* wide, is granted to the Cossacks as their own possession. To the north of this strip begin the sand drifts of the Nogay, or

* Wolves. (Tolstoy's note.)

Mozdok, steppes, which stretch far to the north and merge somewhere, God knows where, with the Trukhmen, Astrakhan and Kirghiz-Kaisatsk steppes. To the south, beyond the Terek, are Greater Chechnya, the Kochkalov range, the Black Mountains, yet another range, and at last the snowy mountains, which are just visible, but where no one has yet set foot. It is this fertile, wooded strip, with its rich vegetation, that since time immemorial has been home to a warlike, handsome and wealthy population of Russian Old Believers[9] called the Grebensk Cossacks.

Very, very long ago their ancestors, the original Old Believers, fled from Russia and settled beyond the Terek, among the Chechens on the Greben, the first range of the wooded mountains of Greater Chechnya. Living among the Chechens, the Cossacks intermarried with them and adopted the customs, way of life and manners of the mountain dwellers; but there, too, they retained the Russian language and the Old Faith in all their former purity. A tradition still fresh among the Cossacks says that Tsar Ivan the Terrible arrived at the Terek, summoned their elders from the Greben into his presence, gave them the land on this side of the river, exhorted them to live in friendship with Russia and promised not to compel them to be Russian subjects or to change their faith. Even to this day, the Cossack clans are considered to be related to the Chechens, and a love of freedom, idleness, pillage and warfare form the principal features of their character. The influence of Russia is expressed only in an unfavourable light: by intimidation at elections, the removal of church bells[10] and the troops that are stationed and pass through there. A Cossack is, by inclination, less disposed to hate the *djigit*[11] mountain dweller who has killed his brother than the soldier who is stationed with him to defend his settlement, but who has filled his hut with tobacco smoke. He respects the mountain dweller as his enemy, but despises the soldier, who for him is an alien and an oppressor. In fact, to the Cossack the Russian muzhik is a foreign, savage and despicable creature, examples of whom he has seen in the itinerant hawkers and Little Russian migrants whom the Cossacks contemptuously call *shapovals*.[12] Smart dressing consists in imitating the Circassians.[13] The best weapons are obtained from the mountain dwellers, and the best horses are bought and also stolen from them. A dashing young Cossack likes to show off his knowledge of the Tatar language, and when out carousing will speak Tatar even to his fellow Cossacks. In spite of all these things, this small Christian people, isolated in a corner of the earth, surrounded by semi-savage Mohammedan tribes and by soldiers, considers itself to be at a high stage of development and acknowledges only the Cossack as a human being; on everyone else it looks with contempt. **23** The Cossack spends most of his time in the cordons, on the march, in hunting or in fishing. He almost never works at home. His presence in the settlement is an exception to the rule – a holiday, and then he drinks. All Cossacks make their own wine, and drunkenness is not so much a tendency common to all as it is a ritual, the non-fulfilment of which would be considered apostasy. The Cossack looks upon a woman as the instrument of his wellbeing; only the unmarried girls are permitted to go drinking; a married woman is compelled to work for her husband from youth to advanced old age, and he views her in terms of the Oriental demands of submission and labour. As a result of this view women are very developed both physically and morally, and although – as everywhere in the East – they are outwardly kept in subjection, their influence and weight in domestic life is incomparably greater than that of their counterparts in the West. Their exclusion from public life and their habituation to heavy male labour

give them all the more importance and power in the home.
A Cossack, who considers it improper to speak affectionately or idly to his wife in front of strangers, involuntarily
feels her superiority when he is alone with her, face to face.
The whole of his house, the whole of his property, the
whole of his economy has been acquired by her and is sustained solely by her efforts and care. Although he is firmly
convinced that physical labour is shameful for a Cossack
and is only proper for a Nogay labourer or a woman, he
vaguely senses that everything he possesses and calls his
own is the product of that labour and that it is within the
power of the woman, his mother or wife, whom he considers his slave, to deprive him of all that he possesses. In
addition, the constant heavy male labour and the cares
entrusted to her hands have given the Grebensk woman a
particularly independent, masculine character, and have
24 wrought in her a remarkable development of physical
strength, common sense, determination and steadfast-
ness. In general, the Cossack women are stronger, more
intelligent, more educated and better-looking than the
Cossack men. The Grebensk woman's beauty is particularly striking for its combination of the purest type of
Circassian face with the broad and powerful build of
Northern women. Cossack women wear Circassian dress:
a Tatar shirt, a *beshmet*[14] and a pair of *chuvyaks,* or slippers;
but their kerchiefs are tied in the Russian manner. Smart-
ness, neatness and elegance of dress and the furnishing of
their huts are a custom and necessity of their lives. In their
relations with men the women, and especially the unmarried ones, enjoy complete freedom. Novomlinsk settlement
was considered the root and heart of Grebensk Cossack-
dom. In it, more than in others, the ways of the old
Grebensk Cossacks had been preserved, and the women
of this settlement have from ancient times been renowned
for their beauty all over the Caucasus. The Cossacks'

livelihood is based on vineyards and orchards, melon and gourd plantations, fishing, crops of maize and millet, and the spoils of war.

Novomlinsk settlement lies three *versts* from the Terek, from which it is separated by dense forest. On one side of the road that passes through the settlement is the river; on the other is a green expanse of vineyards and orchards, and the sand drifts (alluvial sands) of the Nogay Steppe. The settlement is surrounded by earthen ramparts and prickly brambles. One leaves and enters it through a tall gate on posts with a small reed-covered roof, beside which, on a wooden gun carriage, stands a cannon, an ugly thing that has not been fired for a hundred years, captured by the Cossacks at one time or another. A uniformed Cossack, with dagger and rifle, sometimes stands, and sometimes does not stand, on guard at the gate, and sometimes presents arms, and sometimes does not present **25** arms, to a passing officer. Written in black paint on a white board under the roof of the gate are the words: 'Houses 266, male inhabitants 897, female inhabitants 1012'. The Cossacks' houses are all raised on pillars an *arshin* or more from the ground, are neatly thatched with reeds, and have large carved gables. Even if they are not new, they are all straight and clean, with various kinds of tall porches, and are not crammed together, but situated in a spacious and picturesque manner, with wide streets and lanes between them. In front of the large, light windows of many of the houses, beyond the kitchen gardens, dark green poplars and gentle bright-leaved acacias with white scented flowers rise above the huts, and here there are also brazenly gleaming yellow sunflowers and the winding creepers of weeds and vines. On the broad square there are three shops selling drapery, sunflower seeds, peas, beans and spice cakes; and on the other side of a high fence, from behind a row of old poplars, one can see, longer and taller than all the others, the house of the regimental commander, with its shuttered windows. Particularly in summer, few people are seen in the streets of the settlement during weekdays. The Cossacks are on service: in the cordons or in action; the old men are off hunting, fishing or with the women, working in the orchards and kitchen gardens. Only the very old, the very young and the sick remain at home.

5

It was one of those special evenings that occur only in the Caucasus. The sun had gone behind the mountains, but it was still light. The sunset had taken over a third of the sky, and the lustreless white masses of the mountains stood out sharply against it. The air was thin, motionless and resonant. A long shadow, extending for several *versts*, was being cast on the steppe by the mountains. Everywhere – on the steppe, beyond the river, along the roads – was deserted. If at the rarest of intervals men on horseback appeared, the Cossacks watched them from the cordon, as did the Chechens from the *aul*, with surprise and curiosity, trying to guess who these ill-intentioned people might be. As soon as it is evening, people slink off to their dwellings out of fear of one another, and only the beasts and the birds, not fearing man, freely roam in that wilderness. Before the sun goes down, the Cossack women finish tying up the vines and hurry from the vineyards, cheerfully talking. The vineyards, too, become deserted, like all the rest of the environs; but at this time of the evening the settlement grows particularly lively. From all sides, on foot, on horseback, or driving in creaking carts, people move towards the settlement. Girls in tucked-up shirts, holding switches, run to the gates, chatting cheerfully, to meet the cattle that are jostling together in a cloud of dust and gnats, which they have brought from the steppe. Well-fed cows and buffalo cows straggle about the streets, and the Cossack women in coloured *beshmets* scurry among them. One can hear their shrill talk, merry laughter and shrieks, interspersed with the bellowing of the cattle. There a Cossack, armed, on horseback, having requested leave from the cordon, rides up to a hut and, leaning over to the window, knocks on it: in response to the knock the pretty young head of a Cossack girl appears, and smiling, affectionate conversation is heard. There a ragged, high-cheekboned Nogay labourer who has arrived with reeds from the steppe turns his creaking cart around in the Cossack captain's clean broad courtyard, lifts the yoke from the oxen that are tossing their heads, and exchanges shouted conversation with the master. Near a puddle that takes up almost the whole of the street and past which people have walked for so many years, clinging with difficulty to the fences, a barefoot Cossack woman is picking her way with a bundle of firewood on her back, lifting her shirt high above her white legs, and a Cossack returning from a hunting expedition shouts in jest: 'Lift it higher, shameless girl!' – and aims his gun at her; the Cossack woman lowers her shirt and drops the firewood. An old Cossack with rolled-up trousers and uncovered, grey-haired chest, returning from a fishing trip, carries a *sapetka** over his shoulder full of silvery, still wriggling *shamayka* and, in order to take the nearer path, climbs over his neighbour's broken fence, tugging his homespun coat free where it has caught. There a woman is hauling a dry branch, and round the corner one can hear the blows of an axe. Cossack children shriek as they spin their tops anywhere in the streets where there is a smooth place. The women climb the fences in order not to have to go round them. From every chimney rises the fragrant smoke of *kizyak*. In every yard one hears the intensified bustle that precedes the silence of night.

Babuka Ulitka, the wife of a Cossack cornet who is also the schoolteacher, has come out to the gate of her yard like the other women, and is waiting for the cattle which her daughter Maryanka is driving along the street.

---

*   Bast net. (Tolstoy's note.)

Scarcely has she had time to open the wattle fence than an enormous buffalo cow, accompanied by gnats, bellowing, breaks through the gate; well-fed cows slowly follow it, recognizing their mistress, as they rhythmically slap their sides with their tails. The shapely beauty Maryanka passes in through the gate; throwing away her switch, she closes up the fence and, as fast as her nimble legs will carry her, rushes to separate the cattle and drive them into their sheds. 'Take off your slippers, you devil's wench!' shouts her mother, 'you've quite worn them out!' Maryana, not in the slightest insulted by being called a 'devil's wench', takes the words as an endearment and cheerfully continues her task. Maryana's face is covered by the kerchief that is tied round her head; she is wearing a pink shirt and a green *beshmet*. She slips away under the awning of the yard in pursuit of the large, fat cattle, and only her voice can be heard from the shed at the back, as she gently tries to coax **29** the buffalo cow: 'Won't stand still! What a creature you are! Come on now, come on, little mother! . . .' Soon the girl and the old woman cross from the shed to the *izbushka*,* each carrying two large pots of milk – the yield of the current day. From the *izbushka*'s earthenware chimney the *kizyak* smoke is soon rising, as the milk is turned into *kaymak*; the girl kindles the fire while the old woman goes out to the gate. Twilight has already embraced the settlement. Everywhere the air is redolent with the smell of vegetables, cattle and fragrant *kizyak* smoke. Near the gates and along the streets Cossack women are running, carrying lighted rags. In the yard one can hear the snorting and quiet chewing of milked cattle, and only the voices of women and children call to one another across the yards and streets.

---

* *Izbushka* is the Cossack's name for a low, cool hut where the day's milk is scalded and stored. (Tolstoy's note.)

On weekdays it is rare to hear the sound of a man's drunken voice.

One of the female Cossacks, a tall, masculine old woman from the yard opposite, goes over to Babuka Ulitka to ask for a light for her fire; she is holding a rag.

'Well, Babuka, all neat and tidy, eh?'

'The girl is getting the fire lit. Is it fire you need?' says Babuka Ulitka, proud to be able to be of service.

The two Cossack women go inside the hut; coarse hands, unused to small objects, tremblingly prise off the lid of a precious box of matches, which are a rarity in the Caucasus. The masculine Cossack woman sits down on the doorstep with the obvious intention of having a chat.

'Where's your husband, Mother? At the school?' asks the newcomer.

'He's always teaching the children, Mother. He wrote
30 that he'll be back for the holiday,' says the cornet's wife.

'Well, he's a clever man; it all comes in handy.'

'That's right, it does.'

'But my Lukashka's in the cordon, and they won't let him come home,' says the newcomer, in spite of the fact that the cornet's wife has long known this. She needs to talk about her Lukashka, whom she has just sent off to serve with the Cossacks and whom she wants to marry to Maryana, the cornet's daughter.

'He's in the cordon, is he?'

'Yes, Mother. He hasn't been here since the holidays. The other day I sent him some shirts, through Fomushkin. He says that Lukashka's all right, and his superiors approve of him. He says they're looking for Abreks again. He says that Lukashka's cheerful, and not to worry.'

'Well, thank God,' says the cornet's wife. '"Snatcher" is the right name for him.'

Lukashka is nicknamed 'Snatcher' because of his bravery in having hauled a young Cossack boy out of the water, 'snatching' him. And the cornet's wife has mentioned this in order to say something nice to Lukashka's mother, too.

'I thank God, Mother, that he's a good son, a brave young fellow, and everyone approves of him,' says Lukashka's mother. 'If only I could see him married; then I could die in peace.'

'There are plenty of girls in the settlement, aren't there?' answers the sly cornet's wife, as with rough hands she carefully puts the lid back on the box of matches.

'Lots of them, Mother, lots of them,' comments Lukashka's mother, and shakes her head. 'Now your girl, Maryanushka, is one to search the shelf for.'

The cornet's wife knows what Lukashka's mother is aiming at, and although she thinks Lukashka is a good Cossack, she declines to pursue this discussion further, firstly, because she is a cornet's wife, and rich, and Lukashka is the son of a simple Cossack, and fatherless; and secondly, because she does not want to part with her daughter in the near future. Though the real reason is that decorum requires that she not pursue the matter further.

'Oh, Maryanushka needs to grow a bit, and then she'll be marriageable like all the rest,' she says quietly and modestly.

'I'll send the matchmakers, I'll send them, as soon as we get the vineyards cleared we'll come and bow to your favour,' says Lukashka's mother. 'We'll come and bow to Ilya Vasilyevich.'

'Never mind Ilyas!' says the cornet's wife proudly. 'It's me you have to talk to. All in good time.'

By the stern expression on the face of the cornet's wife, Lukashka's mother can see that further talk on this subject is inappropriate, lights her rag with a match, and, getting to her feet, says: 'Don't leave it there, Mother, remember what I have said. I'm going, I must light the fire,' she adds.

As she is crossing the street, brandishing the lighted rag

in her outstretched hand, she meets Maryanka, who bows to her.

'She's a royal queen, that one, and a hard worker, too,' she thinks, as she looks at the pretty girl. 'What does she need to grow any more for? It's time she got married, and into a good home, too, married to Lukashka.'

But Babuka Ulitka has cares of her own, and she remains sitting where she is, in the doorway, thinking about something, until the girl calls her.

6

The male inhabitants of the settlement spend their time on military expeditions and in the cordons, or 'posts', as the Cossacks call them. In the early evening, that same Lukashka the Snatcher of whom the old women had been talking in the settlement stood on the watchtower of the Nizhne-Prototsk post. The Nizhne-Prototsk post is situated right on the bank of the Terek. As he leaned on the railings of the tower, narrowing his eyes, he gazed now into the distance beyond the Terek, now down at his fellow Cossacks, and from time to time he exchanged some words with them. The sun was already approaching the snowy range that gleamed white above the fleecy clouds. The clouds, as they 33 undulated at its foot, were acquiring darker and darker shadows. The air was being suffused with the transparency of evening. From the wild, overgrown forest came a breath of freshness, but near the post it was still hot. The voices of the Cossacks as they talked resonated more sonorously, and hung in the air. The swift, brown Terek was clearly distinguished from its motionless banks in all its moving mass. It was beginning to subside, and here and there wet sand showed brown on the banks and shallow places. Directly opposite the cordon, on the other bank, all was deserted; only the low, unending and uninhabited reeds stretched away to the very mountains themselves. Slightly to the side, on the low bank, some clay houses were visible, the flat roofs and funnel-shaped chimneys of a Chechen *aul*. Through the evening smoke of the peaceful *aul*, the sharp eyes of the Cossack who stood on the watchtower followed the moving figures of the Chechen girls who could be seen in the distance in their blue and red clothes.

Even though the Cossacks hourly expected crossings and attacks by the Abreks* from the Tatar side, especially in May when the forest along the Terek is so thick that it is hard for a person to pass through it on foot, and the river is so shallow that in some places it can be forded on horseback, and even though some two days earlier a Cossack had 'come running'† with a *tsidulka*‡ in which it was announced that, according to intelligence received from spies, a party of eight men was planning to cross the Terek, and therefore ordering special vigilance – no special vigilance was being observed in the cordon. Unarmed, their horses unsaddled, the Cossacks spent their time just as if they had been at home, some in fishing, some in drinking, some in hunting. Only the horse of the man on duty was saddled, moving about in the blackthorn near the forest, and only the Cossack sentry was wearing his Circassian coat,[15] his rifle and his sword. The sergeant, a tall, lean Cossack with an extremely long back and small hands and feet, wearing nothing but an unfastened *beshmet,* was sitting on the earth bank of a hut, with a superior's expression of laziness and boredom, his eyes closed, moving his head from one hand to the other. An elderly Cossack with a broad greyish-black beard, in nothing but a shirt tied with a black belt, was lying right by the edge of the water, lazily surveying the monotonously turbulent and swirling Terek. There were others, also worn out by the heat, half-naked, some rinsing their linen in the Terek, some plaiting a fishing line, some lying on the ground, humming a song, on the hot sand of the bank. One of the Cossacks, with a thin

34

---

* An Abrek is a hostile Chechen who crosses to the Russian side of the Terek with the aim of thieving or plunder. (Tolstoy's note.)

† To 'come running' in Cossack dialect means to arrive on horseback. (Tolstoy's note.)

‡ *Tsidulka* is the name for a circular that is sent round the posts. (Tolstoy's note.)

and sun-darkened face, evidently dead drunk, lay on his back by one of the walls of the hut, which an hour or two ago had been in the shade, but on which the sun's oblique, burning rays now fell.

Lukashka, who stood on the watchtower, was a tall, handsome lad of about twenty, and very like his mother. His face and whole build, in spite of the angularity of youth, expressed great physical and moral strength. Although he had only recently been drafted as a combatant, it was evident from the expression of his face and the calm assurance of his pose that he had already succeeded in acquiring the warlike and somewhat proud bearing typical of Cossacks and in general of people who always carry arms, that he was a Cossack and knew his own merit, no less than genuine. His wide Circassian coat was torn here and there, his cap was tilted back in Chechen fashion, his leggings had fallen below his knees. His clothing was not rich, but it sat on him with that special Cossack flair that consists in the imitation of the Chechen *djigit*. Everything a real *djigit* wears is always wide, ragged and casual; only his weapons are expensive. But this ragged clothing and weaponry are donned, belted and adjusted in a certain distinct manner which is not granted to everyone and is immediately noticed by a Cossack or mountain dweller. Lukashka had this air of a *djigit*. His hands folded under his sword, his eyes narrowed, he kept studying the distant *aul*. Taken individually, the features of his face were not attractive, but, looking at his elegant build and intelligent, black-browed face, anyone would immediately say, in spite of themselves: 'There's a fine fellow!'

'Women, what a lot of women there are in the *aul*!' he said in a sharp voice, lazily parting his dazzling white teeth, and not addressing anyone in particular.

Nazarka, who was lying below, at once quickly raised his head, and observed:

'They must be going for water.'

'Why don't we frighten them with something from a gun?' said Lukashka, laughing. 'That would get them moving!'

'It wouldn't reach.'

'Go on. Mine would reach past them. Wait for a bit, they'll soon be having their feast, I'll go and see Girey-Khan, and drink *buza*,'* said Lukashka, angrily waving away the gnats which had stuck to him.

A rustling in the thicket drew the Cossacks' attention. A pied mongrel gun dog, searching for a scent and eagerly wagging its shabby tail, ran up to the cordon. Lukashka recognized the dog as one belonging to his hunter neighbour, Uncle Yeroshka, and behind it, following it, he discerned the figure of the hunter himself, moving about in the thicket.

36 Uncle Yeroshka was an immensely tall Cossack with a broad beard as white as snow, and such a broad chest and shoulders that in the forest, where there was no one to compare him with, he did not look very tall: so well-proportioned were all his powerful limbs. He was wearing a ragged, tucked-up coat, his feet were shod in deer's hide sandals known as *porshni*,† and on his head there was a small, tattered white cap. Over one shoulder he carried a *kobylka*‡ and a bag containing a hen and a red-footed falcon for luring hawks; over the other shoulder, on a strap, he carried a dead wild cat; stuck under his belt behind his back there were small pouches containing bullets, gunpowder and bread, a horse's tail for warding off the gnats, a large dagger with a torn scabbard stained with old blood,

---

* Tatar beer, made from wheat. (Tolstoy's note.)
† Footwear made of undressed leather, which can only be put on after being soaked in water. (Tolstoy's note.)
‡ A screen for helping one to creep up on pheasants. (Tolstoy's note.)

and two dead pheasants. Taking a glance at the cordon, he stopped.

'Hey, Lyam!' he shouted to the dog in a bass so vibrant that the echo resounded far away in the forest, and, throwing over his shoulder his enormous piston rifle, which Cossacks call a 'flint', he raised his cap.

'Greetings, good folk! Hey!' he addressed the Cossacks in the same powerful and cheerful voice, without any effort, but as loudly as though he were shouting to someone on the other side of the river.

'Greetings, Uncle! Greetings!' the young voices of Cossacks responded from different quarters.

'What's the news? Tell me!' shouted Uncle Yeroshka, wiping the sweat from his broad, red face with the sleeve of his Circassian coat.

'I say, Uncle! There's such a hawk living in the plane tree here! As soon as it's evening, he fairly swoops around,' **37** said Nazarka with a wink, and a twitch of his shoulder and foot.

'Get away with you!' said the old man, mistrustfully.

'It's true, Uncle, you do some sitting,'* said Nazarka, laughing.

The Cossacks began to laugh.

The joker had seen no hawk; but it had long been a custom of the young Cossacks in the cordon to tease Uncle Yeroshka and pull his leg whenever he came to see them.

'Eh, you fool, always telling lies!' said Lukashka from the watchtower, to Nazarka.

Nazarka at once fell silent.

'If I have to do some sitting, I'll sit,' replied the old man, to the great delight of all the Cossacks. 'But have you seen any boar?'

'So that's what's on your mind, is it? Looking out for

---

* 'Sitting' means watching out for a wild creature. (Tolstoy's note.)

boar!' said the sergeant, very glad of the chance of some
entertainment, rolling over and scratching his long back
with both hands. 'It's Abreks we have to try to catch here,
not boar. You wouldn't have heard anything, Uncle, eh?'
he added, narrowing his eyes for no reason and exposing
his white, close-set teeth.

'Abreks?' said the old man. 'No, I haven't heard anything. Say, got any *chikhir*? Give me a drink, there's a good
man. I feel quite exhausted, so I do. When the time comes,
I'll bring you some fresh meat, honest I will. Bring me a
drink!'

'What's your plan, then, are you going to do some sitting?' asked the sergeant, as though he had not heard what
the old man had said.

'I was planning to sit for a night,' replied Uncle Yeroshka, 'maybe I'll bag something in time for the holiday;
I'll let you have some of it then, honest I will!'

'Uncle! Hullo! Uncle!' Luka shouted suddenly from
above, drawing attention, and all the Cossacks looked
round at him. 'Go round to the upper ditch, there's a huge
great herd of boar there. I'm not making it up. Promise!
One of our Cossacks shot one there the other day. It's the
truth, I'm telling you,' he added, adjusting the rifle behind
his back, in a voice that showed he was not laughing.

'Ah, Lukashka the Snatcher is here!' said the old man,
looking up. 'Where were you shooting?'

'You mean you didn't see? You're not tall enough, obviously,' said Lukashka. 'Right beside the ditch, Uncle,' he
added seriously, with a shake of his head. 'We were just
walking along the ditch when we heard a twig snap, and
my rifle was in its cover, so Ilyaska took a pop . . .* I'll show
you the place, Uncle, it's not far from here. Just give me
time. I know all his little paths. Uncle Mosev!' he added

38

---

* To 'pop' in Cossack parlance means to shoot. (Tolstoy's note.)

resolutely and almost commandingly to the sergeant. 'It's time to change the guard!' And, picking up his rifle, without waiting for the order, he began to come down from the watchtower.

'Come down!' said the sergeant, only afterwards, looking around him. 'It's your watch, is it, Gurka? Off you go, then! It's true, that Lukashka of yours has become quite a dab hand,' added the sergeant, addressing the old man. 'Like you, he's always on the go, never stays at home; he killed a boar the other day.'

7

The sun had already disappeared, and the shadows of night were quickly approaching from the direction of the forest. The Cossacks finished their tasks near the cordon and gathered in the hut for supper. Only the old man, still waiting for the hawk, and tugging the falcon that was tied by one leg, remained under the plane tree. The hawk was perching in the tree, but did not come down for the hen. In the very midst of the blackthorn thicket, on the pheasants' path, Lukashka was unhurriedly setting traps, singing one song after another as he did so. In spite of his tall stature and large hands, one could see that any kind of work, great or small, prospered in those hands.

'Hey, Luka!' he heard Nazarka's penetratingly resonant voice call from the thicket close by. 'The Cossacks have gone to have supper.'

Nazarka, a live pheasant under his arm, made his way through the blackthorn and clambered out on to the path.

'Oh!' said Lukashka, falling silent. 'Where did you get that cock pheasant? Must have been in my "springer" . . .'*

Nazarka was the same age as Lukashka, and had also only been on active service since the spring.

He was a plain-looking fellow, thin and puny, with a shrill voice that fairly rang in one's ears. Luka and he were neighbours and companions. Lukashka sat on the grass in Tatar fashion, setting his traps.

'I don't know whose it was. Must have been one of yours.'

'On the other side of the pit, near the plane tree, was it? It's mine, I set it yesterday.'

---

* A trap for catching pheasants. (Tolstoy's note.)

Lukashka rose to his feet and took a look at the captured pheasant. When he had stroked his hand along its dark grey head, which it stretched out in fear, rolling its eyes, he picked it up.

'We'll make a pilau tonight; you go and kill and pluck it.'

'Are we going to eat it all ourselves, or give some to the sergeant?'

'He's got enough already.'

'Killing them scares me,' said Nazarka.

'Give it here.'

Lukashka got out a small knife from under his dagger and quickly jerked it. The pheasant fluttered, but before it could spread its wings, its bloody head bent and quivered.

'That's the way to do it!' said Lukashka, throwing the pheasant down. 'It'll be a good pilau.'

Nazarka gave a shudder as he looked at the pheasant.

'But listen, Luka, that devil will be sending us to the observation post again,' he added, picking up the pheasant, and by 'that devil' referring to the sergeant. 'He's sent Fomushkin for *chikhir,* but it was *his* turn. How many nights we've gone for it! It's always us he singles out.'

Lukashka, whistling, walked along the cordon.

'Take some string with you!' he shouted.

Nazarka obeyed.

'I'll tell him tonight, truly I will,' Nazarka went on. 'Let's say that we won't go, we're worn out, and there's an end of it. You tell him, really, he'll listen to you. I mean, what is this?'

'A fine topic of conversation you've discovered!' said Lukashka, whose thoughts were evidently elsewhere. 'A lot of nonsense! It would be too bad if they kick us out of the settlement for the night. A man can have some fun there, but what is there here? The cordon or the observation post, it's all the same. Get along with you . . .'

'And are you coming to the settlement, then?'

'I'll be there for the holiday.'

'Gurka said that your Dunayka is carrying on with Fomushkin,' Nazarka said suddenly.

'To hell with her!' replied Lukashka, exposing his white, close-set teeth, but without laughing. 'Do you think I can't find another?'

'Gurka said he went to see her, and her husband wasn't there. Fomushkin was sitting there eating pie. Gurka stayed for a while, then went outside and stood under the window: he heard her say: "The devil's gone away. Why aren't you eating your pie, dear? Don't go home to sleep tonight." And Gurka under the window said to himself: "There's a fine thing!"'

'You're lying!'

'Honest, it's true.' Lukashka was silent.

'Well, if she's found someone else, to hell with her: there's plenty of other girls. Anyway, I was sick of her.'

'Oh, you old devil!' said Nazarka. 'You ought to go and pay your regards to Maryanka, the cornet's daughter. Why doesn't she go out with anyone?'

Lukashka frowned.

'What Maryanka is that? They're all the same!' he said.

'You ought to go and put yourself forward . . .'

'And then what do you suggest? There are plenty of them in the settlement, aren't there?' And Lukashka again began to whistle and walked towards the cordon, tearing leaves from branches. As he was passing along the bushes, he suddenly stopped, having noticed a smooth little sapling, took the small knife from under his dagger and cut it down.

'This will make a fine ramrod for my gun,' he said, making the stick whistle in the air.

The Cossacks were sitting at supper in the wattle and daub outhouse of the cordon, on the earthen floor, round a small, low Tatar table, when the talk turned to the question of whose turn it was to man the observation post.

'Who's going tonight?' shouted one of the Cossacks, addressing the sergeant through the open door of the hut.

'Who's going?' replied the sergeant. 'Uncle Burlyak's been, and so has Fomushkin,' he said, not quite confidently. 'You'd better go, don't you think? You and Nazar,' he said, turning to Luka, 'and Yergushov can go, too: with any luck he'll have slept it off by now.'

'You never sleep it off yourself, so why should he?' said Nazarka in a low voice.

The Cossacks laughed.

Yergushov was the same Cossack who had been sleeping, drunk, beside the hut. He had only just tumbled into the outhouse, rubbing his eyes.

Meanwhile, Lukashka had got up and was adjusting his rifle.

'Well, hurry up, and off you go; finish your supper, and go,' said the sergeant. And, without waiting for an expression of agreement, the sergeant shut the door, evidently having little trust that the Cossacks would obey. 'If it wasn't orders, I wouldn't send you, but as it is, well, the *sotnik*[16] might look in. And also, they say about eight Abreks have crossed the river.' 43

'Oh, then we must go,' said Yergushov. 'It's procedure! Nothing for it, such are the times we're living in. I say we go.'

Meanwhile Lukashka was holding a large piece of pheasant to his mouth. Looking now at the sergeant, and now at Nazarka, he seemed quite indifferent to what was taking place, and was laughing at them both. The Cossacks had not yet left for the observation post when Uncle Yeroshka, who had 'sat' beneath the plane tree until nightfall, entered the dark passage.

'Well, lads,' his bass voice began to boom in the low-ceilinged passage, drowning all the other voices, 'I'm coming with you. You'll "sit" for Chechens, and I'll "sit" for wild boar!'

8

It was already quite dark when Uncle Yeroshka and the three Cossacks from the cordon, in *burkas* and with rifles slung over their shoulders, marched along the Terek to the place that had been designated as an observation post. Nazarka did not want to go at all, but Luka shouted at him, and they set off smartly. Having gone a few yards in silence, the Cossacks turned away from the ditch and approached the Terek along a barely evident path through the reeds. On the bank lay a thick black log, thrown up by the water; the reeds around it had been freshly trampled.

'Is this where we're to "sit"?' asked Nazarka.

44 'Why not?' said Lukashka. 'You make yourself at home here, and I'll be back quite soon. I'm just going to show Uncle the way.'

'This is a very good place: we can see, but no one can see us,' said Yergushov. 'We'll sit here; it's a first-class spot!'

Nazarka and Yergushov, spreading out their cloaks, took up positions behind the log, while Lukashka continued onward with Uncle Yeroshka.

'It's not far, Uncle,' said Lukashka, stepping inaudibly in front of the old man. 'I'll show you where they came past. I'm the only person who knows, old fellow.'

'All right, show me; you're a good man, Snatcher,' the old man replied, also in a whisper.

Going forward a few steps, Lukashka stopped, stooped down over a puddle and gave a whistle.

'This is where they came to drink, do you see?' he said in a voice that could scarcely be heard, pointing to the fresh tracks.

'May Christ reward you,' answered the old man. 'It'll

be *karga* on the other side of the ditch, in the *kotluban*,'* he added. 'I'll "sit", and you go back.'

Lukashka tucked his cloak up and walked back along the riverbank alone, quickly glancing to the left – now at the wall of reeds, now at the Terek as it seethed alongside below the bank. 'After all, he'll also be keeping watch and creeping about somewhere,' he thought to himself, imagining a Chechen. Suddenly a violent rustling and splashing in the water made him start and reach for his rifle. From below the river bank there was panting and puffing, a boar leapt forth, and a black figure, standing out for a moment from the shiny surface of the water, vanished in the reeds. Luka quickly whipped out his gun and aimed, but before he had time to shoot the boar had already vanished in the thicket. Spitting with vexation, he walked on further. Approaching the place of the observation post, he again came to a halt and gave a low whistle. The whistle was **45** answered, and he walked over to his companions.

Nazarka, curled up, was already asleep. Yergushov sat cross-legged and moved slightly to the side in order to make room for Lukashka.

'Sitting here's a real pleasure. It really is a good place,' he said. 'Did you take him to the spot?'

'I showed him,' replied Lukashka, spreading out his cloak. 'Hey, I flushed out a truly enormous boar down by the river just now. It must be the same one! Didn't you hear the noise?'

'I did hear an animal. I knew at once it was an animal. What I thought was: "Lukashka's scared an animal",' said Yergushov, wrapping himself in his cloak. 'I'm going to sleep now,' he added. 'You wake me after cockcrow;

* *Kotluban* is the name for the hollow, sometimes merely a puddle, in which the wild boar wallows in mud, rubbing its *kalgan*, or thick, cartilaginous hide. (Tolstoy's note.)

because we must follow procedure. I'll take a nap, we'll sleep in short turns; you'll sleep next, and I'll sit; that's the way to do it.'

'Thanks, but I don't feel like sleeping,' replied Lukashka. The night was dark, warm and windless. Stars shone only from one side of the sky, above the horizon; the other, larger part of the sky, from the mountains, was obscured by a single great thundercloud. This black cloud, blending with the mountains, in the absence of any wind, was slowly advancing further and further, standing out with its curved edges from the deep starry sky. Only ahead of him could the Cossack see the Terek and the distance beyond it; from behind and from the sides he was surrounded by a wall of reeds. From time to time, as if without reason, they began to sway and rustle against one another. From below the swaying heads looked like feathery tree branches against the bright edge of the sky. Directly in front of his feet was the riverbank, below which the torrent seethed. Further away, a shiny, moving mass of brown water rippled monotonously near the sandbanks and shores. Still further away, water, riverbank and thundercloud all merged into an impenetrable gloom. Along the surface of the water trailed black shadows, which the experienced eye of a Cossack recognized as tree stumps carried downstream by the river. Only now and then did summer lightning, reflected in the water as in a black mirror, disclose the outline of the sloping bank opposite. The constant nocturnal sounds of the rustling of the reeds, the snoring of the Cossacks, the humming of the gnats and the flowing of the water were broken from time to time, now by a distant shot, now by the gurgling sound as a piece of the riverbank gave way, now by the splash of a large fish, now by the noise of an animal as it crashed about the wild, overgrown forest. Once an owl flew past along the Terek, brushing wing against wing regularly at every second beat.

Right above the Cossacks' heads it turned towards the forest and, flying down to a tree, not every two beats but at every beat brushed wing against wing and then for a long time fluttered about as it settled down on the old plane. At every such unexpected sound the wakeful Cossack's hearing tensed itself keenly, his eyes narrowed, and unhurriedly he felt for his rifle.

The greater part of the night was now over. The black cloud that had stretched to the west revealed from behind its ragged edges a clear starry sky, and the golden, upturned crescent of the moon began to shine gloriously above the mountains. The air was chilly now. Nazarka woke up, said something, and fell asleep again. Lukashka felt bored, got up, took the small knife from under his dagger, and began to whittle his stick into a ramrod. Through his head meandered thoughts of how up there, in the mountains, lived Chechens, how their brave young men came over to this **47** side, how they were not afraid of the Cossacks and how they might be crossing the river at another place. And he thrust himself forward and looked out along the river, but nothing could be seen. From time to time looking at the river and the distant bank, which stood out faintly from the water in the timid light of the moon, he now stopped thinking about the Chechens and merely waited for it to be time to wake his companions and walk back to the settlement. In the settlement he imagined Dunka, his 'darling', as the Cossacks call a man's mistress, and thought of her with vexation. The signs of morning: a silvery mist began to gleam white above the water, and not far from him young eagles began a piercing whistling and a flapping of their wings. At last the crow of the first cock reached him from far away in the settlement, followed by another, long-drawn-out, which was answered by other voices.

'It's time to wake them,' thought Lukashka, who had

finished his ramrod and felt his eyes growing heavy. Turning to his companions, he could make out which pair of legs belonged to whom; but suddenly it seemed to him that something splashed on the other side of the Terek, and once again he looked round at the brightening horizon of the mountains beneath the upturned crescent, at the outline of the opposite bank, at the Terek and the now clearly visible tree stumps that were floating on it. It seemed to him that he was moving, and the Terek with its tree stumps was motionless; but this only lasted for a moment. Again he began to look closely. One large black stump with a branch particularly drew his attention. Somehow strangely, neither rocking from side to side nor spinning around, this stump was floating right in the middle. It even seemed to him that it was not floating with the current, but was crossing the Terek to a sandbank. Lukashka, craning his neck, began to watch the stump intently. It floated to the sandbank, stopped, and began to move in an odd manner. Lukashka fancied that he saw an arm come out from under the stump. 'Now I'm going to kill an Abrek all by myself!' he thought, grabbed his rifle, swiftly, but without hurry, set up his gun rest, put the rifle on it, positioned it, inaudibly cocked the trigger and, holding his breath, began to aim, still looking intently. 'I won't wake them,' he thought. However, his heart began to beat within his breast so violently that he stopped and listened. The stump suddenly plopped out of sight and then floated again, crossing the water, towards the Russian side. 'So long as I don't let it get away!' he thought, and there, by the faint light of the moon, he glimpsed a Tatar head in front of the stump. He aimed his rifle straight at the head. It seemed quite close, at the other end of the barrel. He glanced across. 'It is, it's an Abrek,' he thought joyfully and, suddenly rising to his knees with a jerk, again aimed the rifle, sought the target, which was just visible at the other end of the long gun, and, saying in Cossack fashion, learned from childhood: 'In the name of the Father and the Son', pressed the knob of the trigger. A flash of lightning illuminated the reeds and the water for a moment. The sharp, abrupt sound of the shot carried along the river and disappeared into a roar somewhere in the distance. The stump was now floating not against the current but with it, spinning and swaying.

'Hold your fire!' cried Yergushov, feeling at his rifle, and half-rising from behind a block.

'Be quiet, damn it!' Luka whispered at him through clenched teeth. 'It's Abreks!'

'Who did you shoot?' asked Nazarka. 'Who did you shoot, Lukashka?'

Lukashka made no reply. He was reloading his gun and watching the stump as it floated away. A short distance away it stopped on a sandbank, and from behind it some- **49** thing large, rocking on the water, came into view.

'What did you fire at? Why don't you say?' the Cossacks repeated.

'I told you, it's Abreks,' Luka repeated.

'Enough of your fibbing! Your rifle went off, didn't it?'

'It's an Abrek I killed! That's what I fired at!' Lukashka said, in a voice that was breaking with excitement, jumping to his feet. 'A man was swimming . . .' he said, pointing to the sandbank. 'I killed him. Look over here.'

'Enough of your lies,' Yergushov repeated, rubbing his eyes.

'What do you mean, lies? Here, look! Look over here!' said Lukashka, seizing him by the shoulders and bending him towards him with such force that Yergushov groaned.

Yergushov looked in the direction in which Luka was pointing, and, discerning the body, suddenly altered his tone.

'There! And there's more where that one came from,'

he said quietly, and began to examine his rifle. 'That was a scout swimming across; they're either already here or they're not far away on the other side; I can tell you for certain.'

Lukashka undid his belt and began to take off his Circassian coat.

'Where are you going, you fool?' cried Yergushov. 'Poke your nose out and you'll be done for, I'm telling you. If you killed him, he won't be going anywhere. Give me some powder to frighten them off with. Have you got any? Nazar! You get back to the cordon at the double, and don't go along the bank: they'll kill you, man.'

'So I have to go alone, do I? Go yourself,' said Nazarka angrily.

Lukashka, who had taken off his coat, walked over to the bank.

'Don't go out there, man,' said Yergushov, putting powder on the pan of his rifle. 'Sheesh, the fellow's not going anywhere, even I can see that. It's not long till morning, let the lads from the cordon come and give us a hand. Off you go, Nazar; you're not scared, are you? Don't be scared, that's an order!'

'Luka! Hey, Luka!' said Nazarka. 'Tell us how you killed him.'

Luka immediately changed his mind about going into the water.

'Go back to the cordon at the double, and I'll "sit". And tell the Cossacks to send a mounted patrol. If they're on this side . . . they have to be caught!'

'That's what I'm saying – they'll get away,' said Yergushov, getting up. 'They have to be caught, right enough.'

And Yergushov and Nazarka got up. Crossing themselves, they set off for the cordon, not along the bank, however, but breaking their way through the thickets of blackthorn, and clambering out on to the forest path.

'Now mind, Luka, don't you move a muscle,' said Yergushov, quietly, 'or they'll cut your throat. Keep all your wits about you, man.'

'I know. Off you go,' said Luka and, having inspected his rifle, sat down on the block again.

Lukashka sat alone, looked at the sandbank and listened for the sound of Cossacks; but it was a long way to the cordon, and he was tormented by impatience; he had thought all along that the Abreks who had been with the one he had killed would get away. He was annoyed, just as he had been about the boar that had got away the previous evening, that the Abreks were going to get away now. He glanced now around him, now at the opposite bank, expecting at every moment to see another man, and he set up his gun rest ready to fire. The thought that he might be killed never even entered his head.

9

It was now starting to get light. The whole of the Chechen's body, which had got stuck, and was gently rocking on the sandbank, could now be clearly seen. Suddenly, not far from the Cossack, the reeds began to rustle, footsteps were heard and the feathery tops of the reeds began to move. The Cossack cocked his rifle at the ready, and said quietly: 'In the name of the Father and the Son.' After the click of the cocking piece, the footsteps died away.

'Hey, Cossacks! Don't kill, Uncle,' a calm, bass voice was heard to say, and, moving the reeds apart, Uncle Yeroshka came right up to him.

52 'I nearly killed you, I swear I did!' said Lukashka.

'What did you shoot?' asked the old man.

The old man's sonorous voice, resonating through the forest and down the river, suddenly destroyed the nocturnal silence and mystery that surrounded the Cossack. Everything suddenly became lighter and more visible.

'You didn't see, Uncle – it was a wild beast I killed,' said Lukashka, lowering the cocking piece and getting to his feet with unnatural calm.

The old man, his gaze trained straight ahead now, was looking at the white back gleaming as the Terek rippled around it.

'He was swimming with a tree stump on his back. I spotted him, and when . . . Look over here! Here! With those blue trousers, and that rifle, he looks like . . . Do you see him?' said Luka.

'How can I help seeing?' the old man said angrily, and something stern and serious displayed itself in his face. 'You've killed a *djigit*,' he said, with evident regret.

'I was sitting here, and then I saw something dark on the other side, wondered what it was. I spotted him while he was still over there, it looked as though someone had gone to the edge and fallen in. Strange, that. And there was a tree stump, a big tree stump floating, not floating with the current but crossing it. I looked, and saw a head peeping out from underneath it. Stranger and stranger! I craned my neck, but I couldn't see because of the reeds; I got up, and he must have heard, the beast, and he climbed out on to the sandbank, looked round. "No you don't," I thought, "you're not getting away." But he climbed out, looked round. (Oh, something stuck in my throat!) I got my rifle ready, kept dead still, waited. He stayed there, stayed there, then started swimming again, and when he swam into the moonlight, I could see his back. "In the name of the Father, the Son and the Holy Ghost." I looked through the smoke, and there he was, floundering. Was it my imagination, or could I hear **53** him groaning? Well, praise the Lord, I thought, I've killed him! And when he ended up on the sandbank it all became clear, he tried to stand up but he didn't have the strength. He struggled, struggled and then lay down. Clear as daylight it was, you could see it all. Sheesh, he wasn't moving, must have bought it. The Cossacks have gone back to the cordon in case the rest of them try to escape!'

'So you got him!' said the old man. 'He's far away now, brother . . .' And again he sadly shook his head. Just then Cossacks on foot and horseback could be heard coming along the bank with loud voices and a cracking of branches.

'Are they bringing the skiff?' cried Lukashka.

'Good lad, Luka! Pull it to the bank!' shouted one of the Cossacks.

Without waiting for the skiff, Lukashka began to take his clothes off, keeping his eyes on his prey as he did so.

'Hang on, Nazarka's bringing the skiff!' shouted the sergeant.

'Don't be a fool! Maybe he's still alive! What if he was pretending? Take a dagger with you!' another Cossack shouted.

'Get along!' cried Luka, pulling off his trousers. Swiftly he undressed, crossed himself and, jumping down, leapt into the water with a splash, dipped in and, with vigorous strokes of his white arms, lifting his back high out of the water and breathing deeply as he struck out against the current, began to cross the Terek towards the sandbank. A crowd of Cossacks were talking on the bank, several resonant voices raised at once. Three men on horseback set off on a detour. The skiff appeared from round the bend. Lukashka stood up on the sandbank, stooped over the body, turned it over a couple of times.

'He's dead, all right!' Luka's sharp voice shouted from the sandbank.

54　The Chechen had been shot in the head. He was dressed in dark blue trousers, a shirt and a Circassian coat, and he had a rifle and a dagger tied to his back. Above all these a large branch was tied, and it was this that had initially deceived Lukashka.

'That's a fine fish someone's landed!' said one of the Cossacks who had gathered around in a circle, as the body of the Chechen, which had been hauled out of the skiff, was laid on the bank, crushing the grass.

'A nice brown one, too!' said another.

'Where have our lads gone to search? The rest of the Chechens are probably on the other side. If he wasn't a scout, he wouldn't have swum like that. Why would he swim alone?' said a third.

'He must have been a smart fellow, got the job before anyone else did. A real *djigit*, obviously!' said Lukashka, mockingly, wringing out his wet clothes on the bank and shivering without let-up. 'His beard's been dyed and trimmed.'

'And he had his coat packed away in a little bag on his back. That's so it was easier for him to swim,' someone said.

'I tell you what, Lukashka,' said the sergeant, holding the dagger and rifle that had been taken from the dead man. You take the dagger and the coat, but about the rifle, if you'll bring it round to my place I'll give you three "coins"[17] for it. Sheesh, it's even got a flaw in it,' he added, blowing down the muzzle. 'So I want it as a souvenir.'

Lukashka made no reply: he evidently found this sort of cadging a source of vexation; but he knew it was unavoidable.

'Sheesh, what a devil!' he said, frowning and throwing the Chechen's coat to the ground. 'If it were a decent coat, but this thing is *baygush*!'

'It'll do for fetching firewood in,' said another Cossack.

'Mosev! I'm going home,' said Lukashka, evidently forgetting his annoyance and anxious to get some advantage from his gift to his superior.

'All right, go then, if you want!'

'Haul him out to the other side of the cordon, lads,' the sergeant addressed the Cossacks, still examining the rifle. 'And we'll need to make a shelter of branches to keep the sun off him. They may come down from the mountains to ransom him.'

'The sun isn't hot yet,' someone said.

'Well, what if a jackal mauls him? Would that be a good thing?' observed one of the Cossacks.

'We'll guard him; if they do come to ransom him, it won't look good if he's been mauled.'

'Well, Lukashka, whatever else you do you'll have to stand the lads a pail of vodka,'[18] the sergeant added cheerfully.

'Yes, that's the custom,' the Cossacks said, joining in. 'Sheesh, God's given you luck: never seen action before, but you go and kill an Abrek.'

'Buy the dagger and the coat. Give me some more money. I'll sell you the trousers, too. God be with you,' said Luka. 'They won't fit me: he was a skinny devil.'

One Cossack bought the coat for a 'coin'. Another gave two pails of vodka for the dagger.

'You'll get drinks, lads, I'll stand you a pail,' said Luka. 'I'll bring it from the settlement myself.'

'And cut up the trousers for kerchiefs for the girls,' said Nazarka.

The Cossacks roared with laughter.

'Enough of your laughter,' the sergeant repeated. 'Haul the body away. What did you put that filthy thing outside the hut for, anyway . . .?'

'What are you standing there for? Drag him this way, lads!' Lukashka shouted to the Cossacks, who reluctantly took hold of the body, and the Cossacks obeyed his command as though he were their superior. Having hauled the body several yards, the Cossacks let go of the legs, which sank down with a lifeless jerk and, stepping apart, they stood in silence for a while. Nazarka walked up to the body and adjusted the flopped-over head so as to make visible the dead man's face, and the round, bloody wound above his temple.

'Sheesh, left his mark on him all right, he did! Smack in the brains!' he said. 'This fellow won't go missing; his masters will recognize him.'

No one made any reply, and again the angel of silence flew above the Cossacks.

The sun had now risen, its fragmented beams illuminating the dewy green grass. The Terek seethed close by; in the awakened forest, greeting the morning, the pheasants called to one another from every side. Silent and motionless, the Cossacks stood around the dead man, looking at him. The brown body, dressed only in the darkened wet blue trousers, drawn in by a small belt over the sagging stomach, was well-formed and handsome. The muscular arms lay straight, along the sides of his ribs. The round, bluish, freshly shaven head with the congealed wound on one side was thrown back. The smooth, sun-burned forehead stood out sharply from the shaven part. The glassy open eyes with their low-frozen pupils looked upward – it seemed, past and beyond everything. On the thin lips, stretched at the corners and jutting from behind a red, trimmed moustache, a thin, good-natured and ironic smile seemed to have remained. The fingers of the small hands, covered with reddish hairs, were bent inward and their nails were dyed red. Lukashka had not yet put his clothes back on, his neck was redder and his eyes were gleaming more than they usually did. The broad cheek-bones quivered; the white, healthy body gave off a barely perceptible vapour in the fresh morning air.

'He was a man, too!' he said quietly, evidently admiring **57** the corpse.

'Yes, if you'd ended up in his hands, he'd have given you no quarter,' one of the Cossacks responded.

The angel of silence had flown away. The Cossacks began to stir, began to talk. Two of them went off to cut brushwood for the shelter. Others took a stroll to the cordon. Luka and Nazarka ran to prepare to return to the settlement.

Half an hour later, passing through the thick forest that divided the Terek from the settlement, Lukashka and Nazarka went home almost at a run, their talk incessant.

'You mind and not tell her I sent you. Go and find out if her husband's at home, will you?' said Luka, sharply.

'And I'll go round to Yamka's – we'll have a good time, eh?' asked the obedient Nazar.

'When will we have it if not tonight,' replied Luka.

Arriving in the settlement, the Cossacks drank and then lay down to sleep until evening.

10

On the third day after the event described, two companies
of a Caucasian infantry regiment arrived to be stationed
at Novomlinsk settlement. Unharnessed, the company
waggon train already stood on the square. Having dug a
pit and from various yards dragged in logs that had lain in
temptation's way, the cooks were now making *kasha*. Sergeant majors were numbering off men. Soldiers from the
transport unit were driving stakes into the ground to make
tethering posts, and the quartermasters, like domestic
servants, were scurrying about showing officers and men
to their quarters. Here were the green ammunition boxes,
standing to attention. Here were the carts and horses of
the artels.[19] Here were the cauldrons in which the *kasha*
was being cooked. Here were the captain, and the lieutenant and Onisim Mikhaylovich, the sergeant major. And
all this was situated in the very same settlement where, it
was rumoured, the companies were to be stationed; as a
result, the companies were at home. Why were they to be
stationed here? Who were these Cossacks? Did they
approve of the prospect of companies being stationed
here? Were they Schismatics,[20] or were they not? This was
none of their business. Dismissed from their detachments,
the exhausted and dust-covered soldiers, noisy and disor-
derly, like a settling swarm, scattered about the squares
and streets. Determinedly ignoring the Cossacks' ill dis-
position, by twos and threes, with merry talk, their rifles
clattering, they entered the huts, hung up their kit,
unpacked their bags and joked with the women. At the
spot most favoured by the soldiers, around the *kasha*, a
large group assembled, and with pipes in their teeth the

men – looking now at the smoke as it rose indistinctly into the hot sky and thickened up aloft like a white cloud, now at the flames of the campfire which trembled like molten glass in the pure air – cracked jokes and made fun of the Cossack men and woman because they did not live at all like Russians. In every yard soldiers could be seen, and it was possible to hear their laughter, and the fierce and penetrating cries of Cossack women as they defended their homes and refused to give the soldiers water or cooking utensils. With frightened astonishment small boys and girls, clinging to their mothers and one another, followed the movements of the army men, the like of whom they had never seen before, running after them at a respectful distance. Old Cossacks came out of their huts, sat down on the earth embankments and, in silent gloom, watched the soldiers' bustling activity, as though they had shrugged it off without understanding what it all might lead to.

Olenin, who had joined the Caucasian Regiment three months earlier as a cadet volunteer, was given a billet in one of the settlement's best houses, in the home of the cornet Ilya Vasilyevich – in other words, Babuka Ulitka's house.

'What's all this then, Dmitry Andreyevich?' said a panting Vanyusha to Olenin, who, mounted, dressed in a Circassian coat, riding a Kabarda horse[21] he had bought in Groznaya,[22] was cheerfully entering the yard of his allotted quarters after a five hours' march.

'How do you mean, Ivan Vasilyich?' he asked, patting his horse and looking cheerfully at the sweating, tousle-haired and distraught face of Vanyusha, who had arrived with the waggon train and was unpacking their things.

Olenin looked quite a different man. Instead of clean-shaven jowls, he now had a youthful moustache and a small beard. Where before his face had been yellowish, dissipated by nocturnal living, now his cheeks, forehead and the skin behind his ears were covered by red, healthy sun-burn. Instead of a clean, new black suit, he now wore a dirty white Circassian coat with wide pleated skirts, and was armed. Instead of fresh, starched collars, the red collar of a silk *beshmet* sat tightly at his sunburned neck. He was dressed in Circassian style, but badly; anyone would have realized he was a Russian, not a *djigit*. It was all as it was meant to be, yet not as it was meant to be. In spite of this, the whole of his outward appearance exuded health, cheer-fulness and satisfaction.

'You think it's funny,' said Vanyusha, 'but go and talk to these people yourself: they don't give you a chance, and that's that. You can't even get a word out of them.' Vanyu-sha angrily threw a metal pail towards the doorway. 'They're not like Russians, really.'

'Well, go and ask the head of the settlement about it.'

60   'I don't know where he is, do I?' Vanyusha replied touchily.

'Who's upsetting you like this?' asked Olenin, looking around him.

'It's them, these damned people! Pah! They've no proper master, they say he's gone to something they call the "kreegah".* And the old woman is such a fiend that the Lord preserve us!' Vanyusha replied, scratching his head. 'How we're going to live here, I don't know. They're worse than the Tatars, I tell you. Even though they also consider themselves Christians. The Tatars may be bad, but even they are more noble. Gone to the kreegah, indeed! What-ever this kreegah they've invented for themselves is, it's a mystery to me!' Vanyusha concluded, and turned away.

'Not like the servants' quarters back home, eh?' said Ole-nin, teasing the man, and not getting down from his horse.

---

* A *kriga* is the name for a place by the riverbank protected by a wattle fence, for fishing. (Tolstoy's note.)

'Let me have your horse,' said Vanyusha, evidently puzzled by an order of things that was new to him, but submitting to his fate.

'So the Tatar is more noble? Eh, Vanyusha?' repeated Olenin, getting down from his horse and slapping the saddle.

'Yes, that's right, laugh! You think it's funny, don't you?' said Vanyusha in an angry voice.

'Come on, don't be angry, Ivan Vasilyich,' replied Olenin, continuing to smile. 'Look, I'll go and speak to the masters of the house, you'll see – I'll sort it all out. You've no idea what a grand time we shall have here! Just don't be anxious.'

Vanyusha did not reply, but narrowing his eyes merely gave his retreating master a contemptuous glance, and shook his head. Vanyusha regarded Olenin solely as his master. Olenin regarded Vanyusha solely as his servant. And they would both have been very surprised if anyone had told them that they were friends. For they were friends, even without being aware of it. Vanyusha had been taken into the house as an eleven-year-old boy, when Olenin was the same age. When Olenin was fifteen he had for a time occupied himself with educating Vanyusha, and had taught him to read French, something of which Vanyusha was immensely proud. Even now, at moments when he was in a good mood, Vanyusha would spout some French words, always laughing stupidly as he did so.

Olenin ran up the front steps of the hut and pushed open the door of the passage. Maryanka, wearing nothing but a pink shirt, as female Cossacks usually do at home, jumped away from the door in fear and, pressing herself against the wall, covered the lower part of her face with the broad sleeve of the Tatar shirt. Opening the door further, Olenin glimpsed in the half-light the tall and shapely figure of the young Cossack woman. With the swift and avid curiosity of youth he involuntarily observed the strong and nubile curves that showed beneath the thin silk shirt, and the beautiful black eyes fixed on him with child-like terror and wild curiosity. 'There she is!' thought Olenin. 'But there will be many more like her' came into his head after that, and he opened the inner door into the hut. Old Babuka Ulitka, also dressed only in a shirt, stooped, with her back to him, was sweeping the floor.

'Hullo, Mother! I've come to see you about my quarters . . .' he began.

The Cossack woman, without unbending, turned her stern but still attractive face towards him.

'Why did you bother? Do you plan to make fun of us? Eh? I'll teach you to make fun of us! May the black plague take you!' she cried, training a sidelong gaze on the new-comer from under frowning brows.

62   At first Olenin had thought that the brave, exhausted Caucasian army, of which he was a member, would be received everywhere, particularly by the Cossacks, their comrades in war, with joy, and so a reception of this kind puzzled him. Without losing his presence of mind, how-ever, he tried to explain that he intended to pay for his billet, but the old woman would not let him finish.

'Why have you come here? Who needs a running sore like you? You and your smarmy mug! Just you wait, the master will come, he'll show you where you belong. I don't need your dirty money. Think we've never seen money before? You'll stink the house out with your filthy tobacco, and want to pay for it with money. Never seen such a run-ning sore! I hope your heart's shot out together with your bowels! . . .' she cried in a piercing voice, interrupting Olenin.

'Evidently Vanyusha was right!' thought Olenin. 'The Tatar is more noble.' And, to the accompaniment of Babuka Ulitka's abuse, he left the hut. As he was leaving,

Maryanka, still clad only in her pink shirt, but now with a white kerchief tied so that it covered her face to just above her eyes, suddenly slipped past him out of the passage. Quickly pattering down the steps on bare feet, she ran from the porch, stopped for a moment, looked round jerkily, with laughing eyes, at the young man, and vanished round the corner of the hut.

Her firm, youthful gait, the wild gaze of her flashing eyes from under the white kerchief, and the shapeliness of the young beauty's strong physique, struck Olenin even more powerfully now. 'She is the one, she must be,' he thought. And thinking even less about his lodgings, and still looking round at Maryanka, he went over to Vanyusha.

'Sheesh, that girl's a wild one,' said Vanyusha, who was still pottering about the cart, though now in a somewhat more cheerful state. 'Like a filly in the herd! *Lafam*!'[23] he added in a loud, pompous voice, and burst out laughing.

11

Towards evening the master of the house returned from his fishing trip and, having learned that someone wanted to pay him for a billet, calmed his wife down and satisfied Vanyusha's demands.

In the new lodgings all the arrangements had been made. The master and mistress moved into the hut where the stove was, while the cadet was given the stoveless hut for three 'coins' a month. Olenin ate some food and then fell asleep. Waking towards evening, he washed, tidied himself up, had some dinner and, lighting a cigarette, sat down by the window that looked on to the street. The heat had subsided. The oblique shadow of the hut with its carved gable spread across the dusty street, even bending at the foot of the house opposite. The steep reed-thatched roof of that house gleamed in the rays of the descending sun. The air grew fresher. Everything was quiet in the settlement. The soldiers had found their billets and had quietened down for a while. The herd had not yet been driven home, and the people had not yet returned from work.

Olenin's lodgings were situated almost on the edge of the settlement. At rare intervals, somewhere far beyond the Terek, in the districts from which Olenin had come, there was the sound of muffled firing – in Chechnya or the Kumyk[24] lowlands. After three months of army camp life, Olenin was feeling in the peak of health. There was a freshness in his washed face, and in the aftermath of the campaign his powerful body felt clean, in an unaccustomed way. All his rested limbs exuded tranquillity and strength. His state of mind also felt fresh and clear. He remembered the campaign, the danger that was past. He remembered that in the face of danger he had borne himself well, that he was no worse than others and was accepted into the comradeship of brave Caucasians. His Moscow memories had now receded God only knew where. His old life was erased, and now a life had begun that was new, entirely new, and as yet contained no errors. Here, as a new man among new men, he could earn a new, positive opinion of himself. He was experiencing a youthful sense of the joy of life and, as he looked now out of the window at the urchins spinning their tops in the shade near the house, now at his new, tidy quarters, he thought of how pleasant it was going to be to adapt himself to the life of the settlement, so new to him. He would also look at the mountains and the sky, and all his memories and dreams would be mixed with a stern dose of majestic nature. His life had begun, not in the way he had expected **65** it would when he left Moscow, but unexpectedly well. The mountains, the mountains, the mountains could be sensed in everything that he thought and felt.

'He's sold his dog and spent it all on drink! Uncle Yeroshka's sold his dog!' the Cossack children who had been spinning their tops under the window began to shout suddenly, turning towards the lane. 'He's sold his dog! He's sold his dagger, too, for drink!' the urchins shouted, crowding together and stepping back.

These cries were directed at Uncle Yeroshka, who was returning from the hunt with his rifle over his shoulder and pheasants at his belt.

'I've done wrong, children! I know I have!' he said, waving his arms about and looking at the windows of the huts on both sides of the street. 'I sold my dog for drink, and that was wrong,' he repeated, evidently angry, but pretending not to care.

Olenin was surprised by the way the urchins behaved

towards the old hunter, but was struck even more by the expressive, intelligent face and powerful build of the man they called Uncle Yeroshka.

'Grandad! Cossack!' he addressed him. 'Come here for a moment.'

The old man glanced at the window and stopped.

'Hail, good man,' he said, raising his cap above the short-cut hair of his head.

'Hail, good man,' replied Olenin. 'Why are the urchins shouting at you?'

Uncle Yeroshka came up to the window.

'Oh, they're just teasing an old man. It doesn't matter. I like it. Let them have their fun with Uncle,' he said with the firm and musical intonation in which old and venerable people speak. 'Are you an army boss?'

'No, I'm a cadet. But where did you kill those pheasants?' asked Olenin.

'I knocked off three of them in the forest,' replied the old man, turning towards the window his broad back, on which three pheasants hung, their heads tucked into his belt, staining his Circassian coat with blood. 'Haven't you seen any?' he asked. 'Take a couple, if you like. Here!' And he handed two pheasants through the window. 'Are you a hunter, then?' he asked.

'Yes, I am. I killed four while we were on the march.'

'Four? So many!' said the old man, sarcastically. 'And are you a drinker? Do you drink *chikhir*?'

'Why not? I like a drink.'

'Aye, I see you're a good man! We'll be *kunaks*, you and I,' said Uncle Yeroshka.

'Come in,' said Olenin. 'We'll have some wine.'

'All right, then,' said the old man. 'But take the pheasants.'

By the old man's face it was evident that he liked the cadet; he had realized at once that he could get a free drink at the cadet's lodgings, and so he could reasonably make him a gift of a couple of pheasants.

A few moments later the figure of Uncle Yeroshka appeared in the doorway of the hut. Only now did Olenin observe the full extent of this man's massive size and powerful build, in spite of the fact that his red-and-brown face with its completely white broad thick beard was furrowed all over with mighty wrinkles that were the mark of old age and toil. The muscles of his legs, arms and shoulders were as plump and barrel-like as those of a young man. Under the short hair, his head showed deep scars. His thick, sinewy neck was covered, like that of a bull, with cellular folds. The horny hands were worn and scratched. He stepped across the threshold lightly and agilely, freed himself from his rifle, put it in a corner, cast a swift glance round the place, assessing the value of the possessions in it, and with feet turned outward, in rawhide sandals, making no sound, moved out to the middle of the room. Together with him, it was permeated by a strong but not unpleasant mixed odour of *chikhir*, vodka, gunpowder and congealed blood.

Uncle Yeroshka bowed before the icons, smoothed out his beard and, going up to Olenin, gave him his thick black hand.

'*Koshkildy!*'; he said. 'That's the Tatar for "how d'you do" – it means "peace to you" in their language.'

'*Koshkildy!* I know,' replied Olenin, giving him his hand.

'Ah, but you don't know the customs, the customs! Don't be a fool!' said Uncle Yeroshka, shaking his head reproachfully. 'If someone says *koshkildy* to you, you have to say *Allah rasi bo sun*, which means "God save you". That's what you say, old chap, and not *koshkildy*. I'll teach you it all. We had a fellow here called Ilya Moseich, one of your crowd, a Russian, and he and I were *kunaks*. He was a good man. A drunkard, a thief and a hunter, oh, what a hunter! I taught him everything.'

'And what will you teach me?' asked Olenin, who was becoming more and more interested in the old man.

'I'll take you hunting. I'll teach you how to fish, I'll show you Chechens, I'll even find you a lassie, if you want one. That's the kind of fellow I am. I'm a joker!' And the old man laughed. 'I'm going to sit down, laddie, I'm tired. *Karga*?' he added, inquiringly.

'And what does *karga* mean?' asked Olenin,

'It means "all right" in Georgian. But it's just something I say; it's a proverb of mine, it's my favourite word: *karga*; when I use that word *karga*, it means I'm "joking". Oh come on, laddie, tell them to bring some *chikhir*. You've got a soldier, an orderly, haven't you? Eh? Ivan!' the old man shouted. 'All your soldiers are Ivans, aren't they. Is your servant an Ivan?'

'Yes, he is. Vanyusha! Fetch some *chikhir* from the mistress of the house and bring it here.'

'"Vanyusha" is the same as Ivan. Why are your soldiers all Ivans? Ivan!' the old man repeated. 'You ask them to give you some *chikhir* from the barrel they've started, man. They've got the best *chikhir* in the settlement. But see that you don't give them more than thirty copecks a quart, for she'd be only too glad, the witch . . . Our folk are stupid, cursed folk,' Uncle Yeroshka repeated in a confidential tone, when Vanyusha had gone. 'They don't even think you're human. To them, you're worse than the Tatars. "The Russians are too worldly," they say. But the way I see it is, even though you're a soldier, you're still a man, you've got a soul in you, too. I'm right, am I not? Ilya Moseich was a soldier, but the man was pure gold! Isn't that so, laddie? It's for saying things like that that our own folk don't like me; but I don't care. I'm a cheerful sort, and he likes everyone, does Yeroshka! That's right, laddie.'

And the old man patted the young man affectionately on the shoulder.

12

Vanyusha, who had meanwhile succeeded in putting his housekeeping arrangements in order and even had himself shaved by the company's barber, pulling his trousers out of his boots as a sign that the company was billeted in spacious quarters, was in the very best of moods. He looked at Yeroshka attentively but disapprovingly, as at a wild animal he had never seen before, shook his head at the floor the old man had stained with mud and, taking two empty bottles from under the bench, set off to see the hosts.

'Good evening, kind hosts,' he said, deciding to be especially meek. 'My master has sent me to buy *chikhir*; please **69** pour some for me, good souls.'

The old woman made no reply. The girl, standing in front of a small Tatar mirror, was adjusting the kerchief on her head; she looked round at Vanyusha in silence.

'I'll pay you money, venerable hosts,' said Vanyusha, jingling the copper coins in his pocket. 'You be kind and we'll be kind, it's better that way,' he added.

'How much do you want?' asked the old woman, abruptly.

'A quart.'

'Go and draw it for them, dear,' said Babuka Ulitka, turning to her daughter. 'Pour it from the barrel that's open, sweetheart.'

The girl took the keys and a decanter, and went out of the hut together with Vanyusha.

'Tell me, please, who is that woman?' asked Olenin, pointing to Maryanka, who was passing the window just then.

The old man winked and nudged the young man with his elbow.

'Wait,' he said, and leaned out of the window. 'Ahem! Ahem!' he coughed, his voice booming. 'Maryanushka! Hey, Maryanka, my lass! Give me your love, darling!'

'I'm a joker,' he added in a whisper, turning to Olenin.

The girl, not turning her head, swinging her arms evenly and powerfully, walked past the window with that special, dashing, boyish gait used by Cossack women. Only slowly did she turn her black, shadowed eyes on Olenin.

'Give me your love, you'll be happy!' cried Yeroshka and, winking, cast a glance of inquiry at Olenin. 'I'm a lad, I'm a joker,' he added. 'That girl's a queen, eh?'

'She is beautiful,' said Olenin. 'Call her here!'

'No, no!' said the old man, quietly. 'That one's to be married to Lukashka. Luka's a fine Cossack, a *djigit*, he killed an Abrek the other day. I'll find you a better girl. I'll find you one who'll walk in silk and silver. My word is my deed; I'll find you a beautiful girl.'

'An old man, and you talk like that!' said Olenin. 'Why, it's a sin!'

'Sin? Where's the sin?' the old man replied decisively. 'Is it a sin to look at a pretty girl? Is it a sin to have a bit of fun with her? Is it a sin to love her? Is that how it is among the people where you come from? No, dear laddie, it's not a sin, it's a salvation. God made you, and God made the girl as well. So it's not a sin to look at a pretty girl. She's made in order to be loved and delighted in. That's how I see it, my good sir.'

Crossing the yard and entering a cool, dark storeroom that was filled with barrels, Maryana approached one barrel and lowered a siphon into it. Vanyusha, standing in the doorway, smiled as he looked at her. He thought it was terribly comical that she was wearing only a shirt, close-fitting behind and tucked up in front, and even more comical that there was a string of fifty-copeck coins around her neck. He thought this was not really Russian, and back in the servants' quarters at home they would have laughed if they had seen a girl like that. '*La feel com say tray bya*,[25] for a change,' he thought. 'Now I'll tell my master.'

'Don't stand in the light, damn it!' the girl cried suddenly. 'Give me the decanter!'

Having filled the decanter full of cold red wine, Maryana handed it to Vanyusha.

'Give the money to my mum,' she said, pushing away Vanyusha's hand with the money.

Vanyusha grinned.

'Why are you so angry, my dear little women?' he said in a good-natured tone, shuffling his feet as the girl closed the barrel.

She began to laugh.

'And are you and your master the kind ones, then?'

'My master and I are very kind,' Vanyusha replied earnestly. 'We're so kind that wherever we stay our landlords are always grateful to us. Because he's a man of nobility.'

The girl paused, listening.

'And is he married, your *pan*?' she asked.

'No! My master is young and unmarried. Because gentlemen of nobility can never marry young,' Vanyusha retorted, in a lecturing tone.

'I'll bet! A well-fed buffalo like that, and too young to marry! Is he the officer of you all then?' she asked.

'My master is a cadet, so he's not an officer yet. But his rank is higher than that of a general – an important man. Because not only our colonel but even the Tsar himself knows him,' Vanyusha explained proudly. 'We're not like the other soldiers – those down and outs, for our papa was a senator; he owned a thousand or more souls, all muzhiks, and each of them sends us a thousand roubles apiece. So everyone always loves us. Another man may be a captain, very well, but he has no money. What's the use of that? . . .'

'Off you go, I'm about to lock up,' the girl interrupted him.

Vanyusha brought the wine and announced to Olenin that *la feel say tray jollee*[26] – and immediately, with a stupid laugh, went away.

13

Meanwhile, on the square, the tattoo sounded. The people had returned from work. At the gates the herd began to low, jostling in a dusty, golden cloud. Girls and women began to bustle about the streets and yards, gathering in the cattle. The sun had completely disappeared behind the distant, snowy mountain range. The same bluish shadow spread across earth and sky. Above the darkened gardens the stars had come out, just visibly, and the sounds of the settlement gradually died away. Having gathered in the cattle, the Cossack women were coming out to the corners of the streets and, cracking seeds in their teeth, settling down on the earthen embankments. It was one of these **73** groups that Maryanka joined once she had finished milking the two cows and the buffalo.

The group was made up of several women and girls, and one old Cossack.

The talk was of the Abrek who had been killed. The Cossack was telling the story and the women were asking questions.

'I expect he'll get a big reward, won't he?' said one of the women.

''Course he will. They say he'll get a medal out of it.'

'Even so, Mosev tried to insult him. Took away his rifle, and the top brass in Kizlyar heard about it.'

'He's a nasty character, that Mosev!'

'They were saying that Lukashka's back,' one of the girls said.

'Nazarka and he are at Yamka's (Yamka was a loose, unmarried Cossack woman who kept a tavern) carousing. They say they've drunk half a pail.'

'He has some luck, that Snatcher!' someone said. 'He certainly is a Snatcher! What can you say? The lad's all right! Smart as you please! A straightforward lad. His father, Daddy Kiryak, was the same; he takes right after his father. When he was killed the whole settlement wailed for him . . . There, that looks like them coming now,' the woman who was speaking continued, pointing at some Cossacks who were advancing down the street towards them. 'Yergushov's managed to join up with them. Sheesh, the drunkard!'

Lukashka, Nazarka and Yergushov, having drunk half a pail, were going to visit the girls. All three of them, especially the old Cossack, were redder than usual. Yergushov was staggering a little, and, laughing loudly, kept nudging Nazarka in the side.

'Come on, starlings, why aren't you singing for us?' he
74 cried to the girls. 'Sing for our carousing, I say.'

'Greetings! Greetings!' could be heard.

'Why should we sing? It's not a holiday, is it?' said a woman. 'You've had a drink or two, so you do the singing.'

Yergushov roared with laughter and nudged Nazarka:

'You sing something! And I'll sing, too, I'm good at it, I'll have you know . . .'

'What, fair ladies, have you gone to sleep?' said Nazarka. 'We've come from the cordon to say a prayer for you.* Lukashka here's already been prayed for.'

Lukashka, approaching the group, slowly raised his cap and stopped, facing the girls. His broad cheekbones and neck were red. He stood and spoke quietly, in a measured way; but in his slow and measured movements there was more strength and animation than in all of Nazarka's

---

* In Cossack language, the word *pomolit* (to say a prayer) means to greet someone over a glass of wine, or to wish them happiness in general; it is used generally in the sense of 'drink'. (Tolstoy's note.)

chatter and bustle. He made one think of a playful colt stopping short on all four legs with a snort and a flourish of its tail. Lukashka stood quietly in front of the girls; his eyes were laughing; he spoke little, looking now at his drunken companions, now at the girls. When Maryana approached the corner, he raised his cap with a slow, even movement, stood to one side, and then again stepped out in front of her, one foot slightly ahead of the other, his large fingers on his belt, and toying with his dagger. In response to his bow, Maryana slowly inclined her head, sat down on the earthen embankment and took some seeds from inside her shirt. Without lowering his eyes, Lukashka gazed at Maryana; cracking seeds in his teeth, he spat them out from time to time. Everyone was quiet when Maryana approached.

'So, how long are you here for?' asked a Cossack woman, breaking the silence.

'Till the morning,' Lukashka replied in measured tones.

'Well, may God grant you some good interest,' said the old Cossack man. 'I'm glad to see you, and was saying so just now.'

'And so say I,' the drunken Yergushov chimed in, laughing. 'What a lot of visitors!' he added, pointing to a soldier who was passing. 'This vodka the soldiers drink is not half bad, I like it!'

'They've sent three devils among us,' said one of the Cossack women. 'Grandad went to the settlement office, but they say there's nothing to be done.'

'Aha! Have you had trouble, then?' said Yergushov.

'Smoked the place out with their filthy tobacco, I'll warrant?' asked another Cossack woman. 'Smoke as much as you like in the yard, I say, but we won't allow it in the hut. Not even if the settlement head comes, I won't *allow* it. They'll steal things, too. Sheesh, I bet none of them are staying with him, the devil.'

'Not giving them any love, are you!' said Yergushov.

'And I've also heard it said that the girls will be told to make the soldiers' beds for them and give them *chikhir* with honey,' said Nazarka, putting one foot in front of the other, like Lukashka, and tilting his cap backwards, like him, too.

Yergushov burst out laughing and, seizing hold of the girl who was sitting closest to him, embraced her.

'It's true, I'm telling you.'

'Get off me, blackguard!' the girl began to squeal. 'I'll tell your old woman!'

'Tell her!' he shouted. 'It's true what Nazarka says; there was a circular, and he can read, you know. It's true.' And he began to embrace the next girl along the line.

'What, come to pester us, have you, dirty pig?' laughing, the rosy-cheeked, round-faced Ustenka squealed, fighting him off with her hands.

The Cossack moved aside, and nearly fell down.

'Sheesh, and they say girls have no strength; you just about killed me.'

'Get out of it – the devil brought you from the cordon!' said Ustenka quietly and, turning away from him, again snorted with laughter. 'You slept through the Abrek, didn't you? He should have cut your throat, that would have been better.'

'I bet you'd have howled!' Nazarka laughed.

'No I wouldn't!'

'Sheesh, she couldn't give a damn. Howled, would she have? Eh, Nazarka?' Yergushov said.

All this time Lukashka had been staring at Maryanka in silence. The stare was evidently embarrassing the girl.

'What's this I hear, Maryanka? They've billeted an officer with you, have they?' he said, moving towards her.

As always, Maryana did not reply at once, and slowly raised her eyes to the Cossacks. Lukashka's eyes were laughing, as though something special, independent of the conversation, had taken place between himself and the girl.

'Aye, they're all right, as they've got two huts,' an old woman intervened for Maryana, 'but at Fomushkin's they've also got an officer billeted on them, and they say he's partitioned off a whole corner with his stuff, and there's no room left for Fomushkin's own family. Never heard anything like it – they've driven a whole horde into the settlement. What are we going to do about it?' she said. 'And what black plague are they going to work on us here?'

'They say they're going to build a bridge across the Terek,' said one of the girls.

'What they told me,' said Nazarka, going up to Ustenka, 'is that they're going to dig a pit and put the girls in it for not giving the lads any love.' And again he played his favourite trick, which made everyone burst out laughing, and Yergushov at once began to embrace an old Cossack **77** woman, missing out Maryanka, who was next in line.

'Why aren't you kissing Maryanka? You ought to do them all in order,' said Nazarka.

'No, this old one is sweeter,' shouted the Cossack, kissing the struggling old woman.

'He'll throttle me!' she cried, laughing.

A steady tramping at the end of the street interrupted the laughter. Three soldiers in overcoats, with rifles on their shoulders, were marching in step to relieve the guard at the company cash box. The corporal, an old decorated soldier, giving the Cossacks an angry glance, led his soldiers past so that Lukashka and Nazarka, who were standing right by the road, had to get out of the way. Nazarka stepped back, but Lukashka, merely narrowing his eyes, turned his head and broad back, and did not move from the spot.

'People are standing here, you have to go round,' he said quietly, but looking askance and with a contemptuous nod in the direction of the soldiers.

The soldiers passed by in silence, keeping up an even tread along the dusty road.

Maryana began to laugh, and with her all the girls.

'What well-dressed lads!' said Nazarka. 'Like a bunch of churchmen in long skirts' – and he marched along the road, mimicking them.

They all burst out laughing again.

Lukashka slowly approached Maryana.

'And where's the officer staying at your place?' he asked.

'He's been given the new hut,' she said.

'Is he old or young?' asked Lukashka, sitting down beside the girl.

'I never asked,' replied the girl. 'I saw him when I took him some *chikhir*, he was sitting at the window with Uncle Yeroshka, he's got red hair, I think. They'd brought a whole cartload of stuff with them.'

And she lowered her eyes.

'I must say I'm glad I managed to get some leave from the cordon!' said Lukashka, moving closer to the girl on the earth embankment, and still staring her in the eyes.

'And how long have you come for?' asked Maryana, smiling a little.

'Till the morning. Give me some seeds,' he added, holding his hand out.

Maryana smiled properly now, and opened the collar of her shirt.

'Don't take them all,' she said.

'I really missed you, honest I did,' said Luka in a calm, suppressed whisper, taking some seeds from the girl's bosom, and, bending even closer to her, began to whisper something, his eyes laughing.

'I won't come, and that's that,' Marya said suddenly in a loud voice, leaning away from him.

'Really . . . There's something I wanted to tell you,' whispered Lukashka, 'honest! Do come, Mashenka.'

78

Maryanka shook her head, but she was smiling.

'Nanyuka Maryanka! Hey, Nanyuka! Mamuka's calling you for supper!' shouted Maryanka's little brother, running up to the Cossack girls.

'I'll be there in a minute,' replied the girl. 'You go, little one, go on your own; I'll follow in a minute.'

Lukashka stood up and raised his cap.

'I can see I'd better go home, too, that will be the best thing to do,' he said, making it sound casual, but scarcely able to repress a smile, and vanished round the corner of the house.

Meanwhile night had completely fallen on the settlement. Bright stars were scattered on the night sky. The streets were dark and deserted. Nazarka remained with the Cossack women on the earth embankment, and their laughter could be heard. But Lukashka, moving away from the girls at a leisurely pace, crouched down like a cat and suddenly ran without a sound, holding on to his dangling **79** dagger, not homewards, but in the direction of the cornet's house. Having run along two streets and turning, he tucked up his Circassian coat and sat down on the ground in the shadow of a fence. 'Sheesh, she's a cornet's daughter!' he reflected, thinking of Maryanka. 'And she doesn't play around, damn it! But give me time.'

The footsteps of a woman approaching diverted him. He began to listen, and laughed to himself. Maryanka, her head lowered, was walking with swift and even steps straight towards him, tapping the stakes of the fence with a long, dry branch. Lukashka got up. Maryanka gave a start, and halted.

'Sheesh, you cursed devil! You frightened me. So you didn't go home after all?' she said, laughing loudly.

Lukashka put one arm around the girl, and with the other took hold of her face.

'There's something I wanted to tell you . . . honest!' His voice was trembling and breaking.

'Fine sort of talk you've got for night-time,' replied Maryanka. 'Mamuka is waiting, and you should be off to see your sweetheart.'

And, freeing herself from his arm, she ran a few paces. Reaching the wattle fence of her yard, she stopped and turned to the Cossack, who was running beside her, still trying to persuade her to wait for a moment.

'Well, what was it you wanted to tell me, midnight man?' And again she laughed.

'Don't laugh at me, Maryanka! Honestly, don't! So what if I do have a sweetheart? The devil take her. Just say the word, and I'll love you – I'll do anything you want. Here it is!' (And he jingled the money in his pocket.) 'Now we shall live. Everyone is full of joy, but what about me? I see no joy from you, Maryanushka!'

The girl made no reply, stood before him and with swift movements of her fingers broke the dry branch into little pieces.

Lukashka suddenly clenched his fists and teeth.

'But why all this waiting and waiting? Don't I love you, little mother? You can do what you like with me,' he said suddenly, frowning angrily and seizing her by both hands.

Maryana did not alter the calm expression of her face and voice.

'Don't try to bully me, Lukashka, but listen to what I have to say,' she replied, not pulling away her hands, but keeping the Cossack at a distance from her. 'Yes, I know I'm just a girl, but you listen to me. My will is not my own, but if you love me, I'll tell you this. Let go of my hands, I'll tell you anyway. I will marry you, but it's no good expecting me to be foolish,' said Maryana, not turning her face away.

'Marry me? Marriage is not within our power. Love me as you are, Maryanushka,' said Lukashka, suddenly changing from being morose and angry to becoming once again meek, submissive and tender, smiling and looking closely into her eyes.

Maryana pressed herself against him and kissed him firmly on the lips.

'Dear boy!' she whispered, pressing him violently to her. Then suddenly, tearing herself away, she ran off and, without turning round, went in through the gate of her house.

In spite of the Cossack's pleas for her to wait another minute to listen to what he had to say to her, Maryana did not stop.

'Go away! You'll be seen!' she said quietly. 'I think that damned lodger of ours is walking about the yard.'

'A cornet's daughter,' Lukashka thought to himself. 'Marry me! Marriage is all very well, but it's your love I want!'

He found Nazarka at Yamka's; then, after they had done some drinking, he went to see Dunyashka and, in spite of her unfaithfulness, spent the night with her. **81**

14

Olenin really had been pacing the yard as Maryanka walked through the gate, and had heard her say: 'That damned lodger's walking about.' He had spent all that evening with Uncle Yeroshka on the porch of his new quarters. He had had a table, a samovar, wine and a lit candle brought out to him, and over a glass of tea and a cigar he listened to the tales of the old man who was sitting at his feet, on the step. Though the air was still, the candle had melted and the flame jumped about in different directions, illuminating now a post of the porch, now the table and crockery, now the old man's white, close-cropped head. Moths hovered about and, scattering the dust from their wings, knocked against the table and in the glasses, now flying into the flame of the candle, now disappearing in the black air, outside the illuminated circle. Olenin and Yeroshka had drunk five bottles of *chikhir*. Each time Yeroshka filled the glasses, he handed one to Olenin, drinking his health, and talked indefatigably. He told stories of the life of the Cossacks in the olden days, about his father, Shiroky, 'The Broad', who had carried on his back, alone, a boar's carcass weighing ten *poods* and had drunk two pails of *chikhir* at one sitting. He told stories of his own days and of his 'nanny'* Girchik, with whom he had ferried *burkas* across the Terek at the time of the plague. He told the story of a hunting trip on which one morning he had killed two deer. He told the story of his 'darling', who at nights had run to see him at the cordon. And all these

---

* 'Nanny' in the straight sense always means an older sister, while in the metaphorical sense it means a friend. (Tolstoy's note.)

stories were told with such eloquence and picturesque vividness that Olenin did not notice the time passing.

'Aye, laddie,' he said, 'you never knew me in my golden days, or I'd have shown you a few things. Nowadays Yeroshka merely licks the jug, but in those days Yeroshka was the talk of the whole regiment. Who had the best horse? Who had a Gurda sword?[27] Who did you visit to get a decent drink, who did you go out on the tiles with? Who did you send to the mountains to kill Akhmet-Khan? Always Yeroshka! Who did the girls love? Yeroshka was always the one who had to answer for it. Because I was a real *djigit*. A drunkard, a thief, a rustler of herds in the mountains, a singer: I turned my hand to everything. There aren't any Cossacks like that nowadays. They're a pretty horrible sight. When they're only this high off the ground' (Yeroshka held his hand an *arshin* off the ground) 'they put on idiotic boots, then keep staring at them, and that's their only joy in life. Or they drink themselves silly; and drink not like men but like I don't know what. But who was I? I was Yeroshka the thief; I was known not only in the settlements but also in the mountains. The *kunak* princes used to come riding. I was *kunaks* with them all: a Tatar with the Tatars, an Armenian with the Armenians, a soldier with the soldiers, an officer with the officers. I didn't care, as long as they were good drinkers. You ought to cleanse yourself of worldly intercourse, they used to say: not go eating with soldiers, drinking with Tatars.'

'Who used to say that?' asked Olenin.

'Oh, our preachers. But just listen to a mullah or a Tatar kadi. They'll say: "You infidels, Giaours,[28] why do you eat pig?" In other words, everyone has his own law. And in my opinion it's all the same. God made everything for the delight of man. There's no sin in anything. Take the creatures as an example. They live in the Tatars' reeds and they live in ours. Wherever they go, they're at home. Whatever

God gives them, they'll eat it. But our folk say we'll lick frying pans in hell for it. I think it's all a fraud,' he added, after a silence.

'What is?' asked Olenin.

'What the preachers say. You know, laddie, we had an army captain in Chervlena – he was a *kunak* of mine. He was a fine chap, a chap like myself. He was killed in Chechnya. He used to say that the preachers make all that stuff up out of their own heads. "When you die," he'd say, "the grass will grow on your grave, and that's it." (The old man began to laugh.) A desperate character, he was!'

'And how old are you?'

'God knows! About seventy. When you had your Empress in Russia, I wasn't a little boy any more. So you can work out how old I am. About seventy, I'll be?'

'You must be. But you're still in fine shape.'

'Well, I thank God that I'm healthy, quite healthy; except that a woman, a witch, has done me some harm . . .'

'How?'

'Oh, just done me some harm . . .'

'So when you die, the grass will grow?' Olenin repeated.

Yeroshka was evidently reluctant to express his thoughts clearly. He said nothing for a while.

'What else do you suppose? Drink!' he cried, handing up the wine with a smile.

15

'So what was I saying, now?' he continued, trying to remember. 'Well, that's the kind of man I am. I'm a hunter. There's no hunter in the whole regiment to compare with me. I'll find and show you any animal or any bird you want; what it is and where it is – I know it all. I have dogs, I have two rifles, and nets, and a screen, and a hawk – I have everything, thanks be to God. If you're a real hunter, and aren't boasting, I will show you everything. What sort of man am I? If I find a track – I know what it is, the creature, I know where it will lie down and where it will go to drink or come to wallow. I'll make a *lopazik** and sit there over-night, keeping watch. What's the good of staying at home? **85** All you do is get into trouble, drink yourself silly. Women come and chatter, boys keep shouting, drives you out of your mind. It's something else to go out at sunset, choose a nice little place, press down the reeds and settle down and sit there, good fellow, and wait. You know everything that takes place in the forest. You look up at the sky – the little stars are moving, you study them to see what time it is. You look around – the forest's rustling, still you wait, in a moment a twig cracks in the undergrowth, a boar is coming to wallow in the mud. You listen for the screech of young eagles, for cocks crowing in the settlement, or the cry of geese. If it's geese – it's not midnight yet, that means. I know all that, too. Or if a rifle goes off somewhere in the distance, thoughts start to come. You wonder: who's that firing? Is it a Cossack, like myself, who was waiting

---

* *Lopazik* – the name for a place for sitting on posts or trees. (Tolstoy's note.)

for a creature to shoot, and hit it, or did he just wound it, the poor thing, and is it smearing the reeds with blood as it goes, for nothing? I don't like that! Oh no, I don't. Why did he wound the creature? The fool! The fool! Or you think to yourself: "Maybe an Abrek has killed a stupid Cossack boy." All that goes through your head. Or once when I was sitting by the river I saw a cradle floating downstream. It was quite intact, except for a broken corner. Then the thoughts really came. Who could the owner of the cradle be? Your damned soldiers must have come to an *aul* and rounded up the Chechen women. Some devil killed an infant; took it by its legs and hit its head against the corner of a house. They do things like that, don't they? Ach, men have no souls! Thoughts like that came to me, I felt pity. I thought: they've thrown the cradle away and driven the woman out, they've burnt her home, and the *djigit* has taken his rifle and gone to our side of the river to plunder us. You sit and think. And when you hear a herd of boar charging through the thicket, something starts to beat inside you. Come on, little mothers, this way! They'll scent me, you think; you sit there, you don't move a muscle, and your heart goes: thump! thump! thump! It fairly throws you. One night this spring a massive herd came close to me, something black reared up. "In the name of the Father and the Son . . ." – my, how I wanted to fire. But just then she snorted at her piglets: "Trouble, children," she seemed to say. "There's a man sitting there." – and they all began to crash off through the bushes again. She was that close I think I could have bitten her.'

'But how could a sow tell her piglets there was a man there?' asked Olenin.

'What do you think? Do you think it's a fool, the creature? No, it's cleverer than a human being, even though you call it a sow. It knows everything. Just to take one example: a man will pass along a track and not notice it, but when a female boar gets on to your track she scents it at once and she's off; that means that she has intelligence, that you don't smell your own stink, but she does. And there's another thing: you want to kill her, but she wants to gad about the forest alive. You have one law, and she has another. She may be a sow, but she's no worse than you are: she's also one of God's creatures. Ekh-ma! Man is stupid, stupid, stupid!' the old man said, repeating it several times and, lowering his head, fell into reflection.

Olenin also became reflective and, going down the steps of the porch, his hands folded behind his back, began to walk about the yard.

Waking up, Yeroshka raised his head and began to stare fixedly at the moths that were hovering around the swaying flame of the candle and falling into it.

'Silly lady, silly thing!' he said. 'Where are you flying to? Silly, silly!' He got to his feet and with his fat fingers began to chase the moths away. **87**

'You'll burn to death, silly lady, look, fly this way, there's lots of room,' he kept repeating in a tender voice, with his fat fingers politely trying to catch a moth by its wings and set it free. 'There you go trying to destroy yourself, but I feel sorry for you!'

He sat for a long time, chatting and sipping from the bottle now and then. Meanwhile, Olenin walked to and fro about the yard. Suddenly a whispering outside the gate caught his attention. Involuntarily holding his breath, he made out a woman's laughter, a man's voice and the sound of a kiss. Deliberately rustling the grass with his feet, he walked over to the other side of the yard. But a little while later the wattle fence began to creak. A Cossack, dressed in a dark Circassian coat with a white tassel on his cap (it was Luka), walked along the other side of the fence, while a tall woman in a white dress went past Olenin. 'You have nothing to do with me, and I have nothing to do with you'

Maryanka's determined tread seemed to say to him. He followed her with his gaze to the porch of the landlords' hut, and even, through the window, observed her take off her kerchief and sit down. And suddenly a feeling of anguish and loneliness, of obscure longings and hopes mixed with a kind of envy of someone, overcame the young man's soul.

The last lights in the huts had been extinguished. The last sounds had died away in the settlement. The wattle fences, the cattle that showed white in the yards, the roofs of the houses, the slender poplars – all, it seemed, slept a healthy, quiet, workaday sleep. Only the ringing, incessant sounds of the frogs floated from the damp distance to the strained hearing. In the east the stars were becoming fewer, and they seemed to be dissolving in the intensifying light. Overhead they were scattered ever deeper and thicker. The old man, his head resting on his hand, had begun to drowse. A cock crowed in the yard opposite. But Olenin kept walking and walking, thinking about something. He approached the fence and began to listen. The young voices of some Cossacks were singing exuberantly, and one young voice stood out from the rest with marked strength.

'Do you know who that is singing?' said the old man, waking up. 'It's Lukashka, the *djigit*. He's killed a Chechen; so he's fairly over the moon. What's there to be so cheerful about? He's a fool, a fool!'

'And have you killed people?' asked Olenin.

'Damn it!' the old man shouted at him. 'What sort of question is that? Don't talk about it. It's a heavy thing, oh, a heavy thing to destroy a human soul! Goodbye, laddie, I've eaten too much and I'm drunk,' he said, getting to his feet. 'Will I come tomorrow and take you hunting?'

'Yes, do.'

'You'll have to get up early, mind, and if you oversleep there'll be a fine.'

'I expect I shall be up before you are,' Olenin replied.

The old man left. The singing died away. Footsteps and merry conversation could be heard. A short while later there was more singing, but further away, and the loud voice of Yeroshka joined the others. 'What people, what a life!' thought Olenin, sighing and returning to his hut alone.

16

Uncle Yeroshka was a retired and solitary Cossack; twenty
years earlier his wife, having converted to Orthodoxy, had
left him and married a Russian sergeant major; he had no
children. He was not boasting when he said that in the old
days he had been the most dashing young man in the settlement. Every man in the regiment knew about his former
daredevilry. More than one slaying, of both Chechens and
Russians, was ascribed to him. He also used to go into the
mountains and steal from the Russians, and had been in
prison twice. The greater part of his life had been passed
on hunting expeditions in the forest, where for days his
90 only nourishment had been a piece of bread, and water his
only drink. In the settlement, on the other hand, he
caroused from morning to night. Returning from Olenin's, he fell asleep for a couple of hours and, waking up
before daybreak, lay on his bed and pondered on the man
he had got to know the evening before. Olenin's 'simplicity' had appealed to him greatly (simplicity in the sense
of not grudging him a drink). And he also liked Olenin
himself. He found it surprising that Russians should all
be so 'simple' and rich and yet, though highly educated,
know nothing. He considered both these questions
and what he might get out of Olenin for himself. Uncle
Yeroshka's hut was rather large and not old, but the absence
of a woman was noticeable in it. In defiance of the usual
Cossack concern for cleanliness, the whole room was dirty
and in a state of the utmost disorder. Thrown on a chair
were a bloodstained coat, half a shortbread biscuit and
beside it a plucked and shredded crow for feeding a hawk.
On the benches, scattered about, lay rawhide sandals, a

rifle, a dagger, a satchel, wet clothes and rags. In a corner, in a tub of dirty, stinking water, more sandals were being steeped; in the same corner were a rifle and a hunting screen. Thrown on the floor were a net and several dead pheasants, while walking about near the table, tied by one leg, pecking in the dirt, was a hen. In the unheated stove was a crock filled with some kind of milky liquid. On top of the stove a falcon was screeching, trying to break free of its string, and a moulting hawk sat peacefully on the edge, looking sideways at the hen and bending its head from right to left from time to time. Uncle Yeroshka himself lay on his back on a short bed arranged between the wall and the stove, in nothing but his shirt, and, with his strong legs raised up on the stove, was picking at the scabs on his hands where they had been scratched by the hawk, which he carried about without wearing gloves. In the whole room, and especially near the old man himself, the **91** air was impregnated with that strong, not unpleasant, hybrid smell that accompanied him everywhere.

'*Uyde-ma, dyadya?*' (that is: Are you at home, Uncle?) he heard, through the window, a sharp voice say, which he at once recognized as that of his neighbour, Lukashka.

'*Uyde, uyde, uyde!*' – 'I'm at home, come in!' cried the old man. 'Neighbour Marka, Luka Marka, have you come to see Uncle? On your way to the cordon, are you?'

The hawk leapt up at the sound of its master's voice and began to flap its wings, straining at its tether.

The old man was fond of Lukashka, who was the only Cossack of the new generation whom he excepted from contempt. Moreover, Lukashka and his mother, being neighbours, not infrequently made him presents of wine, *kaymak* and similar homemade produce, which Yeroshka did not have. Uncle Yeroshka, who had followed the whims of fancy all his life, always explained his motivations in practical terms. 'Why not? They're people of means,' he would say to himself. 'I'll give them some fresh meat, or a chicken, and they won't forget Uncle: they'll bring me pie and biscuits now and then . . .'

'Hullo, Marka! I'm glad to see you,' the old man shouted cheerfully, and with a swift movement threw his bare feet off the bed, leapt upright, took a couple of steps across the creaking floor, looked at his outward turned feet, and suddenly found them comical: he laughed wryly, stamped a bare heel, stamped again and did a 'pirouette'. 'Clever, eh?' he asked, his small eyes gleaming. Lukashka grinned a little. 'Well, on your way back to the cordon?' said the old man.

'Uncle, I've brought you the *chikhir* I promised when we were at the cordon.'

'May Christ thank you and save you!' said the old man quietly, picked up the wide peasant trousers that were lying on the floor, and his *beshmet*, put them on, secured them with a belt, poured some water on his hands from a crock, wiped them on the old trousers, straightened out his beard with a piece of comb, and stood facing Lukashka. 'Ready!' he said.

Lukashka fetched a cup, wiped it, filled it with wine and, sitting down on the bench, handed the cup to Uncle Yeroshka.

'Your health! In the name of the Father and the Son!' said the old man, accepting the wine with solemnity. 'May you obtain what you desire, may you be a fine and brave young man, may you earn a cross!'

Lukashka also took a sip of wine with a prayer, and put the cup on the table. The old man rose, went to fetch some dried fish, placed it on the threshold, beat it with a stick to make it softer and, placing it with his calloused hands on his single blue plate, served it up to the table.

'I have everything, I even have a bite to eat, thanks be to God,' he said proudly. 'Well, and what of Mosev?' asked the old man.

Lukashka told the story of how the sergeant had taken the rifle away, evidently wishing to know the old man's opinion.

'The rifle's not worth bothering about,' said the old man. 'If you don't give him the rifle, you won't get a reward.'

'But Uncle, I mean to say! What sort of reward will a minor* get, everyone says. And it's a good rifle, Crimean, worth eighty "coins".'

'Oh, let it go! I once had a quarrel with a lieutenant over a thing like that; he wanted my horse. Give me your horse, he said, and I'll get you made a cornet. I didn't give it to him, so nothing happened.'

'But look here, Uncle! I have to buy a horse, and they say you can't get one on the other side of the river for less than fifty "coins". Mother hasn't even sold our wine yet.'

'Ach, it never caused us any trouble,' said the old man. 'When Uncle Yeroshka was your age, he was stealing whole herds of horses from the Nogay tribesmen and driving them across the Terek. We used to give away a decent horse for a *shtof*[29] of vodka or a cloak.'

'Why did you part with them so cheaply?' said Lukashka.

'You're a fool, a fool, Marka!' said the old man, contemptuously. 'The whole point of stealing them is so as not to be stingy. I suppose you've never even seen horses being rounded up. Lost your tongue, have you?'

'What is there to say, Uncle?' said Lukashka. 'We're obviously not the same kind of men as you.'

'You're a fool, a fool, Marka! Not the same kind of men, indeed!' replied the old man, mimicking the young Cossack. 'When I was your age I was a different kind of Cossack.'

'How so?' asked Lukashka.

The old man shook his head contemptuously.

---

* 'Minor' is the name for a Cossack who has not yet begun regular mounted service. (Tolstoy's note.)

'Uncle Yeroshka was "straightforward", never grudged a man anything. That's why I was *kunaks* with the whole of Chechnya. A *kunak* would come to see me, I'd give him vodka till he was drunk, make him happy, put him to bed beside me, and when I went to see him I'd take him a present, a *peshkesh*. That's how real men behave, not like nowadays: the only fun the lads get is gnawing a few seeds and spitting out the shells,' the old man concluded scornfully, making faces to represent the present-day Cossacks spitting out the seeds.

'I know,' said Lukashka. 'It's true!'

'If you want to be a hero, then be a *djigit*, not a muzhik. Though even a muzhik will buy a horse, dump the money and take the horse.'

For a while they said nothing.

'I mean, it's so boring, Uncle, in the settlement or at the **94** cordon; and there's nowhere to go and get a bit of entertainment. The lads, the whole bunch of them, are so timid. Take Nazar, for example. The other day we were in the *aul*; well, Girey-Khan summoned us to Nogay for horses, but no one went; and I wasn't going to go alone, was I?'

'And what do you think Uncle would do? You think I've shrivelled up and lost my strength! Well, I haven't. Give me a horse and I'll go to Nogay right away.'

'What's the point of empty talk?' said Luka. 'You'd do better to tell me how to deal with Girey-Khan. Just bring the horses to the Terek, he says, and even if there's a whole herd I'll find room for them. I mean, he's another of these shaven-headed types, you can't trust a word he says.'

'You can trust Girey-Khan, all his family are good people; his father was a faithful *kunak*. You just listen to Uncle, I won't teach you anything bad: tell him to take an oath, then it will be all right; but if you go with him, keep your pistol at the ready all the time. Especially when you start dividing up the horses. A Chechen once nearly killed me that way: I'd asked him for ten "coins" for a horse. Trusting is all very well, but don't go to sleep at night without a rifle by your side.'

Lukashka listened attentively to the old man.

'Hey, Uncle. People say you've got some lovebreak-herb,'[30] he said, after a silence.

'No, I haven't, but I can tell you how to find it: you're a good fellow, you don't forget an old man. You want me to tell you?'

'Tell me, Uncle.'

'You know what a tortoise is? Damn clever thing, a tortoise.'

''Course I do.'

'Go and find a tortoise's nest and make a little fence round it, so it can't get in. When it shows up, it'll go round it and then go straight back where it came from; it'll find some lovebreak-herb, bring it, and destroy the fence. Well, then come back early next morning and take a look: lying in the broken place will be some lovebreak-herb. Take it and carry it anywhere you like. No lock or bar will hold you back.' **95**

'Tried it yourself, have you, Uncle?'

'No I haven't, but good folks have told me about it. The only charm I used to say was the "Hail to thee" whenever I mounted my horse. No one killed me.'

'What's the "Hail to thee", Uncle?'

'Don't you know? Ech, these men! Well, Uncle's the right man to ask. Now listen and say after me:

> Hail to thee living in Zion.
> This is thy King.
> We shall mount our horses.
> Cry out, Sofony,
> Speak, Zakhary.
> Father Mandryk,
> Mankind forever loving.

'Mankind forever loving,' the old man repeated. 'Know it? Well, let's hear you say it, then.'

Lukashka laughed.

'I say, Uncle, was that what stopped them killing you? Maybe it was.'

'You've grown too clever. Learn it all and say it. It won't do you any harm. Anyway, once you've sung "Mandryk", you'll be all right.' And the old man laughed, too. 'Just don't go to Nogay, Luka, that's all!'

'Why?'

'Times are different now, you're not the Cossack men you were, you've turned into rubbish! And you've even brought the Russians down on us! They'll just put you in prison. Really, you might as well give up the idea! What's in it for you? Now in the old days Girchik and I used to . . .'

And the old man was on the point of beginning one 96 of his endless stories. But Lukashka glanced out of the window.

'It's quite light, Uncle,' he interrupted. 'It's time to be off. Drop by and see me some time.'

'May Christ save you, but I'll go to the officer: I promised to take him hunting; he's a good man, I think.'

17

On leaving Yeroshka's, Lukashka called in at home. As he returned, a damp, dewy mist was rising from the ground and enveloping the settlement. Here and there, invisible cattle were beginning to stir. The cocks exchanged their cries more frequently and urgently. The air was becoming transparent, and people were up and about now. Going right over, Lukashka was able to make out the fence of his yard, wet with mist, the porch of the hut and the open storehouse. In the yard the sound of an axe chopping firewood could be heard in the mist. Lukashka entered the hut. His mother had got up and, standing in front of the stove, was throwing firewood into it. His little sister was still asleep in bed.

'Well, Lukashka, had a good night out?' said his mother softly. 'Where have you been?'

'In the settlement,' her son answered reluctantly, taking his rifle out of its case and inspecting it.

His mother shook her head.

Putting some powder on the pan, Lukashka got his satchel, took out some empty cartridge cases and began to fill them, stuffing them thoroughly with a bullet wrapped in a rag. Having tested the filled cases with his teeth and inspected them, he put the satchel down.

'I say, mother, I told you to mend the bags; have you done it?' he said.

'Of course! I think the deaf and dumb lass mended them last night. Is it time for you be going back to the cordon again? I haven't seen anything of you at all.'

'As soon as I've cleared up I'll have to be off,' replied Lukashka, tying up the gunpowder. 'Hey, where is the deaf and dumb lass? Has she gone out?'

'She must be chopping firewood. She's been fretting for you constantly. I won't see him at all, she says. She points to her face like this, makes a clicking sound and presses her hands to her heart, as if she were saying she missed you. Shall I call her in? She understood all about the Abrek.'

'Yes, do,' said Lukashka. 'And I had some tallow out there, please bring it here. I need to grease my sword.'

The old woman went out, and a few minutes later Lukashka's deaf and dumb sister came up the creaking front steps and into the hut. She was six years older than her brother and would have been extremely like him had it not been for the vacant and coarsely changeable expression – common to all who are deaf and dumb – of her face. Her clothing consisted of a coarse shirt, covered in patches; her feet were bare and stained with mud; on her head there was an old blue kerchief. Her necks, arms and face were sinewy, like those of a muzhik. It was clear, both from her clothing and from everything else, that she constantly performed the hard work of a man. She brought in a bundle of firewood and threw it down beside the stove. Then she went over to her brother with a joyful smile that creased the whole of her face, touched him on the shoulder and began to make quick signs to him with her hands, her face and her whole body.

'Good, good! Good lass, Styopka!' replied her brother, nodding his head. 'You've brought and mended everything, good lass! Here's something for you in return!' And, taking two spice cakes from his pocket, he gave them to her.

The face of the deaf and dumb girl flushed, and she began to shriek wildly with joy. Seizing the spice cakes, she began to make signs even more quickly, pointing frequently in one direction and passing a fat finger over her eyebrows and face. Lukashka understood her and kept nodding, smiling slightly. She was saying that her brother should give the girls 'snacks', saying that the girls liked him and that one girl, the best of them all, liked him too. She indicated Maryanka by quickly pointing in the direction of Maryanka's yard, and then to her own eyebrows and face, smacking her lips and shaking her head. 'Likes you,' she mimed, pressing her hands to her breast, kissing her own hand and pretending to embrace someone. Their mother returned to the hut and, on learning what her deaf and dumb daughter was talking about, smiled and shook her head. Her daughter showed her the gingerbread cakes and again began to shriek quietly with joy.

'I was telling Ulitka the other day that I'd send them a matchmaker,' said her mother. 'She took my words well.'

Lukashka looked at his mother in silence.

'How about it, mother? We must sell the wine. I need a horse.'

'I'll sell it when it's time; I'm going to get the barrels ready,' said his mother, evidently reluctant to let her son interfere in household matters. 'When you go,' the old woman told her son, 'take the bag that's out in the passage. I borrowed from some people, got you some things to take back to the cordon. Or should I put them in your *sakvy?**

'Very well,' replied Lukashka. 'And if Girey-Khan comes across the river, send him to the cordon, for I won't be getting any leave for a long time now. I've some business with him.'

He began to get ready to leave.

'I will, Lukashka, I will. You've been drinking at Yamka's all the time, haven't you?' said the old woman. 'At any rate, whenever I got up in the night to see to the cattle, it seemed to be your voice I heard singing.'

Lukashka made no reply, went out into the passage,

---

* *Sakvy* are the bags that Cossacks carry behind their saddles. (Tolstoy's note.)

threw the bags over his shoulder, tucked up his coat, picked up his rifle and stopped in the doorway.

'Goodbye, mother,' he said. His mother saw him to the gate. 'Send me a nice little barrel with Nazarka – I promised the lads; he'll call for it,' he said to her, closing the gate behind him.

'Christ save you, Lukashka! God be with you! I'll send you some, from the new barrel,' the old woman replied, going over to the fence. 'And listen,' she added, leaning over the fence.

The Cossack stopped.

'You had a good time here, well, and thanks be to God! Why shouldn't a young man make merry? Well, and God has given you luck. That's good. But when you get over there, mind out, now, son . . . Don't you ever go and get into trouble with your superiors. That's not on! But I'll sell the wine, I'll find the money to buy a horse, and I'll get you married to that girl.'

'Very well, very well,' her son replied, frowning.

His deaf and dumb sister shouted in order to draw his attention. She pointed to her head and to her arm, which meant: a shaven head, a Chechen. Then, knitting her brows, she went through the gestures of aiming with a rifle, uttered a shriek and began a rapid chanting, shaking her head. She was saying that Lukashka should kill another Chechen.

Lukashka understood, smiled wryly, and with swift, light steps, holding his rifle behind his back under his cloak, disappeared in the thick mist.

Having stood in silence at the gate for a while, the old woman returned to the hut and at once set to work.

18

Lukashka walked to the cordon, while at the same time Uncle Yeroshka whistled to his dogs and, climbing over the wattle fence, went round by the backs of the houses to Olenin's quarters (when going hunting, he did not like to meet women). Olenin was still asleep, and even Vanyusha, awake but not yet risen, was looking around him and wondering if it was time to get up yet, when Uncle Yeroshka, his rifle on his shoulder and wearing all his hunter's gear, opened the door.

'Beat the drum! Sound the alarm!' he cried in his thick voice. 'The Chechens are here! Ivan! Get the samovar ready for your master. And out of bed with you! Hurry up!' shouted the old man. 'That's the way we do it, my good sir. Look, even the girls are up now. Look out of the window, look, she's going to fetch water, and you're asleep.' **101**

Olenin woke up and leapt to his feet. He felt so fresh and cheerful at the sight of the old man and the sound of his voice.

'Hurry up, hurry up, Vanyusha!' he cried.

'Is this how you go hunting?' said the old man. 'Everyone's at breakfast, but you are still asleep. Lyam! Where are you off to?' he shouted at his dog. 'Is your rifle ready?' he shouted, as though there were a whole crowd of people in the hut.

'Well, I'm for it, there's nothing to be done. Powder, Vanyusha! Wads!' said Olenin.

'I'll fine you!' shouted the old man.

'*Doo tay voolay voo?*'[31] said Vanyusha, smirking.

'You're a foreigner! You talk like a damned foreigner!' the old man shouted at Vanyusha, exposing stumps of teeth.

'First offenders are pardoned!' Olenin joked, as he pulled on his tall boots.

'First offenders are pardoned,' replied Yeroshka, 'but if you oversleep another time, the fine will be a pail of *chikhir*. By the time it gets warmer you won't find any deer.'

'And even if you do find them, they'll be cleverer than you are,' said Olenin, echoing the old man's words of the night before. 'You won't pull the wool over their eyes.'

'That's right, laugh all you want! Kill one first, then you can talk. Well, hurry up! Look, here's the landlord coming to see you,' said Yeroshka, looking out of the window. 'Sheesh, he's all dressed up, got a new coat and all, so you'll realize he's an officer. Ach, these men, these men!'

Vanyusha announced that the landlord wished to see the *barin*.

'*Larjong!*'[32] he said with a thoughtful air, warning the *barin* of the import of the cornet's visit. Next, the cornet himself, in a new Circassian coat with officer's stripes on the shoulders, and wearing polished boots – something rare among Cossacks – with a smile on his face, swaying from side to side, entered the room and congratulated Olenin on his arrival.

The cornet, Ilya Vasilyevich, was an 'educated' Cossack, who had lived in Russia, was a schoolteacher and, above all, a 'gentleman'. He wanted to appear a 'gentleman'; but beneath the ugly assumed gloss of frivolity, the self-confidence and the absurd manner of speech, one sensed a man just like Uncle Yeroshka. This was plain just by looking at his sunburnt face, his hands and his reddish nose. Olenin asked him to sit down.

'Good morning, Ilya Vasilyich, sir!' said Yeroshka, getting up and making, it seemed to Olenin, an ironically low bow.

'Good morning, Uncle! You're here already?' replied the cornet, casually nodding to him.

The cornet was a man of about forty, with a grey, wedge-shaped beard, dry, slim and handsome and still very fresh for his forty years. In coming to see Olenin, he evidently feared that he would be taken for an ordinary Cossack, and wished to make his importance felt at once.

'This is our Nimrod of Egypt,' he said, turning to Olenin with a self-satisfied smile, and pointing at the old man. 'A mighty hunter before the Lord. The first among us at every task. Have you already made his acquaintance?'

As Uncle Yeroshka looked at his feet, which were shod in wet rawhide sandals, he shook his head reflectively, as though marvelling at the cornet's adroitness and learning, and repeated to himself: 'Nimrod of Eejit! What will he think of next?'

'Well, we're off hunting, you see,' said Olenin.

'Indeed, sir, yes,' observed the cornet. 'But I have a small matter to discuss with you.'

'What can I do for you?'

'As you are a gentleman,' the cornet began, 'and as I understand that I also bear the rank of officer and thus we can always do business together by stages, like all gentlemen . . . (He paused, glancing with a smile at Olenin and the old man.) However, if you so wish, with my consent, as my wife is a stupid woman in my possession, she could not at the present time fully comprehend your words of the last inst. For my quarters might be let, without stables, to the regimental adjutant for six "coins" – though, as a gentleman, I can always make that gratis. But as it is your wish, then I, myself bearing the rank of officer, can come to an agreement with you personally in everything, and as a resident of this locality, not like the women according to our custom, but in everything am able to observe the conditions . . .'

'He's a plain speaker, isn't he,' muttered the old man.

The cornet went on speaking in the same vein for a long

time. From all of it Olenin was able to gather, not without difficulty, that the cornet was willing to let the quarters for six silver roubles a month. Olenin eagerly agreed to this, and offered his guest a glass of tea. The cornet declined.

'According to our stupid ritual,' he said, 'we consider it almost a sin to use an ordinary glass. Though of course I with my education could understand it, my wife, because of human weakness . . .'

'Well, may I offer you some tea?'

'If you will permit, I shall fetch my own glass, a *special* one,' the cornet replied, and went out to the porch. 'Bring a glass!' he cried.

A few minutes later the door opened and a young, sunburnt arm in a pink sleeve was thrust through the doorway with a glass. The cornet approached, took the glass and whispered something to his daughter. Olenin poured tea into the cornet's *special* glass, and into Yeroshka's *ordinary* one.

'But I do not wish to detain you,' said the cornet, draining his glass and scalding himself. 'I also have a great inclination for fishing and am only here on leave, by way of recreation from my duties, as it were. I also have a desire to try my luck and see if the *gifts of the Terek* may fall to my lot. I hope that you will come and visit us some time to drink the paternal wine,[33] in accordance with our settlement custom,' he added.

The cornet bowed, shook Olenin's hand and went out. While Olenin was preparing to leave he could hear the cornet's clear and commanding voice giving orders to the members of the household. And a few moments later Olenin saw the cornet, in a tattered *beshmet* and trousers rolled up to his knees, walk past his window with a net on his shoulder.

'He's a rogue, though,' said Uncle Yeroshka, finishing

the tea in his *ordinary* glass. 'What, are you really going to pay him six "coins"? It's unheard of! You could have the best hut in the settlement for two. What a monster! Hey, you can have mine for three.'

'No, I think I'll stay here,' said Olenin.

'Six "coins"! It's a fool's money, stands to reason. E-ech!' replied the old man. 'Give us some *chikhir,* Ivan!'

When they had had a snack and drunk some vodka for the road, Olenin and the old man came out on to the street together before eight o'clock.

At the gate they encountered a harnessed ox cart. With a white kerchief down to her eyes, and a *beshmet* on top of her shirt, wearing boots and holding a long dry branch in her hand, Maryana was hauling the oxen forward by a rope that was tied to their horns.

'Mamushka!' said the old man quietly, making it look as though he was going to seize her in his arms.

Maryanka waved her branch at him and glanced at them both cheerfully with her beautiful eyes.

Olenin felt even more cheerful.

'Well, let's be off, let's be off!' he said, throwing his rifle on to his shoulder and sensing the girl's eyes on him.

'Gee up! Gee up!' came Maryana's voice behind them, and then the ox cart began to creak forward.

While the road passed the backs of the houses of the settlement, along the pastures, Yeroshka continued to talk. He could not get the cornet out of his mind, and kept cursing him.

'But why are you so angry at him?' asked Olenin.

'He's mean! I don't like that,' replied the old man. 'When he dies it will all remain behind him. Who is he saving it for? He's built two houses. He's gained another garden from his brother by a lawsuit. And he's a dab hand at the paperwork, too! People come from other settlements to get him to write their documents for them. Whatever he writes, it works out exactly that way. He gets it absolutely right. But who is he saving for? All he's got is a boy, and the girl; when she gets married, there won't be anyone.'

'So he's saving up for her dowry,' said Olenin.

'What dowry? The girl will be taken, she's a fine girl. But he's damn well got to go and get her married to a rich man. He wants to get as much bride money as he can for her. Luka's a Cossack, my neighbour and nephew, a fine lad, the one who killed the Chechen, he's been wooing her for a long time; but he won't let him have her. Now it's one thing, now it's another: the girl's too young, he says. But I know what's in his mind. He wants them to get down on their knees to him. The way he was acting about the girl today was shameful. And yet Lukashka will get her. Because he's the best Cossack in the settlement, he's a *djigit,* killed an Abrek, he'll be given a medal.'

'But what about this? When I was strolling about the yard last night I saw the landlord's daughter kissing some Cossack,' said Olenin.

'You're making it up!' cried the old man, stopping in his tracks.

'I swear to God,' said Olenin.

'Women are the devil,' said Yeroshka, pondering. 'But who was the Cossack?'

'I couldn't see.'

'Well, what sort of band did he have on his cap? A white one?'

'Yes.'

'And a red coat? About your height, was he?'

'No, a bit taller.'

'It was him.' Yeroshka began to laugh. 'It was him, my Marka. It was Lukashka. I call him Marka, for fun. The man himself. I love it! I was like that, my dear fellow. There's no point in trying to keep an eye on them. My "darling" slept in a room with her mother and sister-in-law, but I always got in. She used to live at the top of the house; her mother was a witch, a devil, my God she didn't like me – I used to come with my *nyanya* (my friend, that is), Girchik his name was. I'd go under her window, then I'd stand on his shoulders, push the window up, and feel about. She'd be sleeping there, on the bench. One night I woke her up. My, how she gasped! She didn't recognize me. Who is it? And I couldn't say. Her mother was beginning to stir. I took off my cap and shoved it in her face; then she knew right away by the seam in the cap. Out she jumped. I never went hungry in those days. She'd bring you *kaymak* and grapes, the lot,' Yeroshka added, explaining it all in practical terms. 'And she wasn't the only one. That was a life.'

'And what now?'

'Now we're going to follow a dog, get a pheasant to sit on a tree, and then you can shoot it.'

'Would you have run after Maryanka?'

'You keep an eye on the dogs. I'll tell you tonight,' said the old man, indicating his favourite dog, Lyam.

They fell silent.

Continuing the conversation for a hundred yards or so, the old man stopped again and pointed to a twig that was lying in the road.

'What do you think that is?' he said. 'Do you think that's all right? No. That stick's lying wrong.'

'What do you mean, lying wrong?'

He grinned wryly.

'You don't know anything, do you? Listen to me. When you find a stick like that in the road, you don't step over it, you either go round it or you throw it away and say a prayer: "In the name of the Father, the Son and the Holy Ghost" – and be on your way. It won't do anything to you. That's what the old men taught me.'

'Oh, what rubbish!' said Olenin. 'You'd do better to tell

me about Maryana. What, does she go out with Lukashka, then?'

'Shh! Be quiet now,' the old man said, again interrupting this line of talk in a whisper. 'Just listen. We're going to go round through the forest.'

And the old man, stepping softly in his rawhide sandals, walked forward along a narrow path which led into dense, wild, overgrown forest. Several times, frowning, he looked round at Olenin who, rustling and clattering with his large boots, and, carrying his rifle carelessly, several times got caught on the twigs of trees that had grown across the path.

'Don't make such a noise, go quietly, soldier!' he said to him in angry whispers.

One could feel in the air that the sun had risen. The mist was lifting, but it still covered the tops of the trees. The forest seemed strangely tall. At every step they took forward, the landscape changed. What had seemed to be a tree turned out to be a bush; a reed looked like a tree.

19

The mist was lifting in some places, revealing wet, reed-thatched roofs, and in others turning to dew, moistening the road and the grass near the fences. Everywhere smoke rose from chimneys. The people were leaving the settlement – some for their work, some for the river, some for the cordons. The hunters walked side by side along the damp, overgrown road. The dogs, wagging their tails and looking round at their master, ran at their sides. Myriad gnats hovered in the air and pursued the hunters, covering their backs, eyes and hands. There was a smell of grass and damp forest. Olenin kept looking round at the ox cart in which Maryanka sat, driving the oxen with her long dry branch.

It was quiet. The sounds of the settlement, audible before, now did not reach the hunters; only from time to time the dogs went crashing through the brambles, and there was the occasional cry of a bird. Olenin knew that it was dangerous in the forest, that Abreks always hid in these places. He also knew that for a man on foot in the forest, a rifle is a great protection. Not that he was afraid, but he felt that someone else in his place might be afraid and, straining his eyes, peered into the damp, misty forest, listening to the sparse, faint sounds, he shifted his grasp on his rifle and felt a pleasant sensation that was new to him. Uncle Yeroshka, who had gone on in front, stopped at every puddle where there were the twin tracks of an animal and, carefully studying them, pointed them out to Olenin. He hardly spoke, making only occasional whispered remarks. The road along which they were walking had once been made by an ox cart, and had long ago become overgrown with grass. The forest of elm and plane on both sides was so dense and overgrown that nothing could be seen through it. Almost every tree was twined from top to bottom with wild vines; dark bramble bushes grew thickly at their base. Each small clearing was completely overgrown with blackberry bushes and reeds with grey, swaying heads. In places large animal tracks and small ones, like tunnels, made by pheasants, led down from the road into the thick of the forest. The resilience of the vegetation of this forest, which cattle had not penetrated, struck Olenin at every step: he had never seen anything like it. This forest, the danger, the old man with his mysterious whispering, Maryanka with her shapely, boyish figure and the mountains – to Olenin it all seemed like a dream.

'A pheasant's come down,' whispered the old man, looking round and pulling his cap over his face. 'Hide your face: it's a pheasant.' He waved at Olenin angrily and crawled onward, almost on all fours. 'They don't like a human face.'

Olenin was still behind him when the old man stopped and began to survey a tree. A cock pheasant 'choggled'[34] from a tree at the dog that was barking at it, and Olenin saw the pheasant. But at that same moment there was a bang, like that of a cannon, from Yeroshka's enormous rifle, the cock fluttered up, losing feathers, and fell to the ground. As he walked over to the old man, Olenin startled another. Freeing his rifle, he aimed and fired. The pheasant soared straight up and then, like a stone, getting caught on the branches, fell down into the thicket.

'Good lad!' the old man shouted, laughing, for he was not skilled at shooting birds in flight.

When they had picked up the pheasants they walked on. Olenin, excited by the physical exercise and the praise, kept talking to the old man.

'Wait! Let's go this way!' the old man interrupted him. 'I saw some deer tracks here yesterday.'

Turning off into the thicket and going some three hundred paces, they emerged into a small clearing overgrown with reeds, and flooded in places. Olenin could still not keep up with the old hunter, and Uncle Yeroshka, some twenty paces ahead of him, bent down, nodding and beckoning to him with his arm. On catching up with him, Olenin saw the imprint of a human foot, which the old man was pointing out to him.

'You see?'

'Yes. What of it?' said Olenin, trying to speak as calmly as he could. 'Someone's footprint.'

Involuntarily, thoughts of Cooper's Pathfinder[35] and of Abreks flashed through his mind, but observing the air of mystery with which the old man was walking on, he could not bring himself to ask and was uncertain as to whether danger or hunting was the cause of the mystery.

'No, the footprint's mine, but look there,' the old man replied, pointing to the grass, under which the barely perceptible track of an animal could be seen.

The old man went on. Olenin kept up with him. When they had gone some twenty paces, moving downhill, they came to a thicket and a spreading pear tree, beneath which the earth was black and the fresh dung of an animal had been left.

The vine-entangled place resembled a cosy covered arbour, dark and cool.

'He's been here this morning,' the old man said with a sigh. 'His lair is damp and fresh.'

Suddenly there was a terrible crashing sound in the forest some ten paces from them. Both men started and grabbed their rifles, but nothing was visible; all one could hear was branches breaking. For a moment a swift, rhythmic galloping was heard, and the crashing turned into a rumble, echoing more and more distantly, wider and wider through the quiet forest. Something seemed to snap in Olenin's heart. In vain he stared into the green thicket and at last looked round at the old man. Uncle Yeroshka, his rifle pressed to his chest, stood motionless; his cap was knocked backwards, his eyes burned with an unusual brilliance, and his open mouth, from which worn yellow teeth were malevolently thrust, had frozen in its position.

'An antlered king,' he said quietly. And, throwing down his rifle in despair, he tugged at his grey beard. 'It was right here! We should have approached it from the path! I'm a fool! A fool!' And he seized himself malevolently by the beard. 'Fool! Pig!' he kept repeating, tugging himself painfully by the beard. In the mist, something seemed to fly away over the forest; ever more distant, wider and wider rumbled the galloping of the frightened stag . . .

112   It was twilight when Olenin returned with the old man, tired, hungry and full of energy. The dinner was ready. He ate and drank with the old man until he felt warm and cheerful, and went out on to the porch. Again before his eyes the mountains rose in the sunset. Again the old man told his endless stories of hunting, of Abreks, of sweethearts, of a bold and carefree life. Again the beautiful Maryanka entered and left and crossed the yard. Under her shirt the beautiful girl's powerful, maidenly body was clearly outlined.

20

The next day, this time without the old man, Olenin walked to the place where they had frightened the stag. Instead of going round through the gate, he climbed the prickly hedge, as everyone in the settlement did. And before he had time to pull out the thorns that caught on his Circassian coat, his dog, which ran on ahead, had already startled two pheasants. No sooner had he gone into the brambles than pheasants began to rise at every step he took. (The old man had not shown him this place the previous day, in order to preserve it for hunting with the screen.) Olenin killed five pheasants with twelve shots and, clambering after them through the brambles, became 113 so exhausted that the sweat poured from him in torrents. He called back his dog, released the cocking pieces, placed bullets on the small shot and, warding off the gnats with the sleeves of his coat, slowly walked to the place they had visited the previous day. But it was impossible to restrain the dog, which had found trails on the road itself, and he shot another pair of pheasants, with the result that, detained by retrieving them, only towards noon did he start to recognize the place of the day before.

The day was utterly cloudless, quiet and hot. Even in the forest the morning coolness had withered away, and myriad gnats literally stuck to his face, back and arms. The dog had changed colour from black to grey: its back was entirely covered with gnats. Olenin's Circassian coat, through which they had passed their stings, had turned the same colour. He was ready to flee the gnats: he already had the feeling that life in the settlement was impossible in summer. He was on the point of going home, but remembering that, after all, people did manage to live here, he determined to endure it and began to resign himself to being eaten alive. And, strange to tell, by noon he had even begun to find this sensation a pleasant one. It even seemed to him that, were it not for this gnat-laden atmosphere around him, this gnat-laden paste that was smeared by his hand over his sweaty face, and this restless itching over the whole of his body, the forest here would lose its character and its charm for him. These myriad insects were so suited to this wild, outrageously lavish vegetation, this vast array of birds and beasts that filled the forest, this dark foliage, this hot, pungent air, these channels of muddy water that everywhere seeped from the Terek and gurgled somewhere beneath the overhanging leaves, that he began to find pleasant the very thing that previously had seemed horrible and insupportable. Going round the place where yesterday he had found the animal, and not encountering anything, he began to feel like taking a rest. The sun stood directly above the forest, constantly striking his back and head in vertical fashion whenever he emerged into a clearing or on to a road. The seven heavy pheasants weighed him down painfully at the waist. He found the tracks of yesterday's stag, crept under a bush into the thicket, to that very place where yesterday the stag had lain, and lay down beside its lair. He examined the dark foliage around him, examined the damp place, yesterday's dung, the imprint of the stag's knees, the clod of black earth it had torn up, and his own footprints of yesterday. He felt cool, comfortable; there was nothing in his mind, he had no desires. And suddenly he was assailed by such a strange feeling of causeless happiness and love for everything that, following an old habit of his childhood, he began to cross himself and thank someone. It suddenly occurred to him with great clarity that 'here am I, Dmitry Olenin, a being so separate from all others: now I lie alone, God knows where, in the place where a stag lived, an old stag, a beautiful one, that may never have seen a human being, and in a place where no human being has ever sat and thought this. I sit, and around me stand trees young and old, and one of them is twined with a lattice of wild vines; around me pheasants are moving, chasing one another away and, perhaps, sensing the presence of their slain brothers.' He felt his pheasants, inspected them and wiped his warm, blood-stained hands on his Circassian coat. 'Perhaps the jackals can scent them, and they're making their way in a different direction, with discontented faces; around me, flitting between the leaves, which to them seem like enormous islands, the gnats hang in the air, humming; one, two, three, four, a hundred, a thousand, a million gnats, and all of them for some unknown reason are humming around me, and each of them is a Dmitry Olenin, separate from all others, as I am.' He had a clear impression of what the 115 gnats were humming. 'This way, this way, lads! Here's one for us to eat,' they hummed as they stuck to him all over. And it became clear to him that he was not a Russian nobleman at all, a member of Moscow society, the friend and relative of such and such a person, but just a gnat, or a pheasant, or a stag, like the ones that were living now, all around him. 'Like them, like Uncle Yeroshka, I shall live and die. And what he says is true: "the grass will grow on your grave, and that's it".'

'And what if the grass does grow?' he thought further. 'I must still live, I must be happy; because that is the only thing I want – happiness. It doesn't matter what I am: an animal like all the others on top of whom the grass will grow, and that is all, or a frame in which a part of the one God has been placed – I must nevertheless live in the best way. So how must I live, in order to be happy, and why have I not been happy before?' And he began to remember his past life, and he felt loathing for himself. He appeared to himself as a very demanding egoist, when really he needed nothing for himself. And still he kept looking around him at the foliage with the light shining through it, at the descending sun and the cloudless sky, and felt just as happy as before. 'Why am I happy, and what did I live for before?' he thought. 'How demanding I was for myself, what plans I dreamt up, yet I brought myself only shame and unhappiness! But now I don't need anything in order to be happy!' And suddenly it was as if a new light were revealed to him. 'This is what happiness is,' he said to himself. 'Happiness is to live for others. And that is obvious. The need for happiness has been placed in every human being; therefore it is lawful. In the process of trying to satisfy it egoistically, by seeking wealth, fame, the comforts of life, love, it may happen that circumstances develop in such a way that it will be impossible to satisfy those desires. Consequently, those desires are unlawful, but the need for happiness is not unlawful. But what desires can always be satisfied, in spite of external conditions? What are they? Love, and selflessness.' So overjoyed and excited was he on discovering this – as it seemed to him – new truth, that he leapt to his feet and impatiently began to look for someone for whom he could sacrifice himself, to whom he could do good, whom he could love. 'After all, one needs nothing for oneself,' he kept thinking, 'so why not live for others?' He picked up his rifle and, with the intention of returning home as soon as possible in order to consider all this and find an opportunity of doing good, made his way out of the thicket. On emerging into the clearing, he glanced round: the sun was no longer visible, above the treetops the air was growing cooler, and the landscape seemed to him quite unfamiliar and unlike the one that surrounded the settlement. Everything had suddenly changed – both the weather and the character of the forest: the sky was becoming covered with clouds, the wind was soughing in the treetops, and all around one could see nothing but reeds and broken, untended forest. He began to call his dog, which had run away from him in pursuit of some creature, and his voice came echoing desolately back to him. And suddenly he felt a sense of sinister terror. He began to lose his nerve. Into his head came thoughts of Abreks, murders he had been told about, and he expected that at any time now Chechens would leap out from every bush and he would have to defend his life and die or be a coward. He remembered both God and the life to come more intensely than he had done for a long time. And all around was this same gloomy, severe, wild nature. 'And is there any point in living for oneself,' he thought, 'when very soon one may die, and die without having done any good, and in such a way that no one will ever know?' He walked in the direction where he supposed the settlement lay. Hunting was far from his thoughts now; he felt a crushing weariness and surveyed each bush and tree with extreme attentiveness, almost with horror, expecting at any moment to be called to account for his life. Having wandered in circles for quite a long time, he emerged on to a channel along which cold, sandy water from the Terek flowed, and, in order not to lose his way any further, decided to walk along it. He walked without knowing where the channel would take him. Suddenly behind him the reeds began to snap. He started, and grabbed his rifle. Then he felt ashamed of himself; the overzealous dog, breathing heavily, had thrown itself into the cold water of the channel and begun to lap it.

He drank together with the dog, and then set off in the direction it pulled him in, supposing that it would take him to the settlement. But, in spite of the dog's companionship, everything around him seemed even gloomier. The forest was growing dark, and with ever increasing strength the wind played in the tops of the old, broken trees. Some large birds were hovering and screeching around the nests in these trees. The vegetation was becoming poorer, and more often now he encountered rustling reeds and bare sandy clearings covered with animal tracks. To the howling of the wind was added another cheerless, monotonous howl. All in all, his soul was clouding over. Groping behind him for his pheasants, he discovered that one was missing. The pheasant had got ripped away and been lost, and only the bloody neck and head still stuck out at his waist. He felt more afraid than ever. He began to pray, fearing only one thing – that he would die without ever having done anything kind or good; and he so much wanted to live, live in order to perform an act of selflessness.

21

Suddenly it was as if the sun came out within his soul. He heard the sounds of Russian being spoken, heard the swift and even flow of the Terek, and a few yards ahead of him it all opened up: the brown, advancing surface of the river, with brown, wet sand on the banks and sandbanks, the distant steppe, the watchtower of the cordon distinct above the water, a saddled horse moving through the brambles in its hobble, and the mountains. A red sun emerged from behind a cloud for an instant, for an instant cheerfully gleaming with its last rays on the river, the reeds, the watchtower and the Cossacks gathered in a little group, among whom the vigorous figure of Lukashka **119** caught Olenin's involuntary attention.

For no obvious reason, Olenin felt completely happy again. He had reached the Nizhne-Prototsk post, on the Terek, facing a pacified *aul* on the other side of the river. He greeted the Cossacks, but, as yet finding no occasion to do good to any of them, entered the hut. Neither in the hut did any opportunity present itself. The Cossacks received him coldly. He entered the wattle and daub hut and lit a cigarette. The Cossacks did not pay much attention to Olenin, firstly because he was smoking a cigarette and secondly because they had another diversion that evening. From the mountains had come, with a scout, some hostile Chechens, relatives of the Abrek who had been killed, to ransom the corpse. They were waiting for the Cossack Command to arrive from the settlement. The brother of the Chechen who had been killed, a tall, slim man whose red beard was clipped and dyed in spite of the fact that he was dressed in a most ragged Circassian coat and cap, was as calm and majestic as a tsar. He bore a marked facial resemblance to the dead Abrek. He did not deem anyone worthy of his gaze, never once even glanced at the dead man and, squatting on his heels in the shade, merely spat from time to time as he smoked his pipe, occasionally emitting some guttural sounds of command, to which his fellow traveller attended with deference. It was evident that this was a *djigit* who had several times encountered Russians in rather different circumstances, and that now there was nothing about Russians that could possibly surprise or even interest him. Olenin was on the point of approaching the corpse and had begun to look at it, when the brother, glancing up at him from under his eyebrows with calm contempt, said something abruptly and angrily. The scout hurried to cover the dead man's face with his coat. Olenin was struck by the majesty and severity of the expression on the *djigit*'s face; he began to talk to him, asking what *aul* he was from, but the Chechen barely glanced at him, spat contemptuously and turned away. Olenin was so surprised at the mountain dweller's lack of interest in him that he could only ascribe the man's indifference to stupidity or ignorance of Russian. He turned to the man's companion. The companion, a scout and interpreter, was just as ragged, but with black hair instead of red, restless and fidgety, with extremely white teeth and sparkling black eyes. The scout willingly entered into conversation and asked for a cigarette.

'There were five brothers,' the scout was saying in his broken semi-Russian. 'This is the third brother the Russians have killed, only two are left; he's a *djigit*, a great *djigit*,' the scout said, pointing to the Chechen. 'When they killed Akhmed-Khan' (this was the dead *djigit*'s name), 'this man was sitting in the reeds on the other side; he saw everything: how they put him in the skiff and brought him to the shore. He sat there until night-time; wanted to shoot the old man, but the others would not let him.

Lukashka approached the man who was talking and sat down.

'And which *aul* was he from?' he asked.

'It's in those hills over there,' replied the scout, pointing beyond the Terek, to a misty blueish gorge. 'Do you know Suyuk-su? It's about ten *versts* on the other side of it.'

'Do you know Girey-Khan in Suyuk-su?' asked Lukashka, obviously proud of this acquaintance. 'He's a *kunak* of mine.'

'He's my neighbour,' the scout replied.

'A sterling fellow!' And Lukashka, evidently very interested, began to talk to the interpreter in Tatar.

Soon a Cossack lieutenant and the head of the settlement arrived, with a retinue of two Cossacks. The lieutenant, who was one of the new school of Cossack officers, greeted the Cossacks; but none of them shouted to him in reply, as army men would, 'We wish you health, yer honour!' – and only one or two replied with a simple bow. Some, including Lukashka, rose and stood to attention. The sergeant major reported that everything at the post was in order. All this seemed to Olenin comical: it was as though these Cossacks were playing soldiers. But formality soon gave way to ordinary ways of behaving, and the lieutenant, who was just as skilful a Cossack as the others, began to speak to the interpreter in fluent and flamboyant Tatar. They filled in some form or other, handed it to the scout, took some money from him and approached the body.

'Gavrilov, Luka – which one of you is he?' asked the lieutenant quietly. Lukashka took off his cap and stepped forward.

'I've sent the regimental commander a report about you. I don't know what will come of it, but I've put you forward for a medal – you're too young to be made a sergeant major yet. Can you read and write?'

'Certainly not.'

'But what a fine fellow he is to look at!' said the lieutenant, continuing to play at being top brass. 'Put your cap on. What Gavrilovs does he belong to? Is he one of the Shiroky lot?'

'A nephew,' replied the sergeant major.

'I know, I know. Well, carry on, then, help them,' he said to the Cossacks.

Lukashka's face fairly shone with joy and seemed more handsome than usual. Moving away from the sergeant major and putting his cap on, he sat down beside Olenin again.

When the corpse had been carried to the skiff, the Chechen's brother came across to the riverbank. The Cossacks involuntarily stepped aside to let him pass. With a powerful leg he thrust himself off the bank and jumped into the boat. It was now that for the first time, as Olenin noticed, he took in all the Cossacks with a swift glance and again asked some abrupt question of his companion. The companion made some reply, and pointed to Lukashka. The Chechen's brother glanced at him and, slowly turning away, began to look at the other bank. Not hatred but cold contempt was expressed in that gaze. He said something more.

'What did he say?' Olenin asked the fidgety interpreter.

'Your people kill our people, our people put yours in coffins. It's all the same *khurda-murda*,' said the scout, obviously dissembling, and he began to laugh, baring his white teeth.

The dead man's brother sat without moving a muscle, gazing fixedly at the other bank. He was so full of hatred and contempt that there was not even anything of interest to him here. The scout, standing at one end of the skiff, moving his paddle now to this side, now to that, steered adroitly and spoke without cease. As it cut obliquely across the current, the skiff was becoming smaller and smaller, the voices were growing scarcely audible, and, at last, still within sight, they pulled in to the bank, where their horses stood. There they lifted out the corpse and in spite of the fact that the horse shied, put it across the saddle, mounted their steeds and rode at walking pace along the road past an *aul*, from which a crowd of people came to look at them. As for the Cossacks on this side of the river, they were extremely content and cheerful. Laughter and joking could be heard from every quarter. The lieutenant and the head of the settlement went to be fed and watered at the wattle and daub hut. Lukashka, with a cheerful expression to which he vainly strove to impart an air of gravity, sat beside Olenin, leaning his elbows on his knees and whittling a stick.

123

'Why do you smoke?' he said, as if with curiosity. 'Is it good?'

He evidently said this only because he had noticed that Olenin felt uncomfortable and that he was alone among the Cossacks.

'I just do, it's a habit,' replied Olenin. 'Why?'

'Hm! If one of us were to start smoking, there'd be trouble! It's not far to those mountains,' said Lukashka, pointing to the gorge, 'but you'd never get there! . . . What are you going home on your own for? It's dark. I'll go with you, if you like,' said Lukashka. 'You ask the sergeant major.'

'What a fine fellow,' thought Olenin, looking at the Cossack's cheerful face. He remembered Maryanka and the kiss he had watched by the gate, and he felt sorry for Lukashka, sorry for his lack of education. 'What nonsense and muddle is this?' he thought. 'A man kills another, and is happy, content, as though he'd performed the most magnificent deed. Is there really nothing to tell him that there is no cause for great joy in this? That happiness lies not in killing, but in sacrificing oneself?'

'Well, you'd better not cross his path now, brother,' said one of the Cossacks who had seen the skiff off, addressing his words to Lukashka. 'Did you hear him asking about you?'

Lukashka raised his head.

'Is it about the godson?'[36] said Lukashka, using this word to refer to the dead Chechen.

'The godson's not going to get up again, but the red-haired fellow is the godson's brother!'

'Let him say his prayers and thank God he's still alive,' said Lukashka, laughing.

'What are you so pleased about?' said Olenin to Lukashka. 'What if it was your brother who'd been killed; would you be pleased?'

The Cossack's eyes laughed as they looked at Olenin. It seemed he had understood everything that Olenin was trying to say to him, but was above such considerations.

'So what? It happens! Our brothers get killed, too, don't they?'

22

The lieutenant and the head of the settlement rode away; and Olenin, in order to do something pleasant for Lukashka and also not to have to go back alone through the dark forest, asked that Lukashka be given leave, and the sergeant major gave it. Olenin thought that Lukashka wanted to see Maryanka, and was in any case glad of the companionship of such a pleasant-looking and talkative Cossack. Lukashka and Maryanka were involuntarily combined in his imagination, and he found pleasure in thinking about them. 'He loves Maryana,' Olenin thought to himself, 'and I could love her, too.' And as they walked home through the dark forest he was overcome by a powerful feeling of tenderness 125 that was new to him. Lukashka was also in a cheerful mood. Something resembling love could be sensed between these two young men, so different from each other. Each time they exchanged glances they felt like laughing.

'Which gate do you go in by?'

'The middle one. But I'll see you as far as the marsh. There you really have nothing to fear.'

Olenin began to laugh.

'Do you think I'm afraid? Go back if you like, but thank you – I shall get there alone.'

'That's all very well, but what am I supposed to do? Of course you're afraid – I'm afraid, too,' said Lukashka, also laughing, and trying to bolster Olenin's *amour propre*.

'Why don't you come back to my house? We'll talk, drink, and in the morning you can go.'

'Do you think I can't find a nice little place to spend the night?' Lukashka laughed. 'But the sergeant major asked me to go and see him.'

'I heard you singing last night, and saw you, too . . .'

'It seems that everyone did . . .' And Luka shook his head.

'I say, are you really getting married? Is it true?'

'Mother wants me to get married. And I haven't even got a horse yet.'

'You're not a regular soldier?'

'Of course not, I've only just joined up. I haven't got a horse yet, and there's no way I can get one. So I can't get married, either.'

'And how much does a horse cost?'

'Someone was selling one on the other side of the river a few days ago, and they wanted more than sixty "coins" for it, even though it's a Nogay horse.'

'Will you come and be my drabant? (On military campaigns, a drabant was something similar to an orderly, usually given to officers.) I'll get you transferred and make you a present of a horse,' Olenin said suddenly. 'I mean it. I have two, and I don't need two.'

'Don't need two?' Lukashka said, laughing. 'Why should you make me a present? I'll get by, God willing.'

'No, I'm serious. Or perhaps you don't want to be a drabant?' said Olenin, delighted that it had occurred to him to make Lukashka a present of a horse. For some reason, however, he felt awkward and ashamed. He looked for something to say, and could not find it.

Lukashka broke the silence first.

'Say, do you have a house of your own in Russia?' he asked.

Olenin could not restrain himself from telling him that he had not only one, but several houses.

'A nice house? Bigger than ours?' Lukashka asked good-naturedly.

'Much bigger – ten times, and it has three storeys,' Olenin told him.

'And do you have horses like ours?'

'I have a hundred horses, worth three or four hundred roubles each, but they're not like yours. Three hundred silver roubles! Trotters, you know . . . But even so, I like the horses here better.'

'Now then, did you come here of your own free will or didn't you?' asked Lukashka, still apparently laughing at him. 'This is where you lost your way,' he added, pointing to a path they were walking past. 'You should have turned right.'

'I came here because I wanted to,' replied Olenin. 'I wanted to see your part of the country, and to take part in some expeditions.'

'I feel like going on an expedition today,' said Luka. 'Sheesh, the jackals are howling,' he added, listening.

'So you're not scared by having killed a man?' asked Olenin.

'What's there to be afraid of? But I'd like to go on an expedition,' Lukashka repeated. 'I would, oh, how I would . . .'

'It may be that we'll be going on one together. Our regiment is going before the holidays, and so is your Hundred.'[37]

'I don't know what on earth made you come here! You've a house, you've horses and you've servants. I'd just spend the days having a high old time, so I would. And what's your rank, then?'

'I'm a cadet, but now I've been recommended for a commission.'

'Well, if you're not just boasting about that life of yours, if it were me I'd never have left home. Never have left it, I would. You like it here with us?'

'Yes, I like it very much,' said Olenin.

It was already quite dark when, talking together in this fashion, they approached the settlement. They were still surrounded by the dark gloom of the forest. The wind was roaring high in the treetops. The jackals suddenly seemed to begin howling right next to them, laughing and weeping; but ahead of them, in the settlement, the sound of women talking and the barking of dogs could be heard, the profiles of the huts were clearly distinguishable, lights shone and there was a smell, the peculiar smell of *kizyak* smoke. Olenin really did feel, especially this evening, that here in the settlement were his home, his family and all his happiness, and that nowhere had he lived nor would ever live so happily as in this settlement. This evening he loved everyone, and especially Lukashka! On reaching home, to Lukashka's great astonishment, Olenin personally brought out from the shed a horse he had bought in Groznaya – it was not the one he usually rode, but another, quite a good one, though no longer young – and gave it to him.

128

'Why should you give me a present?' said Lukashka. 'I haven't done anything to deserve it from you.'

'Really, it doesn't cost me anything,' replied Olenin. 'Take it, and you can make me a present of something . . . And then we'll go campaigning together.'

Luka was embarrassed.

'But really, what is this? A horse costs a lot of money, doesn't it?' he said, not looking at the horse.

'Go on, take it! If you don't take it, you'll offend me. Vanyusha, take the grey horse to his house.'

Lukashka took hold of the reins.

'Well, thank you. This is something I never thought or dreamt of . . .'

Olenin was as happy as a twelve-year-old boy.

'Tie it up here. It's a good horse, I bought it in Groznaya, and it gallops like the wind. Vanyusha, serve us some *chikhir*. Let's go into the hut.'

The wine was served. Lukashka sat down and took his

cup. 'God willing, I'll pay you back,' he said, draining it. 'What's your name?'

'Dmitry Andreich.'

'Well, Mitry Andreich, may God thank you. We'll be *kunaks*. Now come and see us. Though we're not rich, we know how to treat a *kunak*. I'll tell mother if there's anything you want – *kaymak* or grapes. And if you come to the cordon, I'll be your servant, take you hunting, across the river, anywhere you like. The other day now, if only I'd known: what a great boar I killed! I shared it out among the Cossacks, but I'd have brought it to you instead.'

'That's good, thank you. But don't harness the horse, for it hasn't travelled much yet.'

'Why harness a horse? And there's something else I'll tell you, if you like,' said Lukashka, lowering his voice. 'I've a *kunak*, Girey-Khan; he invited me to lie in ambush with him, where they come down from the mountains, and we can go there together. I won't give you away, you can be sure of that, I'll be your *murid*.'[38]

'Let's go there, let's go there some time.'

Lukashka, it seemed, was now completely reassured, and understood Olenin's attitude to him. His calmness and the bluntness of his address surprised Olenin, and were even slightly disagreeable to him. They talked for a long time, and it was late when Lukashka, not drunk (he was never drunk), but having imbibed a great deal, shook Olenin's hand and left his quarters.

Olenin glanced out of the window to see what Lukashka would do after leaving him. Lukashka walked slowly, his head lowered. Then, taking the horse out through the gate, he suddenly shook his head, leapt on to the horse like a cat, threw over the reins of the bridle and headed off down the street with a whoop. Olenin had thought that he would go to share his joy with Maryanka; but, in spite of the fact that Luka did not do this, he none the less felt in a better mood than ever. He was as happy as a boy, and not only could not refrain from telling Vanyusha that he had made Luka a present of a horse, but had also to tell him why he had done so, and the whole of his new theory of happiness. Vanyusha did not approve of this theory and declared that *larjong eel nya pah,*[39] and therefore it was all nonsense.

Lukashka paid a quick visit to his home; jumping down from the horse he entrusted it to his mother, instructing her to let it join the Cossack herd; he himself had to return to the cordon that same night. His deaf mute sister undertook to lead the horse down and demonstrated by signs that when she saw the man who had made the present of the horse she would certainly bow down at his feet. The old woman merely shook her head at her son's story, decided inwardly that he had stolen the horse, and therefore told her deaf mute daughter to take it to the herd before daybreak.

130

Lukashka went back to the cordon alone, still thinking about what Olenin had done. Though the horse was not a good one, in his opinion, it was still worth at least forty 'coins', and Lukashka was very glad of the gift. But why the gift had been made he could not understand, and so he felt not the slightest sense of gratitude. On the contrary, vague suspicions wandered through his mind that the cadet might have bad intentions. What these intentions were he could not work out, but to allow the thought that it had just happened, for no reason, that a stranger had given him a horse worth forty 'coins', out of the kindness of his heart, seemed to him impossible. If Olenin had been drunk, then it might have been comprehensible to him: the man was trying to show off. But the cadet was sober, and so had probably been trying to bribe him for some evil purpose. 'Well, you've got the wrong man!' thought Lukashka. 'I have the horse, and so we'll see. I'm nobody's fool either. As for who can trick whom, we shall see!' he thought, sensing a need to be on his guard against Olenin, and therefore arousing within himself a hostile feeling towards him. He told no one how he had acquired the horse. To some he said he had bought it; others he fobbed off with an evasive reply. However, the settlement soon learned the truth. Lukashka's mother, Maryana, Ilya Vasilyevich and the other Cossacks, learning of Olenin's unprompted gift, felt bewildered and began to have misgivings about the cadet. In spite of such misgivings, this action aroused in them a great respect for Olenin's 'simplicity' and wealth.

'Did you hear? Lukashka got a horse worth fifty "coins" from the cadet who's lodging with Ilya Vasilyich!' said one. 'He's a rich man.'

'Yes, I heard,' replied another, with a thoughtful air. 'He must have done him a favour. We shall see, we shall see what becomes of him. Quite a piece of luck for the Snatcher.'

'Those cadets are a crafty lot, watch out!' said a third. 'Next thing you know he'll be burning the place down, or something.'

23

Olenin's life continued with regular monotony. He had little to do with the commanding officers or with his comrades. The position of a wealthy cadet in the Caucasus is particularly advantageous in this respect. He was not sent to work, or made to do drill. For the expedition he had made he was recommended for a commission, and meanwhile he was left in peace. The officers viewed him as an aristocrat, and therefore treated him with dignity. The card games and officers' drinking sessions with singers, which he had experienced during his time in the detachment, seemed to him unattractive, and he, for his part, also avoided the officers' company and the life of the officers in the settlement. The life of the officers in a settlement has long had its own special profile. Just as every cadet or officer in the fortress regularly drinks stout, plays *shtoss*, talks about the rewards for taking part in the expeditions, so in the settlement he regularly drinks *chikhir* with his hosts, treats the girls to snacks and honey, chases after the Cossack women, with whom he falls in love; and sometimes even marries. Olenin always lived his life in his own way and had an unconscious aversion to beaten tracks. And here too he did not follow the well-worn rut of a Caucasian officer's life.

It had become a matter of course with him to wake up with the light. After drinking tea and admiring from his porch the mountains, the morning and Maryanka, he would put on a tattered leather coat and a pair of *porshni*, gird himself with a dagger, take his rifle and a bag containing snacks and tobacco, call his dog to follow him, and before it was six a.m. he would set off into the forest beyond the settlement. Between six and seven in the evening he returned tired and hungry, with five or six pheasants at his belt, sometimes with some creature he had caught, and with his bag of snacks and cigarettes untouched. If the thoughts in his head had lain like the cigarettes in the bag, it might have been possible to observe that during all those fourteen hours not a single one of them had stirred within it. He arrived home strong, mentally refreshed and completely happy. He could not have said what he had been thinking about all that time. Things that were neither thoughts, nor memories, nor dreams roamed about in his head – fragments of all three. He would come to himself, and wonder what he had been thinking about. And catch a glimpse of himself as a Cossack, working in the orchards with his Cossack wife, or as an Abrek in the mountains, or as a wild boar, fleeing from himself. And all the while listening, watching and waiting for a pheasant, a boar or a deer.

Every evening without fail Uncle Yeroshka would sit with him. Vanyusha always brought a quart of *chikhir,* and they sat quietly chatting and drinking, and then went contentedly off to their beds to sleep. The next morning there would again be hunting, again the healthy tiredness, again they would drink over a chat, and again be happy. Sometimes on a holiday or a rest day he spent the whole day at home. Then his chief occupation was Maryanka, whose every movement he eagerly followed from his windows or his porch, without even being aware that he was doing so. He watched Maryanka and loved her (so it seemed to him) in the same way that he loved the beauty of the mountains and the sky, and had no thought of entering into any kind of relationship with her. It seemed to him that there could not exist between the two of them the kind of relationship that was possible between her and the Cossack Lukashka, and even less of the kind that was possible between a rich

133

officer and a Cossack girl. It seemed to him that if he attempted to do what his comrades did, he would exchange his pleasure-filled contemplation for an abyss of torments, disappointments and remorse. Moreover, in relation to this woman he had already performed a feat of self-sacrifice which had afforded him a great deal of pleasure; and, most importantly of all, for some reason he was afraid of Mary-anka, and could never have ventured to say to her a word of love that was not seriously meant.

One day in summer, Olenin did not go hunting, but stayed at home. Quite unexpectedly a Moscow acquaintance of his, a very young man he had met in society, came in.

'Ah, *mon cher*, my dear fellow, how pleased I was when I learned that you were here!' he began in Moscow French, and continued this way, peppering his speech with French words. '"Olenin", they said. What Olenin could that be? I was so glad . . . Fate has simply brought us together! Well, how are you? What are you doing here? Why?'

And Prince Beletsky told the whole of his story: how he had joined this regiment temporarily, how the commander-in-chief had invited him to become an adjutant and how after the campaign he was going to work for him in spite of the fact that he was not at all interested in doing so.

'Doing service in this hole one must at least make a career . . . a medal . . . a rank . . . be transferred to the Guards. All that is essential, though not for myself, but for my family, for my friends. The Prince received me very well; he's a very decent man,' said Beletsky, talking without cease. 'For the expedition I've been recommended for the Order of St Anne.[40] And now I'm going to stay here until the campaign. It's excellent here. What women! Well, and how are you getting on? Our captain was telling me – Startsev, you know; a well-meaning, stupid fellow . . . he said that you're living like an awful savage, you never see anyone. I can understand that you don't feel like associating with the officers here. I'm glad that now you and I will be able to see something of each other. I'm staying at the sergeant major's house here. What a girl there is there, Ustenka! I tell you – charming!'

And more and more French and Russian words poured forth from that world which Olenin had thought he had left behind for ever. The general opinion of Beletsky was that he was a nice, good-natured fellow. Perhaps, indeed, he was; but in spite of his pretty, good-natured face, Olenin found him extremely unpleasant. He fairly reeked of all the filth that Olenin had renounced. But what annoyed Olenin most of all was that he was unable, just did not have the strength, to harshly repel this person from that world, as though that old, former world he had belonged to possessed inalienable rights over him. He was angry with Beletsky, and with himself, and yet against his will he inserted French phrases into his conversation, took an 135 interest in the commander-in-chief and their Moscow acquaintances, and, on the basis of the fact that they were both talking a dialect of French in a Cossack settlement, made contemptuous remarks about his fellow officers and the Cossacks and treated Beletsky in a friendly manner, promising to visit him and inviting him to call. In fact, however, Olenin did not keep his promise. Vanyusha approved of Beletsky, saying he was 'a real *barin*'.

Beletsky at once entered into the usual life of a wealthy Caucasus officer in a settlement. Before Olenin's eyes, in a single month he became a kind of veteran resident of the place: he made the old men tipsy, gave parties and went to parties at the homes of girls, boasted of his conquests and even went so far that for some reason the girls and women gave him the nickname of 'Grandad', while the Cossacks, who had a clear picture of this man who liked wine and women, got used to him and even preferred him to Olenin, who was a mystery to them.

24

It was five o'clock in the morning. Using the leg of a boot
as bellows, Vanyusha was getting the samovar going on the
porch of the hut. Olenin had already gone off on horseback
to bathe in the Terek. (He had recently devised a new
amusement for himself – bathing his horse in the Terek.)
His landlady was in her *izbushka,* from the chimney of
which rose the thick, black smoke of the stove being kindled; the girl was milking the buffalo cow in the shed. 'She
won't stand still, the damned thing!' came her impatient
voice, and then there was the rhythmical sound of milking.
In the street outside the house the lively trot of a horse was
136 heard, and Olenin, riding bareback on a handsome, dark
grey steed that was not yet dry and gleamed with moisture,
rode up to the gate. Maryanka's pretty head, tied with a
plain red kerchief (called a *sorochka*[41]), poked out of the
shed and disappeared again. Olenin wore a red silk shirt,
a white Circassian coat, girded with a belt that held a dagger, and a tall cap. He sat astride the wet back of his
well-fed horse with a slightly refined air and, holding on
to his rifle behind his back, leant down to open the gate.
His hair was still wet, and his face shone with youth and
health. He thought he looked handsome, agile and resembled a *djigit*; but this was not the case. To the eye of any
experienced dweller of the Caucasus he still looked like a
soldier. On observing the head of the girl poking out of
the shed, he bent down with particular liveliness, threw
back the wattle fencing of the gate and, taking the reins,
with a wave of his whip, rode into the yard. 'Is the tea ready,
Vanyusha?' he cried merrily, without looking at the door of
the shed; with pleasure he felt beneath him the beautiful

horse, tensing its quarters, asking for the reins and quivering in every muscle, ready to leap across the fence at full tilt, beat out its trot on the dried clay of the yard. '*Say pray!*'[42] replied Vanyusha. To Olenin it seemed that Maryana's pretty head was still watching from the shed, but he did not look round at her. Jumping down from the horse, Olenin hooked his rifle on the porch, made an awkward movement and looked anxiously at the shed, where no one was visible and the same rhythmical sounds of milking could be heard.

He went inside the hut and a short time later reappeared on the porch, settling down with a book and a pipe for a glass of tea at the side that was not yet suffused with the morning's oblique rays of sunlight. That day he had no plans to go anywhere until dinnertime, and intended to write the letters he had long postponed composing; for some reason, however, he felt loath to abandon his nice little place on the porch and go back into the hut again, as though it were a prison. His landlady finished kindling the stove, the girl drove the cattle into the fields and, returning, began to gather dung and stick it along the fence to make *kizyak*. Olenin read, but did not take in anything of what was written in the book that lay open before him. He kept constantly lifting his eyes from it and looking at the strong young woman who was moving about in front of him. Whenever this woman walked into the damp morning shade that was thrown by the house, or emerged from it into the middle of the yard that was illumined by a joyous, youthful light, and her shapely figure in its bright clothing shone in the sun and cast a black shadow – he was afraid to miss even one of her movements. It delighted him to see how freely and gracefully her figure bowed, how the pink shirt that was her only clothing draped itself about her breast and along her shapely legs; how when her figure straightened the outlines of her panting bosom stood out beneath the ungirdled shirt; how her slender feet, shod in old red shoes, rested on the ground without altering their form; how her powerful arms, with rolled-up sleeves, tensing their muscles, seemed to ply the spade almost as if in anger, and how her deep dark eyes sometimes looked at him. Although her delicate eyebrows frowned, in her eyes there was an expression of pleasure, and a sense of her own beauty.

'Well, Olenin, been up long, have you?' said Beletsky, entering the yard. He wore the frock-coat of a Caucasus officer.

'Ah, Beletsky!' Olenin responded, offering his hand. 'Why are you out so early?'

'What can one do! I've been kicked out. There's a ball at my place tonight. Maryana, you'll be coming to Ustenka's, won't you?' he addressed the girl.

Olenin was surprised that Beletsky was able to address this woman in such plain terms. But Maryana, as though she had not heard, bowed her head and, shouldering the spade, walked off to the *izbushka* with her lively, masculine gait.

'She's ashamed, the poor dear, she's ashamed,' Beletsky said quietly, as she went. 'She's ashamed before you.' And, smiling gaily, he ran up the steps of the porch.

'What, there's a ball at your place? Who kicked you out?'

'Yes, it's at Ustenka's, my landlady's, and you're invited. Well, not really a ball, just a pie and a bevy of girls.'

'But what are *we* going to do there?'

Beletsky smiled slyly and, winking, pointed his head at the *izbushka,* into which Maryana had disappeared.

Olenin shrugged his shoulders and reddened.

'You're a strange fellow, I must say!' he said.

'Well, tell me everything!'

Olenin frowned. Beletsky noticed this, and smiled a searching smile.

'Oh, for mercy's sake,' he said. 'You live in the same house . . . as such a fantastic girl, a marvellous girl, a total beauty . . .'

'Amazingly beautiful! I've never seen women like these,' said Olenin.

'Well, and so?' Beletsky asked, completely failing to understand.

'It may be strange,' replied Olenin, 'but why shouldn't I tell the truth? Since I've been living here it's as if women don't exist for me. And that really is a good thing! Well, and what can we have in common with women like these? Yeroshka's a different matter; he and I have a common passion – hunting.'

'There you go again! Depends what you mean by "common"! What do I have in common with Amalia Ivanovna? It's just the same. Now if what you mean is that they're a bit dirty, that's another matter. *À la guerre, comme à la guerre.*'[43]

'But I've never known any Amalia Ivanovnas, and have never known how to handle them,' replied Olenin. 'Anyway, it's impossible to have any respect for them, while these women I do respect.'

'Well, respect them, then! Who's stopping you?'

Olenin did not reply. He evidently wanted to finish saying what he had begun. It was all too close to his heart.

'I know that I'm an exception. (He was plainly flustered.) But my life has arranged itself in such a way that not only do I see no reason to alter my principles, but I could not live here, let alone live as happily as I am doing, if I were to live as you do. And then, I seek something quite different, see something different in them, from what you seek.'

Beletsky raised his eyebrows sceptically.

'All the same, come to my place this evening, and Maryana will be there, I shall introduce you. Do visit, please! Well, and if you get bored, you can leave. Will you visit us?'

'I'd like to; but, to tell you the truth, I'm afraid of becoming seriously infatuated.'

'Oh, oh, oh!' cried Beletsky. 'Just visit, and I'll put you at your ease. You'll visit? Give me your promise?'

'I'd like to, but I really don't understand what we're going to do, what role we're going to play.'

'Please, I beg you. You'll visit?'

'Yes, perhaps,' said Olenin.

'For heaven's sake, there are gorgeous women here, like nowhere else, and you live like a monk! Where's the sense in that? Why spoil your life and fail to take advantage of what's on offer? Have you heard, our company's moving to Vozdvizhensk?'

'Really? I was told that the 8th company is going there,' said Olenin.

'No, I had a letter from the adjutant. He writes that the Prince himself will take part in the campaign. I'm glad, as I shall see something of him. I'm beginning to get fed up with this place.'

'They say we'll soon be going on a raid.'

'I haven't heard that, but I did hear that Krinovitsyn got the Order of St Anne for a raid. He'd only expected to be made a lieutenant,' said Beletsky, laughing. 'That was a turn up for the books! He's moved to headquarters . . .'

It had begun to grow dark and Olenin started to think about the party. The invitation tormented him. He wanted to go, but the thought of what might happen there was strange, absurd and even slightly alarming. He knew that there would be neither Cossack men nor older women there, only the girls. What on earth would take place? How was one to conduct oneself? What was one to say? What would they talk about? What kind of relations could there be between him and these wild Cossack girls? Beletsky had talked about relations that were so strange, so cynical and at the same time strictly circumscribed relations . . .

He found it strange to think that he would be there in the same hut with Maryana and might perhaps have to talk to her. That seemed impossible to him, when he remembered her majestic bearing. Yet Beletsky said it was all so simple. 'Will Beletsky really talk to Maryana in the same way? That will be interesting,' he thought. 'No, I'd better not go. The whole thing is cheap and sordid, and above all – pointless.' But again he was tormented by the question of what it might be like. And he somehow felt bound by the promise he had given. He set off without having made up his mind one way or the other, but when he reached Beletsky's, he went in.

The hut where Beletsky lived was just like Olenin's. It stood on wooden piles, some two *arshins* off the ground, and consisted of two rooms. In the first room, which Olenin entered up a steep flight of steps, feather beds, rugs, blankets and cushions lay in the Cossack manner, arranged **141** elegantly and attractively next to one another along the main wall. Here too, on the lateral walls, hung brass basins and weapons; under the bench lay watermelons and pumpkins. In the second room were a large stove, a table, benches and some Old Believer icons. Here Beletsky was lodged, with his old folding bed, his saddlebags, a rug on which weapons hung, and, arranged on the table, some portraits and toilet things. A silk dressing-gown had been thrown on the bench. Beletsky himself, good-looking, clean, lay on the bed in his underwear, reading *Les Trois Mousquetaires*.[44]

Beletsky jumped to his feet.

'There, you see how well I'm fixed up. Wonderful, isn't it? Well, it's just as well you've arrived. They're working away like mad. Do you know what a pie is made of? Pastry with pork and grapes. And that's not the half of it. Just look at what's on the boil over there!'

Indeed, looking out of the window they could see an

unwonted bustle in the landlady's hut. Girls were running in from the passage, now with one thing, now with another, and running back again.

'How long will it be?' cried Beletsky.

'Not long now! Getting hungry are you, Grandad?' And from the hut came resonant laughter.

Ustenka, plump, red-cheeked and pretty, with her sleeves rolled up, ran into Beletsky's hut to fetch plates.

'Oh, you! You'll make me break the plates!' she squealed at Beletsky. 'You'd better come and help,' she cried, laughing, to Olenin. 'And get some "snacks"* for the girls.'

'And is Maryanka there?'

'Of course she is! She brought the pastry.'

'You know,' said Beletsky, 'if one were to dress this Ustenka up and give her a clean and a bit of looking after, she'd be better than any of our beauties. Did you ever see that Cossack woman Borshcheva? She married a colonel. The most amazing *dignité*![45] Where do they get it . . .'

'I've never seen Borshcheva, but in my opinion there can be nothing better than those costumes of theirs.'

'Oh, I can get used to all kinds of things!' said Beletsky, sighing cheerfully. 'I'm going to go and see what they're up to.'

He threw on his dressing-gown and ran off.

'And you can see to the "snacks"!' he cried.

Olenin sent the orderly for spice cakes and honey, and he suddenly felt so disgusted at giving money, as though he were bribing someone, that he made no definite answer to the orderly's inquiry as to how many mint cakes and how many honey cakes he should buy.

'As you think best.'

'Shall I spend it all, sir?' the old man asked meaningfully.

* 'Snacks' is what they call spice cakes and candy. (Tolstoy's note.)

'The mint ones are dearer. They were selling them for sixteen copecks each.'

'Yes, yes, spend it all,' said Olenin and sat down by the window, surprised that his heart was thumping as if he were getting ready to do something important and indecent.

He heard the shouting and shrieking when Beletsky entered the girls' hut, and saw him leap out a few minutes later to the accompaniment of shrieking, noise and laughter, and run down the flight of steps.

'I've been kicked out,' he said.

A few minutes later Ustenka entered the hut and solemnly invited the guests, announcing that everything was ready.

When they entered the hut, everything was indeed ready, and Ustenka was arranging the cushions along the wall. On the table, which was covered by a disproportionately small napkin, stood a decanter of *chikhir* and some dried fish. The hut smelt of pastry and grapes. Some six girls, in ceremonial *beshmets*, their heads bare of the usual kerchiefs, were huddled in the corner behind the stove, whispering, laughing and snorting.

'We humbly bid you to "pray" to my angel,' said Ustenka, inviting the guests to the table.

In the throng of girls, who were all without exception beautiful, Olenin discerned Maryana, and he found it painful and vexing that he should meet her in such vulgar and awkward circumstances. He felt stupid and awkward, and made up his mind to do what Beletsky did. Beletsky approached the table rather solemnly, but with casual self-confidence drank a glass of wine to Ustenka's health and invited the others to do the same. Ustenka announced that the girls did not drink.

'With honey, we could,' said a voice from the throng of girls.

The orderly was called, having just returned from the

shop with honey and 'snacks'. From under his eyebrows – whether with envy or with contempt it was not clear – he surveyed the gentlemen, who in his opinion were 'carousing', then carefully and conscientiously handed over a piece of honeycomb and the spice cakes, wrapped in grey paper, and began to expatiate on the subject of the price and the change, but Beletsky chased him away.

After mixing honey in the glasses of ready poured *chikhir,* and extravagantly spreading three pounds of spice cakes over the table, Beletsky dragged the girls out of their corner, sat them down at the table and began to distribute the cakes to them. Olenin could not help noticing as Maryanka's sunburned but diminutive hand took two round mint cakes and one brown one, uncertain what to do with them. The conversation was awkward and difficult, in spite of Ustenka's and Beletsky's free and easy manner, and their desire to cheer up the company. Olenin hesitated, tried to think of something to say, but felt that he was arousing curiosity, and perhaps also ridicule, and that he was passing his embarrassment on to the others. He was blushing, and it seemed to him that Maryana especially felt awkward. 'They probably expect us to give them money,' he thought. 'How are we going to do that? And get it over with as soon as possible, and then leave!'

25

'How is it you don't know your own lodger?' said Beletsky, addressing Maryanka.

'How can one know him if he never comes to see us?' said Maryana, glancing at Olenin.

For some reason, Olenin took fright, blushed and, not really knowing what he was saying, said:

'I'm afraid of your mother. She gave me a fine old scolding the first time I came to see you.'

Maryanka burst out laughing.

'And you were frightened?' she said, looking at him, and then turned away.

Now for the first time Olenin could see the face of this 145 beautiful woman in its entirety, where before he had only seen her in a kerchief that came down to her eyes. Not for nothing was she considered the beauty of the settlement. Ustenka was a pretty girl, small, plump, rosy-cheeked, with merry dark brown eyes and a perpetual smile on red lips that perpetually laughed and chattered. Maryana, on the other hand, was not *pretty* at all, but *beautiful*. The features of her face might have seemed too masculine, and almost coarse, had it not been for her tall, shapely figure and powerful chest and shoulders and, above all, the stern and at the same time tender expression of her long, black eyes surrounded by dark shadow under black brows, and the affectionate expression of her mouth and smile. She seldom smiled, but when she did the effect was always striking. She exuded female strength and health. All the girls were pretty, but they themselves, and Beletsky, and the batman who had brought the cakes all found themselves involuntarily gazing at Maryana and, in turning to the girls, turned to her. Among the others, she seemed like a proud and cheerful empress.

Beletsky, trying to maintain the decorum of the party, chattered incessantly, made the girls pour *chikhir,* fussed over them and kept making improper remarks to Olenin in French about Maryanka's beauty, calling her 'yours', *la vôtre,* and inviting him to do as he did. Olenin was feeling more and more uncomfortable. He was thinking up a pretext for going outside and running away, when Beletsky proclaimed that Ustenka, whose name-day it was, must pour *chikhir* for everyone together with a kiss. She agreed, but on condition that they put money on her plate, as is done at weddings. 'The Devil brought me to this revolting feast!' Olenin said to himself and, getting up, made to leave.

'Where are you going?'

'I'm going to fetch some tobacco,' he said, intending to
146 flee, but Beletsky caught him by the arm.

'I have money,' he said to him in French.

'One can't leave, one has to pay here,' thought Olenin, feeling thoroughly vexed at his own awkwardness. Why can't I just behave like Beletsky? I should never have come, but now that I'm here I mustn't spoil their enjoyment. I must drink in Cossack fashion.' And, taking a *chapura* (a wooden cup containing about eight glassfuls), he filled it with wine and drank nearly all of it. The girls looked at him in bewilderment, and almost in fear, as he drank. To them it seemed strange and improper. Ustenka brought them another glass each, and kissed them both.

'There, girls, now we can have a good time,' she said, shaking the four 'coins' they had put on the plate.

By now, Olenin no longer felt awkward. He talked freely.

'Well, Maryanka, now you must serve us, with a kiss,' said Beletsky, seizing her by the hand.

'And I'll give you such a kiss!' she said, raising her hand against him in jest.

'It's all right to kiss Grandad without money,' another girl chimed in.

'There's a clever one!' said Beletsky, kissing the girl, who fought him off. 'No, you must serve him,' Beletsky insisted, addressing Maryana. 'Serve your lodger.'

And, taking her by the hand, he led her to the bench and sat her down beside Olenin.

'What a beautiful girl!' he said, turning her head to show its profile.

Maryana did not struggle, but, proudly smiling, turned her long eyes on Olenin.

'The girl is beautiful,' Beletsky repeated.

'What a beautiful girl I am!' Maryana's gaze seemed to echo. Without realizing what he was doing, he embraced Maryana and made to kiss her. She suddenly tore herself free, knocked Beletsky off his feet and the top off the table, and jumped away towards the stove. Shouting and laughter began. Beletsky whispered something to the girls, and suddenly they all ran out of the hut into the passage and locked the door.

'Why did you kiss Beletsky, but you won't kiss me?' asked Olenin.

'Oh, I just don't want to, that's all,' she replied, with a jut of her lower lip and brow. 'He's Grandad,' she added, smiling. She went over to the door and began to knock on it. 'Why have you locked the door, you devils?'

'Oh, just let them stay there, and we can be here,' said Olenin, drawing close to her.

She frowned and sternly guided him away from her with her hand. And again she seemed so majestically beautiful to Olenin that he came to his senses and felt ashamed of what he was doing. He went over to the door and began to tug at it.

'Beletsky, open up! What sort of silly joke is this?'

Maryana again laughed her bright, happy laugh.

'Oh, are you afraid of me?'

'Well, you're as bad-tempered as your mother.'

'And you ought to spend more time with Yeroshka, for then the girls would start to love you for it.' And she smiled, looking directly and closely into his eyes.

He did not know what to say.

'And if I came to see you? . . .' he said inadvertently.

'That would be different,' she said quietly, with a shake of her head.

At that moment Beletsky opened the door with a shove, and Maryana jumped back against Olenin, striking his leg with her hip.

'They're all nonsense, all those things I thought before: love, and self-denial, and Lukashka. Happiness is the only thing that matters: he who is happy is right' flashed through Olenin's mind, and with a strength unexpected to himself he seized and kissed the beautiful Maryanka on the temples and cheek. Maryana did not get angry, but merely burst into loud laughter and ran out to the other girls.

With this, the party ended. Ustenka's mother, having returned from work, gave all the girls a good scolding and chased them outside.

26

'Yes,' thought Olenin, as he made his way home. 'I would only need to allow myself a little freedom, and I might fall madly in love with this Cossack girl.' He went to bed with these thoughts, but considered that it would all pass and he would return to his old life again.

But his old life did not return. His relation to Maryanka had changed. The wall that had previously separated them was destroyed. Now Olenin greeted her every time they met.

The landlord, who came to collect the rent and had learned of Olenin's wealth and generosity, invited him to his home. The old woman received him kindly, and from the day of the party onwards Olenin would often go to his hosts of an evening and sit with them until night-time. While it looked as though he were continuing to live in the settlement in his old way, in his soul everything had been turned upside down. He spent the daytime in the forest, but at about eight o'clock, when dusk began to fall, he would go to see his hosts, either alone or with Uncle Yeroshka. His hosts were now so used to him that they were surprised when he did not show up. He paid well for the wine, and he was a quiet man. Vanyusha would bring him tea; he would sit down in the corner facing the stove; the old woman, not minding him, carried on with what she was doing, and over their tea and *chikhir* they would chat about Cossack affairs, about the neighbours, or about Russia, when Olenin did the talking and they asked questions. Sometimes he chose a book and read to himself. Maryana, like a wild goat, with her legs tucked up beneath her, sat on the stove or in a dark corner. She did not take part in the conversation, but Olenin saw her eyes and face, heard her movements, the cracking of seeds, and felt that when he talked she listened with her whole being, and when he read in silence he would sense her presence. Sometimes it seemed to him that her eyes were fixed on him and, encountering their radiance, he would find himself falling silent and looking at her. Then she would instantly hide, while he, pretending that he was much preoccupied with his conversation with the old woman, would listen to her breathing, to her every movement, and again await her gaze. When others were present, she was mostly cheerful and affectionate with him, but when they were alone she was unsociable and coarse. Sometimes he would arrive at their home before Maryana had returned from the street: suddenly her powerful footsteps would be heard, and in the open doorway there was a glimpse of her light blue cotton shirt. She would come out into the centre of the hut, catch sight of him – and her eyes would give a barely perceptible tender smile, and he would feel happy and afraid.

He sought nothing, wished nothing from her, but with each day her presence was becoming more and more indispensable to him.

Olenin had grown so used to the life of the settlement that the past seemed to him something entirely alien, while the future, especially outside the world in which he lived, did not interest him at all. Receiving letters from home, from his family and friends, he found it hurtful that they apparently grieved for him as for a man who was lost, while he in his settlement considered as lost anyone who did not lead the kind of life he did. He was convinced that he was never going to repent of having torn himself away from his previous life and having settled down in his settlement in such a solitary and distinctive way. On the campaigns, in the fortresses he felt at ease; but only here, only from under Uncle Yeroshka's wing, from his forest,

150

from his hut on the edge of the settlement and especially when he remembered Maryanka and Lukashka, did he see clearly all the falsehood in which he had lived before and which even then had made him angry, and now appeared to him unutterably vile and absurd. Here with each day that passed he felt increasingly free, and increasingly human. The Caucasus appeared quite different from what he had imagined it to be. Here he had found nothing that resembled his dreams, or the descriptions of the Caucasus he had heard and read. 'Here there are no *burkas*, rapids, Amalat-Beks, heroes or villains,' he thought. 'People live as nature lives: they die, are born, copulate, are born again, fight, drink, eat, rejoice and die again, and with no restrictions but those unalterable ones that nature has placed on the sun, the grass, the animal and the tree. They have no other laws but those . . .' And so these people, compared to himself, seemed to him beautiful, strong and free, and, looking at them, he felt ashamed and sad about himself. He often seriously had the idea of giving up everything, registering as a Cossack, buying a hut and cattle, and marrying a Cossack woman – only not Maryana, whom he would cede to Lukashka – and live with Uncle Yeroshka, go hunting and fishing with him, and with the Cossacks on their campaigns. 'Why don't I do that? What am I waiting for?' he would ask himself. And he urged himself on, he put himself to shame. 'Or am I afraid of doing what I myself consider right and proper? Is the desire to be a simple Cossack, to live close to nature, to do no harm to anyone, and even to do good to others, is that dream more stupid than those I had before – of being a government minister, for example, or a regimental commander?' But a voice from somewhere told him to wait and not take any decision. He was restrained by an obscure awareness that he could not live completely like Yeroshka and Lukashka, because he had a different idea of happiness – he was restrained by the thought that happiness consists in self-denial. His good deed towards Lukashka continued to gratify him. He constantly sought occasions to sacrifice himself for others, but those occasions did not present themselves. Sometimes he forgot this newly discovered recipe for happiness and believed he was capable of fusing with the life that Uncle Yeroshka led; but then he suddenly came to his senses and at once seized at the thought of conscious self-denial and on its basis calmly and proudly gazed on all human beings and on the happiness of others.

27

Before the grape harvest, Lukashka came on horseback to see Olenin. He looked even more debonair than usual.

'Well, what's this, getting married, are you?' asked Olenin, greeting him cheerfully.

Lukashka did not reply directly.

'I've just exchanged that horse you gave me, on the other side of the river! What a horse I've got! It's a Kabarda Lov-Tavro.* I know a lot about horses.'

They examined the new horse, rode it *djigit*-style around the yard. The horse really was unusually handsome: a broad and long bay gelding with a glossy coat, a feathery tail and a soft, delicate, thoroughbred mane and crest. It was so well fed that one could positively 'go to bed on its back', as Lukashka put it. Its hooves, eyes and teeth were all exquisitely and sharply formed, as is the case only with horses of the very purest blood. Olenin could not help admiring the horse. He had never yet seen such a beautiful one in the Caucasus.

'And its stride!' said Lukashka, patting it on the neck. 'What a sprint it has! And it's clever, too! It fairly runs after its master.'

'How much did you give for it?' asked Olenin.

'Oh, I didn't pay for it,' Lukashka replied, smiling. 'I got it from a *kunak*.'

'The horse is a miracle, a beautiful creature! What will you take for it?'

'They were offering me a hundred and fifty "coins" for

---

* The Kabarda horses from the Tavro stud farm at Lov are considered one of the finest breeds in the Caucasus. (Tolstoy's note.)

it, but I'll give you it for nothing,' said Lukashka, cheerfully. 'Just say the word, and it's yours. I'll unsaddle it, and you can take it. As long as you give me some horse or other for my service duties.'

'No, I can't possibly do that.'

'Well, look, I've brought you a *peshkesh*.' And Lukashka undid his belt and took out one of the two daggers that hung from it. 'I got it on the other side of the river.'

'Well, thank you.'

'And mother has promised to bring you grapes herself.'

'She doesn't need to, we'll settle our accounts eventually. After all, I'm not going to give you any money for the dagger.'

'How could you anyway – we're *kunaks*! It's the same as when Girey-Khan took me into his *saklya*, his mountain hut, on the other side of the river, and said: "choose anything you like". So I took this sword. It's a law with us.'

They went into the hut and had a drink.

'So, are you going to stay here for a bit?' asked Olenin.

'No, I've come to say goodbye. They're sending me from the cordon to a company on the other side of the Terek. I'm going there tonight with my comrade Nazar.'

'And when is the wedding to be?'

'I'll return soon, for the betrothal, and then I'll go back on service,' Luka answered reluctantly.

'What, and not see your fiancée?'

'Yes. What's the point of seeing her? When you're on your next campaign, ask in our company for Lukashka Shiroky. And there are plenty of wild boar there! I've killed two. I'll take you.'

'Well, goodbye! Christ save you.'

Lukashka mounted his horse, and without calling in at Maryanka's, rode out, *djigit*-style, to the street, where Nazarka was already waiting for him.

'What, aren't we going to look in and say hullo?' asked Nazarka, winking in the direction of the hut where Yamka lived.

'You don't say!' said Lukashka. 'Here, take the horse to her, and if I don't show up for a long time, give it some hay. In any case, from tomorrow morning I'll be with the Hundred.'

'But didn't the cadet give you anything else?'

'No! I thanked him by giving him a dagger, or else he'd have started asking for the horse,' said Lukashka, getting down from the horse, and handing it over to Nazarka.

Right under Olenin's window he slipped into the yard and approached the window of the landlords' hut. It was already quite dark. Maryanka, clad only in her shirt, was combing her hair, preparing to go to bed.

'It's me,' the Cossack whispered.

Maryana's face wore an expression of stern indifference; **155** but it suddenly brightened up when she heard her name. She raised the window and stuck her head out, in alarm and delight.

'What is it? What do you want?' she said.

'Open up,' said Lukashka, softly. 'Let me in for a minute. Oh, how I've missed you! Something terrible!'

Through the window he embraced her head, and kissed her.

'Please, open up.'

'What nonsense you talk! I told you, I won't let you in. Well, have you come for long?'

He did not reply, but merely went on kissing her. And she asked no more questions.

'Sheesh, I can't even reach through the window to kiss you properly,' said Lukashka.

'Maryanushka!' came the voice of the old woman. 'Who are you with?'

Lukashka took off his cap, to make himself less conspicuous, and squatted down under the window.

'Go away, quickly!' whispered Maryana.

'Lukashka dropped by,' she replied to her mother. 'He was asking for Dad.'

'Well, send him in, then.'

'He's gone, he says he hasn't enough time.'

Bending down, Lukashka ran swiftly under the windows to the yard, and went to Yamka's hut; Olenin was the only person to see him. When Lukashka and Nazarka had drunk a couple of *chapuras* of *chikhir,* they rode away from the settlement. The night was warm, dark and quiet. They rode in silence, and only the trotting of their horses could be heard. Lukashka began to sing a song about the Cossack Mingal, but before he had finished the first verse he fell silent and turned to Nazarka.

156   'She wouldn't let me in, you know,' he said.

'Oh!' Nazarka responded. 'I knew she wouldn't. Yamka told me that the cadet's started visiting their home. Uncle Yeroshka was boasting that he'd got a flint rifle from the cadet for Maryanka.'

'He's talking through his hat, the old devil!' said Lukasha angrily. 'She's not that kind of girl. The old devil had better watch out, or I'll kick his backside for him.' And he began to sing his favourite song:

> Once from the village of Izmailovo,
> From the master's favourite garden,
> A bright falcon flew out.
> Quickly a young hunter rode after it,
> Tried to lure the bright falcon on to his right hand,
> 'Come, come, falcon, to my right hand,
> Because of you the Russian Tsar
> Wants to hang me by the neck.'

The bright falcon made this reply:
'You could not keep me in a golden cage
And on your right hand you could not keep me,
Now I shall fly to the blue sea;
I will kill a white swan for myself,
I'll have my fill of sweet and "swanly" flesh.'

28

The betrothal was taking place at the landlords' hut. Lukashka had returned to the settlement, but had not called to see Olenin. And, when he received the cornet's invitation, Olenin did not go to the betrothal. He was sadder than he had ever been since he had moved into the settlement. He had seen Lukashka, dressed in his finery, go along to the landlords' hut before evening with his mother, and the thought had tormented him: why was Lukashka so cold towards him? Olenin shut himself up in his hut and began to write his diary.

'I have reflected on many things, and many things have changed of late,' Olenin wrote, 'and I have arrived at what is written in the children's ABC. In order to be happy, one need do only one thing – love, and love with self-denial, love everyone and everything, spread a spider's web of love in all directions: whoever enters it shall be taken. That was how I caught Vanyusha, Uncle Yeroshka, Lukashka, Maryanka.'

As Olenin was finishing this, Uncle Yeroshka came into his room.

Yeroshka was in a most cheerful state of mind. A few days earlier, calling in to see him one evening, Olenin had found him in the yard in front of the carcass of a boar, which he was skinning with a small knife, his face happy and proud. The dogs, and among them his favourite, Lyam, lay nearby, wagging their tails a little as they watched him at his task. The urchins looked at him respectfully through the fence, and did not even tease him as they usually did. The women in the neighbouring huts, who were generally not too fond of him, greeted him and brought him things – a jug of *chikhir,* some *kaymak,* some flour. The following morning, Yeroshka sat in the shed of his hut, covered in blood, doling out the fresh meat a pound at a time – to some for money, to others for wine. On his face was written: 'God granted fortune, slew the beast; now Uncle's in demand, at least.' As a consequence of this, he began to drink, of course, and this was the fourth day of his drinking – he had not ventured out of the settlement. In addition to this, he had had quite a lot to drink at the betrothal.

When Uncle Yeroshka arrived from the landlords' hut to see Olenin, he was dead drunk, his face red, his beard dishevelled, but was wearing a new red *beshmet* embroidered with gold braid, and carrying a pumpkin balalaika[46] he had brought from beyond the river. He had long promised Olenin this pleasure and was in the mood. When he saw that Olenin was writing, he was annoyed.

'Write on, write on, my lad,' he said in a whisper, as though supposing that some kind of spirit sat between him and the paper, and, fearing to frighten it, slowly and soundlessly sat down on the floor. When Uncle Yeroshka was drunk, his favourite position was on the floor. Olenin glanced round, ordered wine to be served, and went on writing. Yeroshka found it boring to drink alone; he felt like talking.

'I was at the landlords', at the betrothal. But oh, those pigs! I didn't want to stay there! I came to see you instead.'

'And where did the balalaika come from?' asked Olenin, continuing to write.

'I was over on the other side of the river, my lad, that's where I got the balalaika,' he said, just as quietly. 'I'm a master player: Tatar, Cossack, gentry or soldiers' songs, whatever you like.'

Olenin glanced at him again, smiled ironically, and went on writing.

This smile encouraged the old man.

'Oh, leave it, my lad! Leave it!' he said suddenly, in a decisive tone. 'So they've insulted you – leave them, spit on them! Well, what are you writing and writing for? What's the point?'

And he mimicked Olenin, tapping his fat fingers on the floor and contorting his fat mug in a contemptuous grimace.

'What do you want to write slander for? Better have a good time, be a lad!'

On the subject of writing there was no room in his head for any idea other than that it was harmful slander.

Olenin burst into laughter. So did Yeroshka. He leapt up from the floor and began to demonstrate his skill on the balalaika and to sing Tatar songs.

'What do you want to write for, good man? You'd better listen to what I'll sing you. You won't hear any songs when you're dead. Have a good time!'

To start with, he sang a song of his own composition, with a dance refrain:

> Oh di-di-di-di-li
> Oh where did you see him?
> At the market in a stall
> Selling pins and that is all.

Then he sang a song that had been taught to him by a friend of his, a sergeant major:

> In love on Monday I did fall,
> All Tuesday I did suffer,
> On Wednesday declared my all,
> On Thursday sought an answer.
> On Friday it arrived at last,
> But any chance I'd had was past.

And on a sunny Saturday
I thought I'd throw my life away;
Salvation then my soul did find:
On Sunday I did change my mind.

And again:

Oh di-di-di-di-li
Oh where did you see him?

Then, winking, jerking his shoulders and dancing, he sang:

I'll embrace you, I will kiss,
Bind with scarlet ribbon, too,
Hope I'll call you, little miss.
Now, my Hope, I question you:
Do you really love me true?

And so worked up did he become that, playing wildly, he performed a dashing gesture and set off dancing round the room on his own.

The songs that went 'di-di-li' and so on, 'gentry' songs, he sang only for Olenin; but then, when he had drunk another three glasses of *chikhir,* he remembered the old days and began to sing genuine Cossack and Tatar songs. In the middle of one of his favourite songs his voice suddenly began to tremble, and he fell silent, continuing only to strum the strings of the balalaika.

'Oh, my friend!' he said.

At the strange sound of his voice, Olenin looked round: the old man was crying. There were tears in his eyes and one was trickling down his cheek.

'You've gone, my dear young days, and you won't return!' he said quietly, sobbing, and fell silent. 'Drink, why don't you drink?' he shouted suddenly in his deafening voice, without wiping away his tears.

One Tavlinsk song in particular moved him. It had few words, but the whole of its charm was contained in the sad refrain: 'Ai! dai! dalalai!' Yeroshka translated the words of the song: 'A young man drove his sheep from the *aul* to the mountains, the Russians came, burnt the *aul*, killed all the menfolk, took all the women captive. The young man came back from the mountains: where the *aul* had been, there was an empty place; his mother was not there, nor his brothers, nor his home; one tree alone remained. The young man sat down under the tree and began to cry. Alone, like you, left all alone, and the young man began to sing: "Ai! dai! dalalai!"' And this wailing, soul-rending refrain the old man repeated several times.

When he got to the end of the last refrain, Yeroshka suddenly grabbed a rifle from the wall, ran hurriedly out into the yard and fired into the air from both barrels. And again began to sing, even more sadly: 'Ai! dai! dalalai a-a!' – and fell silent.

Olenin, going out to the porch after him, gazed silently at the dark, starry sky in the direction where the shots had flashed. In the landlords' house there were lights, and voices could be heard. In the yard girls were crowding around the porch and the windows and running across from the hut to the passage. Some Cossacks darted out of the passage and could not restrain themselves, began to whoop, repeating the ending of Uncle Yeroshka's song, and his shots.

'Why aren't you at the betrothal?' asked Olenin.

'To hell with them! To hell with them!' said the old man quietly; he had evidently been offended by something over there. 'I don't care for them, I don't! Ech, what folk! Let's go back in the hut! They can do their drinking, and we can do ours.'

Olenin went back into the hut.

'And what of Lukashka, is he in good spirits? Won't he come to see me?' he asked.

'Oh, Lukashka! They lied to him and told him I was going to get his girl for you,' said the old man in a whisper. 'But the girl will be ours if we want her: just cough up more money – and she's ours! I'll do it for you, honest.'

'No, Uncle, money won't be any use if she doesn't love me. You'd better drop the subject.'

'You and I are unloved, we're orphans!' Uncle Yeroshka said suddenly, and began to cry again.

Olenin drank more than usual, as he listened to the old man's stories. 'So there it is, my Lukashka's happy now,' he thought; but he felt sad. The old man had drunk so much that evening that he slumped to the floor, and Vanyusha had to summon soldiers to help, who spat as they hauled him outside. So angry was Vanyusha with the old man for **163** his bad behaviour that he even refrained from uttering a single word of French.

29

It was August. For several days in a row there had not been a cloud in the sky; the sun scorched unbearably, and from morning on a warm wind blew, lifting clouds of hot sand in the dunes and along the roads, and carrying it through the air, through the reeds, the trees and the settlements. The grass and the leaves on the trees were covered in dust; the roads and salt marshes were exposed and resonantly firm. The water of the Terek had long ago subsided and had quickly run along the ditches and dried up. The oozy banks of the pond near the settlement had been trampled bare by the cattle, and all day one heard the splashing and shouting of girls and boys in the water. The tall weeds and reed beds of the steppe were already drying up, and the cattle, lowing, roamed away from their field during the afternoons. The wild animals moved on into the distant reed beds and the mountains beyond the Terek. Gnats and midges stood in clouds above the low-lying lands and the settlements. The snowy mountains were covered in grey mist. The air was thin and stank. Abreks, it was said, had crossed the now shallow river and were reconnoitring on this side of it. Each evening the sun set in a hot red glow. It was the time of the most intense labour. The entire population of the settlements swarmed in the melon fields and among the vines. The vineyards were densely overgrown with twining verdure, and everywhere in the cool, thick shade ripe, heavy clusters gleamed black from behind the broad, translucent leaves. Along the dusty road that led to the vineyards the creaking ox carts trundled, piled with heaps of black grapes. On the dusty road, crushed by the wheels, bunches of grapes lay scattered about. Little boys and girls in shirts stained with grape juice, with bunches in their hands and in their mouths, ran after their mothers. On the road one constantly encountered ragged workmen carrying baskets of grapes on their powerful shoulders. *Mamuki,* veiled with kerchiefs to the eyes, led bullocks harnessed to the carts that were piled high with grapes. Soldiers encountering a cart would ask the Cossack girls for grapes, and a Cossack girl, climbing up on the cart as it moved, would take an armful of grapes and pour them into the skirt of the soldier's coat. In some yards people were already pressing the grapes. The odour of *chapra* filled the air. Bloody red troughs could be seen under the sheds, and Nogay workmen with their trousers rolled up and calves stained red could be seen in the yards. Pigs, grunting, gobbled the pressings and wallowed in them. The flat roofs of the *izbushki* were covered with black and amber bunches that were drying in the sun. Crows **165** and magpies, pecking up the seeds, crowded around the roofs and fluttered from place to place.

The fruits of the year's labour were being gathered cheerfully, and this year the fruits were unusually plentiful and good.

In the shady green vineyards, amidst a sea of vines, from all sides one could hear laughter, singing, cheerful female voices, and catch glimpses of the women's brightly coloured garments.

At the height of noon, Maryana was sitting in her vine-yard, in the shade of a peach tree, taking out the dinner for her family from beneath an unharnessed ox cart. Opposite her, on a spread-out horse cloth, sat the cornet, returned from the school, washing his hands from a small jug. A little boy, her brother, who had just come running from the pond, was wiping himself with his sleeves, gazing anxiously at his sister and mother in the expectation of dinner, and breathing heavily. The old mother, her sleeves rolled up on her strong, sunburned arms, was setting out grapes, dried fish, *kaymak* and bread on a low, round Tatar table. The cornet, first rubbing his hands, took off his cap, crossed himself and moved towards the table. The little boy grabbed the jug and began to drink eagerly. Tucking up their legs, the mother and daughter settled down at the table. Even in the shade the heat was unbearable. A stench hung in the air above the vineyard. The strong warm wind, passing through the branches, brought no coolness, but merely bent the tops of the pear, peach and mulberry trees in monotonous fashion. The cornet, saying his prayers again, took from behind his back a jug of *chikhir* covered with a vine leaf, drank from its neck and handed it to the old woman. The cornet was dressed only in a shirt, unbuttoned at the neck, that exposed his muscular, hairy chest. His thin, cunning face was cheerful. Neither in his pose nor in his speech was there any sign of his usual diplomatic canniness: he was cheerful and natural.

'Well, will we have finished the bit beyond the shed by tonight?' he said, wiping his wet beard.

'We'll clear it,' replied the old woman, 'as long as the weather doesn't get in the way. The Demkins haven't cleared half of their yards yet,' she added. 'Ustenka's the only one who's working, killing herself, she is.'

'What are they thinking of?' said the old man, proudly.

'Here, have some of this, Maryanushka!' said the old woman, handing the jug to the girl. 'Now, God willing, we'll have some money for a decent wedding,' the old woman said.

'That's still in the future,' said the cornet, frowning slightly.

The girl lowered her head.

'But why can't we talk about it?' said the old woman. 'The matter's decided, and the day is not far off.'

'Don't guess at the future,' said the cornet, again. 'Right now we've our vineyards to clear.'

'Have you seen Lukashka's new horse?' asked the old woman. 'He hasn't got the one that Mitry Andreich gave him now: he went and exchanged it.'

'No, I haven't seen it. But I was talking to the servant of that lodger of ours today,' said the cornet. 'He says Lukashka got a thousand roubles for that horse.'

'The lodger's a wealthy man, and that's the truth of it,' the old woman confirmed.

The whole family was cheerful and content.

The work was advancing well. There were more grapes, and they were better than they had expected.

When Maryana had finished her dinner, she put out some more grass for the oxen, tucked her *beshmet* under her head and lay down under the ox cart on the trampled, succulent grass. She was wearing only a *krasnaya sorochka*, that is to say a silk kerchief on her head and a faded blue cotton shirt; but she felt unbearably hot. Her face was burning, her feet hurt, her eyes were covered with a moist film of sleep and tiredness; her lips parted involuntarily, and her bosom breathed heavily and deeply.

The working season had begun two weeks earlier, and the heavy, incessant toil had occupied the whole of the young girl's life. In the early morning, at dawn, she would jump up, wash her face in cold water, wrap herself in a shawl and run out barefoot to tend to the cattle. Quickly she put her shoes on, and her *beshmet* and, taking some bread in a small bundle, harnessed the oxen and rode off to the vineyards for the whole day. There she rested for only a brief hour, cut grapes and hauled baskets, cheerful and untiring, pulling the oxen by a rope and driving them with a long stick, and then returning to the settlement. Having gathered in the cattle at twilight, taking some sunflower seeds in the broad sleeve of her shirt, she went out to the corner to laugh and talk with the other girls. But as soon as the light of the sunset had died she returned home to the hut and, after eating supper in the dark *izbushka* with her father, mother and young brother, carefree and healthy, entered the hut, sat down on the stove and in a state of semi-drowsing listened to the lodger's talk. The moment he left, she threw herself on her bed and slept until morning, in a sound and quiet slumber. The next day was the same. She had not seen Lukashka since the day of the betrothal, and was calmly awaiting the day of the wedding. And as for the lodger, she had grown used to him and felt his intent gaze on her with pleasure.

30

In spite of the fact that there was nowhere to escape from the heat, that the gnats hovered in swarms in the cool shade of the ox cart, and her little brother, tossing and turning, kept pushing her, Maryana pulled her kerchief over her head and face, and was on the point of falling asleep when suddenly Ustenka, her neighbour, came running to see her and, ducking beneath the ox cart, lay down beside her.

'All right then, sleep, girls! Sleep!' said Ustenka, settling down under the ox cart. 'Wait,' she said, jumping up. 'This won't do.'

She leapt to her feet, tore off some green branches and 169 hung them on the ox cart's wheels, throwing her *beshmet* over them.

'Let me in!' she cried to the little boy, climbing under the ox cart again. 'Is this any place for Cossacks to be, with girls? Go away!'

Remaining alone with her friend under the cart, Ustenka suddenly seized her friend Maryana in both arms and, pressing against her, began to kiss her on the cheeks and neck.

'Dear sweet man! My darling!' she kept saying, dissolving in her clear, delicate laughter.

'It's easy to see you've learned a thing or two from "Grandad",' Maryana replied, fighting her off. 'Now stop it!'

And the two of them burst into such peals of laughter that the mother shouted at them to be quiet.

'Are you jealous, then?' said Ustenka in a whisper.

'Don't talk nonsense! Let me sleep. Oh, why are you here?'

But Ustenka was persistent:

'I've got something to tell you, that's what!'

Maryana raised herself on one elbow and adjusted the kerchief which had fallen off.

'Well, what is it?'

'I know something about your lodger.'

'There's nothing to know,' replied Maryana.

'Oh, you bad girl!' said Ustenka, nudging her with her elbow and laughing. 'You won't tell me anything. Does he come to see you?'

'Yes, he does. What of it?' said Maryana, blushing suddenly.

'Look, I'm a simple girl, I'll tell anyone who wants to hear. Why should I try to hide?' said Ustenka, and her cheerful, rosy face assumed a pensive expression. 'I'm not doing anyone any harm, am I? I love him, and that's the end of it!'

'Grandad, is it?'

'Well, yes.'

'That's a sin!' retorted Maryana.

'Oh, Mashenka! When can a girl have a good time if not when she still has her girlish freedom? I'll marry a Cossack, I'll bear children and I'll know hardship. And when you marry Lukashka you'll never even think about happiness – it'll be all children and work.'

'Well, other people get married and live happily. It doesn't make any difference!' Maryana replied calmly.

'All right, you tell me then once and for all, what happened between you and Lukashka?'

'What happened? He wooed me. My father put it off for a year; but today we had the betrothal, and in the autumn I'll be married.'

'And what did he say to you?'

Maryana smiled.

'What else would he say? He said he loves me. Kept asking me to go to the vineyards with him.'

'Oh, the blackguard! Well, you didn't go, I hope. And what a daredevil he's become now! A top-class *djigit*. He's forever carousing in the company, too. The other day our Kirka came here and said: "What a wonderful horse Lukashka's got now!" But I expect he's pining for you. What else did he say?' Ustenka asked Maryana.

'You need to know everything, don't you?' Maryana laughed. 'One night he came riding on his horse to my window, drunk. He wanted me to let him in.'

'And you didn't, did you?'

'Of course I didn't! Once I've said a thing, that's it! As firm as a rock,' Maryana replied, seriously.

'And he's a daredevil! He could have any girl he wants, no girl would turn up her nose at him.'

'Let him go to the others, then,' Maryana replied proudly.

'You don't love him?'

'Yes, I do, but I won't do something stupid. It's wrong.' **171**

Ustenka suddenly let her head fall on her friend's breast, seized her in her arms and shook all over with the laughter that was choking her.

'You silly, foolish girl!' she said quietly, out of breath, 'you don't want happiness for yourself.' And she began to tickle Maryana again.

'Hey, stop it!' said Maryana, her girlish screams dissolving into laughter. 'You're smothering Lazutka.'

'Sheesh, the devils, they're playing the fool, and they never get tired of it,' the old woman's sleepy voice came from the ox cart.

'You don't want happiness,' Ustenka repeated in a whisper, and half getting up. 'But you're lucky, my, how lucky you are! How they love you! You've got pockmarks, but they love you. Oh, if I were in your place, I'd soon turn the lodger's head! I got a look at him when you were at our house: he looked as though he could eat you with his eyes. My "Grandad" – what has he ever given me? But they say your fellow is the richest man in Russia. His batman says they have their own servants.'

Maryana got up and, after reflecting, smiled.

'He once said something to me, the lodger,' she said quietly, chewing on a blade of grass. 'He said: "I wish I were a Cossack like Lukashka, or your little brother, Lazutka." Why did he say that, I wonder?'

'Oh, he was just talking whatever nonsense came into his head,' replied Ustenka. 'The things mine says! Like a man with the evil eye!'

Maryana threw her head on to the folded *beshmet*, put her arm on Ustenka's shoulder and closed her eyes.

'He was going to come and work in the vineyards today: father asked him to,' she said softly, after a short silence, and fell asleep.

31

Now the sun had come out from behind the pear tree that had shaded the ox cart, and with slanting rays, even through the branches that Ustenka had twined together, scorched the faces of the girls as they slept underneath. Maryana woke up and began to adjust her kerchief. Looking round, on the other side of the pear tree she caught sight of the lodger, who with his rifle on his shoulder stood talking to her father. She gave Ustenka a nudge and silently, smiling, pointed him out to her.

'I went hunting yesterday, but I didn't find anything,' Olenin was saying, restlessly looking around, unable to see Maryana through the branches.

'Well, you ought to go to the other side, walk straight as the crow flies, over there in the disused vineyard, the "Wilderness" it's called; there are always hares to be found there,' said the cornet, at once altering his manner of speech.

'A fine thing to go looking for hares in the working season! You'd do better to come and give us a hand. You could work with the girls,' said the old woman, cheerfully. 'Now then, girls, up you get!' she cried.

Maryana and Ustenka were whispering together, hardly able to restrain their laughter under the ox cart.

Ever since word had got round that Olenin had made Lukashka a present of a horse worth fifty 'coins', his hosts had grown better disposed towards him; the cornet especially, it seemed, viewed Olenin's association with his daughter with satisfaction.

'But I don't know how to do the work,' said Olenin, trying not to look under the ox cart through the green branches, where he had noticed Maryana's blue shirt and red kerchief.

'Come along, I'll give you some dried peaches and apricots,' the old woman replied.

'It's a bit of traditional Cossack hospitality, just an old woman's silliness,' said the cornet, explaining his wife's words, as if correcting them. 'I should think that in Russia you're more used to pineapple jam and preserves.'

'So there are hares in the disused vineyard?' asked Olenin. 'I shall go over there.' And, throwing a swift glance through the green branches, he doffed his cap and disappeared between the straight green rows of vines.

The sun had already gone behind the fence, and was gleaming with broken rays through the translucent leaves when Olenin returned to his hosts among the vines. The wind was dying down, and a fresh coolness began to spread through the vineyards. By some instinct, while he was still a long way away, Olenin recognized Maryana's light blue shirt through the rows of grapes, and picking some as he went, he approached her. From time to time his overexcited dog also grabbed a low-hanging bunch of grapes in its slavering mouth. Flushed, her sleeves rolled up, her kerchief down below her chin, Maryanka was quickly cutting down the heavy bunches and putting them away in a basket. Without letting go of the vine she was holding, she stopped, smiled and again set to work. Olenin approached, throwing his rifle over his shoulder in order to free his hands. 'But where is your family? God help you! Are you alone?' he wanted to say, but said nothing, and merely doffed his cap. He felt awkward alone with Maryanka, but, as though tormenting himself deliberately, he walked up to her.

'You'll be shooting women if you go on like that,' said Maryana.

'No, I won't.'

They were both silent for a while.

'You could give me a hand.'

He took out a small knife and began to cut in silence. Pulling down from under the leaves a thick, heavy bunch weighing all of three pounds, on which all the grapes were stuck to one another, unable to find enough room, he showed it to Maryana:

'Shall I cut them all? Isn't this bunch too green?'

'Give it here.'

Their hands collided. Olenin took her hand, and smiling, she looked at him.

'Well, so you're going to be married soon?' he said.

Without replying, she turned away and brought her stern eyes to bear on him.

'Do you love Lukashka?' he asked.

'What's it to you?'

'I'm envious.'

'Indeed!'

'It's true, you're so beautiful.'

And suddenly he felt a horrible guilt about what he had said. His words sounded so tawdry, he thought. He flushed, lost his composure and took her by both hands.

'Whatever I am, I'm not for you! Why are you making fun of me?' replied Maryana, but her gaze showed how firmly she knew that he was not making fun.

'Making fun of you? If you knew how I . . .'

The words sounded even more tawdry, even more out of harmony with what he felt; but he went on:

'I don't know all the things I'd be ready to do for you . . .'

'Leave me alone, you blackguard!'

But her face, her shining eyes, her swelling bosom, her shapely legs said something quite different. It seemed to him that she understood how tawdry all the things he was saying to her were, but was above such considerations; it seemed to him that she had long known all the things he yearned to tell her and was unable to, but wanted to hear how he would say them. 'And how can she fail to know,' he thought, 'when all I want to tell her is all that she is? But she doesn't want to know, doesn't want to reply,' he thought.

'Yoo-hoo!' came Ustenka's little voice, quite close, from behind the vine, and her delicate laughter. 'Come and give me a hand, Mitry Andreich. I'm all on my own!' she cried to Olenin, thrusting her round, naïve little face through the leaves.

Olenin made no reply and did not move.

Maryanka went on with her cutting, but kept constantly looking up at the lodger. He began to say something, but stopped, shrugged his shoulders and, throwing on his rifle, swiftly walked out of the vineyard.

32

Once or twice he stopped, listening to the resonant laughter of Maryana and Ustenka, who were shouting something as they met. All evening he walked about the forest, hunting. Without having killed anything, he returned home when it was already twilight. Walking across the yard, he noticed that the door into his hosts' *izbushka* was open, and from it caught a glimpse of a blue shirt. He called Vanyusha particularly loudly, in order to let his arrival be known, and sat down in his usual place on the porch. His hosts had already returned from the vineyards; they came out of the *izbushka,* walked through to their hut, and did not invite him to come in. On two occasions, Maryanka went out through the gate. Once in the half-light it seemed to him that she glanced round at him. He eagerly followed her every movement, watching but unable to bring himself to approach her. When she vanished back into the hut, he came down from the porch and began to walk about the yard. But Maryana did not re-emerge. Olenin spent the whole night without sleep, out in the yard, listening to every sound from the landlords' hut. As the evening wore on, he heard them talking, having supper, hauling out the feather mattresses and going to bed, Maryana laughing at something; then all grew quiet. The cornet was discussing something in a whisper with the old woman, and someone was breathing heavily. He returned to his own hut for a while. Vanyusha was asleep in his clothes. Olenin felt envious of him and again began to pace about the yard, waiting for something; but no one came out, no one stirred; the only sound was the regular breathing of three human beings. He knew Maryana's breathing, and kept listening

177

to it and to the beating of his heart. In the settlement all was quiet, a late moon had risen, and the cattle were more in evidence now, snorting in the yards, lying down or slowly getting up. Olenin angrily wondered: 'What do I want?' – and was unable to tear himself free of this night. Suddenly he heard the clear sound of footsteps and the creak of a floorboard in the landlords' hut. He rushed to the door; but again nothing could be heard except regular breathing, and again after a heavy sigh a buffalo cow turned, rose on the knees of its front legs, then stood up on all fours, waved its tail, shuffled rhythmically on the dry clay of the yard, and lay down again with a sigh in the moonlit darkness . . . He wondered what he should do – and firmly made up his mind to go to bed; but again there were sounds, and in his mind he saw an image of Maryanka, emerging into this misty, moonlit night, and again he rushed to the window, and again heard footsteps. When it was nearly dawn, he went up to the window, gave the shutter a push, ran round to the door, and he really could hear Maryana's sighing and footsteps. He took hold of the latch and knocked. Cautious barefoot steps, which made the floorboards faintly creak, approached the door. The latch began to move, the door squeaked, there was an odour of marjoram and pumpkin, and Maryanka, all of her, appeared in the doorway. He saw her only for an instant in the moonlight. She shut the door and, whispering something, ran back inside with light footsteps. Olenin knocked gently, but there was no response. He ran round to the window and began to listen. Suddenly a harsh, shrill male voice surprised him.

'Lovely!' said a short little Cossack in a white cap, coming across the yard, right up to Olenin. 'I saw it, lovely!'

Olenin recognized Nazarka and was silent, not knowing what to do or say.

'Lovely! Now I'll just go to the settlement office, hand

in my report and tell her father. Sheesh, some cornet's daughter she is! One's not enough for her.'

'What do you want from me, what are you after?' Olenin managed to get out.

'It's all right, I'll tell them when I get to the settlement office.'

Nazarka spoke very loudly, and it appeared that this was deliberate.

'Sheesh, a clever "cadet", and no mistake!'

Olenin trembled and turned pale.

'Come here, come here!' He seized him violently by the arms and led him to his hut. 'Listen, nothing happened, she didn't let me in, and I didn't . . . She's a decent girl . . .'

'Well, we can discuss it down at the office . . .'

'But all the same, I'll give you something . . . Wait a moment!'

Nazarka fell silent. Olenin ran into his hut and brought **179** the Cossack ten roubles.

'Look, nothing happened, but I realize that I'm to blame, so here you are! Only for God's sake don't let anyone find out. And anyway, nothing happened . . .'

'Good luck!' Nazarka said, laughing, and went away.

Nazarka had arrived in the settlement that night at Lukashka's bidding – to prepare a place to hide a stolen horse – and, as he went home along the street, had heard the sound of footsteps. He returned to his company in the morning and, boasting, told his comrade how he had cleverly obtained ten 'coins'. Next morning, Olenin saw his hosts, and none of them knew anything. With Maryana he exchanged no words, and she merely laughed a little as she gazed at him. Again he passed the night without sleep, in futile strolling about the yard. The following day he deliberately went hunting and in the evening, in order to escape from himself, went off to see Beletsky. He was afraid of himself, and promised himself not to visit his

hosts any more. During the night that followed Olenin
was woken by the sergeant major. The company was going
on a raid forthwith. Olenin was glad of this opportunity,
and planned not to return to the settlement again.

The raid lasted for four days. The commander asked to
see Olenin, to whom he was related, and offered to let him
remain at staff headquarters. Olenin declined. He could
not live without the settlement to which he had grown so
attached, and asked to be allowed to go back there. For the
raid he received a soldier's cross, which earlier he had
greatly desired. But now he was completely indifferent to
that cross, and even more indifferent to his promotion to
the rank of officer, which had not yet come through. With
Vanyusha he rode back to the line, without event, several
hours ahead of his company. He spent all evening on the
porch, gazing at Maryana. All night he paced the yard
180 again, without aim or thought.

33

Next morning Olenin woke late. His hosts had already left. He did not go hunting, and now set to reading a book, now went out on the porch and again re-entered the hut and lay down on the bed. Vanyusha thought he was ill. Towards evening Olenin determinedly got up, began to write, and wrote until late at night. He wrote a letter, but did not send it, because no one would have understood what he wanted to say, and there was no reason why anyone should understand it but Olenin himself. This is what he wrote:

'People write letters of condolence to me from Russia; they are afraid that I will perish, having buried myself in this backwater. They say of me: he'll grow coarse, lose touch with everything, start drinking and even, who knows, marry a Cossack girl. It's not for nothing, they say, that Yermolov[47] said: "Any man who serves ten years in the Caucasus will either drink himself to death or marry a loose woman." How terrible! Indeed, I mustn't ruin myself when it might fall to my lot to know the great happiness of becoming the husband of Countess B—, a chamberlain or a marshal of nobility. How repulsive and pathetic you all seem to me! You don't know what happiness is, what life is! One must experience life in all its uncontrived beauty. One must see and understand what every day I see before me: the eternal inaccessible snows of the mountains and a majestic woman in that primordial beauty, in which the first woman must have emerged from her creator's hands, and then it will become clear who is ruining himself, who is living in truth or in a lie – you or I. If you knew how loathsome and pathetic you seem to me in your deluded state! As soon as I picture to myself, in place of my hut, my forest and my love, those drawing-rooms, those women with pomaded hair over false curls stuffed in below, those unnaturally moving lips, those weak limbs, hidden and deformed, and that drawing-room babble, obliged to be conversation and having no right to it – I feel a sense of unbearable revulsion. I picture to myself those stupid faces, those rich fiancées with an expression on their faces that says: "It's all right, you may come near, even though I'm a rich fiancée"; those seatings and changings of seats, that brazen procuring of couples, and that endless gossip and pretence; those rules – with whom to shake hands, to whom to nod, with whom to hold a conversation, and above all that eternal ennui in the blood which passes from generation to generation (and all of it done consciously, with a conviction that it is indis- 182 pensable). Just try to understand one thing, believe one thing. You need only see and understand what truth and beauty are, and all that you say and do, all your wishes for happiness both for me and for yourselves, will crumble to dust. Happiness is being with nature, seeing it, talking with it. "He may even, God forbid, marry a simple Cossack girl and be completely lost to society," I imagine them say- ing about me with sincere compassion. Yet there is only one thing I desire: to be completely lost in your sense, I want to marry a simple Cossack girl and do not dare to because that would be a supreme happiness of which I am not worthy.

'Three months have passed since I saw the Cossack girl Maryana for the first time. The ideas and prejudices of the world from which I had emerged were still fresh in me. At that time I did not believe I could love this woman. I admired her, as I admired the beauty of the mountains and the sky, and could not help admiring her, because she was as lovely as they were. Then I felt that the contemplation of this beauty had become a necessity in my life, and I began to ask myself: did I not love her? But I could not find in myself anything that resembled what I imagined that feeling to be like. This was a feeling that resembled neither the melancholy of loneliness nor the desire for wedlock, nor Platonic love, nor even less carnal love, all of which I have experienced. I needed only to see her, hear her, know that she was near, and I was not only happy, but calm. After the party at which I was together with her and touched her, I felt that between this woman and myself there existed an inseparable though unacknowledged bond, against which it was impossible to struggle. But I did still struggle; I said to myself: "Can I really love a woman who will never understand the sincere interests of my life? Can one really love a woman for her beauty alone, love a woman as though she were a statue?" I asked myself, but I already loved her, even though I did not yet believe in my feeling. **183**

'After the party at which I spoke to her for the first time, our relations altered. Previously she had been for me an alien but majestic object of external nature; after the party she became a human being for me. I began to meet her, talk to her, sometimes go to work for her father and sit for whole evenings with them at their house. And in those close encounters she remained in my eyes just as pure, inaccessible and majestic. She always replied to every question with equal calm, pride and indifferent gaiety. Sometimes she was affectionate, but for the most part her every look, every word, every movement expressed that indifference, not contemptuous but overwhelmingly bewitching. Every day with a feigned smile on my lips I tried to dissemble to some degree and with a torment of passion and desire in my heart engaged her in flippant conversation. She could see that I was pretending: but she would look at me directly, cheerfully and simply. This situation became unendurable to me. I wanted not to lie to her and wanted to tell her everything I was thinking and feeling. I was extremely worked up; this took place in the vineyards. I began to tell her of my love in words I am ashamed to remember. Ashamed, because I ought not to have dared say this to her, because she stood immeasurably higher than those words and the feeling I wanted to express by means of them. I fell silent, and from that day on my situation became unendurable. I did not want to degrade myself by remaining on our previous flippant terms, and I felt that I had not yet grown to the level of direct and simple relations with her. In despair I asked myself: "But what am I to do?" In absurd dreams I imagined her now as my lover, now as my wife, and rejected both the one and the other in disgust. To make her a loose woman would be terrible. It would be murder. To make her a lady, the wife of Dmitry Andreyevich Olenin, like one of the Cossack women here whom one of our officers has married, would be even worse. Now if I could make myself into a Cossack, a Lukashka, steal horses, get drunk on *chikhir,* sing loud songs, kill people and climb in through her window for the night when drunk without a thought of who I am or what I am for, that would be a different matter. Then we might understand each other, and then I might be happy. I tried to abandon myself to that sort of life, but it just made me feel all the more keenly how weak and affected I was. I was unable to forget myself and my complex, disfigured past that lacks all harmony. And my future seems to me even more hopeless. Every day I am confronted by the distant snowy mountains and this majestic, happy woman. And not for me is the only happiness possible in the world, this woman is not for me! The most terrible thing about my situation, and also what is most sweet about it, is that I feel I understand her, and she will never understand me. This is not because she is inferior to me – on the contrary, she ought not to understand me. She is happy; she, like nature, is even, calm, and self-contained. While I, a weak, corrupted being, want her to understand my disfigurement and my torments. For nights I did not sleep, spending them under her windows to no purpose, and without realizing what had happened to me. On the eighteenth our company embarked on a raid. I spent three days outside the settlement. I felt sad and could not care less. In the detachment the singing, cards, drinking bouts, talk of military decorations were even more repulsive to me than usual. Today I returned home, and saw her, my hut, Uncle Yeroshka, and the snowy mountains, from my porch, and such a powerful new emotion took hold of me that I understood everything. I love this woman with a love that is genuine, for the first and only time in my life. I know what has happened to me. I am not afraid to degrade myself by my emotion, am not ashamed of my love, am proud of it. I am not to blame for **185** having fallen in love. It has happened against my will. I tried to run away from my love in self-sacrifice, I tried to invent some joy for myself in the love of Maryanka and the Cossack Lukashka, but merely intensified my own love and jealousy. This is not the ideal, so-called "exalted" love I experienced earlier; not that feeling of attraction in which one admires one's own love, feels within oneself the source of one's feeling and does everything oneself. I have experienced that, too. Even less is it a desire for pleasure, it is something different. Perhaps in her I love nature, the personification of all that is beautiful in nature; but I do not have a will of my own, and what loves her is some elemental force passing through me; all of God's world, all of nature presses this love into my soul and says: "Love". I love her not with my mind, not with my imagination, but with all my being. Loving her, I feel myself to be an inseparable part of all God's happy world. I wrote earlier about my new convictions, which I derived from my solitary life;

but no one can know the toil with which they were elaborated in me, with what joy I became conscious of them and saw a new, open path in life. Nothing was dearer to me than those convictions ... Well ... Love has come, and they are no longer here, nor even any regret for them. Even the thought that I could have prized such a cold, one-sided, cerebral state of mind is difficult for me to entertain. Beauty came and scattered into ash the whole of the Egyptian labour of my inner world. And I have no regret for what has gone! Self-denial – all that is nonsense, rubbish. It is all pride, a refuge from deserved unhappiness, a running away from envy of the happiness of others. Live for others, do good! Why? When in my soul there is only love for myself and the desire to love her and live with her, with her life. Not for others, not for Lukashka do I now desire happiness. Now I do not love those others. Before, I would have told myself that this is wrong. I would have tormented myself with the questions: "What will become of her, of myself, of Lukashka?" Now I don't care. I live not by my own will, and there is something stronger than me that is leading me. I am suffering, but before I was dead, and only now am I alive. Today I will go to their house and tell her everything.'

34

When, late in the evening, he had finished writing this letter, Olenin went to see his hosts. The old woman was sitting on the bench behind the stove, spinning silkworm cocoons. Maryana, her hair uncovered, was sewing by the light of a candle. On seeing Olenin, she jumped up, took her kerchief and walked over to the stove.

'Now then, Maryanushka, sit with us for a bit,' said her mother.

'No, I've nothing on my head.' And she jumped up on the stove.

All Olenin could see of her was one knee, and a shapely lower leg. He helped the old woman to tea. The old woman offered her guest *kaymak,* for which she sent Maryana. However, putting the plate on the table, Maryanka jumped back up on the stove again, and Olenin felt only her eyes. A conversation about household matters ensued. Babuka Ulitka really let herself go, passing into raptures of hospitality. She brought Olenin preserved grapes, a grape tart and some of the best wine, doing it all with that special, proud and coarse peasant hospitality that is found only among people who earn their bread by physical toil. The old woman, who had at first so struck Olenin by her coarseness, now often touched him with her simple tenderness towards her daughter.

'But why make God angry, sir? We have everything, thanks be to God, we've made the *chikhir* and stored it, we'll sell about three barrels, and there'll be plenty left to drink. You stay with us, and don't go away. We'll all have a good time at the wedding.'

'And when is the wedding to be?' asked Olenin, feeling

the blood suddenly rush to his face and his heart start to thump unevenly and painfully.

There was a movement behind the stove, and the sound of seeds being cracked was heard.

'Well, it ought to be next week. We're ready,' the old woman replied simply and calmly, as though Olenin was not there, and did not exist. 'I've got all the things for Marya-nushka, and I've set them in order. We shall give her away properly. But there's just one thing that's not right: our Lukashka has started to behave a bit wild. Very wild! He's up to some mischief! The other day a Cossack from his company came here and said that Luka had made a trip to Nogay.'

'He'd better take care that he doesn't get caught,' said Olenin.

'I tell him that, too. Stop your mischief, Lukashka, I say. Well, he's a young man, so of course he likes to throw his 188 weight around. But I mean, there's a time for everything. Oh, I know, he did some rustling, stole, killed an Abrek, good for him! All right, so now he ought to settle down. Or else there'll be some real trouble.'

'Yes, I saw him a couple of times in the detachment, he's always on the spree. He even sold the horse I gave him,' said Olenin, looking round at the stove.

The large dark eyes gleamed at him with stern hostility. He felt ashamed of what he had said.

'So what? He doesn't do anyone any harm,' Maryana said suddenly. 'It's his own money he spends on his fun.' And, lowering her legs, she jumped down from the stove and went out, slamming the door loudly behind her.

Olenin followed her with his eyes while she was in the hut, then looked at the door and waited, not taking in anything that Babuka Ulitka was saying to him. A few moments later some visitors entered: an old man, Babuka Ulitka's brother, with Uncle Yeroshka, followed by Marya-na and Ustenka.

'Hullo!' piped Ustenka. 'Still having a good time?' she addressed Olenin.

'Yes, I am,' he replied, and for some reason he felt ashamed and awkward.

He wanted to go away, but was unable to. Silence also did not seem an option. The old man helped him: he asked for a drink and they drank. Then Olenin drank with Yeroshka. Then again with the other Cossack. And the more he drank, the heavier did his heart become. But the old men were making merry. The two girls sat up on the stove, whispering to each other, while the men drank until evening. Olenin did not say anything, and drank more than anyone else. The Cossacks were shouting about something. The old woman chased them away and refused to let them have any more *chikhir*. The girls laughed at Uncle Yeroshka, and by the time they all went out to the porch it was nearly ten o'clock. The old men invited themselves **189** along to Olenin's in order to finish their merrymaking there. Ustenka ran off home. Yeroshka took the Cossack to see Vanyusha. The old woman went off to tidy up the *izbushka*. Maryana remained alone in the hut. Olenin felt fresh and cheerful, as though he had just woken up. He noticed everything and, letting the old men go on ahead, he returned to the hut: Maryana was preparing to go to bed. He approached her, wanting to say something to her, but his voice failed him. She sat down on the bed, tucked her legs under her, moved away from him right into the corner, and silently looked at him with a wild and frightened stare. She was plainly afraid of him. Olenin could feel this. He felt sorry and ashamed of himself, and at the same time he experienced a sense of proud satisfaction that he at least aroused this feeling in her.

'Maryana!' he said. 'Will you never take pity on me? I can't tell you how much I love you.'

She moved away even further.

'For shame, that's the wine talking. You won't get anything from me!'

'No, it's not the wine. Please don't marry Lukashka. I'll marry you.' 'What am I saying?' he thought at the very moment he uttered these words. 'Will I say the same thing tomorrow? I will, I'll say it for certain, and I'll say it again now' an inner voice replied to him. 'Will you marry me?'

She gave him a serious look, and her fear seemed now to have passed.

'Maryana! I'm going out of my mind! I'm not my own man. Whatever you tell me to do, I'll do it.' And words of mad tenderness spoke themselves of their own accord.

'Oh, what nonsense is this?' she said, interrupting him, suddenly seizing the arm he was stretching towards her. She did not, however, push his hand away, but pressed it tightly in her strong, hard fingers. 'Do gentlemen marry peasant girls? Go away!'

'But will you marry me? I'll give you anything . . .'

'And where will we put Lukashka?'

He tore away his arm, which she was holding, and violently embraced her young body. But, like a female deer, she leapt up, sprang away on her bare feet, and ran out to the porch. Regaining his senses, Olenin was horrified at himself. Again he found himself unutterably loathsome by comparison with her. But, not for one moment repenting of what he had said, he went home and, without a glance at the old men who were drinking in his lodgings, lay down and fell into a sleep that was sounder than any he had known for a long time.

35

The next day was a holiday. By evening everyone was out in the street, their festive clothes gleaming in the setting sun. More wine than usual had been pressed. The people were freed from their labours. In a month's time the Cossacks would be leaving on a campaign, and in many households preparations for weddings were being made.

On the square, in front of the settlement office and near the two shops – the one selling 'snacks' and sunflower seeds, the other kerchiefs and printed cottons – stood the largest number of people. Sitting or standing on the earthen embankment of the office were old men in grey and black coats, without gold braid or ornaments. Calmly, in measured voices, the old men chatted among themselves about the harvests and the young lads, or about public matters and the old days, surveying the younger generation with majestic indifference. As they walked past them, the women and girls stopped for a moment and lowered their heads. The young Cossacks respectfully slackened their pace and, removing their caps, held them in front of their heads for a while. The old men fell silent. Now sternly, now kindly, they examined the passers-by, slowly taking off their caps and putting them on again.

The Cossack women and girls had not yet begun their round dances; gathering in small groups, dressed in brightly coloured *beshmets* and white kerchiefs that bound their heads and faces, they sat on the ground and on the earthen embankments of the huts, shaded from the sun's slanting rays, resonantly laughing and chattering together. Little boys and girls played *lapta*, throwing the ball high into the clear sky, and running about the square, shouting and squealing. In another corner of the square adolescent girls were already engaged in a round dance, squeaking out a song in their thin, timid voices. Clerks, young lads with privileges and those who had returned from service for the holiday, in smart white or new red Circassian coats, embroidered with gold braid, their faces festive and cheerful, walked in twos and threes, arm in arm, from one group of Cossack women and girls to another and, when they stopped, joked and flirted with them. The Armenian shopkeeper, wearing a blue Circassian coat made of thin cloth, with gold braid, stood awaiting customers at the open door through which tiers of folded coloured kerchiefs could be glimpsed, with an Oriental merchant's pride and an awareness of his own importance. Two red-bearded, shoeless Chechens, who had come from the other side of the Terek to admire the festivities, crouched outside the house of someone they knew, casually puffing their small pipes and spitting, and exchanging remarks, with swift, guttural sounds, as they watched everyone. From time to time an unfestive-looking soldier in an old overcoat hurriedly passed between the brightly coloured groups around the square. Here and there one could hear the drunken singing of Cossacks who had already begun to make merry. All the huts were closed up, and the porches had been scrubbed clean the night before. Even the old women were out in the street. In the dry streets the dust was everywhere, strewn underfoot with the husks of melon and pumpkin seeds. The air was warm and still, the clear sky blue and transparent, while the lustreless white range of mountains visible above the rooftops seemed close, and was turning pink in the rays of the setting sun. Now and then, from somewhere across the river, there came the distant rumble of cannon fire. But above the settlement all kinds of merry, festive sounds floated, mingling with one another.

All morning Olenin had paced about the yard, waiting

for a sight of Maryana. But she, having put on her best clothes, had gone to Mass at the chapel; afterwards she sat on the earth embankment with the other girls, now cracking seeds, or now running off home for a while with her companions, and casting swift, cheerful, friendly glances at the lodger. Olenin was afraid to start talking to her flippantly and in the presence of others. He wanted to finish telling her what he had begun to tell her the previous day, and obtain a definite answer. He was waiting for another moment like the one that had occurred the evening before; but the moment did not arrive, and he felt he had not the strength to remain in such an uncertain state any longer. Maryana went out into the street again, and after a while, not knowing where he was bound, he followed her. He passed the corner where she sat in her resplendent blue satin *beshmet,* and with a sinking heart heard the girls' loud laughter behind him.

Beletsky's hut was on the square. Olenin, as he passed it, heard Beletsky's voice: 'Come in for a bit,' – and he did.

After they had talked for a little, they both sat down at the window. Soon they were joined by Yeroshka, who was wearing a new *beshmet* and settled down on the floor beside them.

'That's the aristocratic set, over there,' said Beletsky, pointing with his cigarette to a brightly coloured group on the corner, and smiling. 'Mine's there, too, do you see? She's the one in the red. It's a new acquisition. But why don't they start the round dance?' cried Beletsky, looking out of the window. 'Just wait, when it gets dark we'll go too. Then we'll invite them to Ustenka's. We must give them a ball.'

'I shall come to Ustenka's, too,' said Olenin, decisively. 'Will Maryana be there?'

'Of course she will, do come!' said Beletsky, not surprised in the least. 'I say, it's very attractive, isn't it?' he added, pointing to the brightly coloured crowds.

'Yes, very!' Olenin agreed, trying to appear indifferent. 'Holidays like this,' he added, 'always make me wonder why in consequence of the fact that, for example, today is the fifteenth of the month, everyone is suddenly cheerful and contented. The holiday is visible in everything. Eyes, faces, voices, movements, clothes, the air, the sun – everything's in holiday mood. Yet back in Russia we don't have holidays any more.'

'Mm,' said Beletsky, who disliked reflections of this kind. 'But why aren't you drinking, old fellow?' he said, turning to Yeroshka.

Yeroshka winked at Olenin, indicating Beletsky:

'My, he's a proud one, this *kunak* of yours!'

Beletsky raised his glass.

'*Alla bir-dy*,'* he said, drinking it all.

'*Sau bul*,'† replied Yeroshka, smiling, and drained his glass. 'A holiday, you say?' he said to Olenin, getting up and looking out of the window. 'What sort of holiday is that? You should have seen how they celebrated in the old days! The women used to come out dressed in *sarafans* trimmed with gold lace. Their breasts were hung with two rows of gold coins. They wore gold headdresses. They made a 'fr, fr' sound as they passed. Each woman was like a princess. They used to come out, the whole flock of them, and they'd start singing so the air was full of their moaning; all night they'd celebrate. And the Cossacks would roll barrels out into the yard, sit down and drink all night until dawn. Or else they'd join hands and move through the settlement like a flood. Whoever they met, they'd take him with them, and they'd go from one house to another.

194

---

* *Alla bir-dy* means: 'God has given'; this is the usual greeting used by natives of the Caucasus when they drink together. (Tolstoy's note.)

† 'Your health.' (Tolstoy's note.)

Sometimes they'd celebrate for three days on end. My dad used to come home, I can still remember it, all red and swollen, without his cap, completely shattered, he'd come in and lie down. My mum knew what to do: she'd give him some fresh caviar and *chikhir* to treat his hangover, and she'd run around the settlement herself to look for his cap. Then he'd sleep for two whole days and nights! That's what men were like in those days! But now what are they?'

'Well, and what about the girls in *sarafans*? Did they celebrate on their own, then?' asked Beletsky.

'Yes, they did! Cossacks would arrive on foot or on horseback, and they'd say: "Let's go and break up the round dance", and off they'd go, but the girls would take up cudgels. At Shrovetide some young lad would come flying along, and they'd use their cudgels, beat his horse, beat him. He'd break through the wall, grab the one he loved, and carry her off. Aye, there were some proper girls in **195** those days! Queens, they were!'

36

At that moment two horsemen rode out of the side street on to the square. One of them was Nazarka, the other Lukashka. Lukashka sat slightly sideways on his well-fed Kabarda bay as it stepped lightly along the hard road, tossing its beautiful head and delicate, glossy withers. The neatly adjusted rifle in its case, the pistol at his back and the *burka* folded behind his saddle were proof that Lukashka had not come from anywhere that was peaceful or close at hand. In his stylish, sideways posture, in the careless movement of the hand with which he scarcely audibly patted the horse on its belly with his whip, and especially in his glittering black eyes, which looked around proudly and narrowly, there was a consciousness of the strength and self-confidence of youth. 'Ever seen such a fine fellow as me before?' his eyes seemed to say, as they gazed from side to side. The elegant horse with the silver decorative plate on its trappings, the weapons and the handsome Cossack rider drew the attention of all the people on the square. Nazarka, thin and short of stature, was much less well dressed than Lukashka. As he rode past the old men, Lukashka stopped for a moment and raised his white curly sheepskin cap above his black and close-cropped head.

'How many Nogay horses have you stolen?' said a rather thin old man, with a dark and frowning look.

'I suppose you've counted them, Grandad, that you should ask,' replied Lukashka, turning away.

'It's not right, taking the lad along with you,' the old man said quietly, with an even darker look.

'Sheesh, the old devil, he knows everything!' Lukashka muttered to himself, and his face took on a worried expression; but then, glancing round the corner, where a lot of Cossack girls were standing, he turned his horse towards them.

'Greetings, girls!' he cried in a strong, harmonious voice, suddenly stopping his horse. 'You've put on years while I was gone, you witches!' And he laughed.

'Greetings, Lukashka! Greetings, dear!' cheerful voices were heard saying. 'How much money have you got with you? Buy the girls some *zakuski*! How long have you come for? We haven't seen you for a while, have we?'

'Nazarka and me are here on a flying visit, and we're going to make a night of it,' replied Lukashka, raising his whip threateningly at his horse, and charging at the girls.

'I think Maryanka's forgotten all about you,' piped Ustenka, nudging Maryana with her elbow, and dissolving in high-pitched laughter.

Maryana moved away from the horse and, throwing her 197 head back, calmly looked at the Cossack with her large, shining eyes.

'You haven't been here for ages! Going to run us down with your horse, are you?' she said dryly, and turned away.

Lukashka seemed unusually cheerful. His face radiated boldness and joy. Maryana's cold reply had evidently given him pause. Suddenly he frowned.

'Step up on the stirrup and I'll whisk you off to the mountains, missy!' he cried suddenly, as though chasing away unpleasant thoughts. *Djigit*-style, he made his horse prance among the girls. He stooped down towards Maryana. 'I'll kiss you, oh I'll kiss you to kingdom come!'

Maryana's eyes met his and she suddenly flushed. She stepped back.

'Damn you, really! You'll crush my legs,' she said and, lowering her head, looked at her shapely legs in their blue, tight-fitting stockings with arrow-shaped patterns, and their new red slippers trimmed with narrow silver braid.

Lukashka turned towards Ustenka, while Maryana sat down beside a Cossack girl who was holding a baby in her arms. The baby stretched out his chubby little hand to the girl and seized the string of necklaces that hung on her blue *beshmet*. Maryana leaned towards the child, casting a sideways glance at Lukashka as she did so. Meanwhile Lukashka was fetching out from under his Circassian coat a small bundle of 'snacks' and seeds which had lain in the pocket of his black *beshmet*.

'It's a present for you all,' he said, handing the bundle to Ustenka, and looked at Maryana with a smile.

Once again, confusion showed in the girl's face. Her beautiful eyes twitched as if in a kind of mist. She lowered her kerchief to below her mouth, and then suddenly, letting her head fall towards the baby's little white face as he held her by the necklace, began to kiss him greedily. The baby supported himself with his small hands on the girl's high breasts and screamed, opening his toothless little mouth.

'What are you smothering the little fellow for?' said the baby's mother, taking him away from her and unfastening her *beshmet* in order to give him the breast. 'You'd do better to go and say hullo to the young lad.'

'I'll get my horse stabled, and then Nazarka and I will be back, and we'll celebrate all night long,' said Lukashka, slapping the horse with his whip and riding away from the girls.

Turning into a side street, Nazarka and he rode up to two huts that stood next to one another.

'Here we are then, brother! Come back quick!' cried Lukashka to his companion, who had dismounted in front of the neighbouring yard, as they cautiously led their horses in through the wattle gates. 'Hullo, Styopka!' he said, addressing the deaf and dumb girl who, also dressed in her festive clothes, came in from the street to take his horse. And by means of signs he instructed her to put the horse to the hay, and not to unsaddle it.

The deaf and dumb girl began to make cooing sounds and smack her lips as she pointed to the horse, and she kissed it on the nose. This meant that she liked the horse and that it was a good one.

'Greetings, mother! Why, I thought you'd be out in the street by now!' cried Lukashka, holding his rifle and climbing up to the porch.

His old mother opened the door to him.

'There now, I never expected, I never guessed,' said the old woman, 'and Kirka kept saying you wouldn't come.'

'Go and fetch some *chikhir,* mother. Nazarka's coming to see me, and we're going to "pray" the holiday in.'

'Right away, Lukashka, right away,' the old woman replied. 'Our womenfolk are celebrating. I expect our deaf and dumb girl's gone too.'

And, taking the keys, she quickly set off for the *izbushka.*

When he had stabled his horse and taken off his rifle, Nazarka entered Lukashka's hut.

199

37

'Your health!' said Lukashka, as he took from his mother a full cup of *chikhir* and carefully raised it to his bowed head.

'This is some business, and no mistake,' said Nazarka. 'Grandad Burlak asked how many horses you'd stolen. He obviously knows!'

'He's a warlock!' Lukashka replied curtly. 'Anyway, what's all the fuss about?' he added with a shake of his head. 'They'll be on the other side of the river by now. Go and look for them!'

'Still, it's not right.'

'What's not right? Take him some *chikhir* tomorrow. That's the way to do it, and then there'll be no trouble. Now we're going to celebrate. Drink!' cried Lukashka, in the same tone of voice with which old Yeroshka used to pronounce that word. 'We'll go out to the street, to the girls, and celebrate. You go and get some honey, or I can send our deaf and dumb girl for some. We'll celebrate till morning.'

Nazarka smiled.

'Going to be here long, then, are we?'

'Let's have a good time! Run and get some vodka! And pay for it!'

Nazarka obediently ran off to Yamka's.

Uncle Yeroshka and Yergushov, like birds of prey, having sniffed out a celebration, tumbled into the hut one after the other, both drunk.

'Bring us another half-pail!' Lukashka shouted to his mother in reply to their greeting.

'Right, now tell us where you stole them, you devil!' shouted Uncle Yeroshka. 'Good lad! I love you!'

'I love you, indeed!' Lukashka replied, laughing. 'You take "snacks" to girls from cadets. Ah, you old codger!'

'It's not true, I'm telling you it's not true! Ach, Marka! (The old man burst into laughter.) Oh, how that devil begged me! Go and fix it up, he said. He was going to give me a rifle, too. No, to hell with him! I might have done it, but I felt sorry for you. Well, tell us: where have you been?' And the old man began to speak in Tatar.

Lukashka replied fluently.

Yergushov, who did not know much Tatar, merely inserted some Russian words now and then.

'I tell you, he's stolen some horses. I know it for a fact,' he confirmed.

'Gireyka and I went together,' Lukashka recounted. (In his calling Girey-Khan 'Gireyka' there was a mettlesome quality that is noticeable in Cossacks.) 'On the other side of the river he kept trying to show me what a fearless fellow he was, telling me that he knew the whole of the steppe and would lead us straight there, but when we rode out it was a dark night and my Gireyka lost his way, began to crawl about, but nothing came of it. He couldn't find the *aul*, and that was that. Gone too far to the right, we had, apparently. We searched for it almost until midnight. Then, thank God, the dogs started howling.'

'Fools,' said Uncle Yeroshka. 'We used to lose our way in the steppe at night like that, too. Who the devil knows his way out there? I used to ride up a hill and howl the way the wolves do, like this! (He put his hands to his mouth and began to howl like a pack of wolves, on one note.) The dogs would answer at once. Well, go on. So did you find them, then?'

'We put the bridles on them quick! Nazarka nearly got caught by some Nogay women, hch!'

'Yes, I nearly did,' Nazarka, who had now returned, said in an offended tone.

'We rode off; then Gireyka lost his way again, nearly led us into the sandhills. We thought we were riding towards the Terek, but we were actually going the other way.'

'You should have guided yourself by the stars,' said Uncle Yeroshka.

'That's what I say, too,' Yergushov chimed in.

'Yes, try doing that when the sky's all dark. Oh, I tried and tried! Caught one of the mares, bridled it, and let my own horse go; it'll lead us there, I thought. And what do you know? It snorted and snorted, put its muzzle to the ground . . . Went galloping on ahead, and led us straight to the settlement. And by then it was quite light; thank goodness; we just had time to hide the horses in the forest. Nagim came from across the river, and took them.'

Yergushov shook his head.

'Cunning, I call that! And how much did you get for them?'

'It's all here,' said Lukashka, slapping his pocket.

At that moment his mother entered the room. Lukashka did not get to the end of what he was saying . . .

'Drink!' he exclaimed.

'You know, late one night Girchik and I went riding . . .' Yeroshka began.

'Here, I don't want to listen to that all over again!' said Lukashka. 'I'm off.' And, finishing the wine in his cup and tightening his belt, Lukashka went out to the street . . .

38

It was already quite dark when Lukashka came out into the street. The autumn night was cool and windless. A full golden moon was floating out behind the dark poplars that rose on one side of the square. Smoke was rising from the chimneys of the *izbushki*, mingling with the mist and spreading above the settlement. Here and there lights shone in the windows. The air was suffused with the odour of *kizyak*, *chapra* and mist. The sounds of talk, laughter, singing and the cracking of seeds blended as they did in the daytime, but were clearer. Little groups of kerchiefs and sheepskin caps were visible in the darkness near the fences and houses.

On the square, in front of the open and illuminated doorway of the shop, a crowd of Cossack men and girls showed black and white, and loud singing, laughter and talk could be heard. Catching one another by the hand, the girls moved in a circle, stepping smoothly across the dusty square. A thin girl, the least attractive of them, began to sing:

> From beyond the forest, the dark forest,
> Ay-da-lyuli!
> From beyond the garden, the green garden
> They walked out, the two young lads.
> Two young lads, and both of them unmarried.
> They walked and then they stopped,
> They stopped, and quarrelled.
> A pretty girl came out to them,
> Came out to them, and spoke to them:
> 'To one of you I'll give myself.'

It was the fair-skinned one who got her,
The fair-skinned lad, the fair-haired one.
He took her, took her by the right hand.
He led her, led her round and round,
To all his comrades boasted he:
'How do you like the missus, lads?'

Nearby the old women stood listening to the songs. The little boys and girls ran about in the darkness, chasing one another. Here and there Cossacks stood, trying to accost passing girls, now and then breaking up the round dance and entering the ring. On the dark side of the doorway stood Beletsky and Olenin in Circassian coats and sheepskin caps, talking together in a manner unlike that of the Cossacks, not loudly but audibly, and sensing that they were attracting attention. Next to each other in the round dance moved the rather fat little Ustenka in a red *beshmet*, and the majestic figure of Maryana in a new shirt and *beshmet*. Olenin and Beletsky were talking about how they might get Maryanka and Ustenka away from the round dance. Beletsky thought that Olenin merely wanted to have a good time, but Olenin was awaiting the resolution of his destiny. He wanted at all costs to see Maryana alone that very day, tell her everything and ask her if she could and would be his wife. Even though he had long ago received a negative answer to this question, he hoped that he would be able to tell her everything he felt, and that she would understand him.

'Why didn't you tell me earlier?' Beletsky was saying. 'I'd have set it up for you through Ustenka. You're such a strange fellow!'

'What can one do? Some day, very soon, I shall tell you all about it. Only now, for God's sake, see to it that she comes to Ustenka's.'

'Right. That's easy . . . Well now, are you going to give

yourself to the fair-skinned lad, Maryanka, eh? And not to Lukashka?' said Beletsky, turning first, for propriety's sake, to Maryanka; and, not waiting for an answer, he went up to Ustenka and began to ask her to bring Maryanka with her. He had not had time to finish what he was saying when the leader of the chorus began to sing another song, and the girls pulled one another round. They sang:

> By the garden, by the garden,
> A young lad went a-walking,
> Along to the end of the street.
> The first time that he went,
> He waved his right hand
> The second time that he went,
> He waved his feathered cap,
> And the third time that he went,
> He stopped,
> Stopped, and went across.
> 'I wanted to come and see you,
> See you and reproach you, dear:
> Why, my dear, do you not
> Go a-walking in the garden?
> Or do you, my dear one,
> Despise me?
> Later, my dear one,
> You will calm down.
> I will send the matchmaker,
> I will woo you.
> When I marry you,
> You will weep because of me.'
> Now I knew what to say,
> But I did not dare reply.
> I did not dare reply.
> Went a-walking in the garden.
> Went into the green garden,

> Bowed to my friend,
> And I, a maiden, bowed,
> And dropped my handkerchief.
> 'Please, my dear one, take
> This in your white hands.
> Take it in your white hands,
> And, maiden, love me.
> I don't know, I'm at a loss,
> For what to give my dear one.
> I shall give my dear one
> A big kerchief, a shawl.
> And for the shawl I'll take
> Five kisses in return.'

Lukashka and Nazarka, who had broken through the round dance, began to walk among the girls. Lukashka joined in the singing with a harsh supporting voice and, waving his arms about, walked in the middle of the group.

'Well, step out, one of you!' he said.

The girls pushed Maryanka; she did not want to leave the ring. Through the singing high-pitched laughter, blows, kisses and whispering were heard.

As he walked past Olenin, Lukashka gave him a friendly nod.

'Mitry Andreich! Come to have a look, too, have you?' he said.

'Yes,' Olenin replied, firmly and coldly.

Beletsky leaned down to Ustenka's ear and said something to her. She was about to answer, but did not have time to and, as she passed by the second time, said:

'All right, we'll go.'

'And Maryana, too?'

Olenin leaned down towards Maryana.

'You'll go? Please do, even if it's only for a minute. I need to speak to you.'

'I'll go if the other girls go.'

'Will you tell me what I asked you?' he asked, leaning down to her again. 'You're cheerful today.'

She was already moving away from him. He went after her.

'Will you tell me?'

'Tell you what?'

'The answer to the question I asked you the other day,' said Olenin, bending down to her ear. 'Will you marry me?'

Maryana thought for a moment.

'I'll tell you,' she replied. 'I'll tell you today.'

And in the darkness her eyes gleamed cheerfully and affectionately at the young man.

He went on following her. It was a delight for him to lean closer to her.

But as he continued to sing, Lukashka tugged her violently by the arm, tearing her out of the round dance and into the centre of the ring. Olenin, who had only had time to say: 'Then come to Ustenka's', went back to his comrade. The song came to an end. Lukashka wiped his lips, and so did Maryanka, and they kissed.

'No, five kisses!' said Lukashka. The smooth motion and smooth sounds were replaced by talk, laughter and running about. Lukashka, who already seemed to be very intoxicated, began handing out the 'snacks' to the girls.

'It's a present for you all,' he said with a proud self-satisfaction that was comically touching. 'But those who want to play around with soldiers can leave the dance now,' he said, with an angry glance at Olenin.

The girls grabbed the snacks from him and, laughing, fought one another for them. Beletsky and Olenin stepped off to one side.

Lukashka, as if embarrassed by his own generosity, taking off his cap and wiping his forehead on his sleeve, went over to Maryanka and Ustenka.

'Or do you, my dear one, despise me?' he said, repeating the words of the song they had just been singing and, turning to Maryanka – 'despise me?' he repeated again angrily. 'When you marry me, you will weep because of me,' he added, putting his arms round Ustenka and Maryana together.

Ustenka tore herself free and, with a wave of her arm, struck him on the back so hard that she hurt her hand.

'Well, are you going to dance some more?' he asked.

'The girls may do as they want,' replied Ustenka. 'But I'm going home, and Maryanka was going to come to our place, too.'

The Cossack, continuing to embrace Maryanka, led her away from the crowd to a dark corner of the house.

'Don't go, Mashenka,' he said. 'Let's enjoy ourselves for the last time. Go home, and I'll come to you.'

208 'What would I do at home? Holidays are for having fun. I'm going to Ustenka's,' said Maryana.

'I'll marry you all the same, you know!'

'All right,' said Maryana. 'We'll see later on.'

'What, are you going?' Lukashka said sternly and, pressing her to him, kissed her on the cheek.

'Hey, leave off! Don't give up, do you?' And Maryana, tearing herself free, walked away from him.

'Ach, girl! . . . It'll end badly,' said Lukashka reproachfully, coming to a halt, and shaking his head. 'You will weep because of me.' And, turning away from her, he shouted at the girls: 'Sing something, will you?'

What he had said seemed to have made Maryana frightened and angry. She stopped.

'What will end badly?'

'It will.'

'What do you mean, it?'

'The fact that you're carrying on with that soldier, the lodger, and the fact that you don't love me any more!'

'I'll do as I please. You're not my mum and dad. What do you want? I'll love whoever I like.'

'Very well!' said Lukashka. 'But remember!' He walked over to the shop. 'Girls!' he cried. 'Why have you stopped? Sing another round of the dance. Nazarka! Run and fetch some *chikhir*.'

'Well, are they coming?' Olenin asked Beletsky.

'They'll be coming in a moment,' Beletsky replied. 'Let's be off, we have to make preparations for the ball.'

39

It was late at night when Olenin left Beletsky's hut, following Maryana and Ustenka. Maryana's white kerchief gleamed white in the dark street. The moon, shining golden, was descending towards the steppe. A silvery mist hung above the settlement. Everything was quiet, there were no lights anywhere and the only sound was that of the women's footsteps as they walked away. Olenin's heart was beating violently. His flushed face was cooled by the damp air. He glanced up at the sky, looked round at the hut from which he had just emerged: the candle there had gone out, and he began to peer at the retreating shadows of the women again. The white kerchief disappeared in the mist. He was afraid to remain alone; he was so happy! He jumped down from the porch and ran after the girls.

'Bother you! Someone will see!' said Ustenka.

'It doesn't matter!'

Olenin ran up to Maryana and embraced her. Maryanka did not struggle.

'Can't get enough kissing, can you?' said Ustenka. 'Get married, then you can kiss all you want, but for now you can wait.'

'Goodbye, Maryana. Tomorrow I'll come and see your father, and tell him myself. Don't you say anything.'

'What would I say?' replied Maryana.

The two girls ran off. Olenin walked on alone, remembering all that had happened. He had spent the whole evening with her tête-à-tête in the corner, near the stove. Ustenka had not left the hut for a single moment, but had romped about with the other girls and Beletsky. Olenin had spoken in whispers with Maryanka.

'Will you marry me?' he had asked her.

'You'll deceive me, you won't take me,' she replied cheerfully and calmly.

'But do you love me? Tell me, for God's sake!'

'Why shouldn't I love you, you're not one-eyed!' Maryana answered, laughing, and with her hard hand squeezing his. 'What whi – ite, whi – te hands you have, they're like *kaymak*,' she said.

'I mean it seriously. Tell me, will you marry me?'

'Why not, if my dad gives me to you?'

'Well, just remember that I shall go mad if you deceive me. Tomorrow I will tell your mother and father, I will come to ask for your hand.'

Maryana suddenly burst into laughter.

'Why are you laughing?'

'It's funny, that's all.'

'I mean it! I'll buy a vineyard, a house, enlist as a Cossack . . .'

'Then mind you don't love other women! That makes me angry.'

Olenin repeated all these words in his imagination with enjoyment. These memories now caused him pain, now took his breath away with happiness. He felt pain because as she talked with him she was just as calm as ever. She did not seem in the slightest disturbed by this new situation. It was as though she did not believe him, and did not think about the future. He had the impression that she loved him only in the present moment and that a future with him did not exist for her. On the other hand, he was happy because all her words seemed to him true, and she had agreed to be his. 'Yes,' he said to himself, 'we shall only understand each other when she is completely mine.

211

For such a love there are no words, it needs life, the whole of a life. Tomorrow all will be made clear. I cannot live like this any more, tomorrow I will tell her father everything, I'll tell Beletsky, the whole settlement . . .'

Lukashka, who had spent two nights without sleep, had drunk so much at the festivities that for the first time ever his legs gave way beneath him, and he slept at Yamka's.

40

Next morning Olenin woke earlier than usual. At the initial moment of waking there came to him the thought of what stood before him, and with joy he remembered her kisses, the squeeze of her hard hands and her words: 'What white hands you have!' He jumped to his feet, and wanted to go to his hosts at once and ask for Maryana's hand. The sun was not yet up, yet it seemed to Olenin that there was an unusual amount of commotion in the street: people were walking, riding to and fro on horseback and talking. He threw on his Circassian coat and leapt out to the porch. His hosts had not yet risen. Five Cossacks were riding past, carrying on a loud conversation about something. In front 213 of them all, on his Kabarda horse, rode Lukashka. The Cossacks were all talking and shouting: it was impossible to make out anything properly.

'Ride up to the Top Post!' shouted one.

'Saddle your horse and catch us up quick,' said another.

'It's quicker to go by the other gate.'

'Use your head,' shouted Lukashka. 'It's the middle gate you need to go out by.'

'That's right, it's quicker from there,' said one of the Cossacks, who was covered in dust and whose horse was in a sweat.

Lukashka's face was red and swollen from the previous night's drinking; his sheepskin cap was pushed back on the nape of his neck. He was shouting imperiously, as though he were an officer.

'What's up? Where are you going?' asked Olenin, drawing the Cossacks' attention only with difficulty.

'We're going to try to catch some Abreks, they've taken

up positions in the sand hills. We're going right now, though there aren't enough of us.'

And the Cossacks, who were continuing to shout and gather, rode further down the street. It struck Olenin that it would not be right for him to stay behind; in any case, he planned to return early. He put on his clothes, loaded his rifle with bullets, jumped on to his horse which had been hastily saddled by Vanyusha, and caught up with the Cossacks at the exit from the settlement. The Cossacks, who had dismounted, were standing in a group and, pouring *chikhir* from a small barrel they had brought with them into a wooden *chapura*, handed it to one another and 'prayed' for the success of their mission. Among them was a young cornet, dressed like a dandy, who happened to be in the settlement and had taken command of the nine Cossacks who had gathered. These Cossacks were all privates, and although the cornet was behaving like an officer, they would only obey Lukashka. Of Olenin they took no notice at all. And when they had all mounted their horses and were on the move, and Olenin rode up to the cornet and began to question him about what was afoot, the cornet, who was usually friendly, addressed him from the height of his majesty. With very great effort, Olenin managed to obtain from him some information about what was going on. A mounted patrol that had been sent to search for Abreks had caught several mountain dwellers some eight *versts* from the settlement, in the sand hills. The Abreks had dug themselves in, firing their rifles and threatening that they would not be taken alive. A sergeant major on patrol with two Cossacks had remained there to keep an eye on the Abreks and sent one Cossack back to the settlement to call the others for help.

The sun was just beginning to rise. Some three *versts* from the settlement the steppe opened out, and one could see nothing but the monotonous, melancholy, arid plain, with the hoof marks of cattle dotting the sand, and here and there withered grass, low reeds in the hollows, rare, scarcely trodden paths, and Nogay nomad encampments visible far, far away on the horizon. What was striking about it all was the absence of shade, and the severe aspect of the landscape. Out on the steppe the sun is red when it sets. When there is a wind, it blows whole mountains of sand about. When it is calm, as it was on that morning, the silence, broken by neither movement nor sound, is especially striking. That morning the steppe was calm and overcast, even though the sun had risen; it was somehow particularly desolate and gentle. The air did not move; all that could be heard was the movement and snorting of horses; and even this sound was faint and died away at once.

The Cossacks rode for the most part in silence. A Cossack always carries his weapons in such a way that they do **215** not clink or jingle. For a Cossack, jingling weapons are the greatest shame. Two Cossacks from the settlement caught them up along the road and exchanged a few words. Lukashka's horse either stumbled or caught its hooves in the grass and began to hurry. Cossacks consider this a bad omen. The Cossacks glanced round at one another and hastily turned away, trying not to pay any attention to this incident, which at the present moment possessed a special importance. Lukashka tugged the reins, frowned sternly, clenched his teeth and brandished his whip above his head. The responsive Kabarda horse suddenly began to dance on the spot with small, light steps as fast as it could, not knowing which leg to put forward, and as if it wanted to rise aloft on wings; but Lukashka gave it a whack of his whip on its sleek sides, gave it another, and another – and the Kabarda, baring its teeth and spreading its tail, snorting, reared on its hind legs and moved several yards away from the group of Cossacks.

'Ech, that's a good mount,' said the cornet.

That he said '*mount*,' and not '*horse*' was a token of especial praise for the animal.

'A lion of a horse,' one of the older Cossacks agreed.

The Cossacks rode silently now at walking pace, now at a trot, and only this one single incident broke for a moment the silence and solemnity of their movement.

Throughout the whole steppe, for some eight *versts* of the way, the only living thing they encountered was a Nogay tent which, placed on an ox cart, was progressing slowly at about a *verst*'s distance from them. This was a Nogay, moving with his family from one nomad territory to another. In a hollow they passed, they also met two ragged, high-cheekboned Nogay women; with baskets on their backs they were gathering dung from the cattle that roamed over the steppe, to make *kizyak*. The cornet, who did not know much Kumyk, began to try to question the women; but they did not understand him and, evidently frightened, kept looking at one another.

Lukashka rode up, stopped his horse, fluently uttered the customary greeting and the Nogay women, who were visibly relieved, began to talk to him freely, as to a brother.

'*Ay, ay, kop Abrek!*' they said plaintively, pointing in the direction the Cossacks were riding. Olenin understood that they were saying: 'Many Abreks.'

Never having seen actions of this kind before, and possessing a notion of them based only on Uncle Yeroshka's stories, Olenin wanted to keep up with the Cossacks and see everything. He admired the Cossacks, scrutinized everything, listened closely and made his own observations. Although he had brought a sabre and a loaded rifle with him, when he noticed that the Cossacks avoided him he decided not to take part in the action, especially as he considered that his bravery had already been proven in the detachment, and, above all, because now he was very happy.

216

Suddenly a shot was heard in the distance.

The cornet grew agitated and began to give the Cossacks instructions on how to split up and from which side to approach. But the Cossacks were apparently paying no attention to these instructions, listening only to what Lukashka said, and looking only at him. Luka's face and figure held an expression of calm and solemnity. He brought his Kabarda horse along at a pace the other horses could not keep up with and, narrowing his eyes, kept peering forward.

'There's a horseman,' he said, reining in his horse and lining up with the others.

Olenin looked as hard as he could, but saw nothing. The Cossacks soon made out two horsemen, and rode slowly straight towards them.

'Are those Abreks?' asked Olenin.

The Cossacks made no reply to the question, which in their view was absurd. The Abreks would have been fools to cross to this side of the river on horses.

'That's our Rodka waving, if I'm not mistaken,' said Lukashka, pointing to the two horsemen, who could now be seen clearly. 'Look, he's coming over to see us.'

Indeed, a few minutes later it became plain that the horsemen were Cossacks on patrol, and the sergeant major rode up to Luka.

41

'How far away are they?' was Lukashka's only question.

At that very moment a sharp, dry report was heard some thirty paces from them. The sergeant major smiled slightly.

'That's our Gurka taking a potshot at them,' he said, indicating the direction of the shot with his head.

Riding a few yards further, they saw Gurka, who was positioned behind a sand hill, loading his rifle. Out of boredom, Gurka was exchanging shots with the Abreks, who were positioned behind another sand hill. A bullet came whistling across from there. The cornet was pale and got confused. Lukashka got down from his horse, thrust it into the care of one of the Cossacks and walked over to Gurka. Olenin did the same and, bending down, followed him. No sooner had they reached the rifle-firing Cossack than two bullets came whistling over their heads. Lukashka, laughing, glanced round at Olenin and bent down.

'It's you they'll be shooting next, Andreich,' he said. 'You'd better go. There's nothing for you here.'

But Olenin was determined to see some Abreks.

From behind the sand hill, some two hundred yards away, he caught sight of caps and rifles. Suddenly a puff of smoke appeared from there, and another bullet came whistling across. The Abreks had taken up positions in a marsh at the foot of the hill. Olenin was struck by the place in which they were hiding. It was just like the rest of the steppe, but because the Abreks were positioned there, it suddenly seemed to detach itself from all the rest and seemed to be marked by something special. It even seemed to him that it was exactly the right place for the Abreks to be positioned in. Lukashka went back to his horse and Olenin followed him.

'We need to get an ox cart full of hay,' said Luka. 'Otherwise they'll slaughter us. Look, behind the sand hill there's a Nogay cart with hay in it.'

The cornet heard him out, and the sergeant major agreed. A cart of hay was brought, and the Cossacks, using it as cover, began to pull the hay out of it on to themselves. Olenin rode up a sand hill, from which he could see everything. The hay cart was moving; the Cossacks huddled behind it. The Cossacks moved; the Chechens – there were nine of them – sat side by side, knee against knee, and did not shoot.

Everything was quiet. Suddenly from the direction of the Chechens there came the strange sounds of a doleful song, reminiscent of Uncle Yeroshka's *ay-da-la-lay*. The Chechens knew that they could not leave, and, in order to rid themselves of the temptation to run away, they had tied **219** themselves with belts, knee to knee, got their rifles ready and begun to sing their song of death.

The Cossacks with their hay cart kept approaching closer and closer, and Olenin expected firing at any moment; but the silence was broken only by the Abreks' doleful singing. Suddenly the singing stopped. There was a sharp report, a bullet thudded into the front of the cart and Chechen curses and screams could be heard. Shot after shot rang out, and bullet after bullet thudded into the cart. The Cossacks did not fire and were no more than five yards away.

Another moment passed and then the Cossacks leapt out with a whoop from both sides of the cart. Lukashka was out in front. Olenin heard only one or two shots, and some shouting and groaning. He saw smoke and blood, or thought he did. Abandoning his horse, in a state of frenzy he ran towards the Cossacks. Horror dimmed his eyes. He could make out nothing, but merely understood that it was all over. Lukashka, white as a sheet, was holding a wounded Chechen by the arms and shouting: 'Don't kill him! I'll take him alive!' The Chechen was that same red-haired brother of the slain Abrek who had come for the body. Lukashka was twisting his arms. Suddenly the Chechen tore himself free and fired his pistol. Lukashka fell. Blood appeared in the region of his stomach. He leapt up, but fell back again, cursing in Russian and Tatar. There was more and more blood on him and under him. The Cossacks went over to him and began to loosen his belt. For a long time before he could attend to him, one of them, Nazarka, was unable to put his sabre back in its scabbard: it would not go in properly. Its blade was covered in blood.

The Chechens, red-haired, with clipped moustaches, lay dead and hacked to pieces. Only the familiar one, the same man who had fired at Lukashka, was still alive, though wounded all over. Like a hawk that had been winged, pale 220 and sombre, covered in blood (it flowed from his right eye), his teeth clenched, staring round in all directions with enormous, angry eyes, he squatted, dagger in hand, preparing to defend himself again. The cornet went up to him and from the side, as though he were going to walk past him, with a swift movement fired a shot from his pistol into the man's ear. The Chechen darted away, but it was too late, and he fell.

The Cossacks, panting with exertion, dragged the slain fighters apart and removed the weapons from them. Each of the red-haired Chechens had been a man, and each had his own particular expression. Lukashka was carried to the ox cart. He kept swearing in Russian and Tatar.

'Don't worry, I'll strangle him with my hands! You won't escape my hands! *Ana seni!*[48] he shouted, making jerky movements. Soon he fell silent from weakness.

Olenin rode home. In the evening he received word that Lukashka was near to death, but that a Tatar from the other side of the river had undertaken to treat him with herbs.

The corpses were dragged off to the settlement office. Women and boys crowded round to look at them.

Olenin returned at twilight and was for a long time unable to recover himself after all he had seen; but by night-time the memories of the evening before came surging over him; he looked out of the window: Maryana was walking to and fro between the house and the shed, clearing up around the yard. Her mother had gone to fetch grapes. Her father was at the directorate. Olenin did not wait for her to finish her clearing up and walked over to her. She was in the hut and stood with her back to him. Olenin thought she was being shy.

'Maryana!' he said. 'Oh, Maryana! May I come in?'

Suddenly she turned round. In her eyes there were barely perceptible tears. In her face there was a beautiful sadness. She looked at him silently and majestically.

Olenin repeated: 'Maryana! I've come to . . .'   **221**

'Stop it,' she said. Her face did not change, but the tears poured from her eyes.

'Why are you crying? What's the matter?'

'The matter?' she echoed, in a rough, hard voice. 'Cossacks have been slaughtered, that's what.'

'Lukashka?' said Olenin.

'Go away, what do you want?'

'Maryana!' said Olenin, going up to her.

'You'll never get anything from me.'

'Maryana, don't say that,' Olenin implored.

'Go away, you hateful man!' the girl cried, stamping her foot and moving towards him threateningly. And such was the revulsion, the contempt and the anger in her face that Olenin suddenly realized he had nothing to hope for, that what he had earlier thought concerning the inaccessibility of this woman was the plain, unvarnished truth. Olenin said nothing to her, and ran from the hut.

42

Returning home, for some two hours he lay motionless on the bed, then set off to see the company commander and requested permission to go back to headquarters. Without saying goodbye to anyone and, having settled his bill with his hosts through Vanyusha, he got ready to leave for the fortress where his regiment was stationed. Uncle Yeroshka was the only person to see him off. They had one drink, then another, and then another. Just as there had been at the time of his departure from Moscow, a coach and troika stood at the entrance. But now Olenin did not settle accounts with himself as he had then, and did not tell himself that everything he had thought and done here was 'wrong'. Now he did not promise himself a new life. He loved Maryanka more than ever, and now knew that he could never be loved by her.

'Well, goodbye, laddie,' said Uncle Yeroshka. 'If you go on a campaign, be sensible, and listen to an old man's advice. When you have to take part in a raid or whatever (I'm an old wolf, after all, and I've seen it all) and they start firing, don't get into a group where there are a lot of others. Because when you fellows get scared, you always bunch up with others: you think it'll be easier to grin and bear it that way. But that's the worst way of all to go about it: they always aim at a crowd. I used to keep away from the others, walk alone: and I was never hit, not once. Oh, the things I've seen in my time!'

'But you've got a bullet in your back,' said Vanyusha, who was clearing up the room.

'That was just Cossacks having some fun,' replied Yeroshka.

222

'Cossacks?' asked Olenin.

'Oh, yes! We were drinking. Vanka Sitkin, he was a Cossack, went on the spree, and he saw fit to fire his pistol right at this place here.'

'Well, and did it hurt?' asked Olenin. 'Vanyusha, make it quick, will you?' he added.

'Ach, what's the hurry? Let me tell you the story . . . Now when he took that potshot at me, the bullet didn't go into the bone, but stayed here. And I said: "Hey, you've killed me, my good fellow. Haven't you, eh? What have you done to me? I'm not letting you go just like that! You can stand me a pail of vodka!"'

'But did it hurt?' Olenin asked again, not really listening to the story.

'Wait and I'll tell you. He stood me a pail. We drank it. But I was still bleeding. The whole room was covered in blood. And Grandad Burlak said: "Here, the fellow's going to croak. Stand us another *shtof* of the sweet stuff, or we'll have you arrested." They brought some more. We swilled and soused . . .'

'But did it hurt?' Olenin asked again.

'What do you mean, hurt? Stop interrupting, I don't like it. Wait and I'll tell you. We swilled and soused, made merry until morning, and then I fell asleep on the stove, drunk. When I woke up the next morning I couldn't straighten myself up no matter how hard I tried.'

'It hurt a lot, then?' Olenin repeated, supposing that now he had finally obtained an answer to his question.

'Did I say it did? No, it didn't, but I couldn't unbend myself, it wouldn't let me walk.'

'So did it heal up again?' said Olenin, even forgetting to laugh: so heavy was his heart.

'Yes, it did, but the bullet's still there. Here, feel it.' And, pulling up his shirt, he showed his mighty back, on which a bullet moved about near the bone.

'Sheesh, feel it moving about,' he said, evidently taking comfort from the bullet, as with a toy. 'It's rolled down to my backside now.'

'How is Lukashka, will he live?' asked Olenin.

'God knows! There's no doctor. They've gone to fetch one.'

'Where will they get one? Groznaya?' asked Olenin.

'No, dear laddie. If I were the Tsar, I'd have hanged all your Russian doctors long ago. All they know is cutting! They made our Cossack Baklashev into a non-human being by cutting off one of his legs. So they're fools, aren't they? What's Baklashev good for now? No, dear laddie, in the mountains there are real doctors. Old Girchik, my *nyanya*, got wounded in this place, in the chest, and your doctors refused to treat him, but Saib came from the mountains and cured him. Herbs is what they know, laddie.'

224 'Well, you've talked enough rubbish now,' said Olenin. 'I'd better send a doctor from staff headquarters.'

'Rubbish!' the old man said, mimicking him. 'Fool, fool! Rubbish! I'll send a doctor! Why, if your doctors could treat them, the Cossacks and Chechens would come to consult them, but in fact what happens is that your officers and colonels send for the doctors from the mountains. Yours are fake, all fake.'

Olenin did not begin to reply. He was all too much in agreement that everything in the world in which he had lived, and to which he was now returning, was fake.

'How is Lukashka? Have you been to see him?' he asked.

'He's lying there like a corpse. Doesn't eat, doesn't drink, and vodka is the only thing his soul will accept. Well, as long as he can drink vodka, he'll be all right. But it would be a shame to lose the fellow. He was a good lad, a *djigit* like myself. I lay dying like that once: the old women were already wailing, wailing they were. There was a fever in my head. They'd dragged me under the icons of the saints. So there I lay, and above me, on the stove, there were all these, all these little drummer boys, who seemed to be beating the tattoo. I shouted at them, but they just drummed all the louder. (The old man laughed.) The women brought the elder from the church, and they were getting ready to bury me; they said: he was *worldly,* went after women, ruined other men's souls, didn't keep the fasts, played the balalaika. Repent, they said. And I began to repent. I have sinned, I said. Whatever the cleric said, I always replied: I have sinned. Then he began to ask me about the balalaika. That's another of my sins, I said. So where is it, the cursed thing, he said, where have you got it? Show it to me and break it to pieces. But I said I hadn't got it. Actually, I'd hidden it in a net in the *izbushka; I* knew they wouldn't find it there. So they gave up on me. And I recovered. When I went to get my balalaika . . . But what am I saying,' he continued. 'Listen to me, keep away from 225 any clusters of men, or you'll be killed for being stupid. I really care about you, you know. You're a drinking man, I love you. You lads always like riding up the hills. We had one of them living here, always riding up hills he was, he had some funny name for them, "holms", or something. As soon as he saw a hill, he went galloping up it. One day he was doing that. Pleased as punch he was. But a Chechen shot him and killed him. Oh, they're good at shooting from their gun rests, those Chechens! Some of them are even better at it than I am. I don't like it when a man is shot because he's stupid. I used to look at your soldiers and be amazed. Such stupidity! The poor lads, they'd go all in a group, with red collars on them and all. How could they fail to be hit? One would be killed, he'd fall down, they'd drag the poor lad away, and another would go in his stead. Such stupidity!' the old man repeated, shaking his head. 'They ought to have spread out in different directions, one at a time. That's the only decent way to go about it. Then the enemy won't be able to get you in his sights. That's the way to do it.'

'Well, thank you! Goodbye, Uncle! God willing, we shall see one another again,' said Olenin, getting up and moving towards the passage.

The old man remained sitting on the floor, and did not get up.

'Is that any way to say goodbye? Fool! Fool!' he said. 'Dear me, what a bunch they've grown into! We've kept one another company, kept company for a whole year, and then it's "goodbye", and off he goes. I mean, I love you, I care about you! You're such a bitter fellow, so alone, always on your own. You're sort of *unloved*! Sometimes when I can't sleep, I think about you, and I really feel sorry for you. As the song says:

> It isn't easy, brother mine,
> Living in a foreign clime!

'That's about you, that is.'

'Well, goodbye,' Olenin said again.

The old man got up and gave him his hand. Olenin shook it, and made to go.

'Your face, give me that face of yours here.'

The old man took him by the head with both of his thick hands, kissed him three times with wet moustaches and lips, and began to cry.

'I love you, goodbye!'

Olenin got into the cart.

'Well, so you're off then? Give me something to remember you by, lad. Give me a rifle. You don't need two, do you?' said the old man, sobbing with tears that were sincere.

Olenin got out a rifle and gave it to him.

'You're not giving that to the old fellow, are you?'

muttered Vanyusha. 'It won't be enough! The old cadger. They're unreliable, the lot of them,' he said quietly, wrapping himself in his coat and taking his seat on the box.

'Shut up, you swine!' cried the old man, laughing. 'Sheesh, you're a mean one!'

Maryana came out of the shed, glanced at the troika indifferently and, with a bow, went into the hut.

'*La feel!*'[49] said Vanyusha, with a wink and a stupid laugh.

'Let's be off!' cried Olenin, angrily.

'Goodbye, laddie! Goodbye! I'll remember you!' shouted Yeroshka.

Olenin glanced round. Uncle Yeroshka was talking to Maryanka, evidently on business of his own, and neither the old man nor the girl looked at him.

Hadji Murat

I was walking home through the fields. It was midsummer. The hay had been carried from the meadows and they were just preparing to cut the rye.

There is a delightful variety of flowers at this time of year: downy, sweet-scented clover, red, white and pink; impudent daisies; milky white ox-eyes with bright yellow centres and their unpleasant, musty, heady odour; yellow charlock with its honeyed smell; tall-standing, tulip-like Canterbury bells, mauve and white; vetches; neat scabious, yellow, red, pink, and mauve; plantains with their pinky down and faint pleasant smell; cornflowers, bright blue in the sunshine when young but paler and redder at evening and as they grow old; and the delicate, almond-scented bindweed flower which blooms and fades in a moment.

I picked a large bunch of different flowers and was walking homewards when I noticed in the ditch a wonderful crimson thistle in full bloom. It was the kind which in our parts is called the Tatar-thistle and reapers are careful to cut around it or if one is accidentally cut they throw it out of the straw so as not to prick their hands on it. I thought I would pick this thistle to put in the middle of my bunch of flowers. I climbed into the ditch and after brushing away a furry bumblebee, which had worked its way into the centre of the flower and fallen into a sweet and languorous sleep, I set about picking the flower. However, this was no easy matter: it was not just that the stalk pricked me at every turn, even through the handkerchief which I had wrapped round my hand; it was so terribly tough that I was five minutes struggling with it, breaking through the fibres one by one. When at last I succeeded in plucking the

flower the stalk was in shreds and the flower itself no longer seemed as fresh and beautiful as before. And, apart
from that, it was too crude and clumsy to go with the delicate flowers I had in my bunch. I was sorry that I had
needlessly destroyed a flower which had been fine where
it was, and threw it away. But what strength and vigour, I
thought, recalling the effort it had cost me to pluck it. How
stoutly it defended itself, and how dearly it sold its life.

The way home was through a fallow field of black earth
which had just been ploughed. I walked along the dusty,
gently rising black-earth road. The ploughed field was
squire's land and very large, so that on either side of the
road and on up the slope you could see nothing but black
evenly furrowed fallow land, as yet unharrowed. The
ploughing was well done and there was not a plant or blade
of grass to be seen across the whole field: it was all black.
232 What a cruel, destructive creature man is. How many different living creatures and plants he has destroyed in order
to support his own life, I thought, instinctively looking for
some sign of life in the midst of this dead black field. Ahead
of me to the right of the road there was a small bush of
some kind. When I got nearer I saw it was a Tatar-thistle,
like the one whose flower I had idly picked and thrown
away.

The Tatar-thistle bush consisted of three shoots. One
had been broken off and the remnant of stalk stuck out
like a severed arm. There was a flower on each of the other
two. The flowers had once been red, but were now black.
One stalk was broken and its upper half with the soiled
flower at the end hung down; the other, though caked with
black mud, still stood erect. It was evident that the whole
bush had been run over by a cart wheel and had then picked
itself up again: for that reason it was standing crookedly,
but still it was standing. It was like having part of its body
torn away, its innards turned inside out, an arm pulled off,

and an eye plucked out. But still it was standing and would not surrender to man who had destroyed all its brethren around.

What strength! I thought. Man has conquered everything, destroyed millions of plants, but still this one will not give in.

And an old tale of the Caucasus came to my mind, part of which I saw myself, part heard from eye-witnesses, and part created in my imagination. The tale as I recalled and pictured it was as follows.

1

It was the end of 1851.

On a cold November evening Hadji Murat rode into Makhket, a Chechen village hostile to the Russians, which lay wreathed in the fragrant smoke of dung fires.

The straining chant of the muezzin had just ended and in the pure, smoke-laced mountain air, over the lowing of cattle and bleating of sheep which picked their way through the honeycomb of jostling huts in the village, you could distinctly hear from the fountain below the guttural tones of men in argument and the voices of women and children.

This Hadji Murat was the *naib* of Shamil,[1] a man famed for his exploits, who whenever he rode out was always accompanied by his standard and some dozens of his *murids* making show of their horsemanship. Now, wrapped in a hood and felt cloak from beneath which a rifle stuck out, Hadji Murat rode with a single *murid*, doing his best to pass unobserved and carefully studying the faces of passing locals with his quick black eyes.

Coming to the centre of the village Hadji Murat did not take the street leading on to the square but turned left into a narrow lane. When he reached the second house, which was built into the side of the hill, he stopped and looked around. There was nobody on the veranda at the front of the house but on the flat roof behind the freshly plastered clay chimney lay a man with a sheepskin coat over him. Hadji Murat gave him a gentle prod with the handle of his whip and clicked his tongue. From under the coat rose an old man in a nightcap and a tattered jacket which was shiny with age. His lashless eyes were red and watery and he blinked to get them open. Hadji Murat gave the customary greeting '*Salam aleikum*' and revealed his face.

'*Aleikum salam*' said the old man with a toothless smile as he recognized Hadji Murat. He got up on his thin legs and began directing his feet into the wooden-heeled shoes that stood by the chimney. Having put his shoes on, he unhurriedly donned the wrinkled coat of plain sheepskin and came backwards down the ladder which was leant against the roof. As he put on his coat and climbed down the old man shook his head on his lean, wrinkled, sunburnt neck and champed toothlessly all the time. Reaching the ground, he hospitably took Hadji Murat's bridle and his right stirrup. But Hadji Murat's *murid*, a sharp, powerful fellow, swiftly dismounted, pushed the old man aside and took his place.

Hadji Murat got off his horse and walked with a slight limp on to the veranda. A boy of fifteen or so came quickly out of the door towards him, and stared in surprise at **235** the visitors with his shining eyes, which were black as ripe currants.

'Run to the mosque and fetch your father,' ordered the old man and, going ahead, he opened for Hadji Murat the light, creaking door into the house. As Hadji Murat went in, there came through an inner door a thin, lean, middle-aged woman wearing blue trousers and a jacket over a yellow smock. She was carrying some cushions.

'Your coming is a happy omen,' she said, and bending over she spread the cushions along the front wall for the guests to sit on.

'May your sons live long,' answered Hadji Murat, taking off his cloak, rifle and sword and handing them to the old man.

The old man carefully hung the rifle and sword on nails next to the weapons of the master of the house and between two large basins which gleamed on the smooth plaster of the cleanly whitewashed wall.

Hadji Murat straightened the pistol at the back of his belt, went over to the cushions the woman had laid out and, drawing his *cherkeska* round him, sat down. The old man squatted opposite him on his bare heels, closed his eyes and lifted his hands with upturned palms. Hadji Murat did the same. Then after a prayer they both drew their hands across their faces, bringing them together at the tip of their beards.

'*Ne khabar?*' Hadji Murat asked the old man – that is, 'What news?'

'*Khabar yok*' – 'Nothing new,' the old man answered, his red lifeless eyes looking not in Hadji Murat's face but at his chest. 'I live at the bee-garden. I have just come today to visit my son. He will know.'

Hadji Murat could see that the old man was unwilling to say what he knew and what Hadji Murat needed to know. He nodded and asked no more.

'There is no good news,' the old man began. 'All that is new is that the hares are all taking counsel to see how they can drive off the eagles. And the eagles go on killing them one by one. Last week the Russian dogs burnt the people's hay on the Michik, curse them,' wheezed the old man venomously.

Hadji Murat's *murid* came in, strode softly across the mud floor on his powerful legs, and, as Hadji Murat had done, took off his cloak, rifle and sword and hung them on the nails along with Hadji Murat's weapons, retaining only his dagger and pistol.

The old man pointed at him and asked 'Who is he?'

'He is my *murid*. His name is Eldar,' said Hadji Murat.

'It is well,' said the old man and indicated a place for Eldar on the felt rug next to Hadji Murat.

Eldar sat down cross-legged and with his handsome sheep's eyes stared silently at the face of the now talkative old man who was telling how the week before their men

had captured two soldiers, one of whom they had killed
and the other sent to Shamil in Vedeno.[2] Hadji Murat listened inattentively, keeping an eye on the door and
listening for sounds outside. Steps were heard on the
veranda at the front of the house. The door creaked and
the master of the house came in.

Sado, the master of the house, was a man of about forty
with a small beard, long nose, and eyes which were as black
though not as shining as those of his son, the fifteen-year-
old boy who had gone to fetch him and who now came in
with his father and sat by the door. Taking off his wooden
shoes at the door, Sado pushed his old well-worn *papakha*
to the back of his head, which was long unshaved and
sprouted a growth of black hair, and at once squatted facing Hadji Murat.

Just as the old man before him, he closed his eyes, lifted
his upturned hands, and after saying a prayer wiped **237**
his hands over his face. Only after this did he speak. He
said that Shamil had ordered Hadji Murat to be taken
dead or alive, that Shamil's messengers had set out only
the day before, that the people were frightened to disobey
Shamil's commands, and that it was necessary therefore
to take care.

'In my house as long as there is life in me no harm shall
come to my *kunak*,' said Sado. 'But when you are in the
open – what then? We must give it thought.'

Hadji Murat listened attentively and nodded his approval.
When Sado had finished, he said:

'Very well. I must now send someone with a letter to the
Russians. My *murid* will go, but he will need a guide.'

'I will send my brother Bata,' said Sado. He turned to
his son. 'Tell Bata to come.'

The nimble-footed boy sprang up like a jack-in-the-box,
and with a flurry of arms raced from the house. In ten
minutes he was back with a wiry, short-legged Chechen,

tanned black by the sun, who wore a yellow *cherkeska* with splitting seams and tattered cuffs and black leggings which hung round his ankles. Hadji Murat greeted the new arrival and came straight to the point, asking briefly:

'Can you get my *murid* through to the Russians?'

'Yes, I can,' replied Bata, speaking quickly and cheerfully. 'I can manage everything. No other Chechen could get through the way I can. He might go, and promise everything, but do nothing. But I can.'

'Good,' said Hadji Murat. 'For your service you shall have three,' he said, holding out three fingers.

Bata nodded to show that he understood, but said that he did not value the money and was ready to serve Hadji Murat for the honour of doing so. Everyone in the mountains knew Hadji Murat and the way he had beaten the Russian pigs.[3]

'All right,' said Hadji Murat. 'A long rope is good – a speech is better short.'

'I will say no more,' said Bata.

'Where the Argun bends there is a clearing on the side opposite the cliff. There are two haystacks there. Do you know the place?'

'Yes, I know it.'

'I have three horsemen waiting for me there,' said Hadji Murat.

'*Aya*,' said Bata, nodding.

'Ask for Khan-Mahoma. Khan-Mahoma knows what to do and what to say. He has to be taken to the Russian commander, to the prince Vorontsov.[4] Can you do that?'

'Yes, I will take him.'

'Take him and bring him back. You can do that?'

'Yes, I can do that.'

'You will take him and return to the forest. I will be there.'

'All this I shall do,' said Bata. He got up, put his hands to his chest and left.

'We must send someone to Gekhi[5] too,' said Hadji Murat to his host after Bata had gone. 'In Gekhi we need . . .' he took hold of one of the cartridge cases on the breast of his *cherkeska*, but stopped speaking and dropped his hand on seeing two women come in.

One of the women was Sado's wife, the same thin, middle-aged woman who had put out the cushions. The other was a young girl dressed in red trousers and a green jacket with loops of silver coins hanging across her breast. A silver rouble hung from the rather short, broad plait of coarse black hair that fell between her shoulders down her thin back; she had the same black, currant-like eyes as her father and brother and they shone merrily out of her young face which was trying to look serious. She did not look at the visitors, though it was obvious that she felt their presence.

Sado's wife carried a low round table on which were tea, patties, pancakes in butter, cheese, *churek* – bread made in a flat loaf – and honey. The girl carried a basin, ewer and towel.

Neither Sado nor Hadji Murat spoke while the women, moving quietly in their red unsoled slippers, set out before the guests the refreshments they had brought. As long as the women were in the room Eldar sat still as a statue, his sheep's eyes fixed on his crossed legs. Only when they had gone and their soft footsteps had died away on the other side of the door did Eldar give a sigh of relief and Hadji Murat take one of the cartridge cases from the front of his *cherkeska*, unplug the bullet and draw out a rolled-up note which lay underneath.

'Give this to my son,' he said, showing the note to Sado.

'Where does the answer go?' Sado asked.

'To you, and you will pass it on to me.'

'It shall be done,' said Sado and transferred the note to a cartridge case on his own *cherkeska*. Then he picked up the ewer and moved the basin towards Hadji Murat. Hadji Murat turned back the sleeves of his jacket over his muscular arms, which were white above the wrist, and placed his hands under the stream of cold clear water which Sado poured from the ewer. Then, after wiping his hands dry on the clean, rough towel he turned to the food. Eldar did the same, and while his guests ate Sado sat facing them, several times thanking them for their visit. His son, who sat by the door and never for a moment took his black shining eyes off Hadji Murat, smiled as if confirming with his smile his father's words.

Although it was over twenty-four hours since he had last eaten, Hadji Murat ate only a little bread and cheese, and some honey which he scooped out and spread on his bread with a small knife taken from beneath his dagger.

'Our honey is good. It is a year of years for honey: it is plentiful and good,' said the old man, obviously pleased that Hadji Murat was eating his honey.

'Thank you,' said Hadji Murat, moving away from the food.

Eldar was still hungry, but like his *murshid* he left the table and handed Hadji Murat the basin and ewer.

Sado knew that he was putting his life at stake by receiving Hadji Murat, because after his quarrel with Shamil an announcement had gone out to all who lived in Chechnya forbidding them on pain of death to receive Hadji Murat. Sado knew that at any moment the villagers might learn of Hadji Murat's presence in his house and demand his surrender. But he was actually pleased rather than concerned by that. Sado considered it his duty to protect his guest, his *kunak*, even if it should cost him his life, and he rejoiced and prided himself on doing what was proper.

'As long as you are in my house and my head is on my

shoulders, no harm shall come to you,' he told Hadji Murat once more.

Hadji Murat looked intently into his shining eyes and saw that it was true. He said with some solemnity:

'May life and happiness be yours.'

Sado silently pressed his hand to his chest in gratitude for Hadji Murat's kindly words.

When he had closed the shutters and kindled some logs in the fireplace Sado left the guest room feeling particularly cheerful and keyed up and went to the part of the house occupied by his family. The womenfolk, not yet asleep, were talking of the dangerous visitors who were spending the night in their guest room.

2

The same night, ten miles from the village where Hadji Murat was staying, three soldiers and an NCO left the frontier fort of Vozdvizhenskaya[6] by the Shakhgiri gate. They were dressed as soldiers commonly were at that time in the Caucasus: in sheepskin coats and *papakhas*, with rolled greatcoats across their shoulders and large topboots coming above the knee. At first the soldiers went along the road with shouldered arms, but after some five hundred yards they left the road and, with their boots rustling the dry leaves, went some twenty paces to the right. They stopped by a broken plane tree whose black trunk was visible even in the darkness. It was this tree that the Russians generally used as a listening post.

The bright stars which had seemed to be floating over the tree tops while the soldiers were going through the forest now stood still, shining brightly through the bare branches of the trees.

'It's dry, that's one good thing,' said Panov, the corporal, unslinging his long rifle with fixed bayonet and leaning it with a rattle against the tree trunk. The three soldiers did the same.

'Sure enough, I've lost it,' grumbled Panov in annoyance. 'Either I left it behind or else it fell out on the way.'

'What is it you are looking for?' asked one of the soldiers, in a jolly, cheerful voice.

'My pipe, damme. I don't know where it's got to.'

'Have you got the stem all right?' asked the cheerful soldier.

'Yes, here's the stem.'

'Why not just shove it in the ground?'

'That's no good.'

'We'll fix it in a jiffy.'

Smoking in a listening post was forbidden, but this was hardly a listening post; it was more a kind of forward sentry post which was placed there to ensure that the Chechens did not move up a cannon unnoticed, as had happened in the past, and shoot at the fort. This being so, Panov saw no need to go without his smoke and fell in with the suggestion made by the cheerful soldier. The latter took a knife out of his pocket and began digging at the ground. When he had made a small hollow, he patted it smooth, fixed the pipe stem, filled the hollow with tobacco, pressed it firm – and the pipe was ready. A sulphur match flared, momentarily lighting the prominent cheekbones of the cheerful soldier lying flat on his stomach. The pipe stem wheezed, and Panov caught the pleasant aroma of kindled tobacco.

243

'Fixed it?' he asked, rising to his feet.

'Course I have.'

'Good lad, Avdeev! You're a regular genius. How about it, then?'

Avdeev rolled on to his side to make room for Panov, releasing the smoke from his mouth.

When they had had their smoke, the soldiers began talking.

'I hear the company commander's had his hand in the till again. Gambling debts, I suppose . . .?' said one soldier in a lazy drawl.

'He'll pay it back,' said Panov.

'Of course he will. He's a good officer,' agreed Avdeev.

'Oh, he's good, all right,' the soldier who had started the conversation went on gloomily. 'But if you ask me, the whole company ought to have it out with him and tell him that if he's taken some money he must say how much and when he's going to pay it back.'

'It must be as the company decides,' said Panov, breaking away from his pipe.

'That's right,' agreed Avdeev. 'It's the company which has the say.'

'But look, we've got to buy in oats and get boots for the spring. For that we need money, and if he's taken it . . .' persisted the disgruntled soldier.

'I say it's as the company wants,' repeated Panov. 'It's not the first time it's happened: he'll pay it back all right.'

At that time in the Caucasus each company ran its own economy through a chosen committee. The company received an official allowance of six roubles fifty copecks per man and saw to its own provisioning: planted cabbages, cropped hay, had its own carts and took pride in showing off the company's well-fed horses. The company funds were kept in a cash box, the keys of which were held by the company commander, and it was a common occurrence for the company commander to borrow from these funds. That had happened now and it was this that the soldiers were talking about. Nikitin, the gloomy one, wanted the company commander called to account, while Panov and Avdeev thought this unnecessary.

Nikitin had a smoke after Panov, then spread out his greatcoat and sat down, leaning against the tree. The soldiers fell silent. The only sound was that of the wind stirring in the tree tops high overhead. Suddenly through this steady gentle sound came the whining, shrieking, weeping and laughing cries of jackals.

'There they go, off again, curse 'em,' said Avdeev.

'They're laughing at you and your ugly mug,' came the thin Ukrainian voice of the fourth soldier.

Again all was quiet except for the wind which stirred the branches of the trees, now hiding, now revealing the stars beyond.

'What about you, Antonych?' the cheerful Avdeev suddenly asked Panov. 'Do you ever get fed up?'

'How do you mean – fed up?' replied Panov without enthusiasm.

'Well, sometimes I get that fed up I don't know what I might do to myself.'

'Go on with you,' said Panov.

'Like when I blew all that money drinking – it was only because I was fed up. It just got on top of me, so I had the notion to go and get drunk.'

'It's often worse after you've been drinking.'

'It was too. But what can you do?'

'What is it you're fed up about then?'

'Me? I'm homesick.'

'Were you well off then?'

'No, we weren't exactly rich, but we lived well. It was a good life.'

And Avdeev began telling the story he had told Panov many times before.

'You see, I joined up voluntary in place of my brother,'[7] said Avdeev. 'He had four kids, and I was only just married, and Mother wanted me to go. And I thought, it's all the same to me, maybe they'll remember a good turn. So I went to see the master. He was a good man, our master, and he said to me "Good lad! You do that!" So I went and joined up in place of my brother.'

'Well, that's fine,' said Panov.

'But now I'm fed up, Antonych. Don't you see? And what gets me down most of all is why I joined up instead of my brother. Now he's living like a lord and I lead a dog's life. And the more I think about it, the worse it gets. That's a sin, I suppose.'

Avdeev said nothing for a while, then asked:

'What about another smoke?'

'Why not – you set it up.'

But the soldiers were not to get their smoke. As soon as Avdeev got up and was about to fix the pipe again, through the rustling of the wind came the sound of footsteps on the roadway. Panov took his rifle and prodded Nikitin with his foot. Nikitin rose and picked up his greatcoat. The third soldier, Bondarenko, also got up.

'My, what a dream I just had, mates . . .'

Avdeev hissed at Bondarenko, and the soldiers became dead still, listening. The soft footsteps of men not wearing boots drew closer. The crackling of leaves and dry twigs in the darkness became clearer and clearer. Then came the sound of voices talking in that strange guttural tongue spoken by the Chechens. Now the soldiers not only heard, but could see two shadows passing through the trees. One was shorter, the other taller. As they came abreast of the soldiers, Panov with his rifle at the ready stepped into the roadway with his two comrades.

'Halt! Who goes there?' he cried.

'Chechen, friendly,' said the shorter of the two. This was Bata. 'No gun. No sword,' he said, pointing to himself. 'We see prince.'

The taller one stood by his companion, saying nothing. He also had no weapons on him.

'It's a scout, so he'll have to go to the CO,' Panov explained to his comrades.

'Prince Vorontsov, must see. Very big business,' said Bata.

'All right, all right, we'll get you there,' said Panov. 'Well now, what about it – you,' he said to Avdeev, 'you take them with Bondarenko, hand them over to the orderly officer and come back here. Watch your step and make them go in front. They're smart, these cropheads, if you don't watch them.'

'What's this for then?' said Avdeev, feinting a thrust

with his rifle and bayonet. 'One prod with this and he's done for.'

'But what good is he if you bayonet him?' said Bondarenko. 'Come on, quick march.'

When the footsteps of the two soldiers and the scouts had died away, Panov and Nikitin returned to their former position.

'What the devil brings them out at night?' said Nikitin.

'Must be something important,' said Panov. 'It's got chilly, though,' he added and, unrolling his greatcoat, he put it on and sat against the tree.

A couple of hours later Avdeev and Bondarenko came back.

'Well, did you hand them over all right?' asked Panov.

'Yes. They were still awake up at the CO's, so they took them straight along. Really good lads they are too, these crop-heads. They really are! I got talking to them 247 splendid.'

'You would, of course,' said Nikitin, disgruntled.

'They really are just like Russians. One is married. Got a missus? I ask. Yes, he says. Any nippers? Yes, he says. Many? Just a couple, he says. We had a fine talk. Good lads!'

'Oh, yes, good lads,' said Nikitin. 'You just come up against him on your own and he'll cut your tripes out.'

'It should soon be getting light,' said Panov.

'Yes, the stars are going faint,' said Avdeev, sitting down.

And they lapsed again into silence.

3

The windows of the barracks and the soldiers' billets had long been in darkness, but in one of the best houses of the fort all the windows were still ablaze. This was the house of the commander of the Kura Regiment, Prince Semen Mikhailovich Vorontsov, son of the commander-in-chief and an imperial *aide-de-camp*. Vorontsov lived there with his wife, Marya Vasilevna, a celebrated St Petersburg beauty, and in this small Caucasian fort he lived in greater style than anyone before him. To Vorontsov and particularly to his wife the life they led there was not merely modest, but full of all manner of deprivations; the local inhabitants on the other hand were astonished at the extraordinary luxury in which they lived.

It was midnight now, and in the large drawing-room with its carpeted floor and curtains drawn across the doors the hosts sat with their guests playing cards at a card table lit by four candles. One of those playing was Vorontsov himself, a fair-haired colonel with a long face, wearing the ciphers and aiguillettes of an *aide-de-camp*; his partner was a graduate of St Petersburg University, a morose-looking young man with tousled hair, recently engaged by Princess Vorontsov as tutor to her small son by her first husband. Playing against them were two officers: one was Poltoratsky,[8] a company commander with a broad ruddy face, who had formerly been in the guards, the other the regimental adjutant, who sat very straight with a frigid look on his handsome face. Marya Vasilevna herself, a full-bodied beauty with large eyes and black eyebrows, sat by Poltoratsky, touching his legs with her crinoline and looking over his cards. In the way she spoke and looked and smiled, in every movement of her body and in the scent of her perfume there was something that made Poltoratsky oblivious of everything but the sense of her proximity and he made blunder after blunder to the increasing annoyance of his partner.

'Oh no, that really is too bad! You have hung on to the ace again!' said the adjutant, his face flushing all over, as Poltoratsky played the ace to his partner's trick.

As if just waking up, Poltoratsky gazed uncomprehendingly at the displeased adjutant with his wide-set, black, good-natured eyes.

'You must forgive him,' said Marya Vasilevna with a smile. To Poltoratsky she said: 'You see, I told you.'

'But what you told me was quite wrong,' replied Poltoratsky, smiling.

'*Was* it?' she said and smiled too. This answering smile so much agitated and delighted Poltoratsky that he flushed crimson, snatched up the cards and began shuffling them. **249**

'It isn't your turn to shuffle,' said the adjutant severely, and with his white, ringed hand himself began dealing the cards as if his sole concern was to be rid of them as quickly as possible.

The prince's valet came into the drawing-room and told the prince that the orderly officer wished to see him.

'Excuse me, gentlemen,' said Vorontsov, speaking Russian with an English accent.[9] 'Marie, will you take my place?'

'Does no one mind?' asked the princess, with a rustle of silk rising quickly and lightly to her full imposing height and smiling the radiant smile of a happy woman.

'I am always agreeable to everything,' said the adjutant, very pleased that he would now be playing against the princess who had no idea of the game. Poltoratsky simply spread his hands and smiled.

The rubber was ending when the prince returned to the drawing-room. He was unusually cheerful and elated.

'Do you know what I suggest?' he said.

'No, what?'

'That we have some champagne.'

'I never say no to that,' said Poltoratsky.

'That would be very nice,' said the adjutant.

'Vasilii, bring some champagne,' said the prince.

'What were you wanted for?' asked Marya Vasilevna.

'It was the orderly officer and someone he had with him.'

'Who was it? What did they want?' asked Marya Vasilevna hastily.

Vorontsov shrugged. 'I am not able to say,' he said.

'You are not able to say,' repeated his wife. 'We shall see about that!'

Champagne was brought in. The guests all had a glass, and, having finished their game and settled their debts, began to take leave.

'Is it your company detailed for forest clearing tomor-250 row?' the prince asked Poltoratsky.

'Yes, it is. Why?'

'Then we shall meet tomorrow,' said the prince with a half-smile.

'Delighted,' said Poltoratsky, not really following what Vorontsov was saying and concerned only that he was about to press Marya Vasilevna's large white hand.

Marya Vasilevna, as always, not only pressed Poltoratsky's hand firmly, but shook it hard as well. She again reminded him of the mistake he made in leading diamonds and gave him a smile that seemed to Poltoratsky charming, tender and significant.

Poltoratsky walked home in that uplifted mood which can only be understood by men such as he, brought up in high society, when after months of isolated camp life they again meet a woman from their old milieu – and a woman at that like Princess Vorontsov.

On reaching the house which he shared with a fellow

officer, he gave the outer door a shove, but found it locked. He knocked. The door did not open. Annoyed at this, he began kicking and beating at the locked door with his sword. Footsteps sounded inside and Vavilo, Poltoratsky's serf servant, undid the latch.

'What did you go and lock up for, you idiot?'

'Aleksey Vladimirovich, really you can't . . .'

'Drunk again! I'll show you I really can . . .'

He was about to hit Vavilo, but changed his mind.

'To hell with you. Light me a candle.'

'Yesshir, straight away.'

Vavilo was in fact the worse for drink, and this was because he had been to the quartermaster's name-day party. When he got home he started thinking how different his life was from that of Ivan Makeich, the quartermaster. Ivan Makeich had money coming in, was married and in a year's time was hoping to get his discharge. But Vavilo **251** had been taken into domestic service by his master as a boy and here he was now past forty with no wife and living his life in army camps with his feckless master. Poltoratsky was a good master, he did not hit him much, but what kind of a life was it? He's promised I can have my freedom when he gets back from the Caucasus. But where is there for me to go when I am free? It's a dog's life, thought Vavilo. And he had felt so tired that he had secured the latch to keep out intruders and gone to sleep.

Poltoratsky went into the bedroom which he shared with his fellow officer, Tikhonov.

'How did you get on? Lose?' asked Tikhonov, waking up.

'Not at all. I won seventeen roubles and we had a bottle of Cliquot.'

'And you gazed at Marya Vasilevna?'

'And I gazed at Marya Vasilevna,' repeated Poltoratsky.

'It will soon be time to get up,' said Tikhonov. 'We have to be off at six.'

'Vavilo,' shouted Poltoratsky. 'Call me at five, and make sure I'm awake.'

'How am I supposed to wake you up when you hit me?'

'You wake me up, I tell you. Understand?'

'Very well.'

Vavilo went out, taking their boots and clothes.

Poltoratsky got into bed, smiling as he lit a cigarette and put out the candle. In the darkness he saw before him the smiling face of Marya Vasilevna.

At the Vorontsovs' they did not settle down straightaway either. After the guests had gone, Marya Vasilevna went up to her husband, stopped in front of him and said severely:

'*Eh bien, vous allez me dire ce que c'est?*'

'*Mais, ma chère . . .*'

'*Pas de "ma chère"! C'est un émissaire, n'est-ce pas?*'

'*Quand même je ne puis pas vous le dire.*'

'*Vous ne pouvez pas? Alors c'est moi qui vais vous le dire!*'

'*Vous?*'[10]

'Was it Hadji Murat? Well, was it?' said the princess, who for several days had heard of the negotiations with Hadji Murat and presumed that her husband had been visited by Hadji Murat himself.

Vorontsov could not deny it, but disappointed his wife when he said that it had not been Hadji Murat himself but only a scout coming to say that Hadji Murat would come over to him the next day at the place detailed for forest clearing.

The young Vorontsovs, both husband and wife, were very glad of this event, which broke the monotony of life in the fort. They talked a while about how pleased Vorontsov's father would be to receive the news, then, after two, they went to bed.

4

After the three sleepless nights he had spent fleeing from
the *murids* sent by Shamil to capture him, Hadji Murat fell
asleep the moment Sado left after bidding him goodnight.
He slept fully dressed, resting on one arm, his elbow sunk
deep in the red down cushions his host had provided for
him. Eldar slept a short distance away, by the wall. He lay
on his back, with his strong young limbs stretched out so
that his full chest, surmounted by the black cartridge cases
of his white *cherkeska*, was higher than his blue, freshly
shaved head which was thrown back and had slipped off
its cushion. His upper lip with its faint covering of down
pouted like a child's and seemed to be sipping something 253
as it rose and fell. He slept as Hadji Murat did – fully
dressed with his pistol and dagger in his belt. The dying
fire burnt in the fireplace, and a night light glowed faintly
in the recess of the stove.

In the middle of the night the guest room door creaked
and at once Hadji Murat was on his feet, pistol in hand. Into
the room came Sado stepping softly over the mud floor.

'What is it?' asked Hadji Murat, alert as if he never slept
at all.

'We have to think,' said Sado, squatting down in front
of Hadji Murat. 'A woman on a roof saw you come. She
told her husband and now it's all over the village. A neighbour has just been to see my wife, and she says the old men
are meeting at the mosque and want to stop you.'

'I must go,' said Hadji Murat.

'The horses are ready,' said Sado and went swiftly out.

'Eldar,' whispered Hadji Murat, and Eldar, on hearing
his name but chiefly on hearing his *murshid's* voice, sprang

powerfully to his feet, straightening his *papakha*. Hadji Murat put on his weapons and cloak. Eldar did the same. Then both went out on to the veranda. The black-eyed boy brought their horses. At the clatter of hooves along the beaten roadway a head poked from the door of a neighbouring house and some person ran with wooden shoes tapping up the hill to the mosque.

There was no moon, but the stars shone brightly in the black sky and in the darkness you could make out the rooftops of the houses and, standing above the other buildings, of the mosque and minaret at the top of the village, where a buzz of voices could be heard.

Hadji Murat, swiftly grasping his rifle, put his foot into the narrow stirrup, silently, inconspicuously swung his body over and without a sound took his seat on the high padded saddle.

254 'May God reward you!' he said to Sado, feeling for the other stirrup with an accustomed movement of his right foot. He lightly touched the boy holding his horse with his whip to tell him to stand away. The boy stepped back, and the horse, as if knowing what it had to do, set off at a brisk walk, out of the lane and on to the main street. Eldar rode behind. Sado in a fur topcoat, his arms swiftly swinging, followed them almost at a run, switching from side to side of the narrow street. At the end of the village a shadow moved across the road, then another.

'Halt! Who is it? Stop!' cried a voice, and several men blocked the roadway.

Instead of stopping, Hadji Murat snatched his pistol from his belt and spurred his horse straight at the men blocking the way. They scattered, and without looking back Hadji Murat set off down the road at a fast ambling pace with Eldar following at a quick trot. A couple of shots rang out behind them, the bullets whistled past without touching Hadji Murat or Eldar. Hadji Murat rode on at the same pace. After about three hundred yards he pulled up his gently panting horse and listened. Ahead and below was the sound of rushing water. Behind he could hear the cocks in the village answering each other. Over these noises he heard the beat of horses' hoofs and the sound of voices getting closer. Hadji Murat touched his horse and set off at the same steady ambling pace.

The riders behind were galloping and soon caught up with him. There were about twenty mounted men: the villagers who had decided to detain Hadji Murat or at least clear themselves with Shamil by showing they had tried. When they were near enough to be seen in the darkness Hadji Murat stopped, dropped his reins and, undoing the cover of his rifle with a practised move of his left hand, drew the gun out with his right. Eldar did the same.

'What do you want?' Hadji Murat shouted. 'You want to capture me, do you? Come on, take me then!' And he **255** raised his rifle. The villagers stopped.

Rifle in hand, Hadji Murat began descending the gully. The horsemen followed, keeping their distance. When Hadji Murat reached the far side of the gully the men following him called on him to listen to what they had to say. Hadji Murat replied with a shot from his rifle and put his horse into a gallop. When he stopped there was no longer any sound of pursuit; the village cocks could not be heard either, but the sound of running water in the forest and the occasional lament of the eagle owl had grown more distinct. The black wall of the forest was now quite close. This was the forest where Hadji Murat's *murids* were awaiting him. As he came up to the trees, Hadji Murat halted, took a deep breath and whistled. He stopped and listened. After a minute a similar whistle came from the forest. Hadji Murat turned off the track and rode into the trees. When he had gone about a hundred yards he saw through the trees a fire with shadowy figures sitting round it, and a saddled horse in hobbles half lit by the light of the fire.

One of the men by the fire rose quickly and, coming up to Hadji Murat, took hold of the rein and one stirrup. This was Khanefi, an Avar, Hadji Murat's sworn brother who was in charge of his affairs.

'Put out the fire,' said Hadji Murat, dismounting. The men began scattering the fire, stamping out the burning wood.

'Has Bata been here?' asked Hadji Murat, walking over to a cloak spread on the ground.

'Yes, he was here. He went off long ago with Khan-Mahoma.'

'Which road did they take?'

'That one,' replied Khanefi, pointing in the direction opposite to the way Hadji Murat had come.

'That's all right,' said Hadji Murat. He took off his rifle and began loading it. 'We must keep a lookout. I was pursued,' he said to one of the men putting out the fire.

This man was Gamzalo, a Chechen. He came over to the cloak, picked up a rifle that lay in its cover there and without a word walked to the edge of the clearing to the point where Hadji Murat had entered it. Eldar had dismounted; he took his horse and Hadji Murat's and tethered them to the trees with their heads pulled up high; then, like, Gamzalo, with his rifle on his back he posted himself at the other end of the clearing. The fire was now out and the forest looked less black than before and, though faint, there were stars shining in the sky.

Looking at the stars and seeing the Pleiades already halfway up the sky, Hadji Murat reckoned it was well past midnight and long since time for his nightly prayers. He asked Khanefi to bring the ewer which he always carried in his saddlebags and, putting on his cloak, went down to the water.

When he had taken off his shoes and performed the ritual washing, Hadji Murat stood on the cloak in his bare feet, then facing eastwards knelt, sitting back on his legs, and said the usual prayers with eyes closed and ears blocked by his fingers.

When he had finished his prayers he returned to his place, where the saddlebags were, sat down on the cloak, and with his elbows on his knees and head bent forward he fell to thinking.

Hadji Murat had always trusted in his luck. When planning some venture he was always perfectly sure in advance that he would succeed – and he always did. With few exceptions it had been this way throughout his turbulent life of fighting. And he hoped it would be this way now. With the troops which Vorontsov would give him he could see himself attacking Shamil, making him his prisoner and taking his revenge. He could see the Russian tsar rewarding him, and he would rule once more, not only in Avaria but all over Chechnya which would submit to him. Thinking these thoughts, without noticing it he fell asleep. 257

He dreamt of descending on Shamil with his men to the sound of singing and cries of 'Hadji Murat comes upon you!'; he dreamt of seizing Shamil and his wives and he heard the wives weeping and sobbing. He woke up. The chant of '*La ilaha*,'[11] the shouts of 'Hadji Murat comes upon you', the weeping of Shamil's wives – these were the whining, crying and laughing of the jackals which had woken him up. Hadji Murat lifted his head, looked at the sky now lightening in the east between the trees, and asked the *murid* sitting nearby what news there was of Khan-Mahoma. Hearing that he was still not back, Hadji Murat lowered his head and again dozed off.

He was woken by the cheerful voice of Khan-Mahoma who had returned with Bata from his mission. Khan-Mahoma at once sat down by Hadji Murat and began telling him how they had come upon the soldiers and been taken direct to the prince, how he had talked in person to the prince, who had been delighted at the news and promised to meet them the next day across the Michik at the Shali clearing, where the Russians would be tree-felling. Khan-Mahoma was continually interrupted by Bata who kept adding details of his own.

Hadji Murat questioned them closely about the exact words used by Vorontsov in answer to his proposal to go over to the Russians. Khan-Mahoma and Bata replied in unison that the prince had promised to receive Hadji Murat as a guest and to be responsible for his wellbeing. Hadji Murat also asked about the way there, and after Khan-Mahoma had assured him that he knew the way well and could take him straight to the place, Hadji Murat took out his money and paid Bata his promised three roubles. He told his men to get from the saddlebags his gold-inlaid weapons and his *papakha* with the turban, and instructed his *murids* to clean themselves up so as to look well when they came to the Russians. While they cleaned their weapons, saddles, harness and horses, the stars faded, it became quite light, and an early morning breeze stirred in the air.

5

Early that morning while it was still dark two companies under the command of Poltoratsky, equipped with axes, marched out seven miles beyond the Shakhgiri gate, and at first light, after posting a line of sharpshooters, they began their tree-felling operation. By eight o'clock the mist, mingling with the fragrant smoke of green branches that hissed and crackled on the campfires, began to rise and the felling parties, who had been unable to see more than five yards and had so far only heard each other, could now see the fires and the tree-littered road that passed through the forest. The sun appeared intermittently as a bright blob in the mist. In a clearing a little way from the **259** road sat a group of men using drums as seats. These were Poltoratsky and his subaltern Tikhonov, two officers of No. 3 company and Baron Frézier, a former Horse Guards officer and comrade of Poltoratsky at the Corps of Pages,[12] who had been reduced to the ranks on account of a duel. Food wrappings, cigarette ends and empty bottles lay round the drums. The officers had had some vodka and something to eat and were now drinking porter. A drummer was opening the eighth bottle. Poltoratsky for all his lack of sleep was in that particular mood of animation and jovial unconcern which always came on him when he was with his men and his comrades in a spot where there might be danger.

The officers were having a lively discussion about the latest news, the death of General Sleptsov.[13] Nobody there saw his death as the supreme moment of his life – the moment of its ending and return to the source from which it came – they only saw in it the gallantry of a dashing officer who had charged, sword in hand, at the mountain dwellers and furiously cut them down.

Everybody (especially the officers who had seen action) knew and had opportunity to know that warfare at that time in the Caucasus – or at any time anywhere – never actually involved the hand-to-hand fighting with swords which is always supposed to occur and invariably appears in descriptions (when there *is* fighting with swords or bayonets it only means cutting down and bayoneting men in flight); nevertheless the officers accepted this fiction and it gave them the cool pride and gaiety which they felt as they sat on the drums, some in dashing poses, others quite unassumingly, smoking, drinking and jesting, with never a thought for death which might at any moment strike them as it had Sleptsov. And in fact while they were talking, as if to justify their expectation, there came from the left of the road the sharp, attractive, exhilarating crack of a rifle shot and a bullet whistled gaily through the misty air and thudded into a tree. There were a few ponderous bangs as the soldiers' muskets returned the enemy fire.

'Ho, ho!' cried Poltoratsky gaily. 'That's in the picket line. Here's a stroke of luck for you, Kostya, old boy,' he said to Frézier. 'Go back to your company. We'll lay on a lovely battle and get you a commendation.'

The demoted baron leapt to his feet and went smartly off into the area of smoke where his company was. Poltoratsky was brought his little dark-bay Kabarda horse,[14] mounted, then, mustering his company, led it off towards the picket line where the firing was. The picket line was on the edge of the forest where the ground fell away into a bare gully. The wind was blowing towards the forest and not only the near slope of the gully but also its farther side were clearly visible.

As Poltoratsky came up to the pickets the sun peeped through the mist and several horsemen could be seen on

the far side of the gully a couple of hundred yards away on
the edge of another belt of thin forest. These were the
Chechens who had pursued Hadji Murat and who wanted
to see him arrive for his meeting with the Russians. One
of them had fired a shot at the pickets, and some of the
soldiers had replied. The Chechens drew back and the
firing ceased. But when Poltoratsky came up with his company he ordered them to open fire, and no sooner was the
order given than from all along the picket line came a
merry exhilarating rattle of musket fire with prettily
spreading puffs of smoke. The soldiers were delighted
with this diversion and hastily reloaded, discharging one
shot after another. The Chechens were evidently put on
their mettle and galloped forward in turn to let off a few
shots at the soldiers. One of the shots wounded a soldier –
it was Avdeev, the soldier who had been in the listening
post. When his comrades got to him he lay face down **261**
swaying rhythmically with both hands clutching a wound
in his stomach.

'I was just going to load and I heard a thud,' said the
soldier who had been paired with Avdeev. 'I looked round
and saw he'd dropped his gun.'

Avdeev was in Poltoratsky's company and Poltoratsky,
seeing the group of soldiers, rode up to him.

'Are you hit, lad?' he asked. 'Whereabouts?'

Avdeev made no reply.

'I was just going to load, sir,' began the soldier paired
with Avdeev, 'when I heard a thud. I looked round and saw
he'd dropped his gun.'

Poltoratsky clicked his tongue.

'Too bad. Does it hurt much, Avdeev?'

'No, it doesn't hurt, but I can't walk. If I could have a
drink, sir.'

Vodka, or rather the liquor drunk by soldiers in the
Caucasus, was produced and Panov, frowning severely,

brought a tot of it to Avdeev. Avdeev started to drink, but at once pushed it away.

'I can't get it down. You have it,' he said.

Panov drank what was left. Avdeev made another effort to get up, but again sank back. A greatcoat was spread out and Avdeev was laid on it.

'Sir, the colonel is coming,' said the sergeant major to Poltoratsky.

'All right. You carry on,' said Poltoratsky and with a switch of his whip set off at a brisk trot to meet Vorontsov.

Vorontsov was riding his chestnut English thorough-bred stallion and was accompanied by the regimental adjutant, a Cossack and a Chechen interpreter.

'What's been happening here?' he asked Poltoratsky.

'A party of Chechens came out and attacked the pickets,' Poltoratsky replied.

'I know, and it was all arranged by you.'

'It really wasn't me, Prince,' said Poltoratsky, smiling. 'They came of their own accord.'

'I hear a soldier was wounded?'

'Yes. A great pity. He's a good man.'

'Is it bad?'

'Seems like it. He got it in the stomach.'

'And do you know where I am going?' asked Vorontsov.

'No, I don't.'

'And can't you even guess?'

'No.'

'Hadji Murat has come over and is just going to meet us.'

'Never!'

'He sent us a scout yesterday,' said Vorontsov, with difficulty suppressing a delighted smile. 'He is supposed to be waiting for me now at the Shali clearing, so you post your riflemen up as far as the clearing and then come to me.'

'Very good, sir,' said Poltoratsky, raising his hand to his

papakha, and rode back to his company. He moved the picket line on the right-hand side himself and ordered the sergeant major to do the same on the left. In the meantime four soldiers carried the wounded man back to the fort.

Poltoratsky was already on his way back to Vorontsov when he noticed a group of horsemen closing on him from behind. He stopped and waited for them.

At their head on a white-maned horse rode an impressive looking man wearing a white *cherkeska*, a *papakha* wound with a turban, and weapons mounted with gold. This man was Hadji Murat. He rode up to Poltoratsky and said something to him in Tatar. Poltoratsky raised his eyebrows, spread his hands to indicate that he could not understand, and smiled. Hadji Murat smiled back at him, and Poltoratsky was struck by the childish good nature of his smile. It was not at all what Poltoratsky had expected the fearsome mountain dweller to be like. He had expected someone grim, cold and distant, yet here was this totally unaffected person smiling so good-naturedly that he did not seem to be a stranger at all but an old familiar friend. The only remarkable thing about him was the wide-spaced eyes which looked you calmly and acutely in the eye.

There were four men in Hadji Murat's suite. One of these was Khan-Mahoma, who had gone to see Vorontsov the night before. He was ruddy and round-faced, with bright, black, lashless eyes, and a beaming look of happiness. One of the others was stocky with a lot of hair and eyebrows that met together. This was Khanefi, a hillman, who looked after all Hadji Murat's property. He was leading a spare horse which carried tightly packed saddlebags. The other two men of Hadji Murat's suite were particularly striking: one was a young, handsome fellow, slim-waisted like a woman, but broad in the shoulders, with the beginnings of a light brown beard and eyes like a sheep – this was Eldar; the other was blind in one eye, had neither eyebrows nor eyelashes, wore a trimmed ginger beard and had a scar running across his nose and face – this was the Chechen Gamzalo.

Vorontsov had come into view along the road and Poltoratsky pointed him out to Hadji Murat. Hadji Murat set off in his direction and when he came up to him put his right hand to his chest and said something in Tatar, at the same time halting his horse. The Chechen interpreter translated:

'He says he surrenders himself to the will of the Russian tsar. He wants to serve him, he says, and wanted to long ago, but Shamil would not let him.'

After listening to the interpreter, Vorontsov extended to Hadji Murat his suede-gloved hand. Hadji Murat looked at the hand and hesitated for a moment, then shook it firmly and spoke again, looking at the interpreter and Vorontsov in turn.

264 'He says he wanted to come only to you, because you are the son of the *sardar*. He much respects you.'

Vorontsov nodded his thanks. Hadji Murat said something else, pointing to his suite.

'He says these men are his *murids*, and will serve the Russians as he will.'

Vorontsov turned and nodded to them as well.

The merry Khan-Mahoma, with his lashless black eyes, also nodded and said something to Vorontsov which was evidently funny, for the shaggy-haired Avar smiled, baring his bright white teeth. The red-haired Gamzalo merely flashed his single red eye at Vorontsov for a second, then fixed his gaze once more on his horse's ears.

When Vorontsov and Hadji Murat, accompanied by his followers, rode back to the fort, the soldiers relieved from picket duty were standing in a group and made comments as they passed:

'How many souls that devil's done for, and now you just see how they'll butter him up,' said one.

'What do you expect? He was Shamble's chief lootenant, he was. Now, I daresay . . .'

'That young one's a proper *djigit,* that's a fact.'

'Just look at him with the ginger hair. He's got a vicious look in his eye.'

'A right dog he'll be.'

They all particularly noticed the red-haired one.

At the site of the tree-felling the soldiers nearest the road ran over to watch. An officer shouted at them, but Vorontsov stopped him.

'Let them have a look at their old acquaintance. Do you know who this is?' he asked one of the soldiers nearest to him, speaking slowly in his English accent.

'No, sir.'

'It's Hadji Murat. Have you heard of him?'

'That I have, sir. We've given him many a licking.'

'Yes, and he's given as good as he's got.'

'Indeed he has, sir,' replied the soldier, pleased with the chance to converse with his commanding officer.

Hadji Murat realized that they were talking about him and a merry smile gleamed in his eyes. Vorontsov returned to the fort in the very best of spirits.

6

Vorontsov was very pleased that it was he and no one else who was responsible for the defection and reception of the man who, after Shamil, was Russia's principal and mightiest enemy. There was only one snag, and that was that the military commander in Vozdvizhenskaya was General Meller-Zakomelsky,[15] and strictly speaking the whole affair should have been conducted through him. Vorontsov had handled it entirely on his own without making any report to him, and so there could be some unpleasantness. The thought of this somewhat marred Vorontsov's pleasure.

On reaching his house Vorontsov left Hadji Murat's *murids* in the hands of the regimental adjutant and took Hadji Murat himself inside.

Princess Marya Vasilevna, elegantly dressed and smiling, met Hadji Murat in the drawing-room together with her son, a good-looking, curly-headed boy of six. Hadji Murat put his hands to his breast and through the interpreter who had come in with him said somewhat ceremoniously that as the prince received him in his home he considered himself his *kunak* and the whole family of a *kunak* was as sacred as the *kunak* himself. Marya Vasilevna liked both the look and bearing of Hadji Murat, and she was even more disposed in his favour by the way he flushed and turned red when she gave him her large white hand. She invited him to sit down and after inquiring if he drank coffee ordered some to be served. But when the coffee was brought Hadji Murat declined it. He understood a little Russian, but could not speak it, and when he did not understand he smiled, and his smile appealed to Marya Vasilevna just as it had to Poltoratsky. Meanwhile, Marya Vasilevna's curly bright-eyed son (whom she called Bulka)[16] stood by his mother with his eyes fixed on Hadji Murat, of whom he had heard as a great warrior.

Leaving Hadji Murat with his wife, Vorontsov went to the regimental office to make arrangements for notifying the higher authorities of Hadji Murat's defection. After writing a report to General Kozlovsky,[17] commander of the Left Flank, in Groznaya, and a letter to his father, Vorontsov hurried home, afraid that his wife would be annoyed at his having imposed on her this strange, terrible man who needed careful handling so as neither to offend nor to encourage him too much. But he need not have worried. Hadji Murat was seated in an armchair with Bulka (Vorontsov's stepson) on his knee, tilting his head as he listened attentively to the interpreter's translation of what the laughing Marya Vasilevna was saying. Marya Vasilevna was telling Hadji Murat that if he were to give to every *kunak* whatever he happened to praise then he would soon be going round in the state of Adam ...

When Vorontsov came in, Hadji Murat put Bulka off his knee – which surprised and upset the boy – and he rose, his playful expression at once giving way to a stern and serious one. He sat down only when Vorontsov did. Going back to their conversation he replied to Marya Vasilevna that such was their law that one must give to a *kunak* any object that he took a liking to.

'Your son – my *kunak*,' he said in Russian, stroking Bulka's curly hair, the boy having once more climbed on his knee.

'He really is charming, this brigand of yours,' Marya Vasilevna said to her husband in French. 'Bulka was admiring his dagger so he made him a present of it.'

Bulka showed the dagger to his stepfather.

'*C'est un object de prix,*' said Marya Vasilevna.

'*Il faudra trouver l'occasion de lui faire cadeau,*'[18] Vorontsov replied.

Hadji Murat sat with lowered eyes, stroking the boy's curls and saying:

'*Djigit, djigit.*'

'It's a beautiful dagger, beautiful,' said Vorontsov, half unsheathing the sharpened steel dagger which was grooved down the centre. 'Thank you.'

'Ask him if there is anything I can do for him,' he said to the interpreter.

The interpreter translated, and Hadji Murat at once replied that he wished for nothing, but requested that he might now be given some place where he could pray. Vorontsov called his valet and told him to see to Hadji Murat's request.

As soon as Hadji Murat found himself alone in the room allotted to him his countenance changed: the look of pleasure, the shifting expressions of tenderness and solemnity vanished and a worried look appeared.

His reception by Vorontsov was much better than he had expected. But the better the reception the less Hadji Murat trusted Vorontsov and his officers. He had all kinds of fears, and one was that he would be seized and sent in chains to Siberia or simply be killed, and he was therefore on his guard.

Eldar came in and he asked him where his *murids* were quartered, where the horses were and whether they had had their weapons taken from them.

Eldar answered that the horses were in the prince's stable, that Hadji Murat's men had been put in one of the outbuildings, their weapons had been left them and they were being given food and tea by the interpreter.

Hadji Murat shook his head in bewilderment and, taking off his outer clothes, knelt to pray. When he finished praying he ordered his silver dagger to be brought, put on his clothes and belt, and sat with his feet up on the ottoman to await events.

A little after four o'clock he was summoned to dinner with the prince.

At dinner, Hadji Murat ate nothing except some pilaff, which he took from that part of the dish from which Marya Vasilevna had served herself.

'He is afraid we might poison him,' Marya Vasilevna said to her husband. 'He took his from the same place as I did.' And she at once turned to Hadji Murat and asked through the interpreter when he would next pray. Hadji Murat raised five fingers and pointed to the sun.

'Soon, then.'

Vorontsov took out his Bréguet watch[19] and pressed the spring. The watch struck a quarter past four. Hadji Murat was evidently intrigued by the striking of the watch and asked if Vorontsov would make it strike again and allow him to see it.

'Voilà l'occasion. Donnez lui la montre,'[20] Marya Vasilevna said to her husband.

Vorontsov promptly offered it to Hadji Murat. He put his hand to his heart and took it. He pressed the spring a few times, listened and shook his head approvingly.

After dinner the prince was told that Meller-Zakomelsky's *aide-de-camp* was there.

The *aide-de-camp* informed the prince that the general had heard of Hadji Murat's defection and was very displeased at having received no report of the matter and that he required Hadji Murat to be brought to him forthwith. Vorontsov said that the general's order would be carried out. He then told Hadji Murat through the interpreter what the general wanted and asked him to go with him to Meller.

When she discovered the purpose of the *aide-de-camp*'s visit, Marya Vasilevna realized at once that there was liable to be some unpleasantness between her husband and the general. Despite her husband's efforts to dissuade her she made ready to accompany him and Hadji Murat to the general.

'Vous feriez beaucoup mieux de rester, c'est mon affaire, mais pas la vôtre.'

'Vous ne pouvez pas m'empêcher d'aller voir madame la générale.'[21]

'You could see her some other time.'

'But I want to see her now.'

There was nothing for it but to agree and the three of them set off together.

When they went in Meller, grimly polite, conducted Marya Vasilevna to his wife and ordered his *aide-de-camp* to take Hadji Murat into the drawing-room and keep him there until further orders.

'After you,' he said to Vorontsov, opening the door to his study and letting the prince go in first.

Once inside he stood in front of the prince and, without inviting him to sit down, said:

'I am military commander here and therefore all negotiations with the enemy must be conducted through me. Why did you not report this business of Hadji Murat to me?'

'A scout came and told me that Hadji Murat wanted to give himself up to me,' said Vorontsov, turning pale with emotion in expectation of rough treatment by the furious general, but also himself infected by his anger.

'I want to know why you did not report it.'

'I was going to do so, Baron, but . . .'

'You don't address me as "Baron", but as "Your Excellency".'

And the baron suddenly gave vent to his long-suppressed annoyance and delivered himself of all the feeling that had been building up inside him.

'I haven't served the Emperor for twenty-seven years just so that people who joined the service yesterday can use their family connections to take charge of things that are none of their business, and that under my very nose.'

'Your Excellency, I beg you not to speak unjustly . . .' Vorontsov interrupted him.

'I am saying what is true, and I will not have . . .' the general began more irritably than before.

At that moment there was a rustle of skirts and Marya Vasilevna came into the room followed by a rather short lady of unassuming appearance, the wife of Meller-Zakomelsky.

'Now, now, Baron. Simon never meant to cause you any trouble,' said Marya Vasilevna.

'That is not what I am saying, Princess . . .'

'Well, I think it would be best to call the matter closed. You know – "a bad argument is better than a good quarrel". 271 Oh dear, what am I saying . . .' She laughed.

And the angry general succumbed to the enchanting smile of the beautiful Marya Vasilevna. A smile flickered beneath his whiskers.

'I confess I was wrong,' said Vorontsov, 'but . . .'

'Well, I was too hasty myself,' said Meller and gave the prince his hand.

Peace was restored and it was decided to leave Hadji Murat with Meller for the time being and then despatch him to the commander of the Left Flank.

Hadji Murat sat in the next room and although he did not understand what they were saying he understood all that was necessary: that they were quarrelling about him and that his defection from Shamil was a matter of immense importance for the Russians and that therefore, provided they did not exile or kill him, he could demand a lot from them. In addition, he understood that although Meller-Zakomelsky was the commander, he counted for less than Vorontsov, his subordinate, and that it was Vorontsov, not Meller-Zakomelsky, who mattered. As a result, when Meller-Zakomelsky summoned Hadji Murat and began interrogating him, Hadji Murat's manner was proud and dignified. He said that he had come out of the mountains in order to serve the White Tsar[22] and that he would give a full account of things only to the Tsar's *sardar*, that is to the commander-in-chief, Prince Vorontsov, in Tiflis.

7

The wounded Avdeev was taken to the hospital, a small building with a boarded roof on the way out of the fort, and put into an empty bed in the general ward. There were four other patients in the ward: a typhus case tossing feverishly on his bed, a man with malaria, pallid, with dark rings under his eyes, waiting for the next paroxysm and yawning continuously, and two men wounded in a raid three weeks earlier – one in the hand (he was walking about), the other in the shoulder (he sat on his bed). Except for the man with typhus they all gathered round the new arrival and questioned the men who brought him.

'It might be grapeshot the way they fire sometimes and nobody gets hurt, but this time there weren't more than half a dozen shots,' said one of the bearers.

'One had his name on it.'

'Ah!' Avdeev gave a sudden loud groan, fighting the pain as they began putting him on the bed. When they had laid him there he frowned and groaned no more, only kept up a continuous twitching with his feet. He held his hands to his wound and gazed fixedly into space.

The doctor arrived and ordered the wounded man to be turned over so that he could see if the bullet had passed out through his back.

'What's this?' the doctor asked, pointing to the crisscross of white scars on Avdeev's back and buttocks.

'That's old stuff, sir,' said Avdeev, moaning.

These were the marks of the punishment he had received for misapplying the money he had got drunk on.

Avdeev was turned over again and for some time the doctor probed in his stomach. He found the bullet but could not extract it. After dressing the wound and fixing it with sticking plaster, the doctor left. All the time his wound was being probed and dressed Avdeev lay with his teeth clenched and eyes closed, but when the doctor had gone he opened his eyes and looked around in surprise. His eyes were looking towards the other patients and the orderly, but he appeared to see not them, but some other thing that surprised him greatly.

Avdeev's comrades Panov and Seregin came. He still lay there, staring ahead in surprise. It was a long time before he recognized his comrades, although he was looking directly at them.

'Any message you want sent home, Pete?' asked Panov.

Avdeev was looking Panov in the face, but he made no reply.

'I asked if you wanted any message sent home,' repeated **274** Panov, touching Avdeev's cold, broad-boned hand.

Avdeev seemed to come to.

'Ah, Antonych is here.'

'Yes, I'm here. Is there no message you want sent home? Seregin could write it.'

'Seregin,' said Avdeev, with difficulty shifting his gaze to Seregin. 'You'll write it? . . . Then say this – "Your son Peter has passed away." I envied my brother. I was telling you last night. Well, now I'm glad. Let him be. Good luck to him, I'm glad. Write that.'

After this he said nothing for a long time, his eyes fixed on Panov.

'Did you find your pipe, then?' he asked suddenly.

Panov shook his head and did not answer.

'Your pipe, your pipe – did you find it?' Avdeev repeated.

'It was in my knapsack.'

'There now! Now let me have a candle. I'm going to die,' said Avdeev.

Just then Poltoratsky came to enquire after his man.

'Feeling bad, old chap?' he asked.

Avdeev closed his eyes and shook his head. His face with its high cheekbones was pale and stern. He did not answer, only repeated again to Panov:

'Get me the candle. I'm dying.'

They placed a candle in his hand but his fingers would not bend, so they put it between his fingers and held it for him. Poltoratsky left. Five minutes after he had gone the orderly put his ear to Avdeev's chest and said that he was dead.

In the report despatched to Tiflis Avdeev's death was described in the following manner: 'On 23 November two companies of the Kura Regiment proceeded from the fort for tree-felling. In the early afternoon a considerable force of mountain dwellers made a sudden attack on the felling party. The pickets began to withdraw and at this point No. 2 company charged the enemy with fixed bayonets and **275** routed them. In the course of this action two privates were slightly wounded and one killed. The mountain dwellers' losses were about a hundred killed and wounded.'

8

On the day that Avdeev died in the hospital at Vozdvizhen-skaya his old father, the wife of his brother (the one he had joined the army for), and his elder brother's daughter, a girl of marriageable age, were threshing oats on the frost-bound threshing-floor. There had been a thick fall of snow the evening before and a hard frost overnight. The old man had woken at cockcrow and, seeing the bright moonlight through the frosted pane, had got down from his bed over the stove, put on his boots, his fur-lined coat and cap and gone to the threshing-barn. For some two hours he worked there before going back to the house and rousing his son and the womenfolk. When the women arrived the threshing-floor was already cleared. A wooden shovel was stuck in the white powdery snow and by it an upturned besom; sheaves of oats were laid out in two rows, sheaf-heads together, forming a long line across the clean floor. They sorted out the flails and began threshing, rhythmic-ally timing their strokes: the old man struck hard with his heavy flail, crushing the straw, the girl beat steadily from overhead, and the son's wife did the turning.

The moon went down and it began to grow light. They had almost finished the line when the elder son Akim, in a sheepskin jacket and cap, came out to them.

'What are you shirking for?' his father shouted at him, pausing from his threshing and leaning on his flail.

'I've got to muck out the horses.'

'I've got to muck out the horses,' his father mimicked. 'Your old mother can do that. Get a flail. You've got too fat. Drunken sot!'

'Not your liquor though, was it?' muttered his son.

'What's that you say?' asked the old man menacingly, frowning and missing a stroke with his flail.

Akim said nothing, took a flail and the work went on with four flails going thwack-thwack-thwack-thud, as the old man's heavy flail followed the other three.

'Your neck's that fat anybody would think you was gentry. There's not enough on me to keep my trousers up,' said the old man, missing a stroke and just moving the swingle in the air to keep the rhythm.

They got to the end of the line and the women began raking off the straw.

'Peter was a fool to go off into the army for you. If you were a soldier they'd knock some sense into you, and Peter was worth five of your sort at home.'

'Oh, don't keep on, Dad,' said his daughter-in-law, tossing aside the crushed bindings.

'It's all very well. I'm supposed to feed six mouths and 277 there's not a stroke of work from any of you. Peter, he used to do two men's work, not like . . .'

Along the path trodden in the snow from the house came the old woman, crunching over the snow in new bast shoes which she wore over tightly wrapped woollen leggings. The two men raked the unwinnowed grain into a heap while the women swept up.

'The elder sent round to say everybody's wanted at the master's for carrying bricks,' said the old woman. 'I've got some breakfast ready. You'll be going, I suppose.'

'All right. You harness the roan and go,' the old man said to Akim. 'And see I'm not called to book on your account like I was the other day. Just you keep Peter in mind.'

'When he was home you were always on at him,' Akim this time snapped back at his father. 'And now he's gone you've got your knife into me.'

'And it's no more than you deserve,' said his mother no less angrily. 'You're not a patch on our Peter.'

'All right, all right,' said Akim.

'It isn't all right. You go and drink the money for the flour and then say it's all right.'

'What's the good of harping on what's past?' said the daughter-in-law, and they all set down their flails and went to the house.

The bad blood between father and son had begun long ago, soon after Peter had been sent off as a recruit. Even then the old man had a feeling that he had given a cuckoo for a hawk. Certainly it was right in law as the old man saw it that a man without children should go before a man with a family. Akim had four children and Peter none, but when it came to work Peter was like his father: handy, smart, strong, tough and, above all, industrious. He was always working. Like his father, he would never go by anyone working without lending a hand – he would scythe a couple of swaths, load a wagon of hay, cut down a tree or chop a pile of wood. The old man was sorry to lose him but there was no other way. Going for a soldier was like dying. Once a soldier he was gone for good: there was no point in fretting yourself with memories. Only occasionally when, as today, he wanted to get in a dig at his elder son did the old man recall Peter. His wife often thought about her younger boy and for a long time – more than a year – she had been asking her husband to send him a little money. But the old man never made any answer.

The Avdeevs' holding was a prosperous one and the old man had money put away, but he would never take the step of touching his savings. Hearing him speak of Peter now, his wife decided to ask him again and suggest he might send him something when he sold the oats, if only a rouble. This she did. After the others had gone off to work at the master's and she was alone with her husband she persuaded him to send Peter a rouble out of the money for the oats. So when from the pile of winnowed oats twelve quarters had been taken and tipped on to sacking in three sledges and the sacking carefully fastened with wooden pins she gave the old man a letter she had dictated to the sexton and he promised to put a rouble with it and send it off when he was in the town.

The old man, dressed in a new sheepskin coat, caftan and clean white woollen leggings, took the letter, put it in his pouch and, after saying a prayer, got into the leading sledge and set off for the town. His grandson rode on the last sledge. In the town the old man got the doorkeeper to read him the letter and he listened attentively and with approval.

In her letter Peter's mother first sent him her blessing, then greetings from everybody, news of his godfather's death and finally told him that Aksinya (his wife) 'no longer wants to live with us and has gone off to live her own life. They say she is doing well and living respectable.' The letter mentioned the rouble gift they were sending and ended with the following words straight from the heart of the grieving old woman who had told the sexton with tears in her eyes to write them down just as she said them: 279

'And Peter, my sweet, my own dear boy, I have cried my eyes out grieving for you. Why did you ever go and leave me, my own darling boy?' At this point the old woman had let out a wail and burst into tears.

'That will do,' she said.

And it was left like that in the letter, but Peter was fated never to receive the news that his wife had left home, or the rouble, or his mother's last words. The letter and money came back with the announcement that Peter had been killed in action 'defending Tsar, Fatherland and the Orthodox Faith'. That was how the military clerk put it.

On receiving this news the old woman wailed for as long as she had time, then set about her work. The following Sunday she went to church and handed out pieces of communion bread 'to good souls that they might pray for God's servant Peter'

Aksinya, his wife, also lamented when she heard of the death of her 'dear husband with whom she had known but a year of married life'. She was sorry for Peter and sorry for the way her whole life had been ruined. In her lament she recalled 'Peter Mikhailovich, his curly fair hair, his love, and the hard life she would have with their orphaned Vanka', and she reproached her Peter bitterly for having pity on his brother, but not on her he had left unhappily 'to shift among strangers'.

In her heart of hearts Aksinya was glad of Peter's death. She was expecting again from the bailiff in whose house she lived, and now nobody could abuse her, and the bailiff would be able to marry her just as he promised when trying to win her round.

9

Prince Mikhail Vorontsov,[23] brought up in England as son of the Russian ambassador, was a man of rare European education for a high Russian official of that time; he was ambitious, gentle and kindly towards his subordinates and a subtle courtier in dealing with his superiors. He had no conception of life without authority and submission. He held all the highest ranks and orders and was credited with being a skilful general, victor even over Napoleon at Craonne. In 1851 he was over seventy, but very well preserved; he was brisk in his movements and – the most important thing – he retained all the agility of his subtle and engaging mind, which he applied to maintaining his authority and establishing and extending his popularity. He possessed great wealth (his own and that of his wife, who was a Countess Branitsky), received an enormous salary as Viceroy, and spent most of his money on fitting out his palace and gardens on the southern shore of the Crimea.

On the evening of 7 December 1851 a courier's troika drove up to his palace in Tiflis. The weary officer, black with dust, who brought the news from General Kozlovsky of Hadji Murat's defection to the Russians, walked past the sentries, stretching the cramp from his legs, and entered the broad portico of the Viceroy's palace. It was six o'clock and Vorontsov was about to go into dinner when the courier's arrival was announced to him. He received him at once and so arrived a few minutes late for dinner. As Vorontsov entered the drawing-room the dinner guests – there were about thirty of them, some sitting round Princess Vorontsov, others standing in groups near the windows – all stood up and turned towards him.

Vorontsov wore his usual black military frock-coat with no epaulettes, only shoulder straps and a white cross at his throat. There was an affable smile on his clean-shaven, foxy face and he screwed up his eyes as he surveyed those present.

He came into the room with soft hurried steps, apologized to the ladies for being late, exchanged greetings with the men, and then went up to the Georgian princess Manana Orbeliani,[24] a good-looking woman of forty-five, oriental in build, tall and portly, to whom he gave his arm to conduct her to dinner. Princess Vorontsov gave her arm to a visiting general with gingery hair and bristling whiskers. The Georgian prince escorted Countess Choiseul,[25] Princess Vorontsov's friend; Dr Andreevsky,[26] the *aides-de-camp* and others, with or without ladies, followed these three couples in. Footmen wearing caftans with stockings and shoes moved the chairs for the guests as they sat down and a butler ceremoniously ladled steaming soup from a silver tureen.

Vorontsov sat in the middle of the long table. Opposite him were his wife and the visiting general, on his right sat the lady he had brought in, the beautiful Orbeliani, and on his left was a young Georgian princess, a shapely, dark, ruddy-cheeked girl, brilliantly adorned, who smiled continuously.

'*Excellentes, chère amie,*' replied Vorontsov to his wife's inquiry what news the courier had brought. '*Simon a eu de la chance.*'[27]

And he began recounting so that all at the table could hear the startling news (totally unexpected to all but himself who knew that negotiations had been going on for some time) – that the celebrated Hadji Murat, Shamil's most courageous supporter, had surrendered to the Russians and would be brought in a day or two to Tiflis.

There was a hush and everyone listened, even the

younger ones – the *aides-de-camp* and officers who sat at the ends of the table and had just before been quietly laughing about something.

When Vorontsov had finished speaking, his wife asked her neighbour, the red-haired general with bristling whiskers:

'Did you ever meet this Hadji Murat, General?'

'Oh, several times, Princess.'

And the general told the story of how after Gergebil[28] had been captured by the mountain dwellers in 'forty-three Hadji Murat had come upon General Passek's column and how almost before their eyes he had killed Colonel Zolotukhin.[29]

Vorontsov listened to the general, smiling agreeably, evidently pleased to hear him holding forth. But his face suddenly took on a vacant, sombre look.

The general was in full flow and had begun recounting another episode in which he had encountered Hadji Murat.

'Your Excellency will remember it,' said the general. 'It was in the "Hard Tack" expedition[30] – he was the one who ambushed us during the relief.'

'Where was that?' inquired Vorontsov, screwing up his eyes.

The fact was that the gallant general had mentioned the word 'relief' in reference to the action in the ill-fated Dargo campaign when a whole column under Vorontsov's command would actually have been wiped out if fresh troops had not come to their relief. Everyone knew that the Dargo campaign, led by Vorontsov, in which the Russians had suffered heavy casualties and lost several guns, had been a shameful affair, and because of this if ever it was mentioned in the presence of Vorontsov it was only in the terms used by Vorontsov in his despatch to the Tsar, which presented it as a brilliant feat of Russian arms. To use the word 'relief' was a direct reminder that it was not a brilliant achievement, but a blunder that had cost many lives. Everyone realized this: some pretended to be unaware of the implications of what the general said, some waited in apprehension of what would come next, while others smiled and exchanged glances.

Only the red-haired general with the bristling whiskers failed to notice anything amiss and, carried away by his tale, calmly replied to Vorontsov's question:

'In the relief, Your Excellency.'

And once launched on a favourite subject the general gave a detailed account of how 'this fellow Hadji Murat had cut the column so neatly in two, that if the relief had not come' – he seemed to repeat the word 'relief' with special affection – 'none of us would have got out alive, for . . .'

The general never finished, because Manana Orbeliani, seeing the situation, interrupted him to ask whether his quarters in Tiflis were comfortable. The general in surprise looked round at everyone and at his *aide-de-camp* who was shooting him hard meaning glances from the end of the table. It suddenly dawned on him. Without replying to the princess, he frowned, stopped speaking and hurriedly began eating the elegant food on his plate, swallowing it whole, unaware of what it was or even how it tasted.

There was general embarrassment, but the awkward situation was saved by the Georgian prince, a very stupid man, but as a sycophant and courtier remarkably subtle and astute, who was sitting on the other side of Princess Vorontsov. As if nothing had happened he loudly began telling the story of Hadji Murat's abduction of the widow of Akhmet-Khan[31] of Mekhtuli.

'He went into the village by night, took what he came for and galloped off with his whole band.'

'But why this woman in particular?' asked the princess.

'Her husband was his enemy. Hadji Murat hunted after him, but the khan died before he ever caught up with him so he took revenge on his widow.'

The princess translated this into French for her old friend the Countess Choiseul, who was sitting by the Georgian prince.

'*Quelle horreur!*'[32] said the countess, closing her eyes and shaking her head.

'Not at all,' said Vorontsov, smiling. 'I heard that he treated his prisoner with chivalrous respect and then let her go.'

'Yes, for a ransom.'

'Naturally. But nonetheless he behaved like a perfect gentleman.'

The prince's words set the tone for further anecdotes about Hadji Murat. Those in attendance realized that the more they emphasized the importance of Hadji Murat, the more agreeable it would be to Vorontsov.

'The man's daring is astonishing. He's quite remarkable.'

'He really is. In 'forty-nine he raided Shura and plundered the shops in broad daylight.'

An Armenian at the end of the table who had been in Shura at the time gave the details of this feat of Hadji Murat.

Most of the dinner passed in tales about Hadji Murat. They all vied with each other to praise his courage, cleverness, and magnanimity. Someone recounted an incident when he had ordered the killing of twenty-six captives, but even then there was the usual reply:

'It can't be helped. *À la guerre comme à la guerre.*'[33]

'He is a very considerable man.'

'If he had been born in Europe he might have been another Napoleon,' said the Georgian prince with the gift for flattery.

He knew that any mention of Napoleon would please

Vorontsov: it was for his victory over Napoleon that Vorontsov wore the white cross round his neck.

'Well, perhaps not Napoleon, but at least a dashing cavalry general, certainly,' said Vorontsov.

'If not Napoleon, Murat.'[34]

'He's got the same name – Hadji Murat.'

'Now that Hadji Murat has defected that will be the end of Shamil,' said someone.

'They can tell they haven't got a chance now,' said someone else ('now' meaning 'with Vorontsov in command').

'*Tous cela au grâce de vous,*'[35] said Manana Orbeliani.

Prince Vorontsov tried to restrain the showers of flattery which were beginning to overwhelm him. But he found it agreeable and was in an excellent mood when he escorted his partner into the drawing-room.

After dinner as coffee was being served in the drawing-room Vorontsov was especially pleasant to everyone and going up to the general with the bristling ginger whiskers made every effort to show that he had not noticed his gaffe.

After circulating among all his guests, the prince sat down to play cards. He only played the old-fashioned game of *l'hombre*. Playing with him were the Georgian prince, the Armenian general (who had learnt the game from Vorontsov's valet), and Dr Andreevsky, who was well known for the power he wielded.

Vorontsov placed at his elbow a gold snuff-box with a portrait of Alexander I, broke open the glossy cards and was about to lay them out, when his valet, an Italian called Giovanni, came in with a letter on a silver tray.

'Another courier has arrived, Your Excellency.'

Vorontsov put down the cards, with a word of apology unsealed the letter and began reading.

The letter was from his son. He gave in it an account of Hadji Murat's defection and the brush he had had with Meller-Zakomelsky.

The princess came over and asked what was in her son's letter.

'*Il a eu quelques désagréments avec le commandant de la place. Simon a eu tort.*'[36] "But all is well that ends well",' he said, handing the letter to his wife. He turned then to his respectfully waiting partners and requested they take their cards.

When the first hand had been dealt Vorontsov opened his snuff-box and did what he always did when in an especially good mood: he took a pinch of French snuff into his aged wrinkled white hand, lifted it up and tipped it into his nose.

10

The next day, when Hadji Murat came to be received by Vorontsov, the prince's waiting-room was full of people. There was the general with bristling whiskers of the previous evening, wearing full uniform and decorations, who had come to take his leave; there was a regimental commander who was under threat of court martial for misappropriations from the regiment's victualling account; there was a wealthy Armenian, a protégé of Dr Andreevsky, who held the concession for selling vodka and was now seeking a renewal of the contract; there was a woman in black, the widow of an officer who had been
288 killed, who had come to ask if she might receive a pension or have her children supported by the state; there was a Georgian prince in magnificent Georgian costume who was trying to solicit for himself a church estate that had fallen vacant; there was a district commissioner with a large scroll containing the plans of a new way to subjugate the Caucasus; and there was a khan, whose sole purpose in coming was to be able to say at home that he had visited the prince.

All waited their turn and one by one were conducted into the prince's study by a handsome, fair-haired boy, who was Vorontsov's *aide-de-camp*.

When Hadji Murat, limping slightly, strode briskly into the waiting-room, all eyes turned to him and he heard his name whispered in different corners of the room.

He was wearing a long white *cherkeska* over a brown jacket, the collar of which was decorated with fine silver lace. He had on black cloth leggings and soft leather boots of the same colour which fitted tightly over his feet like gloves; on his shaven head he wore a *papakha* wound with a turban – the same turban which had led to his arrest by General Klugenau[37] after Akhmet-Khan had informed on him and which had been the cause of his going over to Shamil. Hadji Murat walked quickly across the parquet floor of the waiting-room, his slender frame swaying from the slight limp which was caused by his having one leg shorter than the other. His widely set eyes looked calmly straight ahead and appeared to see no one.

The handsome *aide-de-camp* greeted him and asked him to take a seat while he announced him to the prince. But Hadji Murat declined and remained standing with feet apart and one hand at his dagger, scornfully surveying those present.

Prince Tarkhanov,[38] the interpreter, went up to Hadji Murat and began talking. Hadji Murat replied curtly, reluctantly. A Kumyk prince who was lodging a complaint about the district commissioner came out of Vorontsov's study, followed by the *aide-de-camp* who summoned Hadji Murat, took him to the study door and showed him in.

Vorontsov received Hadji Murat standing at the edge of his desk. The old white face of the commander-in-chief was not smiling as it had been the day before, rather it was stern and solemn.

On entering the large room with its enormous desk, large windows and green shutters, Hadji Murat put his rather small sunburnt hands to his chest where the sides of his white *cherkeska* met and with lowered eyes, speaking deliberately, distinctly and respectfully in Kumyk, which he knew well, he said:

'I surrender to the mighty protection of the great tsar and of yourself. I promise to serve the White Tsar faithfully, to the last drop of my blood, and I hope to be of service in the war against Shamil, who is my enemy and yours.'

Vorontsov listened to the interpreter, then looked at Hadji Murat. Hadji Murat, too, looked Vorontsov in the face.

As they met, the eyes of these two men said much that words could not express and not at all what the interpreter had said. Without a word passing between them each stated the plain truth about the other: Vorontsov's eyes declared that he did not believe a single word of what Hadji Murat had said, that he knew he was the enemy of everything Russian and always would be, and that he was submitting now only because he was forced to. Hadji Murat understood this, but nonetheless assured him of his loyalty. At the same time his own eyes were saying that this old man ought to be thinking about death rather than war, but, old as he was, he was sly and he would have to be on his guard. Vorontsov understood, too, but nonetheless explained to Hadji Murat what he considered necessary for a successful outcome of the war.

'Tell him,' said Vorontsov to the interpreter (he used the familiar mode of address in Russian as he did to all young officers), 'tell him that our sovereign is as gracious as he is mighty and will probably grant my request to pardon him and take him into his service. Have you said that?' he asked, looking at Hadji Murat. 'Until I know the gracious decision of my master, tell him that I undertake to receive him and to make his stay with us agreeable.'

Hadji Murat again pressed his hands to the middle of his chest and animatedly began speaking.

The interpreter conveyed what he said, which was that before, in 1839, when he had governed Avaria, he had faithfully served the Russians and would never have broken faith with them had it not been for his enemy Akhmet-Khan, who had wished to destroy him and had falsely denounced him to General Klugenau.

'Yes, yes, I know,' said Vorontsov (who, if he had ever

known, had long since forgotten it). 'I know,' he said, sitting down and waving Hadji Murat to an ottoman by the wall. But Hadji Murat remained standing, signifying with a shrug of his powerful shoulders that he would not presume to sit in the presence of so important a person.

'Akhmet-Khan and Shamil are both my enemies,' Hadji Murat continued, turning to the interpreter. 'Tell the Prince that Akhmet-Khan is dead, I could not revenge myself on him, but Shamil is alive and I shall not die till I have settled scores with him,' he said, frowning and clenching his jaws.

'Yes, of course,' said Vorontsov composedly. 'How does he intend to settle with Shamil?' he asked the interpreter. 'And do tell him he can sit down.'

Hadji Murat again refused a seat and in reply to the question that was conveyed to him he said that he had come over to the Russians for the very purpose of helping them destroy Shamil.

'Good, good,' said Vorontsov. 'What is it exactly he wants to do? Do please sit down . . .'

Hadji Murat sat down and said that if they would only send him to the Lezghian Line[39] and give him a force of men he would guarantee to raise the whole of Daghestan and Shamil would have to give in.

'Yes, good idea. That could be done,' said Vorontsov. 'I will think it over.'

The interpreter told Hadji Murat what Vorontsov said. Hadji Murat became pensive.

'Tell the *sardar*,' he said, 'that my family are in the hands of my enemy and as long as they are in the mountains my hands are tied and I cannot help. If I move openly against Shamil he will kill my wife, my mother and my children. The Prince has only to rescue my family, give some prisoners in exchange for them, and I will destroy Shamil or die in the attempt.'

'Good, good,' said Vorontsov. 'We will think it over. For the present he should go to the chief-of-staff and make a detailed statement of his present position, his intentions and his wishes.'

Thus ended the first meeting between Hadji Murat and Vorontsov.

That evening there was a performance of an Italian opera in the new theatre which was decorated in oriental style. Vorontsov was in his box when the conspicuous limping figure of Hadji Murat wearing a turban appeared in the stalls. He came in with Loris-Melikov,[40] one of Vorontsov's *aides-de-camp* who had been attached to him, and took his seat in the front row. Hadji Murat sat through the first act with oriental, Muslim dignity, expressing no surprise, seeming rather indifferent; he then rose and calmly surveying the audience, went out, the centre of everyone's attention.

292

The following day was Monday, the Vorontsovs' customary 'at home' evening. In the large brightly lit ballroom there was music, played by an orchestra. Young women, and women not so young, in dresses which revealed their necks, their arms and practically their bosoms too, spun in the embrace of men in brightly coloured uniforms. At the mountainous buffet footmen in red frock-coats, stockings and shoes, served champagne and handed confections to the ladies. The *sardar*'s wife who, despite her advancing years, was also half-naked, walked among her guests, smiling affably, and through the interpreter said a few kindly words to Hadji Murat, who was regarding the guests with the same indifference he had shown in the theatre the day before. The hostess was followed by other women with their bodies exposed who came up to Hadji Murat and stood shamelessly before him, smiling and asking the same question: how did he like what he saw? Vorontsov himself, wearing epaulettes and aiguillettes, the white cross at his throat and the ribbon of an order, came up to him and asked the same question, evidently assured as were all who asked that Hadji Murat could not fail to like what he saw. And Hadji Murat replied to Vorontsov as he replied to everyone else: that they had none of this – without saying if it was good or bad that this was so.

At the ball too Hadji Murat made an effort to speak to Vorontsov about ransoming his family, but Vorontsov pretended not to hear and walked away. Loris-Melikov later explained to Hadji Murat that it was not the place for talking business.

When it struck eleven, Hadji Murat checked the time on the watch he had been given by Marya Vasilevna and asked Loris-Melikov if he might go. Loris-Melikov said that he could, but that it would be better if he stayed. Despite this, Hadji Murat did not stay and drove back to the quarters that had been assigned to him in the phaeton provided for his use.

293

11

On the fifth day of Hadji Murat's stay in Tiflis, Loris-Melikov, the Viceroy's *aide-de-camp,* came to see him on orders from the commander-in-chief.

'My head and my hands are glad to serve the *sardar,*' said Hadji Murat with his usual diplomatic expression, inclining his head and putting his hands to his chest. 'Tell me your command,' he said, looking Loris-Melikov kindly in the eyes.

Loris-Melikov sat down in the armchair by the table, Hadji Murat sank on to the low ottoman opposite him and, resting his hands on his knees, bent his head forward and **294** listened attentively to what Loris-Melikov said. Loris-Melikov, who spoke Tatar fluently, told him that the prince, although he knew Hadji Murat's past, wished to have a full account of it from him personally.

'You tell me,' said Loris-Melikov, 'and I will write it down, then I will translate it and the Prince will send it to the Tsar.'[41]

Hadji Murat was silent for a moment (he never interrupted anyone speaking and always waited after they had finished to see if they would say more); he then raised his head, tossing back his *papakha,* and smiled with that special, child-like smile with which he had earlier captivated Marya Vasilevna.

'Yes, I can do that,' he said, evidently flattered by the idea that his story would be read by the Tsar.

'Start from the beginning and tell me everything. There is no need to hurry,' said Loris-Melikov, taking a notebook from his pocket.

'I can do this, but there is much, very much to tell. Many things happened,' said Hadji Murat.

'If it is too much for one day you can finish it on another,' said Loris-Melikov.

'Shall I start at the beginning?'

'Yes, at the very beginning: where you were born, where you lived.'

Hadji Murat lowered his head and sat like that for a long time. Then he picked up a stick lying by the ottoman, drew from beneath his ivory-handled, gold-mounted dagger a steel knife, sharp as a razor, and began carving the stick, at the same time telling his story.

'Write this down. I was born in Tselmes, a small village, the size of an ass's head, as we say in the mountains,' he began. 'Not far from us – two shots' distance – was Khunzakh,[42] where the khans lived. Our family was on very close terms with them. My mother had been nurse to 295 the eldest khan, Abununtsal-Khan, and that is how I became connected with them. There were three khans: Abununtsal-Khan, who was foster-brother to my brother Osman, Umma-Khan, who was my own sworn brother, and Bulach-Khan, the youngest, the one Shamil threw over the cliff. But that was later. When I was about fifteen the *murids* began coming round the villages. They beat on stones with wooden swords and cried out "Muslims, *ghazavat!*" All the Chechens went over to the *murids* and the Avars began to as well. I lived in the palace then. I was like a brother of the khans: I did whatever I wanted and was rich. I had horses, weapons, and money, too. I enjoyed life and gave no thought to anything. And so I lived until Kazi-Mullah was killed and Hamzad took his place.[43] Hamzad sent envoys to the khans to say that if they did not accept the *ghazavat* he would destroy Khunzakh. It needed careful thought. The khans feared the Russians and were afraid to accept the *ghazavat*, so the khanoum sent me and her second son Umma-Khan to Tiflis to ask the chief commander of the Russians to help us against Hamzad. The chief commander was Rosen, Baron Rosen.[44] He did not see me or Umma-Khan. He had us told that he would help, but he did nothing. Only his officers began visiting us and playing cards with Umma-Khan. They gave him wine to drink and took him to evil places and he lost all that he had playing cards with them. In body he was strong as an ox and brave as a lion, but in spirit he was weak like water. He would have lost the last of his horses and weapons, if I had not taken him away. After Tiflis I thought differently and tried to persuade the khanoum and young khans to take up the *ghazavat*.

'What made you think differently?' asked Loris-Melikov. 'Did you not like the Russians?'

296 For a moment Hadji Murat said nothing.

'No, I did not like them,' he said firmly. He closed his eyes. 'And another thing happened that made me want to accept the *ghazavat*.'

'What was that?'

'Near Tselmes the khan and I came upon three *murids*. Two got away, but the other one I killed with my pistol. When I went to take his weapons he was still alive. He looked up at me. "You have killed me," he said. "For me it is well. But you are a Muslim, you are young and strong. Accept the *ghazavat*. It is God's command."'

'And did you accept it?'

'No, I did not. But I began to think,' said Hadji Murat, taking up his story again. 'When Hamzad came up to Khunzakh, we sent old men to him to say that we would accept the *ghazavat*, but that he should send us a learned man to explain how we were to uphold it. Hamzad had the old men shaved of their whiskers, their nostrils pierced and sent them back with small cakes hung to their noses.[45]

The old men said that Hamzad was willing to send a sheikh to instruct us in the *ghazavat*, but only on condition that the khanoum sent him her youngest son as a hostage. The khanoum trusted Hamzad and sent him Bulach-Khan. He received him well and sent a message to us summoning the older brothers too. He said that he wished to serve the khans as his father had served their father. The khanoum was weak and foolish and headstrong as all women are who live by their own will. She was afraid to send both her sons and sent only Umma-Khan. I went with him. A mile or so from his camp his *murids* met us, singing, shooting and showing off their riding tricks. And when we arrived Hamzad came out of his tent, went up to Umma-Khan's stirrup and received him like a khan. He said "I have done no harm to your house and wish none. I ask only that you do not kill me or prevent me from bringing people to the *ghazavat*. And I will serve you with all my warriors as my father served your father. Let me dwell in your house. I will assist you with my advice and you can do as you wish." Umma-Khan was slow-witted in speech. He did not know what to say and was silent. Then I said that if it were as Hamzad said he should go to Khunzakh, and the khanoum and khan would receive him with honour. But I was cut short, and it was now I had my first clash with Shamil. He was there by the Imam and said to me, "No one asked you. Let the khan answer." I said no more, and Hamzad took Umma-Khan into his tent. Then Hamzad summoned me and told me to go with his envoys to Khunzakh. So I went. The envoys tried to persuade the khanoum to send her eldest son to Hamzad as well. I saw their treachery and told the khanoum not to send him. But a woman has as much wit as an egg has hair. The khanoum trusted them and told her son to go with them. Abununtsal did not want to. Then she said: "I see you are afraid." Like a bee she knew where the sting hurt most. Abununtsal flushed. He

said nothing more to her and ordered his horse to be saddled. I went with him. Hamzad welcomed us even better
than he had Umma-Khan. He came two shots' distance
down the hill to meet us. Horsemen with pennants rode
after him chanting "*La ilaha illa allah*", shooting and making show with their horses. When we reached the camp
Hamzad took the khan into his tent. I stayed with the
horses. I was down the hill when suddenly there was shooting in Hamzad's tent. I ran up to it. Umma-Khan was flat
on his face in a pool of blood and Abununtsal was fighting
the *murids*. Half his face had been cut away and was hanging down. He had hold of it with one hand and held his
dagger in the other, cutting down anyone who came near.
I saw him cut down Hamzad's brother and he was just
going for another of them but the *murids* started shooting
and he fell.'

298   Hadji Murat stopped. His tanned face flushed a reddish
brown and his eyes turned bloodshot.

'Fear came upon me and I ran away.'

'You did?' said Loris-Melikov. 'I thought you were never
afraid of anything.'

'Afterwards I was not. Ever since I have remembered
the shame of that day and when I remember it I am afraid
no more.'

12

'That is enough for now. I must pray,' said Hadji Murat. He took Vorontsov's watch from the inner breast pocket of his *cherkeska*, carefully touched the spring and, cocking his head and suppressing a childish smile, he listened. The watch chimed twelve times and one quarter.

'My *kunak* Vorontsov *peshkesh* – gave me,' he said smiling. 'A good man.'

'Yes, he is a good man,' said Loris-Melikov. 'And it is a good watch too. You say your prayers then, and I will wait.'

'*Yakshi*, it is well,' said Hadji Murat, and went to his bedroom.

When he was alone Loris-Melikov wrote down in his 299 notebook the substance of what Hadji Murat had told him, then lit a cigarette and walked round the room. As he came to the door opposite the bedroom Loris-Melikov heard the animated voices of men talking rapidly in Tatar. He guessed it would be Hadji Murat's *murids,* so opened the door and went in.

The room had that particular sour leathery smell characteristic of the mountain dwellers. Sitting by the window on his cloak spread on the floor was the one-eyed, ginger-haired Gamzalo in a tattered greasy jacket, assembling a bridle. He was speaking heatedly in his hoarse voice, but when Loris-Melikov came in he immediately fell silent and, taking no notice of him, continued with his task. Standing opposite him was the cheerful Khan-Mahoma, who kept repeating something with his white teeth grinning and a sparkle in his black lashless eyes. The handsome Eldar, with sleeves rolled up over his powerful arms, was scouring the girth straps of a saddle hanging on a nail.

Khanefi, who did most of the work and looked after the domestic side of things, was not in the room. He was in the kitchen cooking dinner.

Greeting Khan-Mahoma, Loris-Melikov asked him what they were arguing about.

'He still goes on praising Shamil,' said Khan-Mahoma, giving Loris his hand. 'He says Shamil is a great man: a scholar, holy man, and *djigit.*'

'How can he forsake him and still praise him?'

'He did and he does,' grinned Khan-Mahoma, his eyes sparkling.

'Do you then reckon him a holy man?' asked Loris-Melikov.

'If he was not a holy man the people would not listen to him,' Gamzalo retorted.

'Mansur[46] was a holy man, but not Shamil,' said Khan-Mahoma. 'He was a real holy man. When he was Imam the people were different. He went into the villages and the people came out to him, they kissed the hem of his *cherkeska*, repented of their sins and vowed to do no evil. The old men said that in those times everyone lived like a holy man; people did not smoke and drink or miss their prayers, they pardoned offences, yes, even bloodshed. In those days a man who found money or anything else would tie it to a pole and stand it by the road. And God made the people prosper in all things then, not like today,' said Khan-Mahoma.

'In the mountains people don't drink and smoke today either,' said Gamzalo.

'Your Shamil is a *lamoroi*,' said Khan-Mahoma, with a wink to Loris-Melikov.

Lamoroi was a scornful term for the mountain dwellers.

'A *lamoroi* lives in the mountains, and that is where the eagles live,' replied Gamzalo.

'Good man! You got me nicely there,' said Khan-Mahoma with a grin, enjoying the apt retort of his opponent.

Seeing the silver cigarette case in Loris-Melikov's hand, he asked him for a cigarette. Loris-Melikov remarked that surely they were not allowed to smoke. Khan-Mahoma winked and with a nod towards Hadji Murat's bedroom said that it was all right as long as nobody saw. And he straightaway began to smoke, without inhaling, awkwardly shaping his red lips as he blew out the smoke.

'It is bad,' said Gamzalo sternly and left the room. Khan-Mahoma gave a wink in his direction and while he smoked questioned Loris-Melikov about the best place to buy a silk jacket and a white *papakha*.

'Have you got such a lot of money, then?'

'I have money enough,' replied Khan-Mahoma winking.

'Ask him where he got it,' said Eldar, turning his handsome smiling face towards Loris.

'I won it,' said Khan-Mahoma and launched into the tale of how the day before he had been strolling in Tiflis and 301 had come on a group of Russian batmen and Armenians playing heads-or-tails. There was a lot of money in the kitty: three pieces of gold and a lot of silver. Khan-Mahoma got the hang of the game at once and jingling the coppers in his pocket joined the circle, saying he would play for the lot.

'The lot? But you never had that much, did you?' asked Loris-Melikov.

'All I had was twelve copecks,' said Khan-Mahoma, grinning.

'And what if you had lost?'

'I had this.'

Khan-Mahoma pointed to his pistol.

'Would you have given them that?'

'What for? I would have run for it and killed anybody who tried to stop me. And that would be that.'

'So you won?'

'*Aya*. I took the lot and went.'

Loris-Melikov understood Khan-Mahoma and Eldar perfectly. Khan-Mahoma was a wag, a rake, with no idea how to use the brimming life within him, always cheerful, frivolous, playing with life – his own and that of others; for him coming over to the Russians was all part of the game one day, but he might equally well go back to Shamil the next. Eldar too was perfectly easy to understand. This was a man completely devoted to his *murshid*, cool, strong and tough. It was only Gamzalo that Loris-Melikov was unable to make out. He could see that he was devoted to Shamil and that he also felt an insuperable loathing, scorn, disgust and hatred for all Russians. Because of this Loris-Melikov could not understand why he had come over to the Russians. The same thought occurred to him as was held by some of those in higher authority – that Hadji Murat's defection and the tale of his enmity towards Shamil were a blind, and that his only reason for surrendering was to spy out the weak points in the Russian defences before making off to the mountains once more and directing Shamil's forces to the places where the Russians were less strong. Gamzalo's whole being seemed to support this supposition. The others and Hadji Murat himself know how to hide their intentions, thought Loris-Melikov. But Gamzalo with his unconcealed hatred gives the game away.

Loris-Melikov tried talking to him. He asked if he found it dull here. But Gamzalo went on with what he was doing and casting a sideways glance at Loris-Melikov with his single eye barked hoarsely and abruptly:

'No, it's not dull.'

All other questions he answered in the same manner.

While Loris-Melikov was in the room, Hadji Murat's fourth *murid* came in – the Avar Khanefi, with face and neck thick with hair and a shaggy barrel chest which might have been covered with fur. He was the workman, unthinking, stalwart, always engrossed in his work, and, like Eldar, unquestioningly obedient to his master.

When he came into the *nukers'* room to fetch some rice Loris-Melikov stopped him and asked where he came from and how long he had served Hadji Murat.

'Five years,' answered Khanefi. 'We come from the same village. My father killed his uncle and they were going to kill me,' he said, calmly looking Loris-Melikov in the face from under his eyebrows, which grew together in a single line. 'Then I asked them to take me as a brother.'

'What does that mean: take you as a brother?'

'For two months I neither shaved my head nor cut my nails, then I went to them. They sent me in to Patimat, his mother. She gave me her breast to suck and I became his brother.'

Hadji Murat's voice sounded in the next room. Eldar knew at once that he was calling, wiped his hands and hastened with long strides into the drawing-room.

'He wants you,' he said, coming back.

And Loris-Melikov, giving the cheerful Khan-Mahoma another cigarette, went in to Hadji Murat.

13

When Loris-Melikov came into the drawing-room Hadji Murat greeted him with a cheerful look.

'Shall we go on then?' he said, seating himself on the ottoman.

'By all means,' said Loris-Melikov. 'I have just called in on your *nukers* and had a talk with them. One of them is a cheerful fellow,' Loris-Melikov added.

'Yes, Khan-Mahoma is a light-minded man,' said Hadji Murat.

'I liked the young man, the good-looking one.'

'Oh, Eldar. He is young and hard, like iron.'

For a moment they were silent.

'Shall I go on then?'

'Yes, please do.'

'I told you how they killed the khans. Well, they killed them, and Hamzad rode into Khunzakh and set himself up in the place of the khans,' Hadji Murat began. 'The khanoum, their mother, was still there. Hamzad sent for her. She began to rebuke him. He gave a sign to his *murid* Aselder and he felled her from behind and killed her.'

'But why should he have her killed?' asked Loris-Melikov.

'What else could he do? If the front legs are over the back legs must follow. The whole family had to be wiped out, and that is what they did. Shamil killed the youngest khan: he threw him down a cliff. The whole of Avaria submitted to Hamzad: my brother and I alone would not submit. We had to have his blood for that of the khans. We pretended to submit, but our only thought was how we could have his blood. We took counsel with our grandfather and decided to wait for a time when Hamzad left the palace and we would lie in wait and kill him. But some-one heard us and told Hamzad. He sent for our grandfather and said to him: "See now, if it is true that your grandsons plot evil against me, you and they shall hang on the same gallows. I am doing God's work and no one shall hinder me. Go and remember what I have said." Grandfather came home and told us. We decided then not to wait but to do our deed in the mosque on the first day of the feast. Our comrades refused, so there was just my brother and me. We took a pair of pistols each, put on our cloaks and went to the mosque. Hamzad came in with thirty of his *murids,* all with drawn swords. At Hamzad's side was Aselder, his favourite *murid,* the one who had cut off the khanoum's head. When he saw us, he shouted at us to take off our cloaks. He came up to me, my dagger was in my hand – I killed him and went for Hamzad. But already my brother Osman had shot him. Hamzad was still alive and **305** went for my brother with his dagger, but I got him in the head and finished him off. There were thirty *murids,* and two of us. They killed Osman, but I fought them off, jumped out of the window and got away. When it was known that Hamzad had been killed the whole people rose up and the *murids* fled, and any who did not were all killed.'

Hadji Murat stopped and breathed in deeply.

'All this was very good,' he continued, 'but then every-thing went wrong. Shamil took the place of Hamzad. He sent envoys to say I must join him against the Russians, and if I refused he said he would destroy Khunzakh and kill me. I told him I would not go to him nor let him come at me.'

'Why would you not join him?' asked Loris-Melikov.

Hadji Murat frowned and did not answer at once.

'I could not. The blood of my brother Osman and of Abununtsal-Khan was on his head. I did not go to him. Rosen, the general, sent to me: he made me an officer and

commander of Avaria. All this was good, but before that
Rosen had put Avaria under Mahomet-Mirza, the khan
of Kazikumykh, and afterwards under Akhmet-Khan.
And Akhmet-Khan hated me. He had tried to marry his
son to the khanoum's daughter Saltanet. They refused him
and he thought I was to blame. So he took hate against me
and sent his *nukers* to kill me, but I got away. Then he
accused me falsely to General Klugenau. He said I forbade
the Avars to supply wood to the soldiers, and he also said
that I had donned the turban – this turban,' said Hadji
Murat, pointing to the turban on his *papakha,* 'and that
this meant I had gone over to Shamil. The general did not
believe him and said I should be left alone. But when the
general went away to Tiflis Akhmet-Khan took matters
into his own hands. With a company of soldiers he seized
me and had me put in chains and tied me to a gun. Six days
they kept me like that, and on the seventh day they untied
me and took me to Shura. They took me under guard –
forty soldiers with loaded muskets. My hands were tied
and the order was to kill me if I tried to escape. I knew that.
As we were getting close, near Moksokh, the path was
narrow and on the right-hand side there was a drop of
three or four hundred feet. I moved away from the soldier
to the right on to the edge of the cliff. The soldier tried to
stop me, but I jumped over and dragged him after me. He
was killed outright, but as you see I survived. Ribs, head,
arms, leg – all broken. I tried to crawl, but could not. I came
over giddy and fell asleep. I woke up soaked in blood. A
shepherd saw me, he called some people and they took me
to a village. My ribs and head got better, and so did my leg,
except it was shorter.'

Hadji Murat stretched out his crooked leg.

'It gets me about and that is good enough,' he said. 'The
people heard about me and came to visit me. I got better
and moved to Tselmes. The Avars wanted me to come and

rule them again,' said Hadji Murat with calm and confident pride. 'And I agreed to do so.'

Hadji Murat quickly rose, and, getting a folder from his saddlebags, took out two letters yellow with age which he handed to Loris-Melikov. Loris-Melikov read them. The first letter was as follows:

'Ensign Hadji Murat: You served under me and I was well satisfied and thought you to be a good man. I was recently informed by Major General Akhmet-Khan that you were a traitor, that you had donned the turban, that you were in league with Shamil and that you had instructed the people to disobey the Russian authorities. I ordered you to be arrested and brought to me, but you ran away. Whether this makes things better or worse I do not know, since I do not know whether or not you are guilty. Heed now what I say. If your conscience is clear towards the great tsar, if you are guilty of nothing, then appear before me. You have nothing to fear from anyone – I am your protector. The khan will not harm you: he is himself under my command, so you have nothing to fear.'

Klugenau went on to say that he always kept his word and was just, and he again urged Hadji Murat to return.

When Loris-Melikov finished the first letter, Hadji Murat took the other one, but before handing it to Loris-Melikov he told him how he had answered the first letter.

'I wrote and told him that I wore the turban not for Shamil but to save my soul. I wrote that I had no desire to go over to Shamil and could not do so because through him my father, brothers and kinsmen had been killed, but neither could I go back to the Russians since they had dishonoured me. At Khunzakh while I was tied up some cur —— on me. And I could not go over to the Russians until this man had been killed. But most of all I was afraid of that double-dealer Akhmet-Khan. Then the general sent me this letter,' said Hadji Murat, handing Loris-Melikov the second faded sheet.

'You replied to my letter and I thank you,' read Loris-Melikov. 'You write that you are not afraid to come back, but are prevented by the dishonour inflicted on you by a *giaour*.[47] I can assure you that the Russian law is just, and you yourself will witness the punishment of the man who dared to offend you – I am already having this investigated. Listen, Hadji Murat. I have just cause to be dissatisfied with you, because you do not trust me and my honour. However, this I excuse you, knowing as I do the generally mistrustful nature of you mountain dwellers. If your conscience is clear, if you really have donned the turban only to save your soul, then you are in the right and can boldly face the Russian government and myself. You may rest assured that the man who dishonoured you will be punished, that *your property will be returned,* and that you will see and know what the Russian law means. And besides, Russians take a different view of things and consider it no disgrace to you that some scoundrel dishonoured you. I have myself allowed the people of Gimri to wear the turban and I take a right view of their deeds. So, I repeat, you have nothing to fear. Come back with the man I am now sending to you. He is loyal to me, and is *not the servant of your enemies,* but the friend of a man who enjoys the special consideration of the government.'

Klugenau then once more urged Hadji Murat to return.

'I did not trust this letter,' said Hadji Murat when Loris-Melikov had finished reading. 'And I did not go to Klugenau. For me the main thing was to be revenged on Akhmet-Khan and that I could not do through the Russians. At that time Akhmet-Khan surrounded Tselmes, wishing to capture me or to kill me. I did not have enough men and could not fight him off. It was just then that an envoy brought me a letter from Shamil. He promised to help me beat off Akhmet-Khan and kill him, and he offered to make me ruler of all Avaria. I gave it much thought and went over to Shamil. And ever since I have been fighting the Russians.'

Hadji Murat then gave an account of all the actions he had fought. They were very numerous and Loris-Melikov knew part of them already. All his campaigns and raids were astonishing for the extraordinary swiftness of his movements and the boldness of his attacks, which were always successful.

'There was never any friendship between me and Shamil,' said Hadji Murat, as he ended his story, 'but he feared me and had need of me. It so happened then that someone asked me who would be Imam after Shamil, and I said it would be the man whose sword was sharp. This was passed on to Shamil and he decided to get rid of me. He sent me to Tabasaran and I went and carried off a thousand sheep and three hundred horses. But he said the thing I had done was wrong and he replaced me as *naib* and commanded me to send him all the money I had. I sent him one thousand gold pieces. He sent his *murids* and took away all my property. Then he summoned me, but I knew that he wanted to kill me and did not go. He sent his men to capture me, but I fought my way out and came over to Vorontsov. Only I did not bring my family. My mother, my wife and my son are with Shamil. Tell the *sardar*: while my family is there I can do nothing.'

'I will tell him,' said Loris-Melikov.

'See to it, do everything you can. All I have is yours if only you will help me with the Prince. I am bound hand and foot and the end of the rope is in Shamil's hand.'

With these words Hadji Murat ended his story to Loris-Melikov.

14

On 20 December Vorontsov wrote the following letter to
Chernyshev, the Minister of War.[48] He wrote in French.

'My dear Prince, I did not write to you with the last post,
since I wished first to decide what course to follow with
Hadji Murat and I was also unwell for two or three days.
In my last letter I informed you of Hadji Murat's arrival
here: he arrived in Tiflis on the 8th; I met him the following day and for eight or nine days I had talks with him and
considered what eventually he might do for us and particularly what we should do about him now. He is much
concerned about the fate of his family and says with what
seems to be perfect candour that as long as his family are
in Shamil's hands he is paralysed and cannot do us any
service to show his gratitude for the pardon and good
reception we have given him. The uncertainty concerning
those dear to him has thrown him into a state of feverish
anxiety and those persons whom I detailed to reside with
him assure me that he does not sleep at night, eats practically nothing, is continually praying, and asks only for
permission to go riding with a few Cossacks – for him the
only possible diversion and exercise, which the habit of
years has made a necessity. Every day he has come to
ask me if I have any news of his family and he begs me
to collect all the prisoners we have on the various lines
of the frontier and offer them to Shamil in exchange,
together with a small sum of money which he would provide himself. There are people who would give him money
for this purpose. His constant theme has been: first rescue
my family, and then give me the chance to serve you (he
thinks on the Lezghian Line would be best); if in a month

I fail to do you a major service, you may punish me as you think fit.

'I have told him that all this seems to me very reasonable and that in fact there are many people on our side who would be reluctant to trust him if his family did remain in the mountains rather than under our care, where they would be a guarantee of his good faith. I said that I would do all I could to collect the prisoners held in our frontier posts and that although our regulations prevented me from adding any ransom money to what he might raise himself I might find some other means to assist him. I then frankly expressed my view that in no event would Shamil release his family and that Shamil might tell him so outright, promising him a free pardon and reinstatement if he returned, but threatening to kill his mother, wife and six children if he did not. I asked if he could honestly say what he would do if he received such a declaration from Shamil. Hadji Murat raised his eyes and hands to heaven and said that everything was in the hands of God, but that he would never put himself in the power of his enemy, because he was perfectly certain that he would not be pardoned by Shamil and that his days then would be numbered. As for the destruction of his family he doubted whether Shamil would undertake this lightly: firstly, so as not to render Hadji Murat an even more desperate and dangerous enemy, and secondly, because there were many people in Daghestan, some with considerable influence, who would dissuade him. He ended by saying several times over that whatever may be God's will for the future, he for the present was only concerned with the ransom of his family; that he begged me for God's sake to help him and allow him to return to the neighbourhood of Chechnya, where with the permission and assistance of our military command he could have contact with his family and receive regular information about their condition and about possible means to secure their release; that many persons and even some *naibs* in that part of enemy territory are more or less loyal to him; that among the people as a whole – neutrals as well as those under Russian authority – he can, with our help, easily establish contacts, which would be extremely useful for achieving the purpose by which he is driven day and night and whose fulfilment will bring him peace of mind and enable him to act for our benefit and to reward the trust we have shown him. He wants to be returned to Groznaya[49] with an escort of twenty or thirty brave Cossacks, who could protect him against his enemies and for us to provide a guarantee of the sincerity of his intentions.

'You will realize, my dear Prince, that I have been much perplexed by all this, for whatever steps I take, a grave responsibility falls upon me. It would be exceedingly rash 312 to trust him entirely. But if we wished to deprive him of all means for escape we should have to lock him up, and in my view this would be neither just nor politic. News of such a measure would quickly spread throughout Daghestan and it would be very damaging to our interests there since it would discourage all those – and there are many – who are prepared to go more or less openly against Shamil and who take a special interest in the situation of the most courageous and resourceful of the Imam's lieutenants, who has found himself obliged to place himself in our hands. Once we treat Hadji Murat as a prisoner the beneficial effect of his desertion of Shamil will be totally lost to us.

'I think therefore that I could not have acted otherwise than I did, though conscious that I might be held guilty of a major error of judgement if Hadji Murat should decide to go off again. In service life and in such involved affairs as this it is difficult, if not impossible, to follow a clear-cut course without risking error and accepting responsibility, but once the course looks clear one should follow it regardless of the consequences.

'I request you, my dear Prince, to present this matter for his Imperial Majesty's consideration, and I shall be happy if our sovereign master is gracious enough to approve my action. I have communicated all that I have written above to General Zavodovsky[50] and General Kozlovsky to aid him in his direct relations with Hadji Murat, whom I have informed that he should do nothing and go nowhere without Kozlovsky's approval. I told him that it would be better still from our point of view if he took to riding out with our escort, since Shamil might otherwise spread it abroad that we are keeping him under lock and key. But in suggesting this I made him promise that he would never go to Vozdvizhenskoe since my son, to whom he first surrendered and whom he considers his *kunak* (i.e. friend), is not in command there and there might be some misunderstanding. In any case, Vozdvizhenskoe is too near to a large population hostile to us, while Groznaya is convenient in every respect for the contacts he wishes to have with his agents.

'Besides the twenty picked Cossacks who at his own request will never leave his side, I have also sent with him Captain Loris-Melikov, a worthy, distinguished and highly intelligent officer who speaks Tatar; he knows Hadji Murat well and appears to enjoy his full confidence. During the ten days he spent here Hadji Murat resided in the same house as Lieutenant Colonel Prince Tarkhanov, who is commander of the Shusha district and here at present on official business. He is a truly worthy man in whom I have every confidence. He has also won Hadji Murat's trust and, since he speaks excellent Tatar, he has been our sole intermediary during the talks we have had on the most delicate and secret matters.

'I asked Tarkhanov's advice about Hadji Murat and he

entirely agreed with me that it is a matter either of acting as I have done, or of putting him in prison and keeping him in the strictest possible confinement (since once you treat him badly he would be hard to hold), or else of removing him right out of the country. But both the last two measures would not merely destroy the whole benefit to us of Hadji Murat's quarrel with Shamil, it would also inevitably put an end to any development of the mountain dwellers' discontent with Shamil and to the possibility of their rising against him. Prince Tarkhanov told me that he was himself convinced Hadji Murat was telling the truth and that Hadji Murat firmly believes Shamil will never forgive him and, despite any promise of pardon, would have him executed. The only thing which caused Tarkhanov concern in his dealings with Hadji Murat was Hadji Murat's devotion to his religion, and he is frank about the possibility that Shamil might work on him from this angle. But, as I already said above, Shamil will never make Hadji Murat believe that, if he returned, he would not kill him at once or within a short time.

'And that, my dear Prince, concludes what I wished to tell you concerning this episode in our local affairs.'

15

Vorontsov's report was despatched from Tiflis on 24 December. On the eve of the New Year, 1852; the courier – with a dozen worn-out horses and bloodied coachmen's noses left behind him – delivered it to Prince Chernyshev, then Minister of War.

And on 1 January Chernyshev took Vorontsov's report with various other papers to the Emperor Nicholas.

Chernyshev did not like Vorontsov for a number of reasons – the universal esteem in which he was held, his enormous wealth, the fact that Vorontsov was a real aristocrat while he, Chernyshev, was a mere *parvenu,* and principally because of the special favour showed him by the Emperor. Because of this Chernyshev took every opportunity to do what he could to damage Vorontsov. In his last report on Caucasian affairs he had caused Nicholas to be displeased with Vorontsov over the fate of a small column which through the laxness of the higher command had been practically wiped out by the mountain dwellers. On this occasion he intended to present Vorontsov's proposals concerning Hadji Murat in an unfavourable light. He wished to suggest to the Emperor that Vorontsov, who was always protecting and even indulging the natives, especially to the detriment of the Russians, had acted unwisely; that in all probability Hadji Murat had surrendered merely in order to spy out our defences and that it would therefore be best to send him into central Russia and make use of him only after his family had been rescued from the mountains, when one could be quite certain of his loyalty.

But Chernyshev's plan failed for the simple reason that on the morning of 1 January Nicholas was in a particularly bad mood and out of sheer contrariness would not have accepted any proposal from anyone. Still less was he inclined to accept the proposal of Chernyshev, whom he only tolerated because for the time being he regarded him as indispensable, but knowing how he had attempted to bring ruin on Zakhar Chernyshev[51] during the Decembrists' trial and take over his property, he considered him a thorough-going scoundrel. So because of Nicholas's bad mood Hadji Murat remained in the Caucasus and his fate was not affected as it might have been had Chernyshev made his report at some other time.

It was half past nine when in the haze of a twenty-degree frost Chernyshev's fat, bearded coachman in a blue velvet pointed cap drove up to the side entrance of the Winter Palace on the box of a small sledge identical to that in which the Emperor himself rode. He gave an amicable nod to his friend, Prince Dolgoruky's[52] coachman, who, having dropped his master, had already been waiting a long time at the palace entrance with his reins tucked under his fat quilted rump while he rubbed his chilled hands.

Chernyshev was wearing a greatcoat with a soft grey beaver collar and a cocked hat with a plume of cock's feathers worn in the regulation manner. Throwing back the bearskin rug, he carefully lifted out his numbed feet (he wore no galoshes and took pride in never doing so) and, livening up, walked with jingling spurs along the carpet and through the door respectfully opened before him by the porter. In the hall an old footman hastened forward to relieve him of his greatcoat, after which Chernyshev went to a mirror and carefully removed his hat from his curled wig. After regarding himself in the mirror he gave a twist to his curls at the front and sides with a familiar touch of his aged hands, straightened his cross, aiguillettes and the large epaulettes with the imperial cipher and, moving feebly on his aged, unresponsive legs, he began to climb the shallow, carpeted staircase.

Passing doors at which footmen in ceremonial dress obsequiously bowed to him, Chernyshev entered the Emperor's anteroom. He was respectfully greeted by the duty *aide-de-camp*, who had been recently appointed and was resplendent with his new uniform, epaulettes, aiguillettes and his ruddy, as yet unjaded, face with its trim black moustache and the hair at his temples combed forwards just like the Emperor's. Prince Vasilii Dolgoruky, the Deputy Minister of War, with a bored look on his dull face (bedecked with moustache, side-whiskers and hair combed forwards at the temples just like the Emperor's), rose and greeted Chernyshev as he entered.

'*L'empereur?*' Chernyshev asked the *aide-de-camp*, with an inquiring glance at the door of the Emperor's study.

'*Sa Majesté vient de rentrer*,'[53] the *aide-de-camp* answered, **317** evidently pleased with the sound of his own voice, then, gliding so smoothly that a glass of water on his head would not have spilled, he went to the door which swung silently open and, demonstrating with his whole being the veneration he felt for the place he was entering, he disappeared through the door.

Dolgoruky meanwhile had opened his despatch case and was checking through the papers inside.

Chernyshev, knitting his brow, walked up and down, easing his legs and remembering all the things he had to report to the Emperor. He was by the study door when it opened once more and the *aide-de-camp* appeared, even more resplendent and respectful than before, and signalled to the Minister and his deputy that they should go in to the Emperor.

The Winter Palace had long since been restored after the fire,[54] but Nicholas continued to reside on the upper floor. The study in which he received ministers and the most senior officials who came to report to him was a very tall room with four big windows. A large portrait of Alexander I hung on the main wall. Two bureaux stood between the windows. Along the walls were several chairs and in the middle of the room an enormous desk, with an armchair for Nicholas and ordinary chairs for his visitors.

Nicholas sat at his desk in a black frock-coat with shoulder straps and no epaulettes, his huge figure with its tightly laced paunch thrown back in his chair. Without moving, he gazed lifelessly at his visitors. His long white face with the huge sloping forehead that bulged between the smoothly brushed hair at his temples (which was so artistically joined to the toupee covering the bald patch on his head) was particularly cold and fixed that day. His eyes, which were always dull, looked duller than usual; his lips **318** compressed beneath the upturned points of his moustache, his plump cheeks freshly shaved around the regular sausage-shaped side-whiskers and supported by his tall collar, and his chin pressed down on the collar gave his face a look of displeasure, even of anger. The cause of this mood was tiredness. And the cause of his tiredness was that the night before he had attended a masked ball. Wearing his Horse Guards helmet topped with a bird, he had moved among the throng that pressed towards him but timidly withdrew before his huge, assured figure, and he had met again the masked lady – the one who at the previous ball had roused his senile passion by her white skin, beautiful figure and tender voice, and who had then vanished after promising to meet him at the next masked ball. At yesterday's ball she had approached him and he did not let her go. He took her to the private chamber kept ready for this purpose, where they could be alone. Without speaking, Nicholas reached the door of the chamber and looked round for the attendant, but he was not there.

Nicholas frowned and pushed the door open himself, allowing his partner to go in first.

'*Il y a quelqu'un,*' said the masked lady, stopping. The chamber was indeed occupied. Sitting close to each other on a velvet couch were an Uhlan officer and a pretty young woman with blonde curls in a domino with her mask removed. Seeing the angry figure of Nicholas drawn up to its full height, she hastily replaced her mask, and the Uhlan officer, transfixed with horror, not rising from the couch, stared blankly at Nicholas.

However accustomed Nicholas was to the terror he inspired in others, he always found it agreeable and some-times took pleasure in confounding his terror-struck victims by addressing them in a paradoxically gentle way. He did so on this occasion.

'You are a bit younger than me, my boy,' he said to the officer, who was numb with terror. 'You can make room **319** for me.'

The officer sprang to his feet, going pale and red in turn, and bending low, silently followed his partner out of the chamber, leaving Nicholas alone with his lady.

The latter turned out to be a pretty and innocent girl of twenty, the daughter of a Swedish governess. She told Nicholas that ever since she was a child she had been in love with him from his portraits, that she worshipped him and had decided at all costs to make him take notice of her. And now she had succeeded and, as she put it, she wanted nothing else. The girl was conveyed to the place where Nicholas customarily kept his assignations with women and he spent over an hour with her.

That night when he had returned to his room and got into the hard, narrow bed, on which he prided himself, and covered himself with his cloak, which he considered (and declared) to be as famous as Napoleon's hat, he was unable to get to sleep. He recalled the frightened and exalted look on the white face of the girl, then he thought of the powerful, rounded shoulders of his regular mistress Nelidova[55] and compared the two of them. That it was wrong for a married man to engage in debauchery was something that never occurred to him and he would have been very surprised if anyone had condemned him for it. But though he was convinced that what he had done was right and proper, it still left a nasty taste in his mouth, and in order to suppress this feeling he turned his mind to a subject which never failed to soothe him – his own greatness.

Although he had gone to sleep late, he rose, as always, before eight. He performed his usual toilet, rubbed his large, well-fed body with ice and said his prayers, repeating the familiar prayers he had said as a child – 'Mother of God', 'I believe', 'Our Father' – attaching no significance to the words. He then went out by the side entrance on to the embankment wearing a greatcoat and peaked cap.

Halfway along the embankment he met a law school student dressed in uniform and hat who was enormously tall like himself. Seeing the uniform of the law school, which he detested for its freethinking ways, Nicholas frowned, but his displeasure grew less as he noted the tallness of the student, the keenness with which he stood to attention and the exaggerated pointing of his elbow as he saluted.

'What is your name?' he asked.

'Polosatov, Your Majesty.'

'You are a fine fellow.'

The student still stood with his hand at the salute. Nicholas stopped.

'Do you want to join the army?'

'No, Your Majesty.'

'Idiot!'

Nicholas turned away and walked on. He began talking

to himself aloud, saying whatever came into his head. 'Koperwein, Koperwein,' he repeated several times – it was the name of the girl of the previous night. 'Squalid business.' He was not thinking what he was saying, but by listening to himself as he spoke he stifled his feeling of unease. 'What would Russia be without me?' he said to himself, sensing a return of his feeling of dissatisfaction. 'And not only Russia, but what would Europe be without me?' And he thought of his brother-in-law, the King of Prussia,[56] and how feeble and stupid he was, and shook his head.

As he came back towards the steps he saw the Grand-duchess Yelena Pavlovna's[57] carriage with a footman in red drive up to the Saltykov entrance. For him Yelena Pavlovna was the embodiment of those futile people who spent their time talking not only about science and poetry, but also about government, and had the 321 idea that people were capable of governing themselves better than he, Nicholas, could. He knew that however much he trod these people down they would keep raising their heads. And he remembered his brother Mikhail who had recently died. A feeling of vexation and sadness came over him. He frowned darkly and again began whispering whatever came into his head. He stopped doing so only when he entered the palace. He went to his apartments, smoothed his side-whiskers, the hair at his temples and the toupee on the crown of his head in front of the mirror, and then, giving a twirl to the moustache, he went straight to the study where he received reports.

He received Chernyshev first. Chernyshev at once saw from Nicholas's face and especially his eyes that he was in a particularly bad mood that day and, knowing of Nicholas's activities the night before, he realized the cause. After a chilly greeting Nicholas invited Chernyshev to sit down and fixed him with his lifeless eyes.

The first matter in Chernyshev's report concerned the peculations of certain Commissariat officials which had come to light; then there was the matter of transferring troops on the Prussian frontier; then the question of New Year awards for certain persons omitted from the first list; then came Vorontsov's report about the surrender of Hadji Murat; and finally the unpleasant case of a student at the Medical Academy who had attempted to kill one of the professors.

Nicholas pressed his lips together in silence and, smoothing his papers with his large white hands, one of which had a single gold ring on the third finger, he listened to the report about the peculations, his eyes fixed on Chernyshev's forehead and the lock of hair above it.

Nicholas was convinced that everyone was engaged in peculation. He knew that in the present case he would have to punish the officials and decided to send them all to serve as common soldiers, but he also knew that this would do nothing to stop the officials who replaced them doing the same thing. Officials had it in their nature to steal, he had a duty to punish them, and however irksome it was he conscientiously carried this duty out.

'It seems there is only one honest man in Russia,' he said.

Chernyshev understood at once that this single honest man was Nicholas himself and gave an approving smile.

'Such must be the case, Your Majesty,' he said.

'Leave it and I will write in the decision,' said Nicholas, taking the paper and putting it on the left side of his desk.

Chernyshev then began on the matter of the awards and of the transfer of troops. Nicholas looked through the list, deleted a few of the names on it, and then gave brief, decisive instructions for the movement of two divisions to the Prussian frontier.

Nicholas could never forgive the King of Prussia the constitution he had granted after 1848[58] and therefore, while professing in letters and speeches the most amicable feelings for his brother-in-law, he considered it prudent to maintain troops on the Prussian border. The troops might be required in the event of a popular uprising in Prussia (on every hand Nicholas saw the prospect of uprisings); he could then advance them to the defence of his brother-in-law's throne, just as he had moved his troops in to defend Austria against the Hungarians. The troops on the border were also necessary to add weight and import to any advice he gave to the Prussian king.

'Yes, what would Russia be now without me?' he thought once more.

'Well, what else is there?' he asked.

'A courier from the Caucasus,' said Chernyshev and he reported what Vorontsov had written about the surrender of Hadji Murat.

'So,' said Nicholas. 'That is a good start.'

'Your Majesty's plans are clearly beginning to bear fruit,' said Chernyshev.

Nicholas was particularly gratified by this praise of his strategic skill, because although he took pride in his skill as a strategist, deep down he was aware that in fact he had none. He wished now to hear himself praised in more detail.

'What is your view, then?' he asked.

'My view is that if we had followed Your Majesty's plan sooner – gradual, if slow, advance, clearing the forest and destroying food supplies – then the Caucasus would have been subdued long ago. I put down Hadji Murat's surrender entirely to this. He has realized that they cannot hold out any longer.'

'That is true,' said Nicholas.

The plan for achieving a slow advance into enemy territory by forest clearance and the destruction of food supplies had been put forward by Yermolov and Velyaminov.[59] It was the exact opposite of Nicholas's own plan,

323

which proposed the immediate seizure and destruction of the brigands' nest where Shamil had his residence and which had led to the Dargo expedition of 1845 that had cost so many lives: despite this, however, Nicholas also claimed credit for the policy of slow advance by forest clearing and destruction of supplies. One would have supposed that in order to believe that the plan of slow advance was his plan, he would find it necessary to conceal the fact that he had actually insisted on carrying out the operation of 1845 which was its complete opposite. But he did not conceal it and, despite the obvious contradiction, prided himself both on his plan for the 1845 expedition and on the plan for slow advance. The blatant, unceasing flattery of those around him had so far detached him from reality that he was no longer aware of his own inconsistency and ceased to relate his words and actions to reality, logic or plain common sense, fully convinced that all his decisions, however senseless, unjust and inconsistent they were in fact, became sensible, just and consistent simply by virtue of having been made by him.

It was the same with his decision in the case of the medical student to which Chernyshev turned after his report on the Caucasus.

The facts of the case were that the student had retaken an examination which he had failed twice before and when once more the examiner failed him the student, a neurotic type, considering the result unfair, seized a penknife and in a fit of frenzy attacked the professor, inflicting a few trivial wounds.

'What is his name?' asked Nicholas.

'Brzezowski.'

'A Pole?'

'He is of Polish origin and a Catholic,' replied Chernyshev.

Nicholas frowned.

He had done much harm to the Poles[60] and to explain this it was necessary to believe that all Poles were scoundrels. Nicholas considered that to be so and hated the Poles in proportion to the harm he had done them.

'Just wait a moment,' he said and, shutting his eyes, bent his head.

Chernyshev had heard this many times before. He knew that when Nicholas wished to decide some major problem he had only to concentrate for a few moments and inspiration would come to him and the perfect decision would be spontaneously made, as if dictated by some inner voice. Nicholas was now considering how he might best assuage his malice for the Poles which had been roused afresh by this case of the student and, prompted by his inner voice, he made the following decision. Taking the report, he wrote in his bold hand: 'Warrants the death penalty. But in Russia, thank God, there is no capital punishment. And it is not for me to introduce it. Let him run the gauntlet – twelve times through one thousand men. Nicholas.' He signed his name with an enormous unnatural flourish.

Nicholas knew that twelve thousand lashes meant not only certain, painful death, it was also a piece of excessive cruelty, since five thousand lashes would suffice to kill even the strongest man. But he liked to be implacably cruel – as he liked to reflect that there was no capital punishment in Russia.

When he had finished writing, he pushed his decision on the student across to Chernyshev.

'There. Read it,' he said.

Chernyshev read it and bent his head in token of his respectful amazement at the sagacity of the decision.

'And have all the students brought on to the square to see him punished,' added Nicholas.

'It will be good for them,' he thought. 'I will destroy this revolutionary spirit, root and branch.'

'I will attend to it,' said Chernyshev, and after a brief silence and adjustment of his hair he returned to the report on the Caucasus.

'What answer should be made then to Prince Vorontsov?'

'Keep firmly to the system I have laid down – destroy the Chechens' homes and harry them with raids,' said Nicholas.

'What are your orders concerning Hadji Murat?' asked Chernyshev.

'Well, doesn't Vorontsov say he wants to use him in the Caucasus?'

'Isn't that rather risky?' said Chernyshev, avoiding Nicholas's gaze. 'I'm afraid Vorontsov is too trusting.'

'What would you think then?' retorted Nicholas sharply, seeing through Chernyshev's intention to present Vorontsov's proposal in a disadvantageous light.

326

'I would think it safer to send him into Russia.'

'You would think that, would you?' taunted Nicholas. 'Well, I don't. I agree with Vorontsov. Write to him to that effect.'

'Very well,' said Chernyshev and, rising, began to take his leave.

Dolgoruky, who throughout the audience had spoken only a few words in reply to questions put by Nicholas on the troop movements, also withdrew.

After Chernyshev Nicholas received Bibikov,[61] the Governor-General of the Western Provinces, who had come to take leave of the Emperor. Nicholas approved the measures taken by Bibikov against the peasants who had refused to embrace Orthodoxy and ordered him to try all the recalcitrants by court martial – which meant condemning them to run the gauntlet. He also ordered that the editor of a newspaper be conscripted into the army for printing information about the transfer to crown ownership of several thousand state peasants.

'I am doing this because I consider it necessary,' he said. 'And I will not have it discussed.'

Bibikov was fully aware of the harshness of the orders for dealing with the Uniate peasants and the injustice of transferring state peasants (the only free peasants at that time) to crown ownership – to be, that is, serfs of the imperial family. But it was impossible to object. To fail to agree with any of Nicholas's instructions would mean the total loss of the brilliant position he now held which had taken forty years to achieve. And for that reason he humbly bowed his black, greying head in token of his obedience and readiness to fulfil His Majesty's cruel, senseless and dishonest wishes.

When he had dismissed Bibikov, Nicholas, with a sense of duty well done, stretched, looked at the clock and went to dress for his *sortie*. He put on uniform complete with epaulettes, orders and sash and went out into the reception rooms where over a hundred people – men in uniform and women in elegant, low-cut dresses – all in their appointed places, tremblingly awaited his appearance.

With his lifeless gaze, chest puffed out, and tight-laced paunch swelling out below and above its corseting, Nicholas came out to the waiting courtiers and, sensing that all eyes were turned with trembling obsequiousness on him, put on an even more dignified air. As he encountered familiar faces and recalled who was who, he stopped and spoke a few words in Russian or French and, piercing them with his cold, lifeless gaze, listened to what they said.

Having accepted their good wishes for the New Year, Nicholas went into the chapel.

Just as the laity had done, so too God through his servitors greeted and praised Nicholas, and, however tedious these greetings and praises had become to him, Nicholas received them as his due. All this had to be because on him depended the well-being and happiness of the whole world,

327

and although it wearied him he could not refuse the world his help. When at the end of the Eucharist the splendid deacon, with his well-combed hair and beard, intoned the words 'Grant, God, many years . . .' which were taken up by the beautiful voices of the choristers, Nicholas looked round and, catching sight of Nelidova standing by the window with her magnificent shoulders, gave her best over the girl of the previous night.

After the Eucharist he called on the Empress and passed some minutes with his family, joking with his children and his wife. He then went through the Hermitage to see Volkonsky,[62] the Minister of the Court, and among other things instructed him to pay from his special fund an annual pension to the mother of the girl of the previous night. From there he set off on his usual morning drive.

Dinner that day was served in the Pompeian Hall. Apart
328 from Nicholas and Mikhail, the younger sons of the Emperor, the guests were Baron Liven,[63] Count Rzhevussky,[64] Dolgoruky, the Prussian ambassador, and an *aide-de-camp* of the King of Prussia.

While waiting for the Emperor and Empress to appear, the Prussian ambassador and Baron Liven engaged in an interesting discussion about the recent disquieting news from Poland.

'*La Pologne et le Caucase, ce sont les deux cautères de la Russie,*' said Liven. '*Il nous faut cent mille hommes à peu près dans chacun de ces deux pays.*'

The ambassador feigned surprise.

'*Vous dites de la Pologne,*' he said.

'*Oh, oui, c'était un coup de maître de Maeternich de nous en avoir laissé l'embarras . . .*'[65]

At this point the Empress came in with her shaking head and fixed smile, followed by Nicholas.

At table Nicholas told them of Hadji Murat's surrender and said that in consequence of his orders to constrict the mountain dwellers by clearing the forest and building forts the war in the Caucasus would soon be over.

The ambassador, having exchanged a fleeting glance with the Prussian *aide-de-camp,* with whom he had the same morning discussed Nicholas's unfortunate weakness of considering himself a great strategist, warmly applauded the plan as further evidence of Nicholas's great strategic skill.

After dinner Nicholas went to the ballet, where hundreds of unclad women paraded in tights. One in particular took his fancy and summoning the ballet master, Nicholas thanked him and instructed that he should be presented with a diamond ring.

The following day when Chernyshev came with his report, Nicholas once more confirmed his instructions to Vorontsov that with the surrender of Hadji Murat he should step up the raids on Chechnya and hem it in with a line of military posts.

Chernyshev wrote to Vorontsov to this effect and another courier – wearing out horses and bloodying coachmen's noses – galloped off to Tiflis.

16

In prompt execution of Nicholas's instructions a raid on Chechnya was carried out in January 1852.

The column detailed to make the raid consisted of four infantry battalions, two squadrons of Cossacks and eight guns. The column advanced along the road, flanked on either side by a continuous line of sharpshooters in high boots, sheepskin jackets and *papakhas,* who marched with shouldered muskets and cartridge belts over their shoulders, climbing up and down the gullies that crossed their way.[66] As always, the column advanced through hostile territory with the minimum of noise. Only occasionally the guns clanked as they jolted over a shallow ditch, or a limber horse – understanding nothing of orders to keep silent – snorted, or an irate officer shouted in a hoarse, subdued voice, berating his men for extending the flank lines or being too close or too far from the column. Only once was the silence broken, when a goat with a grey back and white rump and belly leapt out of a thorn patch between the column and the flank line, followed by a he-goat with similar markings and small horns thrown back on its shoulders. With bounding strides, tucking their forelegs up to their chests, these handsome, frightened animals ran so close towards the column that some of the soldiers chased them, laughing and shouting, hoping to stick them with their bayonets, but the goats turned back, darted through the flank line and flew off like birds into the hills, pursued by a few regimental dogs.

It was still winter, but the sun was beginning to reach higher in the sky and by midday, when the column after its early morning start had covered seven or eight miles, it was hot and it hurt to look at the steel of the bayonets and the sudden glinting lights that flashed like miniature suns on the brass of the guns.

Behind the column lay the clear, swift river they had just crossed, ahead cultivated fields and meadows with shallow gullies running across them, further ahead lay black, mysterious hills covered with forest and beyond them projecting crags, then high on the horizon the ever enchanting, ever changing snow-clad mountains sparkling like diamonds.

At the head of No. 5 company in a black frock-coat and *papakha* with his sword slung from his shoulder marched the tall handsome figure of Butler, an officer recently transferred from the guards. He was feeling cheerful – a feeling compounded of *joie de vivre,* mortal danger, eagerness for action, and the consciousness of being part of one enormous whole controlled by a single will. This was Butler's second action and it was pleasant to think that at any moment they would be under fire and that he would not duck when a cannonball passed overhead or pay heed to the whistling bullets, but rather, as before, he would lift his head higher and with smiling eyes look round at his fellow officers and men and talk very casually about something completely different.

The column turned off the good road on to a little-used one which passed through fields of maize stubble. They were now nearing the forest, when – it was impossible to see where from – a cannonball whistled ominously overhead and landed in a maize field by the side of the road halfway down the baggage train, showering it with earth.

'It's starting,' said Butler with a merry smile to the officer by his side.

And sure enough, after the cannonshot a dense throng of mounted Chechens carrying pennants appeared out of the trees. In the middle of them was a large green standard and the old company sergeant major, who had a very good eye, informed the short-sighted Butler that it must be Shamil himself. The Chechens rode down the hill and appeared on the rise above the next gully on the right; they began descending into it. The little general wearing a warm black frock-coat and a *papakha* with a large white tassel rode up to Butler's company on his ambler and ordered him to move rightwards against the descending horsemen. Butler quickly led his company in the direction indicated, but before they reached the bottom of the gully he heard behind him two cannonshots, one after the other. He looked round and saw two clouds of blue-grey smoke rise over the cannon and drift along the gully. The Chechens, who had evidently not been expecting artillery, turned back. Butler's company opened fire on the retreating mountain dwellers, and the whole gully was clouded with gunsmoke. Only higher up, out of the gully, could one see the mountain dwellers retreating hastily and firing to keep off the pursuing Cossacks. The column continued to advance after the mountain dwellers and on the slope of the next gully they came upon the village.

Butler and his company entered the village at the double after the Cossacks. The inhabitants were all gone. The soldiers were ordered to burn the corn and hay and the houses too. An acrid layer of smoke spread through the village; in the smoke soldiers rushed about carrying off what they could find from the houses, but chiefly chasing and shooting the chickens which the villagers had been unable to take with them. The officers sat down away from the smoke, and had lunch and something to drink. The sergeant major brought them honeycombs on a board. There was no sound of the Chechens. Soon after midday the order was given to withdraw. The companies formed into a column at the back of the village and Butler had to bring up the rear. As soon as they moved off, the Chechens reappeared and followed, firing parting shots into the column.

When the column reached open ground the mountain dwellers fell back. None of Butler's men was wounded and on the way back he was in a most cheerful and jolly mood.

After fording the river they had crossed in the morning the column marched on, stretching across the maize fields and meadows; the chorus leaders of each company came to the front and the sound of songs burst forth. There was no wind, the air was fresh and pure and so clear that the snowy mountains seventy miles off seemed no distance away, and when the singers stopped you heard the even tramp of feet and the clank of the guns as the background against which the songs began and ended. The song sung in Butler's No. 5 company had been made up by one of the cadets in honour of the regiment and was sung to the tune of a dance with the refrain: 'Sharpshooters, sharpshooters! **333** We're the best, we're the best!'

Butler was on horseback riding alongside his immediate superior, Major Petrov, with whom he shared quarters. He was feeling delighted that he had decided to leave the guards and go off to the Caucasus. His main reason for leaving the guards had been that after losing heavily at cards in St Petersburg he was completely broke. He feared that if he stayed in the guards he would be unable to stop himself gambling and he had nothing left to lose. Now that was all over and done with. He had a different life now, a good, dashing life. He had forgotten all about being ruined and the debts he could not pay. The Caucasus, the war, the men, the officers, this brave, good-natured, hard-drinking Major Petrov – it all seemed to him so splendid that at times he could hardly believe he was not in St Petersburg, in some smoke-laden rooms staking his bets as he played against the bank, hating the banker and feeling that pressing pain in his head, rather than here in this marvellous country among these fine fellows of the army of the Caucasus.

'Sharpshooters, sharpshooters! We're the best, we're the best!' sang the chorus leaders. His horse strode merrily along to the music. Trezorka, the shaggy, grey company dog, with its tail up and a busy look, ran ahead of Butler's company as if in command. Butler was feeling bright, cheerful and at ease. War, as he saw it, was simply a matter of subjecting himself to danger, risking death, and in return gaining awards and the respect of his comrades here and of his friends in Russia. The other face of war – the men, officers and mountain dwellers killed and wounded – oddly never occurred to him. To maintain his poetic view of war he even subconsciously avoided looking at the dead and wounded. It was the same today – on the Russian side three men were killed and twelve wounded. He went past a dead body lying on its back and only out of the corner of his eye did he observe the odd position of the wax-like hand and the deep-red blotch on the head: he did not look closer. The mountain dwellers as far as he was concerned were just daredevil horsemen you had to defend yourself against.

'Well, there you are, old chap,' said the major, between songs. 'Not like your way of things in Petersburg – with your "right dress!", "left dress!". We've done a job of work, and now home. Dear old Masha will have a pie for us and some decent cabbage soup. That's the life, isn't it? Come on, let's have "At morn's first light",' he said, giving the order for his favourite song.

The major lived with the daughter of the camp surgeon. She used to be known as Mashka, but then became Marya Dmitrievna.[67] She had no children and was a good-looking, blonde woman of thirty with a mass of freckles. Whatever her past, she was now the major's faithful companion and looked after him like a child, which was just what the major needed, since he frequently drank himself into a stupor.

When they reached the fort everything was as the major had anticipated. Marya Dmitrievna produced a solid, tasty meal for him, Butler and two officers from the column they had invited to join them, and the major ate and drank till he was past talking and went off to his bedroom to sleep. Butler, who was also tired, but well content and somewhat tipsy after too much *chikhir,* went off to his room, and was hardly undressed before he fell into an unbroken, dreamless sleep, with one hand under his handsome, curly head.

17

The village laid waste by the raiding party was the one in which Hadji Murat had spent the night before going over to the Russians.

Sado, with whom he had stayed, took his family away to the mountains when the Russians approached the village. When he came back he found his house destroyed: the roof was caved in, the door and the post supporting the veranda were burnt and the inside befouled. His son, the good-looking boy with shining eyes who had regarded Hadji Murat with such rapture, was brought into the mosque dead on the back of a horse draped with a cloak. He had been bayoneted in the back. The fine-looking woman who had waited on Hadji Murat during his visit stood over her son with her hair loose and the smock she was wearing rent at the chest to reveal her old, sagging breasts. She stood clawing her face till the blood ran and wailing without stop. Sado took a pick and shovel and went with his kinsmen to dig a grave for his son. The old grandfather sat by the wall of the ruined house, whittling a stick and gazing blankly into space. He had just come back from his bee-garden. The two small hayricks he had there were burnt; the apricot and cherry trees which he had planted and tended were broken and scorched; and, worst of all, every one of his hives had been burnt together with the bees. The wailing of women sounded in every house and in the square where two more bodies were brought. The young children wailed with their mothers. The hungry animals howled, too, and there was nothing to give them. The older children played no games and watched their elders with frightened eyes.

The fountain had been befouled, evidently on purpose, so no water could be drawn from it. The mosque, too, had been defiled and the mullah and his pupils were cleaning it out.

The village elders gathered in the square and squatted on their heels to discuss the situation. Nobody spoke a word of hatred for the Russians. The emotion felt by every Chechen, old and young alike, was stronger than hatred. It was not hatred, it was a refusal to recognize these Russian dogs as men at all, and a feeling of such disgust, revulsion and bewilderment at the senseless cruelty of these creatures that the urge to destroy them – like the urge to destroy rats, venomous spiders or wolves – was an instinct as natural as that of self-preservation.

The villagers were faced with a choice: either to remain as before and by terrible exertions restore all that had been created with such labour and so easily and senselessly **337** destroyed, while every minute expecting a repetition of the same thing, or they could act contrary to the law of their religion and, despite the revulsion and scorn they felt for the Russians, submit to them.

The old men prayed and resolved unanimously to send envoys to ask Shamil for help, and straightaway they set about rebuilding what had been destroyed.

18

The second day after the raid, not too early, Butler went out into the street by way of the back door, intending to have a stroll and a breath of fresh air before his morning tea, which he normally took with Petrov. The sun was already clear of the mountains and it was painful to look at the white daub houses where it shone on the right-hand side of the street. It was, though, as cheering and soothing as ever to look leftwards at the black tree-clad mountains rising higher and higher in the distance and, visible beyond the ravine, the lustreless chain of snow-capped mountains pretending as always to be clouds.

338   Butler looked at the mountains, filled his lungs, and felt happy to be alive and to be just who he was, living in this beautiful world. He was quite happy, too, about his conduct in the previous day's action, both during the advance and in particular during the march back when things were quite hot; and he was happy to recall the way Masha, otherwise Marya Dmitrievna (the woman Petrov lived with) had entertained them after they had got back from the raid, and the especially unaffected, kindly way she had treated everyone, being particularly nice to him, it had seemed. With her thick plait of hair, her broad shoulders, full bosom, and kindly beaming face covered with freckles, Marya Dmitrievna could not help attracting Butler who was a young, vigorous, unmarried man, and he even had an idea that she was keen on him. But he thought it would be a shabby way to treat his simple, good-natured comrade and always behaved towards Marya Dmitrievna with the utmost simplicity and respect and it gladdened him that he did so. He was thinking of this just now.

His thoughts were disturbed by the drumming of many horses' hoofs on the dusty road ahead of him. It sounded like several horsemen galloping. He raised his head and saw at the end of the street a party of riders approaching at a walk. There were a couple of dozen Cossacks with two men riding at their head: one wore a white *cherkeska* and a tall *papakha* wound with a turban, the other was a dark, hook-nosed officer in the Russian service, dressed in a blue *cherkeska* with a lavish amount of silver on his clothing and weapons. The horseman in the turban rode a handsome palomino with a small head and beautiful eyes; the officer was mounted on a tall, rather showy Karabakh.[68] Butler, who was very keen on horses, appreciated at a glance the resilient power of the first rider's horse and stopped to find out who they were. The officer spoke to him.

'That house of commandant?' he asked, pointing with his whip at Ivan Matveevich's (Petrov's) house, and betraying by his accent and defective grammar his non-Russian origin.

'Yes, that's it,' said Butler. 'And who might that be?' he asked, going closer to the officer and with a glance indicating the man in the turban.

'That Hadji Murat. He come here and stay with commandant,' said the officer.

Butler knew about Hadji Murat and that he had surrendered to the Russians, but he had never expected to see him here, in this small fort.

Hadji Murat was looking at him in a friendly fashion.

'How do you do. *Koshkoldy*,' said Butler, using the Tatar greeting he had learnt.

'*Saubul*,' replied Hadji Murat, nodding. He rode across to Butler and offered his hand from which his whip hung on two fingers.

'Commandant?' he asked.

'No, the commandant is inside. I'll go and fetch him,' Butler said to the officer, going up the steps and pushing at the door.

But the 'front door', as Marya Dmitrievna called it, was locked. Butler knocked, but getting no reply went round by the back way. He called for his batman, but got no answer, and being unable to find either of the two batmen went into the kitchen. Marya Dmitrievna was there, with face flushed, her hair pinned up in a kerchief and sleeves rolled up over her plump, white arms. She was cutting pie cases from a rolled-out layer of dough as white as her arms.

'Where have the batmen got to?' asked Butler.

'Gone off drinking,' said Marya Dmitrievna. 'What is it you want?'

'I want the door opened. You've got a whole horde of mountain dwellers outside. Hadji Murat has come.'

340 'Go on, tell me another one,' said Marya Dmitrievna, smiling.

'It's not a joke. It's true. They are just outside.'

'What? Really?' said Marya Dmitrievna.

'Why should I want to make it up? Go and look – they are just outside.'

'Well, there's a thing!' said Marya Dmitrievna, rolling down her sleeves and feeling for the pins in her thick plait of hair. 'I'll go and wake up Ivan Matveevich, then!'

'No, I'll go. You, Bondarenko, go and open the door,' said Butler.

'That's all right by me,' said Marya Dmitrievna and returned to her work.

When he learned that Hadji Murat had arrived, Petrov, who had heard already that he was in Groznaya, was not in the least surprised. He sat up in bed, rolled a cigarette, lit it and began to get dressed, loudly coughing to clear his throat and grumbling at the high-ups who had sent 'that devil' to him. When he was dressed, he ordered his batman to bring his 'medicine', and the batman, knowing what he meant, brought him some vodka.

'You should never mix your drinks,' he growled, drinking the vodka and eating a piece of black bread with it. 'I was drinking *chikhir* last night and now I've got a thick head. All right, I'm ready,' he said finally and went into the parlour, where Butler had taken Hadji Murat and the escorting officer.

The officer handed Ivan Matveevich the orders from the commander of the Left Flank in which he was instructed to take charge of Hadji Murat and, while allowing him contact with the mountain dwellers through scouts, to ensure that he never left the fort except with an escort of Cossacks.

Ivan Matveevich read the paper, looked hard at Hadji Murat, and studied the paper again. After several times shifting his gaze from the paper to his visitor, he finally **341** fixed his eyes on Hadji Murat and said:

'*Yakshi, bek-yakshi.* Very well. Let him stay then. But you tell him that my orders are not to let him loose. And orders are orders. As to quarters, what do you think, Butler? We could put him in the office.'

Before Butler could reply, Marya Dmitrievna, who had come from the kitchen and was standing in the doorway, said to Ivan Matveevich:

'Why in the office? Let him stay here. We can give him the guest room and the store room. At least he'll be where you can keep an eye on him,' she said. She glanced at Hadji Murat, but meeting his eyes turned hurriedly away.

'Yes, I think Marya Dmitrievna is right,' said Butler.

'Go on, off with you!' said Ivan Matveevich, frowning. 'Womenfolk have no business here.'

Throughout this conversation Hadji Murat sat with his hand behind the handle of his dagger and a faintly disdainful smile on his lips. He said it mattered nothing where he lived. All he needed was what the *sardar* had granted – to have contact with the mountain dwellers, and he wished therefore that they be allowed access to him. Ivan Matveevich said that this would be done and asked Butler to look after their guests while something to eat was brought and the rooms made ready. He would go to the office to fill in the necessary papers and give the necessary instructions.

Hadji Murat's relations with these new acquaintances immediately became very clearly established. From their first meeting Hadji Murat felt nothing but repugnance and scorn for Ivan Matveevich and was always haughty in his treatment of him. He particularly liked Marya Dmitrievna, who cooked and served his food. He liked her simple manner, her particular, for him foreign, type of beauty, and the unconsciously conveyed attraction which she felt for him. He tried not to look at her, or to speak to her, but his eyes turned automatically towards her and followed her movements.

With Butler he struck up an immediate friendship and took pleasure in the long talks he had with him, asking Butler about his life and telling him of his own, passing on the news brought by the scouts about the situation of his family and even asking his advice as to what he should do.

The news brought by the scouts was not good. In the four days he had been at the fort they had come twice and on both occasions the news was bad.

19

Shortly after Hadji Murat's surrender to the Russians his family was taken to the village of Vedeno and kept there under guard waiting for Shamil to decide their fate. The women – Hadji Murat's old mother Patimat and his two wives – together with their five small children lived under guard in the house of Ibrahim Rashid, one of Shamil's captains; Yusuf, his eighteen-year-old son, was kept in a dungeon, a deep pit dug eight or nine feet into the ground, with four criminals who, like him, were awaiting Shamil's decision on their fate.

But no decision came, because Shamil was away campaigning against the Russians.

On 6 January 1852 Shamil returned home to Vedeno after a battle with the Russians in which, according to the Russians, he had been beaten and fled to Vedeno, but in which, according to the view of Shamil and all his *murids,* he had been victorious and put the Russians to flight. In this engagement – and it happened very rarely – he himself had fired his rifle and with drawn sword would have charged straight at the Russians if his escort of *murids* had not held him back. Two of them were killed at his side.

It was midday when Shamil arrived at his destination, surrounded by his party of *murids* showing off their horsemanship, firing rifles and pistols and chanting endlessly *'La ilaha illa allah'.*

All the people of Vedeno, which was a large village, were standing in the street and on the roofs of the houses to greet their master, and they too celebrated the event with musket and pistol fire. Shamil rode on a white Arab, which merrily sought to have its head as they neared home. The horse's trappings were extremely plain with no gold or silver ornament – a red leather bridle, finely made and grooved down the middle, metal bucket stirrups and a red saddle cloth showing from under the saddle. The Imam wore a fur coat overlaid with brown cloth, the black fur projecting at the collar and cuffs; it was drawn tight about his tall, slim frame by a black leather strap with a dagger attached to it. On his head he wore a tall, flat-topped *papakha* with a black tassel and white turban round it, the end of which hung below his neck. On his feet were green soft leather boots and his legs were covered with tight black leggings edged with plain lace.

The Imam wore nothing at all that glittered, no gold or silver, and his tall, erect, powerful figure in its plain clothes in the midst of the *murids* with their gold- and silver-ornamented dress and weapons, created on the people exactly the impression of grandeur which he desired and knew how to create. His pale face, framed by his trimmed red beard, with its small, constantly screwed-up eyes, wore a fixed expression as if made of stone. Passing through the village he felt thousands of eyes turned on him, but his own eyes looked at no one. The wives and children of Hadji Murat went on to the veranda with the other occupants of the house to watch the Imam's entry. Only Patimat, Hadji Murat's old mother, did not go, but remained sitting as she was on the floor of the house with her grey hair dishevelled and her long arms clasped round her thin knees, while she blinked her fiery black eyes and watched the logs burning down in the fireplace. She, like her son, had always hated Shamil, now more than ever, and had no wish to see him.

Hadji Murat's son also saw nothing of Shamil's triumphal entry. From his dark, fetid pit he could only hear the shots and chanting and he experienced such anguish as is only felt by young men, full of life, when deprived of their freedom. Sitting in the stinking pit and seeing only the same wretched, filthy, emaciated creatures he was confined with, who mostly hated one another, he was overcome by a passionate envy for people who had air and light and freedom and were at this moment prancing round their leader on dashing horses and shooting and chanting in chorus '*La ilaha illa allah*'.

After processing through the village Shamil rode into a large courtyard next to an inner one where he had his harem. Two armed Lezghians met Shamil at the opened gates of the first courtyard. The yard was full of people. There were people from distant parts here on their own account, there were petitioners, and there were those whom Shamil himself had summoned for judgement. When Shamil rode in everyone in the courtyard rose and respectfully greeted the Imam with their hands placed to their chests. Some knelt and remained kneeling while Shamil crossed the courtyard from the outer to the inner **345** gateway. Although Shamil recognized in the waiting crowd many disagreeable people and many tiresome petitioners who would be wanting his attention, he rode past them with the same stony expression on his face and went into the inner court where he dismounted alongside the veranda of his residence to the left of the gate.

The campaign had been a strain, mental rather than physical, for although he had proclaimed it a victory, Shamil knew that the campaign had been a failure, that many Chechen villages had been burnt and destroyed, and that the Chechens – a fickle and light-headed people – were wavering and some of them, nearest to the Russians, were already prepared to go over to them. It was all very difficult and measures would have to be taken, but for the moment Shamil did not want to do anything or think about anything. All he wanted was to relax and enjoy the soothing delights of family life provided by his favourite wife Aminet, a black-eyed, fleet-footed Kist girl[69] of eighteen.

But not only was it out of the question to see Aminet at this moment – though she was only on the other side of the fence which separated the women's apartments from the men's quarters in the inner courtyard (and Shamil had no doubt that even as he dismounted Aminet and his other wives would be watching through the fence) – not only could he not go to her, he could not even lie down on a feather mattress and recover from his fatigue. Before anything else he had to perform his midday devotions. He felt not the least inclination to do so, but it was necessary that he should, not only in his capacity as religious leader of the people, but also because to him personally it was as essential as his daily food. So he carried out the ritual washing and praying. At the end of the prayers he summoned those who were waiting.

The first to come in to him was his father-in-law and
346 teacher, Jemel-Edin, a tall fine-looking old man with grey hair, snowy white beard and a rubicund face. After a prayer to God, he began to question Shamil about the campaign and to recount what had happened in the mountains while he was away.

There were all manner of events to report – blood-feud killings, cattle-stealing, alleged breaches of the *Tarikat* – smoking tobacco, drinking wine, and Jemel-Edin also told Shamil that Hadji Murat had sent men to take his family over to the Russians, but that this was discovered and the family had been moved to Vedeno, where they were now under guard awaiting the Imam's decision. The old men were gathered in the adjoining guest room for the purpose of considering all these matters, and Jemel-Edin advised Shamil to dismiss them today since they had already waited three days for him.

Shamil took dinner in his own room, where it was brought by Zaidet, the senior of his wives, a sharp-nosed, dark, ill-favoured woman for whom he did not care. He then went into the guest room.

There were six men in Shamil's council – old men with white, grey and ginger beards. They wore tall *papakhas* with or without turbans, new jackets and *cherkeskas* with leather belts and daggers. They rose to greet him. Shamil was a head taller than any of them. They all, including Shamil, lifted their upturned hands and with closed eyes recited a prayer, then wiped their hands across their faces, drew them down over their beards and joined them. This done, they sat down, with Shamil sitting on a higher cushion in the middle, and began their deliberations of the business in hand.

The cases of those accused of crimes were decided according to the *Shariat*: two thieves were condemned to have a hand cut off, another to have his head cut off for murder, and three were pardoned. They moved on then to the main business – to consider what measures should be taken to prevent the Chechens going over to the Russians. In order to halt these defections Jemel-Edin had drawn up the following proclamation:

'May you have peace everlasting with Almighty God. I hear that the Russians show favours to you and call for your submission. Believe them not, do not submit, but be patient. For this you will be rewarded, if not in this life, then in the life to come. Remember what happened before when your weapons were taken from you. If then, in 1840,[70] God had not shown you the light, you would now be soldiers and carry bayonets instead of daggers, and your wives would not wear trousers and would be defiled. Judge the future by the past. It is better to die at war with the Russians than to live with the infidels. Be patient, and I shall come with the Koran and the sword to lead you against the Russians. For the present I strictly command

you to have neither intention nor even any thought of submitting to the Russians.'

Shamil approved the proclamation, signed it and
decreed that it should be despatched to all parts.

When this business was finished the question of Hadji
Murat was discussed. This was a very important matter
for Shamil. Although he did not care to admit it, he knew
that if Hadji Murat had been on his side, with his skill,
daring, and courage, what had now happened in Chechnya
would never have occurred. It would be good to settle his
quarrel with Hadji Murat and make use of him once again;
but if that could not be done, he must still ensure that he
did not aid the Russians. In either case, therefore, he must
send for him and, when he came, kill him. This could be
done either by sending a man to Tiflis to kill him there, or
by summoning him and putting an end to him here. The
348 only way to do that was to use Hadji Murat's family, above
all his son, whom, as Shamil knew, he adored. It was therefore necessary to work through his son.

When the councillors had talked it over, Shamil closed
his eyes and fell silent.

The councillors knew what this meant: Shamil was now
listening to the voice of the Prophet telling him what should
be done. After five minutes' solemn silence Shamil opened
his eyes, screwing them more tightly than before and said:

'Fetch me the son of Hadji Murat.'

'He is here,' said Jemel-Edin.

Indeed, Yusuf, thin, pale, ragged, and stinking, still handsome though in face and figure, and with the same fiery
black eyes as Patimat, his grandmother, was standing at the
gate of the outer courtyard waiting to be summoned.

Yusuf did not feel about Shamil as his father did. He did
not know all that had happened in the past, or if he knew, it
was only at second-hand, and he could not understand why
his father was so doggedly opposed to Shamil. Yusuf only

wanted to go on living the easy, rakish life that he, as son of the *naib,* had led in Khunzakh, and he could see no point in being at odds with Shamil. In defiant opposition to his father he greatly admired Shamil and regarded him with the fervent veneration that was generally felt for him in the mountains. He experienced a particular feeling of awe and reverence for the Imam now as he entered the guest room. He stopped at the door and was fixed by Shamil's screwed up eyes. He stood for a few moments, then went up to Shamil and kissed his large white hand with long fingers.

'You are the son of Hadji Murat?'

'Yes, Imam.'

'You know what he has done?'

'I know, Imam, and am sorry for it.'

'Do you know how to write?'

'I was studying to be a mullah.'

'Then write to your father and say that if he returns to 349 me now, before *Bairam,* I will pardon him and all will be as of old. But if he will not and remains with the Russians, then . . .' – Shamil frowned menacingly – 'I shall give your grandmother and mother to be used in the villages, and I shall cut off your head.'

Not a muscle twitched on Yusuf's face. He bowed his head to signify he had understood what Shamil said.

'Write that and give it to my messenger.'

Shamil was then silent and took a long look at Yusuf.

'Write that I have decided to spare you. I will not kill you but will have your eyes put out, the same as I do to all traitors. Go.'

Yusuf appeared to be calm while in the presence of Shamil, but when he was led out of the guest room he threw himself on his escort, snatched his dagger from its sheath and tried to kill himself. But he was seized by the arms, bound and taken back to the pit.

*

That evening when the evening prayers were over and dusk fell, Shamil put on a white fur topcoat and passed through the fence into the part of the courtyard where his wives lived. He went straight to Aminet's room. But Aminet was not there; she was with the older wives. Trying to keep out of sight, Shamil stood behind the door of her room to wait for her. But Aminet was angry with Shamil because he had given some silk to Zaidet and not to her. She saw him come out and go to look for her in her room and she deliberately did not return to her room. She stood a long time in Zaidet's doorway, laughing quietly as she watched the white figure go in and out of her room. It was nearly time for the midnight prayers when Shamil, after waiting in vain, went back to his own quarters.

20

Hadji Murat had been a week at the fort living in the house of Ivan Matveevich. Although Marya Dmitrievna had quarrelled with the shaggy-haired Khanefi (Hadji Murat had with him only two men: Khanefi and Eldar) and had several times ejected him from her kitchen – for which he nearly cut her throat – she evidently felt a particular respect and sympathetic concern for Hadji Murat. She no longer served him his dinner, a task she had passed on to Eldar, but she took every opportunity to see him and do anything she could to please him. She also took a very keen interest in the negotiations about his family; she knew how many wives he had, how many children and what ages they were, and each time a scout came she asked whom she could to discover how the negotiations were going.

In the course of this week Butler had become firm friends with Hadji Murat. Sometimes Hadji Murat would call on him in his room, at other times Butler would visit him. They sometimes conversed through an interpreter, otherwise they used their own resources – signs and, particularly, smiles. Hadji Murat had evidently taken a liking to Butler. This was clear from the way that Butler was treated by Eldar. Whenever Butler came into Hadji Murat's room Eldar greeted him, flashing his teeth in a cheerful grin, hastened to put cushions on his seat and helped him off with his sword if he was wearing it.

Butler also got on good terms with the shaggy-haired Khanefi, who was Hadji Murat's sworn brother. Khanefi knew many songs of the mountains and sang them well. To please Butler Hadji Murat would summon Khanefi and tell him to sing, mentioning the songs he thought good.

Khanefi had a high tenor voice and sang with great clarity and expression. There was one song Hadji Murat was particularly fond of and Butler was much struck by its solemn, sad refrain. Butler asked the interpreter to tell him the words in Russian and wrote it down.

The song was about vengeance – the vengeance that Khanefi and Hadji Murat had pledged to each other.

It went as follows:

'The earth will dry on my grave, and you, my own mother, will forget me. Grave grass will grow over the graveyard and will deaden your grief, my old father. The tears will dry in my sister's eyes and sorrow will fly from her heart.

'But you, my elder brother, will not forget me till you have avenged my death. You, my second brother, will not forget me till you lie by my side.

'Bullet, you are hot and the bearer of death, but were you not my faithful slave? Black earth, you will cover me, but did I not trample you beneath my horse's hoofs? Death, you are cold, but I was your master. The earth shall take my body, and heaven my soul.'

Hadji Murat always listened to this song with his eyes closed, and, as its last lingering note faded away, he would say in Russian:

'Good song, wise song.'

With the arrival of Hadji Murat and his close acquaintance with him and his *murids,* Butler was even more captivated by the poetry of the peculiar, vigorous life led by the mountain dwellers. He got himself a jacket, *cherkeska* and leggings, and he felt he was a mountain dweller too, living the same life as these people.

On the day Hadji Murat was to leave Ivan Matveevich gathered a few of the officers to see him off. The officers were sitting at two tables, one for tea, dispensed by Marya Dmitrievna, and the other laid with vodka, *chikhir* and hors d'oeuvre, when Hadji Murat, armed and dressed for the road, came limping with quick, soft steps into the room.

Everyone rose and one after the other shook hands with him. Ivan Matveevich invited him to sit on the ottoman, but Hadji Murat thanked him and sat on a chair by the window. He was clearly not in the least put out by the silence which fell when he came in. He closely studied the faces of those present, then fixed his eyes indifferently on the table with the samovar and food on it. Petrokovsky, one of the officers more spirited than the rest, who had not seen Hadji Murat before, asked him through the interpreter if he had liked Tiflis.

'*Aya*,' said Hadji Murat.

'He says he does,' the interpreter answered.

'What did he like in particular?'

Hadji Murat made some reply.

'He liked the theatre best.'

'Did he enjoy the commander-in-chief's ball?'

Hadji Murat frowned.

'Every people has its own customs. Our women do not wear such clothes,' he said, glancing at Marya Dmitrievna.

'What didn't he like?'

'We have a saying,' Hadji Murat said to the interpreter. 'A dog asked a donkey to eat with him and gave him meat, the donkey asked the dog and gave him hay: they both went hungry.' He smiled. 'Every people finds its own ways good.'

The conversation stopped there. The officers began drinking tea or eating. Hadji Murat took the glass of tea he was offered and put it in front of him.

'Now, would you like some cream? Perhaps a bun?' asked Marya Dmitrievna, serving him.

Hadji Murat inclined his head.

'Well, goodbye then,' said Butler, touching him on the knee. 'When shall we meet again?'

353

'Goodbye, goodbye,' Hadji Murat said in Russian, smiling. '*Kunak* Bulur. I your good *kunak*. Now time – off we go,' he said, tossing his head as if to show the direction he had to go.

Eldar appeared in the doorway with something large and white over his shoulder and a sword in his hand. Hadji Murat beckoned him and Eldar with his long strides came over and gave him the white cloak and the sword. Hadji Murat took the cloak and, dropping it over his arm, gave it to Marya Dmitrievna, saying something for the interpreter to translate.

'He says: you admired the cloak – take it,' said the interpreter.

'But what for?' said Marya Dmitrievna, blushing.

'Must do. *Adat tak*, it is the custom,' said Hadji Murat.

'Well, thank you,' said Marya Dmitrievna, taking the cloak. 'God grant you may rescue your son. He is a fine boy – *ulan yakshi*,' she added. 'Tell him I hope he can rescue his family.'

Hadji Murat looked at Marya Dmitrievna and nodded in approval. Then he took the sword from Eldar and gave it to Ivan Matveevich. Ivan Matveevich took it and said to the interpreter:

'Tell him he must take my brown gelding. That is all I can give in return.'

Hadji Murat waved his hand in front of his face to show that he did not want anything and would not accept it. Then he pointed first to the mountains, then to his heart, and went to the door. Everyone followed. Some of the officers, who remained inside, drew the sword and after inspecting the blade decided it was a genuine *gurda*.[71]

Butler accompanied Hadji Murat on to the steps outside. But just then something totally unexpected happened which might have cost Hadji Murat his life but for his quick reactions, determination and skill.

The villagers of Tash-Kichu, a Kumyk village, held Hadji Murat in high esteem and on many occasions had come to the fort just to have a look at the celebrated *naib*. Three days before Hadji Murat's departure they sent messengers inviting him to attend their mosque on Friday. However, the Kumyk princes who resided at Tash-Kichu hated Hadji Murat and had a blood feud with him, and when they heard of the villagers' invitation they would not allow him into the mosque. The people were roused by this and there was a fight between the villagers and the princes' supporters. The Russian authorities restored peace among the mountain dwellers and sent a message to Hadji Murat instructing him not to attend the mosque. Hadji Murat did not go and everybody thought the matter was ended.

But at the very moment of Hadji Murat's departure, when he went out on to the steps and the horses stood waiting outside, one of the Kumyk princes, Arslan-Khan, **355** who was known to Butler and Ivan Matveevich, rode up to the house.

Seeing Hadji Murat he drew his pistol from his belt and aimed it at him. But before Arslan-Khan could fire, Hadji Murat, despite his lameness, sprang like a cat from the steps towards him. Arslan-Khan fired and missed. Hadji Murat meanwhile had run up to him, and with one hand seized his horse's bridle and with the other pulled out his dagger, shouting something in Tatar.

Butler and Eldar rushed up to the enemies at the same time and seized them by the arms. Hearing the shot, Ivan Matveevich also appeared.

'What do you mean by this, Arslan – creating mischief in my house!' he said, on discovering what had happened. 'It's no way to behave. Have it out with each other by all means, but keep it "out" and don't go slaughtering people in my house.'

Arslan-Khan, a tiny man with a black moustache, got

down from his horse, pale and shaking, and with a vicious look at Hadji Murat went off with Ivan Matveevich into the parlour. Hadji Murat went back to the horses, breathing heavily and smiling.

'Why did he want to kill you?' Butler asked him through the interpreter.

The interpreter translated Hadji Murat's reply: 'He says that it is our law. Arslan has blood to avenge on him, that is why he wanted to kill him.'

'And what if he catches up with him on his journey?' asked Butler.

Hadji Murat smiled.

'What of it? If he kills me, it will be the will of Allah. Well, goodbye,' he said once more in Russian, and grasping his horse by the withers, looked round at those seeing him off and affectionately encountered Marya Dmitrievna's eye.

356 'Goodbye, good lady,' he said to her. 'Thank you.'

'May God only grant you can get your family free,' repeated Marya Dmitrievna.

Hadji Murat did not understand what she said, but he understood her concern for him and nodded to her.

'Be sure you don't forget your *kunak*,' said Butler.

'Tell him I am his true friend and will never forget him,' Hadji Murat replied through the interpreter. Then, despite his crooked leg, as soon as his foot touched the stirrup he swung his body quickly and effortlessly on to the high saddle and, straightening his sword and with a customary hand fingering his pistol, he rode off from Ivan Matveevich's house with that particular proud, warlike air the mountain dwellers have when on horseback. Khanefi and Eldar also mounted and, after bidding friendly farewells to their hosts and the officers, set off at a trot after their *murshid*.

As always happens, a discussion started about the person who had left.

'He's a great fellow!'

'It was just like a wolf the way he went for Arslan-Khan. There was a completely different look on his face.'

'He will do us down,' said Petrokovsky. 'He must be a right rogue.'

'Then I wish there were more Russian rogues like him,' interposed Marya Dmitrievna with sudden annoyance. 'He was with us for a week and he couldn't have been nicer,' she said. 'Polite and wise and fair-minded he was.'

'How did you find all that out?'

'I just did.'

'Fallen for him, have you?' said Ivan Matveevich, coming in. 'It's a fact.'

'All right, so I've fallen for him. What's that to you? I just don't see why you speak ill of somebody when he is a good man. He may be a Tatar, but he is a good man.'

'Quite right, Marya Dmitrievna,' said Butler. 'Good for **357** you to stand up for him!'

21

The life of those living in the advanced fortresses on the Chechnya Line went on as before. In the interval there had been two alarms; footsoldiers came running out, Cossacks and militia galloped in pursuit, but on neither occasion were they able to apprehend the mountain dwellers. They got away, and on one occasion at Vozdvizhenskaya drove off eight Cossack horses which were being watered and killed a Cossack. There had been no Russian raids since the one which had destroyed the village. But a major expedition into Greater Chechnya was expected following the appointment of Prince Baryatinsky[72] as commander of the Left Flank.

On arriving in Groznaya, being now in command of the whole Left Flank, Prince Baryatinsky (a friend of the Crown Prince and former commander of the Kabarda Regiment) at once assembled a force to continue the fulfilment of the Emperor's instructions which Chernyshev had communicated to Vorontsov. The column set out from Vozdvizhenskaya, where it had assembled, and took up position on the road to Kurinskoe. The troops camped there and engaged in forest clearing.

Young Vorontsov lived in a magnificent fabric tent; his wife, Marya Vasilevna, would drive out to the camp and often stayed overnight. Baryatinsky's relations with Marya Vasilevna were a matter of common knowledge, and she was coarsely abused by the officers unconnected with the court and by the ordinary soldiers, who because of her presence in the camp were sent out on night picket duty. It was usual for the mountain dwellers to bring up their cannon and fire into the camp. The shots they fired mostly missed their target so as a rule no action was taken against them. But to prevent the mountain dwellers bringing up their guns and frightening Marya Vasilevna pickets were sent out. To go on picket every night to save a lady from being frightened was an insult and an offence, and the soldiers and the officers not received in the best society had some choice names for Marya Vasilevna.

Butler took leave from the fort and paid a visit to the column in order to see old comrades from the Corps of Pages and his regiment, now serving in the Kura Regiment or as *aides-de-camp* or adjutants on the staff. He found it all very enjoyable from the start. He stayed in Poltoratsky's tent and there found a number of people he knew who were delighted to see him. He also went to see Vorontsov, whom he knew slightly, having once served in the same regiment with him. Vorontsov made him very welcome. He introduced him to Prince Baryatinsky and invited him 359 to the farewell dinner he was giving to General Kozlovsky, Baryatinsky's predecessor as commander of the Left Flank.

The dinner was splendid. Six tents had been brought up and pitched together in a row. Their whole length was taken up by a table laid with cutlery, glasses and bottles. It was all reminiscent of the guards officers' life in St Petersburg. They sat down to table at two o'clock. In the centre of the table sat Kozlovsky on one side, and Baryatinsky on the other. Vorontsov sat on Kozlovsky's right, his wife on his left. The whole length of the table on either side was filled by officers of the Kabarda and Kura Regiments. Butler sat by Poltoratsky and they chatted gaily and drank with the officers sitting by them. When they got to the main course and the orderlies began filling the glasses with champagne, Poltoratsky – with genuine apprehension and regret – said to Butler.

'Old "um-er" is going to make a fool of himself.'

'What do you mean?'

'Why, he's got to make a speech. And how can he?'

'Yes, old boy, it's a bit different from capturing barricades under fire. And on top of that he's got the lady next to him and all these court fellows. It really is pitiful to watch,' said the officers one to another.

But the solemn moment arrived. Baryatinsky rose and, lifting his glass, addressed a short speech to Kozlovsky. When he had finished, Kozlovsky got up and in a reasonably firm voice began to speak:

'By his Imperial Majesty's command I am leaving you, gentlemen,' he said. 'We are parting, but always consider me – um-er – present with you . . . You, gentlemen, know the truth of the – um-er – saying that you cannot soldier on your own. And so all the rewards that have come to me in my – um-er – service, everything that has been – um-er – bestowed upon me, the generous tokens of His Majesty's favour, my – um-er – position, and my – um-er – good name, all this, absolutely everything' – his voice quivered – 'I – um-er – owe to you and to you alone, my dear friends.' And his wrinkled face wrinkled still more, he gave a sob, and tears came to his eyes. 'I give you my – um-er – sincere and heartfelt thanks . . .'

Kozlovsky could not go on and stood to embrace the officers who came up to him. Everyone was very touched. The princess covered her face with her handkerchief. Prince Vorontsov pulled a face and blinked hard. Many of the officers, too, were moved to tears. And Butler, who did not know Kozlovsky well, was also unable to restrain himself. He found it all exceptionally agreeable. After this there were toasts to Baryatinsky, to Vorontsov, to the officers, to the other ranks, and finally the guests left, intoxicated by wine and the rapturous martial sentiment to which they were anyway specially inclined.

The weather was superb – sunny and calm, and the air fresh and invigorating. On every side was the sound of

campfires crackling and men singing. Everyone seemed
to be celebrating. Butler went to call on Poltoratsky in the
most happy and serene frame of mind. Some of the officers
were gathered there, a card table had been set up and an
aide-de-camp had gone banker with a hundred roubles.
Twice Butler left the tent holding on to the purse in
the pocket of his trousers, but in the end he succumbed
and, despite the vow he had made to his brothers and to
himself, began playing against the bank.

Before an hour was past Butler, flushed and sweating,
covered with chalk, was sitting with his elbows on the
table, writing down his bets beneath the crumpled cards.
He had lost so much that he was now afraid of counting
what was scored against him. He knew without reckoning
that if he used all the pay he could get in advance and whatever his horse would fetch he could still not make up the
whole of what he owed to this unknown *aide-de-camp*. He 361
would have gone on playing, but the *aide-de-camp* put
down the cards with his clean white hands and began tot-
ting up the column of chalk entries under Butler's name.
Butler with embarrassment apologized that he was unable
to pay all his losses immediately and said he would send
the money on; as he said it he saw they were all sorry for
him and everyone, even Poltoratsky, avoided his gaze. It
was his last evening. All he had had to do was to avoid
gambling and go to Vorontsov's where he had been invited.
Everything would have been fine, he thought. But far from
being fine, everything now was disastrous.

After saying goodbye to his comrades and friends, he
left for home and on arriving went straight to bed and slept
for eighteen hours at a stretch, as people usually do after
losing heavily. Marya Dmitrievna could tell he had lost
everything by his request for fifty copeks to tip his Cossack escort, by his melancholy look and terse replies, and
she set on Ivan Matveevich for giving him leave.

It was after eleven when Butler woke on the following day and when he recalled the situation he was in he would have liked to sink back into the oblivion from which he had just emerged, but this could not be done. He had to take steps to repay the four hundred and seventy roubles which he owed to this total stranger. One step was to write a letter to his brother, repenting for his misdeed and begging him to send for the last time five hundred roubles on account of his share in the mill which they still owned jointly. Then he wrote to a skinflint relative begging her to let him have five hundred roubles, too, at whatever interest she wanted. Then he went to see Ivan Matveevich and knowing that he, or rather Marya Dmitrievna, had money, asked for a loan of five hundred roubles.

'I'd be glad to: I'd let you have it like a shot, but Masha wouldn't part with it. These damned womenfolk are that tight-fisted. But you've got to get off the hook somehow. What about that sutler, hasn't he got any money?'

But there was no point even trying to borrow from the sutler, so Butler's only source of salvation was his brother or the skinflint relative.

22

Having failed to achieve his purpose in Chechnya, Hadji Murat returned to Tiflis. He went daily to see Vorontsov, and when Vorontsov received him he begged him to collect the mountain dwellers held captive and exchange them for his family. He repeated again that unless this were done he was tied and could not, as he wished, serve the Russians and destroy Shamil. Vorontsov promised in general terms to do what he could, but deferred giving a decision until General Argutinsky[73] arrived in Tiflis and he could discuss it with him. Hadji Murat then asked Vorontsov's permission to go for a time to Nukha,[74] a small town in Transcaucasia where he thought it would be easier to conduct negotiations about his family with Shamil and his supporters. Besides that, Nukha was a Muslim town with a mosque and it would be easier for him there to perform the prayers required by Muslim law. Vorontsov wrote to St Petersburg about this, and meanwhile allowed Hadji Murat to go to Nukha.

The story of Hadji Murat was regarded by Vorontsov, by the authorities in St Petersburg and by the majority of Russians who knew of it either as a lucky turn in the course of the war in the Caucasus or simply as an interesting episode. But for Hadji Murat, especially more recently, it was a drastic turning point in his life. He had fled from the mountains partly to save his life and partly because of his hatred for Shamil. Despite all difficulties, he had succeeded in escaping, and initially he had been delighted with his success and actually considered his plans for attacking Shamil. But getting his family out, which he had supposed would be easy, had proved harder than he thought. Shamil had seized his family and now held them captive, promising to despatch the women into the villages and to kill or blind his son. Now Hadji Murat was going to Nukha to try with the help of his supporters in Daghestan by guile or force to rescue his family from Shamil. The last scout to call on him at Nukha told him that the Avars who were loyal to him were going to carry off his family and bring them over to the Russians, but as they were short of men ready to undertake this they were reluctant to attempt it in Vedeno where the family was held and would only do it if they were moved from Vedeno to some other place. They would then take action while they were being moved. Hadji Murat ordered him to tell his friends that he would give three thousand roubles for the release of his family.

At Nukha Hadji Murat was allotted a small house with 364 five rooms not far from the mosque and the khan's palace. Living in the same house were the officers and interpreter attached to him and his *nukers*. Hadji Murat spent his time waiting for and receiving the scouts who came in from the mountains and in going for the rides he was allowed to take in the neighbourhood of Nukha.

On 8 April when he returned from riding Hadji Murat learned that in his absence an official had arrived from Tiflis. Despite his anxiety to find out what news the official brought him, Hadji Murat did not go at once to the room where the official and the local commissioner were waiting, but went first to his own room to say his midday prayers. After he had prayed, he went into the other room which served him as a sitting-room and reception room. The official from Tiflis, a chubby state councillor called Kirillov, conveyed to him that Vorontsov wished him to be in Tiflis by the 12th for a meeting with Argutinsky.

'*Yakshi*,' said Hadji Murat sharply.

He did not take to this official Kirillov.

'Have you brought the money?'

'Yes, I have it,' said Kirillov.

'It is for two weeks now,' said Hadji Murat, holding up ten fingers then four more. 'Give it to me.'

'You will have it directly,' said the official, getting a purse from his travelling bag. 'What does he want money for?' he said to the commissioner in Russian, presuming that Hadji Murat would not understand. But Hadji Murat did understand and looked angrily at Kirillov. As he was taking out the money Kirillov, who wanted to strike up some conversation with Hadji Murat in order to have something to report to Vorontsov on his return, asked him through the interpreter if he found life tedious in Nukha. Hadji Murat gave a scornful sideways glance at this fat little man in civilian clothes who carried no weapons, and made no answer. The interpreter repeated the question.

'Tell him I have nothing to say to him. Let him just give me the money.'

With this, Hadji Murat again sat down at the table and prepared to count the money.

When Kirillov had produced the gold ten-rouble pieces and laid out seven piles each of ten coins (Hadji Murat received fifty roubles in gold per day), he pushed them across to Hadji Murat. Hadji Murat dropped the coins into the sleeve of his *cherkeska,* rose and, as he left the room, quite unexpectedly rapped the state councillor on the top of his bald head. The state councillor leapt to his feet and commanded the interpreter to say that he had better not treat him like that because he was equivalent in rank to a colonel. The commissioner agreed. Hadji Murat merely nodded to indicate that he knew that and left the room.

'What can you do with him?' said the commissioner. 'He will stick his dagger in you, and that's that. There's no coming to terms with these devils. And he's getting his blood up, I can see.'

As soon as dusk fell two scouts, hooded to the eyes, came in from the mountains. The commissioner took them into Hadji Murat's quarters. One of the scouts was a dark, portly tribesman from the hills, the other a skinny old man. For Hadji Murat the news they brought was cheerless. Those of his friends who had undertaken to rescue his family were now backing out completely for fear of Shamil, who threatened the most horrifying deaths to any who helped Hadji Murat. Having heard their account, Hadji Murat put his elbows on his crossed legs, bowed his head (he was wearing his *papakha*) and for a long time was silent. He was thinking, thinking positively. He knew that he was thinking now for the last time, that he must reach a decision. Hadji Murat raised his head and, taking two gold pieces, gave one to each of the scouts.

'Go now.'

'What will be the answer?'

'The answer will be as God wills. Go.'

The scouts got up and left. Hadji Murat remained sitting on the rug, his elbows on his knees. He sat there for a long time.

'What should I do? Trust Shamil and go back to him? He is a fox and would play me false. And even if he did not, I could still not submit to this ginger-haired double-dealer. I could not because, now that I have been with the Russians, he will never trust me again,' thought Hadji Murat.

And he recalled the tale told in the hills about the falcon which was caught, lived among people and then returned to his home in the mountains. The falcon returned wearing jesses on his legs and there were bells still on them. And the falcons spurned him. 'Fly back to the place where they put silver bells on you,' they said. 'We have no bells, nor do we have jesses.' The falcon did not want to leave his homeland and stayed. But the other falcons would not have him and tore him to death.

Just as they will tear me to death, thought Hadji Murat.

'Should I stay here? Win the Caucasus for the Russian tsar, gain fame and wealth and titles?

'Yes, I could do that,' he thought, recalling his meetings with Vorontsov and the old prince's flattering words.

'But I have to decide now, or he will destroy my family.'

All night Hadji Murat was awake, thinking.

23

Halfway through the night he had made up his mind. He decided that he must flee to the mountains and with the Avars who were loyal to him force his way into Vedeno and either free his family or die in the attempt. Whether or not to bring his family back to the Russians or flee to Khunzakh with them and fight Shamil he did not decide. He knew only that he must now get away from the Russians and into the mountains. And he began at once to put this decision into effect. He took his black quilted jacket from beneath the cushion and went to his *nukers'* quarters. They lived across the hall. As soon as he stepped out into the hall, the door of which was open, he was enveloped by the dewy freshness of the moonlit night and his ears were filled by the whistling and warbling of nightingales in the garden by the house.

Hadji Murat crossed the hall and opened the door of his *nukers'* room. There was no light in the room, only the new moon in its first quarter shining through the windows. A table and two chairs stood to the side and all four *nukers* lay on rugs and cloaks spread on the floor. Khanefi was sleeping outside with the horses. Gamzalo, hearing the door creak, raised himself, looked round and, seeing it was Hadji Murat, lay down again. Eldar, however, who lay next to him sprang up and began to put on his jacket, expecting some command. Kurban and Khan-Mahoma slept on. Hadji Murat put his jacket on the table and there was the knock of something hard as he did so: the gold pieces sewn in the lining.

'Sew these in as well,' said Hadji Murat, handing Eldar the gold pieces he had received that day.

Eldar took the money and, going into the light, at once got a knife from beneath his dagger and began cutting open the lining of the jacket. Gamzalo half rose and sat with crossed legs.

'Gamzalo, tell the men to check their guns and pistols and prepare some cartridges. Tomorrow we shall travel far,' said Hadji Murat.

'There is powder and bullets. All will be ready,' said Gamzalo and he growled some incomprehensible remark.

Gamzalo knew why Hadji Murat was ordering them to get their guns loaded. Right from the start he had had only one desire, which as time went on had grown ever stronger: to kill and cut down as many of the Russian dogs as he could and escape to the mountains. He now saw that Hadji Murat wanted this too, and he was content.

When Hadji Murat had gone, Gamzalo roused his companions and all four spent the night looking over their rifles and pistols, checking the touch-holes and flints, replacing poor ones, priming the pans with fresh powder, filling their cartridge pockets with measured charges of powder and bullets wrapped in oiled rags, sharpening their swords and daggers and greasing the blades with lard.

Near daybreak Hadji Murat again went into the hall to fetch water to wash before praying. The singing of the nightingales as they greeted the dawn was louder and more sustained than in the night. From the *nukers'* room came the even sound of steel grating and shrilling on stone as a dagger was sharpened. Hadji Murat ladled some water from the tub and had reached his own door when he heard another sound coming from the *murids'* room besides that of sharpening: it was the thin voice of Khanefi singing a song Hadji Murat knew. Hadji Murat stopped and listened.

The song told how the *djigit* Hamzad and his men drove off a herd of white horses from the Russian side, and how later across the Terek the Russian prince came on him and surrounded him with a great army as thick as a forest. The song went on to tell how Hamzad slaughtered the horses and with his men held fast behind this bloody rampart of dead horses and fought the Russians as long as there were bullets in their guns and daggers at their belts and blood still flowed in their veins. But before dying Hamzad saw some birds in the sky and cried out to them: 'You birds of the air, fly to our homes and tell our sisters, our mothers and fair maidens that we died for the *Ghazavat*. Tell them our bodies shall lie in no grave, our bones will be carried off and gnawed by ravening wolves and black crows will pick out our eyes.'

With these words, sung to a doleful refrain, the song ended, to be followed at once by the cheerful voice of the merry Khan-Mahoma who, as the song finished, bawled *'La ilaha illa allah'* and let out a piercing yell. Then all was quiet and again the only sound was the chugging and singing of the nightingales in the garden and, through the door, the even grating and occasional shrilling note of steel slipping rapidly over stone.

Hadji Murat was so lost in thought that he did not notice he was tipping the jug and spilling water over himself. He shook his head reprovingly and went into his room.

When he had finished his morning prayers, Hadji Murat checked his weapons and sat on his bed. There was nothing else to do. To ride out he had to ask permission from the commissioner. It was still dark outside and the commissioner was still asleep.

Khanefi's song reminded Hadji Murat of another song, which his mother had made up. It was about an actual event – something that had happened just after he was born, but which he had heard from his mother.

The song was this:

'Your damask blade slashed open my white breast, but I pressed to it my darling boy, and washed him in my hot blood, and the wound healed without help of herbs and roots. I did not fear death, no more will my boy-*djigit*.'

The words of the song were addressed to Hadji Murat's father. The point of it was that when Hadji Murat was born the khanoum also gave birth to a son (Umma-Khan, her second son) and sent for Hadji Murat's mother to be his wet nurse as she had been for the khanoum's elder son Abu-nuntsal. But Patimat had not wanted to leave her son and refused to go. Hadji Murat's father got angry and ordered her to. When she still refused he stabbed her with his dagger and would have killed her if she had not been taken away. So, after all, she did not give up her son but raised him, and made up this song about what had happened.

Hadji Murat remembered his mother singing it to him as she put him to bed alongside her, under the fur topcoat on the roof of their house, and he asked her to show him her side where the scar was. He could see his mother just as she was – not all wrinkled and grey with missing teeth as when he left her now, but young and beautiful and strong, so strong that even when he was five or six and heavy she carried him in a basket on her back to see his grandfather over the mountains.

And he remembered his grandfather with his wrinkled face and small grey beard. He was a silversmith and Hadji Murat remembered him engraving the silver with his sinewy hands and making him say his prayers. He remembered the fountain at the bottom of the hill where he went with his mother to fetch water, holding on to her trousers. He remembered the skinny dog that used to lick his face, and especially the smell and taste of smoke and sour milk when he followed his mother into the barn where she milked the cow and warmed the milk. He remembered the first time his mother shaved his head and how surprised he had been to see his little round head all blue in the shining copper basin that hung on the wall.

And remembering his childhood, he remembered too his own beloved son Yusuf, whose head he himself had shaved for the first time. Now Yusuf was a handsome young *djigit*. He remembered him as he last saw him. It was on the day he left Tselmes. His son brought his horse for him and asked if he could ride out and see him off. He was ready dressed and armed and holding his own horse by the bridle. Yusuf's young, ruddy, handsome face and everything about his tall slender figure (he was taller than his father) had seemed the very expression of youthful courage and the joy of living. His shoulders, broad for one so young, his very wide youthful hips and long slender body, his long powerful arms, and the strength, suppleness and dexterity of all his movements were a constant joy to his father and Hadji Murat always regarded his son with admiration.

'You had better stay,' Hadji Murat had said. 'You are the
372 only one at home now. Take care of your mother and grandmother.'

And Hadji Murat remembered the look of youthful spirit and pride with which Yusuf, pleased and blushing, had replied that, as long as he lived, no one would harm his mother or grandmother. Yusuf had then, after all, mounted and gone with his father as far as the stream. There he turned back, and since that time Hadji Murat had not seen his wife, mother or son.

And this was the son whose eyes Shamil was going to put out. Of what would happen to his wife he preferred not to think.

Hadji Murat was so agitated by these thoughts that he could not sit still any longer. He jumped up and limped quickly to the door. He opened it and called Eldar. The sun was not yet up, but it was fully light. The nightingales still sang.

'Go and tell the commissioner I want to go riding, and get the horses saddled,' he said.

24

Butler's only consolation at this time was the romance of military life, to which he surrendered himself not only when on duty but also in his private life. Dressed in Circassian costume, he performed the riding tricks of the natives and with Bogdanovich had twice gone out and lain in ambush, though on neither occasion did they catch or kill anyone. These daring deeds and friendship with Bogdanovich, who was well known for his bravery, seemed to Butler a pleasant and important part of life. He had paid off his debt by borrowing the money from a Jew at an enormous rate of interest – which meant that he had simply deferred settling his still unresolved situation. He tried not to think about his situation and, as well as in military romancing, he also sought oblivion in wine. He was drinking more and more heavily and every day advanced his moral decay. He was no longer the handsome Joseph where Marya Dmitrievna was concerned, on the contrary he made coarse advances to her, and, much to his surprise, had received a resolute rebuff which put him thoroughly to shame.

At the end of April a column arrived at the fort under orders from Baryatinsky to make a new advance through all those parts of Chechnya which were considered impassable. There were two companies of the Kabarda Regiment and, according to established custom in the Caucasus, they were received as the guests of the units stationed at Kurinskoe. The soldiers were taken off to the different barracks and were not only given supper of beef and millet porridge but also served with vodka. The officers took up quarters with the local officers, who, as was customary, entertained their visitors.

373

The party ended with drinking and singing. Ivan Matveevich, who was very drunk and no longer red, but pale
and grey in the face, sat astride a chair cutting down imagin-
ary enemies with his drawn sword; he was swearing,
laughing, embracing people and dancing to his favourite
song, 'In years gone by Shamil rose up, Ho-ro-ro, Shamil
rose up'.

Butler was also present. In this, too, he tried to see the
romance of military life, but deep down he felt sorry for
Ivan Matveevich, though there was no way of stopping
him. And Butler, feeling slightly drunk, quietly left and
set off home.

A full moon was shining on the white houses and on
the stones in the road. It was so light you could see every
small stone, every piece of straw and dung on the road. As
he approached the house Butler met Marya Dmitrievna
374 wearing a shawl over her head and shoulders. After the
rebuff she had given him Butler had rather shamefacedly
avoided her. But now in the moonlight and under the influence of the wine he had drunk Butler was glad to meet her
and tried again to make up to her.

'Where are you going?' he asked.

'To see what the old man is up to,' she answered amic-
ably. She had been quite sincere and positive in her rejection
of Butler's advances, but she was displeased that he had
been avoiding her of late.

'What's the point of going after him? He'll come back.'

'But will he?'

'If he doesn't, they'll carry him back.'

'That's just it, and it really isn't good enough,' said
Marya Dmitrievna. 'You think I shouldn't go then?'

'No, I shouldn't. We had best go home.'

Marya Dmitrievna turned back and began walking to
the house with Butler. The moon was so bright that around
their shadows moving along the roadside was a moving

halo of light. Butler watched this halo round his head and wanted to tell Marya Dmitrievna that he found her as attractive as ever, but did not know how to begin. She waited for him to speak. Walking thus in silence they had almost reached the house when round the corner appeared some horsemen. It was an officer and escort.

'Who on earth is that?' said Marya Dmitrievna, stepping to the side. The moon was behind the officer and it was only when he was practically level with them that Marya Dmitrievna saw who it was. The officer was Kamenev, who served at one time with Ivan Matveevich and so was known to Marya Dmitrievna.

'Peter Nikolaevich,' she said. 'Is that you?'

'In person,' said Kamenev. 'Ah, Butler! How are things? Not asleep yet? Walking out with Marya Dmitrievna, are you? You look out or you'll catch it from Ivan Matveevich. Where is he?'

'You can hear him,' said Marya Dmitrievna, pointing to where there was the sound of singing and a bass drum. 'They're having a binge.'

'Your chaps, is it?'

'No. A column is in from Khasav-Yurt and they're giving them a party.'

'Ah, a good thing. I'll get to it myself. I only want to see him for a minute.'

'Is something up?' asked Butler.

'Just a small matter.'

'Good or bad?'

'Depends who for. It's good for us, but tough on others.' And Kamenev laughed.

The couple walking and Kamenev had meanwhile reached Ivan Matveevich's house.

Kamenev called one of the Cossacks:

'Chikhirev! Here!'

A Don Cossack moved forward from the rest and came

up to them. He was in the ordinary Don Cossack uniform, wearing knee-boots and greatcoat, and had saddlebags slung at the back of his saddle.

'Get it out,' said Kamenev, dismounting.

The Cossack also got off his horse and from one of the saddlebags drew out a sack with something in it. Kamenev took the sack from the Cossack and put his hand in it.

'Shall I show you the latest, then? You won't be frightened?' he said, turning to Marya Dmitrievna.

'What is there to be afraid of?' said Marya Dmitrievna.

'There you are then,' said Kamenev and he pulled out a man's head and held it up in the moonlight. 'Do you recognize him?'

It was a shaven head, with prominent bulges of the skull over the eyes, trimmed black beard and clipped moustache; one eye was open, the other half-closed; the shaven skull was split and hacked about and the nose covered with black clotted blood. The neck was wrapped in a bloody towel. Despite all the wounds on the head, there was in the set of the now blue lips a childish, good-natured expression.

Marya Dmitrievna took one look and without a word turned and went quickly into the house.

Butler could not take his eyes off the terrible head. It was the head of that same Hadji Murat with whom he had recently spent his evenings having such friendly chats.

'How did it happen? Who killed him? Where?' he asked.

'He tried to make a break for it and they caught him,' said Kamenev, and handing the head back to the Cossack he went into the house with Butler.

'He died like a real man,' said Kamenev.

'But how did it all happen?'

'Hang on a minute. When Ivan Matveevich comes I'll give you all the details. That's what I've been sent for. I have got to go round all the forts and villages showing them.'

Ivan Matveevich had been sent for and came back to the house drunk, with two other officers also much the worse for drink, and began embracing Kamenev.

'I have come to see you,' said Kamenev. 'I have brought you the head of Hadji Murat.'

'Go on with you! Has he been killed?'

'Yes, he tried to escape.'

'I always said he would do us down. Where is it then? His head – let's see it.'

The Cossack was called and came in with the sack containing the head. The head was taken out, and for a long time Ivan Matveevich gazed at it with his drunken eyes.

'He was a fine fellow just the same,' he said. 'Let me kiss him.'

'He was a daredevil chap, that's a fact,' said one of the officers.

When they had all inspected the head they gave it back **377** to the Cossack. The Cossack replaced it in the sack, lowering it carefully so as not to bump it too hard on the floor.

'What do you do, Kamenev – do you say something when you show it round?' asked one of the officers.

'But I want to kiss him,' shouted Ivan Matveevich. 'He gave me a sword.'

Butler went out on to the porch. Marya Dmitrievna was sitting on the second step. She looked round at Butler and at once turned angrily away.

'What's the matter, Marya Dmitrievna?' Butler asked.

'You are just a lot of butchers. You make me sick. Butchers, that's what you are.'

'It can happen to anyone,' said Butler, not knowing what to say. 'That's war.'

'War!' cried Marya Dmitrievna. 'What's war? You are butchers, and that's all there is to it. A dead body should be decently buried and they make mock of it. Butchers, that's what you are!' she repeated and went down the steps and into the house by the back door.

Butler went back to the parlour and asked Kamenev to tell him in detail what had happened.

And Kamenev told him.

It happened like this.

25

Hadji Murat was allowed to go riding in the neighbourhood of the town provided that he went with a Cossack
escort. There was only one troop of Cossacks altogether
in Nukha; of these a dozen were detailed for staff duties
and if, according to orders, escorts of ten men were sent
out it meant that the remaining Cossacks had to do duty
every other day. Because of this, after the first day when
ten Cossacks were duly sent out, they decided to send only
five men, at the same time requesting Hadji Murat not to
take his whole party of *nukers*. However, on 25 April all
five of them accompanied Hadji Murat when he set off for
his ride. As Hadji Murat was mounting, the commandant **379**
noticed that all five *nukers* were preparing to go and told
Hadji Murat that he could not take them all, but Hadji
Murat, appearing not to hear, spurred his horse, and the
commandant did not insist. One of the Cossacks was a
corporal, Nazarov, who had the St George Cross,[75] a
young, healthy, fresh-faced fellow with light-brown hair
cut in a fringe. He was the oldest child of a poor family of
Old Believers;[76] he had grown up with no father and kept
his old mother, three sisters and two brothers.

'See he doesn't go too far, Nazarov,' shouted the
commandant.

'Very good, sir,' replied Nazarov. Then, rising in his
stirrups and steadying the rifle across his back, he set off
at a trot on his big, trusty, long-muzzled chestnut stallion.
The other four Cossacks followed him: Ferapontov, who
was lean and lanky, the troop's leading pilferer and fixer –
he it was who had sold powder to Gamzalo; Ignatov, who
was middle-aged and nearing the end of his service, a

healthy peasant type who boasted how strong he was; Mishkin, just a weedy boy, too young for active service, of whom everyone made fun; and Petrakov, young and fair-haired, his mother's only son, who was always amiable and cheerful.

It was misty first thing but by breakfast-time it was bright and fine with the sun shining on the freshly burst leaves, the young virginal grass, the shooting corn and the swift, rippling river on the left of the road.

Hadji Murat rode at a walk. The Cossacks and his *nukers* followed, keeping pace with him. Thus they rode out along the road behind the fort. On their way they met women carrying baskets on their heads, soldiers on waggons and creaking carts drawn by oxen. When they had gone a couple of miles Hadji Murat spurred his white Kabarda horse to a canter, and his *nukers* went into a quick trot. The Cossacks did the same.

'Ay, that's a good horse he's got,' said Ferapontov. 'I'd have him off it, if he was still a hostile like he used to be.'

'Yes, mate, three hundred roubles they offered for that horse in Tiflis.'

'But I'd beat him on mine,' said Nazarov.

'That's what you think!' said Ferapontov.

Hadji Murat continued to increase the pace.

'Hi there, *kunak,* you mustn't do that! Not so fast!' shouted Nazarov, going after Hadji Murat.

Hadji Murat looked back. He said nothing and went on without slackening pace.

'Watch out, those devils are up to something,' said Ignatov. 'Look how they're going!'

They rode like this towards the mountains for half a mile or so.

'Not so fast, I'm telling you,' Nazarov shouted again.

Hadji Murat did not answer or look back. He simply went faster and put his horse into a gallop.

'Don't think you'll get away,' shouted Nazarov, stung by this.

He gave his big chestnut stallion the whip and, standing in the stirrups and leaning forward, rode flat out after Hadji Murat.

The sky was so clear, the air so fresh, Nazarov felt so full of the joy of life as he flew along the road after Hadji Murat, merging into one with his powerful, trusty horse that the possibility of anything wrong or sad or terrible happening never even occurred to him. He was delighted that with every stride he was gaining on Hadji Murat and getting close to him. Hearing the hoofbeats of the Cossack's big horse getting nearer Hadji Murat realized that he would very soon catch up with him and, seizing his pistol with his right hand, used his left to steady his excited Kabarda which could hear the beat of hoofs behind.

'Not so fast, I say,' shouted Nazarov, now almost level with Hadji Murat and reaching out to seize the bridle of his horse. But before he could catch hold of it a shot rang out.

'What's going on?' cried Nazarov, grasping at his heart. 'Get them, lads!' he said as he swayed and fell forward over the pommel of his saddle.

But the mountain dwellers were quicker with their weapons than the Cossacks and fell on them with pistols firing and swords swinging. Nazarov hung on the neck of his terrified horse which carried him in circles round his comrades. Ignatov's horse fell and crushed his leg. Two of the mountain dwellers drew their swords and without dismounting hacked him across the head and arms. Petrakov dashed to his aid but before he could reach him was struck by two bullets, one in the back and one in the side, and he toppled from his horse like a sack.

Mishkin turned his horse back and galloped for the fort. Khanefi and Khan-Mahoma chased after him, but he had too good a start and the mountain dwellers could not overtake him.

Seeing they could not catch up with him Khanefi and Khan-Mahoma returned to their companions. Gamzalo despatched Ignatov with his dagger and pulled Nazarov down from his horse before slitting his throat too. Khan-Mahoma took off the dead men's cartridge pouches. Khanefi was going to take Nazarov's horse, but Hadji Murat shouted to him to leave it and set off down the road. His *murids* galloped after him, trying to drive off the horse of Petrakov which followed them. They were already in the rice fields two or three miles from Nukha when the alarm was sounded by a gunshot from the tower.

Petrakov lay on his back with his stomach slit open, his young face turned to the sky, gasping like a fish as he lay dying.

382 'Merciful heavens above, what have they done!' cried the commander of the fort, clasping his head as he listened to Mishkin's report and heard of Hadji Murat's escape. 'They've done for me! Letting him get away – the villains!'

A general alarm was raised. Every available Cossack was sent off in pursuit of the fugitives, and all the militia from the peaceable villages who could be mustered were called in as well. A thousand-rouble reward was offered to anyone bringing in Hadji Murat dead or alive. And two hours after Hadji Murat and his companions had ridden away from the Cossacks more than two hundred mounted men were galloping after the commissioner to seek out and capture the fugitives.

After travelling a few miles along the main road Hadji Murat pulled in his panting white horse, which was grey with sweat, and stopped. Off the road to the right were the houses and minaret of the village of Belardzhik, to the left were fields, on the far side of which was a river. Although the way to the mountains lay to the right Hadji Murat turned left in the opposite direction, reckoning that pursuers would be sure to head after him to the right. He meanwhile would make his way cross-country over the Alazan and pick up the highway again where no one expected him, take the road as far as the forest, then recrossing the river go on through the forest to the mountains. Having made this decision, he turned to the left. But it proved impossible to reach the river. The rice field which they had to cross had just been flooded, as happened every spring, and it was now a quagmire in which the horses sank up to their fetlocks. Hadji Murat and his *nukers* turned right and left, expecting to find a drier part, but the field they had struck on was evenly flooded and sodden all over. The horses dragged their feet from the sticky mud with a sound like popping corks and every few paces stopped, panting heavily.

They struggled on like this for so long that when dusk fell they had still not reached the river. To the left was a 383 small island with bushes in first leaf, and Hadji Murat decided to ride into the bushes and stay there till night, resting their exhausted horses.

When they were in the bushes Hadji Murat and his *nukers* dismounted, hobbled their horses and left them to graze. They themselves ate some of the bread and cheese they had brought with them. The new moon that had been shining sank behind the mountains and the night was dark. There was an unusual abundance of nightingales in Nukha; there were also two in these bushes. In the disturbance caused by Hadji Murat and his men as they rode into the bushes the nightingales fell silent, but as the human noises ceased the birds once more burst into song, calling and answering each other. Hadji Murat, straining his ears to the sounds of the night, listened involuntarily.

The singing of the nightingales reminded him of the song of Hamzad which he had heard the previous night when he went to get the water. Any time now he could find himself in the same situation as Hamzad. It struck him that it would indeed end like that and his mood suddenly became serious. He spread out his cloak and said his prayers. He had scarcely finished when sounds were heard coming towards the bushes. It was the sound of a large number of horses' feet trampling through the quagmire. The keen-eyed Khan-Mahoma ran to one edge of the bushes and in the darkness picked out the black shadows of men on foot and on horseback approaching the bushes. Khanefi saw another large group on the other side. It was Karganov,[77] the district commandant, with his militia.

We'll fight them as Hamzad did, thought Hadji Murat.

After the alarm was sounded Karganov had set off in hot pursuit of Hadji Murat with a squadron of militia and Cossacks, but he could find no sign of him or his tracks anywhere. Karganov had given up hope and was on his way back when towards evening they came upon an old Tatar. Karganov asked the old man if he had seen six horsemen. The old Tatar said he had. He had seen six horsemen riding to and fro across the rice field and then go into the bushes where he collected firewood. Taking the old man with him, Karganov had gone back along the road and, seeing the hobbled horses, knew for certain that Hadji Murat was there. So in the night he had the bushes surrounded and waited till morning to take Hadji Murat dead or alive.

Realizing that he was surrounded, Hadji Murat discovered an old ditch in the middle of the bushes where he decided to make his stand and fight as long as he had ammunition and strength to do so. He told his comrades and ordered them to raise a rampart along the ditch. His *nukers* at once began cutting off branches and digging earth with their daggers to make a bank. Hadji Murat joined in the work with them.

As soon as it began to get light the commander of the militia squadron rode up close to the bushes and called out:

384

'Hey there, Hadji Murat! Surrender! You're outnumbered!'

By way of reply there was a puff of smoke from the ditch, the crack of a rifle and a bullet struck the horse of one of the militiamen, which shied and fell. After this there was a rattle of fire from the rifles of the militia positioned on the edge of the bushes. Their bullets whistled and hummed, clipping the leaves and branches and landing in the rampart, but none of them hit the men behind. All they hit was Gamzalo's horse which had strayed off. It was wounded in the head but did not fall; snapping its hobble, it crashed through the bushes to the other horses, nestling against them and spilling its blood on the young grass. Hadji Murat and his men only fired when one of the militiamen showed himself and they seldom missed. Three militiamen were wounded and their comrades not only hesitated to charge Hadji Murat and his men, but dropped farther and farther back, firing only random shots at long range.

This went on for over an hour. The sun had risen halfway up the trees and Hadji Murat was just considering whether to mount and attempt a break for the river when the shouts of a fresh large force of men were heard. This was Hadji-Aha[78] of Mekhtuli and his men. There were about two hundred of them. At one time Hadji-Aha had been a *kunak* of Hadji Murat and lived with him in the mountains, but he had then gone over to the Russians. With him was Akhmet-Khan,[79] the son of Hadji Murat's enemy. Hadji-Aha began as Karganov had done by calling on Hadji Murat to surrender, but as on the first occasion Hadji Murat replied with a shot.

'Out swords and at them!' cried Hadji-Aha, snatching his own from its sheath, and there was a sound of hundreds of voices as men charged shrieking into the bushes.

The militiamen got among the bushes, but several shots in succession came cracking from the rampart. Three or four men fell and the attackers halted. They now opened fire from the edge of the bushes too. They fired and, running from bush to bush, gradually edged towards the rampart. Some managed to get across, while others fell to the bullets of Hadji Murat and his men. Hadji Murat never missed; Gamzalo's aim was no less sure and he gave a delighted yelp each time he saw his bullet strike home. Kurban sat by the edge of the ditch chanting '*La ilaha illa allah*'; he took his time in firing, but rarely got a hit. Meanwhile, Eldar was quivering all over in his impatience to rush the enemy with his dagger; he fired often and at random, continually looking round at Hadji Murat and showing himself above the rampart. The shaggy-haired Khanefi continued his role as servant even here. With rolled-up sleeves he reloaded the guns as they were handed to him by Hadji Murat and Kurban, carefully ramming home the bullets in oiled rags with an iron ramrod and priming the pans with dry powder from a horn. Khan-Mahoma did not keep to the ditch like the others, but kept running across to the horses to get them to a safer place, all the time shrieking and casually firing without resting his gun. He was the first to be wounded. He was struck by a bullet in the neck and collapsed backwards spitting blood and cursing. Hadji Murat was wounded next. A bullet went through his shoulder. He tore some wadding from his jacket to plug the wound and went on firing.

'Let's rush them with our swords,' urged Eldar for the third time. He rose above the rampart ready to charge the enemy, but was instantly struck by a bullet. He staggered and fell backwards across Hadji Murat's leg. Hadji Murat looked at him. His handsome sheep's eyes stared earnestly up at him. His mouth, with its upper lip pouting like a child's, quivered but did not open. Hadji Murat freed his leg and went on taking aim. Khanefi bent over Eldar's dead body and quickly began taking the unused cartridges from his *cherkeska*. Meanwhile Kurban went on chanting, slowly loading and taking aim.

The enemy, whooping and screeching as they ran from bush to bush, were getting nearer and nearer. Hadji Murat was hit by another bullet in the left side. He lay down in the ditch and plugged the wound with another piece of wadding from his jacket. This wound in his side was mortal and he felt that he was dying. One after another images and memories flashed through his mind. Now he saw the mighty Abununtsal-Khan clasping to his face his severed, hanging cheek and rushing at his enemies with dagger drawn; he saw Vorontsov, old, feeble and pale with his sly, white face and heard his soft voice; he saw his son Yusuf, Sofiat his wife, and the pale face, red beard and screwed up eyes of his enemy Shamil.

And these memories running through his mind evoked no feelings in him, no pity, ill will or desire of any kind. It all seemed so insignificant compared to what was now beginning and had already begun for him. But his powerful body meanwhile continued what it had started to do. Summoning the last remnants of his strength, he lifted himself above the rampart and fired his pistol at a man running towards him. He hit him and the man fell. Then he crawled completely out of the ditch and, with his dagger drawn and limping badly, went straight at the enemy. Several shots rang out. He staggered and fell. A number of militiamen rushed with a triumphant yell towards his fallen body. But what they supposed was a dead body suddenly stirred. First his bloodstained, shaven head, its *papakha* gone, then his body lifted; then, holding on to a tree, Hadji Murat pulled himself fully up. He looked so terrifying that the advancing men stopped dead. But suddenly he gave a shudder, staggered from the tree, and like a scythed thistle fell full length on his face and moved no more.

He did not move, but could still feel, and when Hadji-Aha, the first to reach him, struck him across the head with his great dagger, he felt he was being hit on the head with a hammer and failed to understand who was doing this and why. This was the last conscious link with his body. He felt no more, and the object that was trampled and slashed by his enemies had no longer any connection with him. Hadji-Aha put a foot on the body's back, with two strokes hacked off its head and rolled it carefully away with his foot so as not to get blood on his boots. Blood gushed over the grass, scarlet from the neck arteries, black from the head.

Karganov, Hadji-Aha, Akhmet-Khan and the militiamen gathered over the bodies of Hadji Murat and his men (Khanefi, Kurban and Gamzalo were bound) like hunters over a dead beast, standing among the bushes in the gunsmoke, gaily chatting and celebrating their victory.

The nightingales, which were silent while the shooting lasted, again burst into song, first one nearby, then others in the distance.

This was the death that was brought to my mind by the crushed thistle in the ploughed field.

Notes

The Cossacks

Historical Note

The name 'Cossack' (R. *kazak*) derives from the Turkic word *kazak*, meaning 'free person', and was originally applied to groups of semi-independent Tatars who lived in the region of the River Dnieper. It was later used to refer to runaway serfs from Poland, Lithuania and Muscovy who had fled to the regions of the Dnieper and the Don. The Cossacks were noted for their military prowess, and were granted special privileges by the Russian government in return for serving in the army. They were used as frontier guards, and also as an advance guard for the expansion of Russia's empire. While the Don Cossacks, like their Grebensk cousins, lived in the Caucasus, there were also Cossacks further to the east, in Siberia. Since the sixteenth century the Don Cossacks had a virtually independent province on the fertile steppes along the lower course of the River Don. Their principal town was Novocherkassk. They were governed by a popular council, the Rada, and an elected chief, the Ataman. Under Stenka Razin, who in 1667 led an uprising, their raids and exploits became the subject of legends and – later, in the nineteenth century – of literary works. Although their self-government was recognized by the Tsar, they engaged in frequent rebellions, culminating in that of Pugachev (1773). This resulted in the loss of many of their privileges.

1. *Amalat-Beks*: Amalet-Bek is the hero of the novella of the same name by the 'Byronic' Russian author, literary critic, poet, military hero and revolutionary Alexander Bestuzhev-Marlinsky (1797–1837), whose work was popular in the 1820s and 1830s.
2. *Circassian*: Native of Cherkessia (see note 13, below).
3. *Notre-Dame de Paris*: *The Hunchback of Notre Dame*, the novel of 1831 by Victor Hugo (1802–85).
4. *Don Cossacks*: See Historical Note, above.
5. *Nogay*: From the name of Khan Nogay, grandson of Genghis Khan. When the Cossacks began to settle on the Don in the

389

seventeenth century the Nogay of the northern Caucasus were separated from the Nogay in the south. The Nogay of the northern Caucasus were used by the Russian army in the fight with the Ottoman Empire in the Crimea.

6. *the line of the Terek*: The River Terek rises in the Caucasus, in Georgia, in the glaciers west of Mount Kazbek. It flows north through the Daryal gorge past Vladikavkaz, then east past Grozny and north-east into the Caspian Sea. The 'Line' referred to is the eastern section of the general Caucasus defence Line, which followed the course of the river.

7. *Abreks*: 'Abrek' was the Cossack name for north Caucasian (mostly Chechen) fighters who resisted the Russian military forces in small bands and groupings after the 'pacification' of the North Caucasus. See also Tolstoy's note on p. 34.

8. *pacified*: i.e. under Russian military control.

9. *Old Believers*: Christians who split from the Russian Orthodox Church in opposition to the Russian Church Reform introduced in 1653–66 by Patriarch Nikon, and use only the old liturgical books. They suffered periodic persecution both from Church and state and many took refuge by settling in outlying parts of the empire. See also note 20, below.

10. *removal of church bells*: The removal of bells from a church was a punishment given by the Russian authorities to dissident religious communities, such as the Old Believers.

11. *djigit*: In the Caucasus and Central Asia, a *djigit* is a member of the semi-feudal retinue of a prince, *bek, naib*, emir, khan, sultan, etc, serving his master in various capacities, both administrative and military. The *djigit* owns his own specially allocated horse, and is a rider of extremely high proficiency. The term *djigit* is in general usage as a term for a skilled horseman and fighter – somewhat similar to the American Indian 'brave'.

12. *shapovals*: Literally 'hat felters', people who made felt hats.

13. *Circassians*: A Muslim people, natives of Cherkessia, whose Russian name is *cherkes*, living in the area between the Black Sea, the Kuban River and the Caucasus.

14. *beshmet*: Among Turks, Tatars, Mongols and some Asiatic peoples, a sleeveless costume or upper garment made from light quilted material (usually silk or cotton).

15. *Circassian coat*: The Circassian national costume is the *cherkeska*, or 'Circassian coat' – a long, collarless, narrow-waisted garment made of strongly woven wool, with cloth cases attached to the part covering the chest in which rifle cartridges were kept. The costume is girded by a narrow leather belt, from which

the national dagger (*kinzhal*) is hung. A shirt, trousers and *besh-met* are worn under the coat, and over it the large semi-circular felt cloak, the *burka*, is worn. This costume became the national Caucasian dress. The *cherkeska* was adopted as standard wear by the Cossacks.

16. *sotnik*: A lieutenant in a Cossack *sotnya*, or 'hundred' (division of troops).
17. *'coins'*: Metal one-rouble coins.
18. *a pail of vodka*: a 'pail' (R. *vedro*) = one-fortieth of a barrel, twenty bottles or 12.3 litres.
19. *artels*: Specialized craft, trade and work groups.
20. *Schismatics*: *raskolniki* (separatists or apostates), also known as *starovery* (Old Believers) – see note 9, above.
21. *Kabarda horse*: A valuable local north Caucasus breed.
22. *Groznaya*: The fortress town located on the River Stunzha in Chechnya built by the Russian forces in 1818, subsequently (as Grozny) the capital of the region.
23. *Lafam!* [*La femme*]: The woman! (The translation follows Tol-stoy's crude phonetic transcription of Vanyusha's garbled French.)
24. *Kumyk*: A Caucasian people who speak a Turkic language and live mainly in the lowlands of north-eastern Daghestan.
25. *'La feel com say tray bya'* [*La fille comme c'est très bien*]: A girl like [that] is very good.
26. *la feel say tray jollee* [*la fille c'est très jolie*]: The girl is very pretty.
27. *Gurda sword*: A special type of ancient and prized sword named after the sword-smith who made them.
28. *Giaours*: From Turkish *giaur*, 'infidel', especially a Christian.
29. *shtof*: One-eighth or one-tenth of a *vedro*, or 'pail'.
30. *lovebreak-herb*: *Razryv-trava*, traditionally placed under the head of one's bed to stimulate prophetic dreams.
31. *'Doo tay voolay voo?'* [*Du thé voulez-vous?*]: Do you want some tea?
32. *'Larjong!'* [*L'argent*]: Money!
33. *the paternal wine*: *Roditel'skoye vino*, wine made from grapes.
34. *'choggled'*: The Russian verb in Tolstoy's text is an onomatopoeic invention – *tordoknut*.
35. *Cooper's Pathfinder*: The hero of the American James Fenimore Cooper's (1789–1851) novel *The Pathfinder* (1841). There are numerous echoes of the book in Tolstoy's narrative.
36. *godson*: Lukashka uses the Russian word *krestnik*, which, with its obviously Christian associations, cannot fail to sound ironic in this situation.
37. *Hundred*: A *sotnya* – see note 16, above, on *sotnik*.

38. *murid*: Here, mentor, adept or skilled guide – though in the context of Muridism the word means 'disciple' or 'follower'.
39. *Larjong eel nya pah* [*L'argent il n'y a pas*]: There ain't no money.
40. *the Order of St Anne*: A prestigious Russian military decoration. Also known as the St Anne Ribbon.
41. *sorochka*: The word's usual meaning is 'camisole', or 'nightdress'.
42. *'Say pray!'* [*C'est prêt*]: It's ready!
43. *'À la guerre, comme à la guerre'*: 'In war as in war' (i.e. 'You have to take things as they are').
44. *Les Trois Mousquetaires*: *The Three Musketeers*, the popular historical novel (1844) by Alexandre Dumas the elder (1802–70).
45. *dignité*: Dignity, bearing.
46. *a pumpkin balalaika*: The instrument was made from a long, narrow and inedible pumpkin – *travyanka* – from which bowls and other vessels were commonly made.
47. *Yermolov*: General A. P. Yermolov (1772–1861). As commander of the Russian army in the Caucasus between 1816 and 1827, his name was a byword for cruelty.
48. *'Ana seni!'*: A particularly violent oath.
49. *'La feel!'* [*La fille*]: The girl!

392

Hadji Murat

Historical Note

Wars with Turkey and Persia in the eighteenth century had drawn Russia into the Caucasus. Gradually a line of forts and Cossack outposts was established along the northern boundary of the Caucasus as a shield against invasion and a base for expansion southwards. With the absorption of Georgia (south of the main Caucasus range) into the Russian Empire in 1800, the Russians set about the conquest of the remainder of the Caucasian isthmus. It was no easy task: the terrain was difficult and they faced stiff resistance from the local tribes, who were fiercely independent, warlike and skilled in the raiding and harassing tactics suited to the country.

The policy of subjugation was first vigorously pursued by General Yermolov, who was commander-in-chief in the Caucasus from 1816 to 1826. His destructive campaigns extended Russia's control of territory, but at the same time united the otherwise factious tribes in opposition to the invader. This union was reinforced by their common Muslim faith, which was then undergoing a revival with the spread of Muridism – a movement directed towards personal spiritual perfection, in which a *murid* ('one who desires') subjected himself to the discipline and instruction of a *murshid* ('one who shows'). In the context of an infidel invasion of Muslim lands Muridism readily took on a political significance, and a call for holy war (*ghazavat*) against the Russians was given in the 1820s by the Imam Kazi-Mullah (killed fighting the Russians in 1832), and then by his successors as Imam: Hamzad (killed by Hadji Murat in 1834) and Shamil, the most skilful and formidable of all Caucasian leaders. The Murid War ended only with Shamil's defeat in 1859.

The base for Russian operations in the Caucasus was the so-called 'Line', a chain of forts and Cossack stations stretching from the Black Sea to the Caspian along the River Kuban in the west and the River Terek in the east. The Line was divided into two commands, the western 'Right Flank' and the eastern 'Left Flank': it was on the Left Flank facing Chechnya and Daghestan that the events described in *Hadji Murat* took place.

1. *naib of Shamil*: Shamil was, like Hadji Murat, an Avar. He was born around 1798 and after rigorous spiritual and martial training became Imam of Daghestan in 1834. He succeeded in uniting most of the Caucasian tribes in holy war against the Russians and for twenty-five years engaged Russia in a bitter and costly struggle for control of the Caucasus. He was finally defeated and captured in 1859. In captivity he was well treated by the Russians and resided in honourable exile in Kaluga, south of Moscow. In March 1870 he was permitted to go to Mecca, where he died in 1871. After his break with the Russians in 1840, Hadji Murat had been appointed by Shamil *naib* (governor) of his home territory of Avaria in Daghestan.

2. *Vedeno*: A village in the mountains of southern Chechnya, which became Shamil's base after he was displaced from Dargo in 1845.

3. *beaten the Russian pigs*: During his years as a supporter of Shamil, Hadji Murat gained renown for his many successful actions against the Russians – fighting, raiding and stock-thieving.

4. *the prince Vorontsov*: Prince S. M. Vorontsov (1823–82), the son of the Viceroy of the Caucasus, Field Marshal Prince M. S. Vorontsov (see note 23), was then colonel commanding the Kura Chasseur Regiment.

5. *Gekhi*: A village in Chechnya, home of Hadji Murat's mother-in-law. From there he had intended to make his move into Russian-controlled territory, but found it occupied by Shamil's men.

393

6. *Vozdvizhenskaya*: A fort in the advanced line south of Groznaya and base of the regiment commanded by Vorontsov.

7. *in place of my brother*: In the periodic conscriptions to the Russian army it was possible for a conscript to gain exemption if a substitute was provided.

8. *Poltoratsky*: In fact, a real person – V. A. Poltoratsky (1828–89), who served in the Caucasus from 1846 to 1854, before being wounded and retiring from the army (he later returned to military service and became a major general). His memoirs, published in 1893, were an important source for Tolstoy, in particular for the details of Hadji Murat's reception by the younger Vorontsov and the account of Kozlovsky's farewell dinner. Poltoratsky also refers in his memoirs to his admiration of Marya Vasilevna.

9. *with an English accent*: The Vorontsovs had close associations with England. Vorontsov's grandfather was the Russian ambassador in London, 1784–1800, and his father, the Viceroy, had grown up there.

10. *'Eh bien, vous allez me dire ce que c'est' . . . 'Vous?'*: 'Well, are you going to tell me what it is all about?' – 'But, my dear . . .' – 'Don't "my dear" me! It was an envoy, wasn't it?' – 'I still can't tell you.' – 'You can't? – Then I'll tell you what it was myself!' – 'You?'

11. *'La ilaha'*: The opening phrase of the Muslim creed *La ilaha illa allah* – 'There is no God but God . . .'.

12. *Corps of Pages*: A select military training school, admission to which was restricted to the sons of higher officials.

13. *General Sleptsov*: General N. P. Sleptsov (1815–51), commander of the Sunzha Cossack Regiment, was killed in action in December 1851.

14. *Kabarda horse*: Kabarda in the northern Caucasus was a celebrated area for horse-breeding.

15. *General Meller-Zakomelsky*: Baron P. P. Meller-Zakomelsky (1806–69) was commander of the garrison at Vozdvizhenskoe and so Vorontsov's superior. His clash with the Viceroy's son resulted in his transfer to another post and ended his service in the Caucasus.

16. *(whom she called Bulka)*: 'Bulka' (bun) was the child of her first marriage, born in 1843.

17. *General Kozlovsky*: General V. M. Kozlovsky (1796–1873) was acting commander of the Left Flank of the Caucasian Line, 1850–51.

18. *'C'est un objet . . . de lui faire cadeau'*: 'It's very valuable.' – 'We must find an opportunity to make him a present, too.'

19. *Bréguet watch*: Bréguet watches (and clocks) produced in the workshops founded by the distinguished French horologist A.-L. Bréguet (1747–1823) were renowned for their quality.

20. *'Voilà l'occasion. Donnez lui la montre'*: 'Here is an opportunity. Give him the watch.'

21. *'Vous feriez beaucoup . . . madame la générale'*: 'It would be much better if you stayed at home. It is my affair, not yours.' – 'You cannot stop me going to see the general's wife.'

22. *White Tsar*: The title 'White Tsar' for the Tsar of Russia originated with the Tatars, for whom 'white' was a designation of 'west'.

23. *Prince Mikhail Vorontsov*: Field Marshal Prince M. S. Vorontsov (1782–1856) was a distinguished soldier and administrator, well characterized here by Tolstoy. In 1823 he was appointed Governor-General of 'New Russia' (the territory of the southern Ukraine north of the Black Sea and the Sea of Azov), and in 1844 Viceroy of the Caucasus.

24. *Manana Orbeliani*: The Orbelianis were a leading family of the Georgian aristocracy. Manana, a noted beauty, played a prominent part in Tiflis society in the 1850s.

25. *Countess Choiseul*: The Russian wife of the French Count Choiseul-Gouffier, who was adjutant to Prince Vorontsov.

26. *Dr Andreevsky*: Dr E. S. Andreevsky (1809–1872) was a member of the Caucasian military medical establishment and personal physician to Prince Vorontsov.

27. *'Excellentes, chère amie . . . Simon a eu de la chance'*: 'Excellent, my dear . . . Simon has had a stroke of good fortune.'

28. *Gergebil*: A town and fortress in Daghestan, which more than once changed hands between the Russians and Shamil's forces in the 1840s. General D. V. Passek (1808–45) played a prominent part in the operations against Shamil and was killed in action during the Dargo expedition (see note 30, below).

29. *killed Colonel Zolotukhin*: Colonel Zolotukhin was killed by Hadji Murat in hand-to-hand fighting at Ozen in 1851.

30. *'Hard Tack' expedition*: During the campaign conducted by Vorontsov in 1845 Russian troops occupied Shamil's stronghold of Dargo, but were virtually cut off in hostile territory. One episode in the campaign was the despatch of troops from Dargo to escort a column bringing much-needed supplies – this was the 'Hard Tack' expedition, in which both the supply train and the escorting troops suffered heavy losses.

31. *Akhmet-Khan*: An old enemy of Hadji Murat, whose scores against him included the murder of three of his cousins. The abduction of his widow took place in 1846.

32. *'Quelle horreur!'*: 'How frightful!'
33. *'Á la guerre comme à la guerre'*: 'War is war.'
34. *Murat*: Marshal Joachim Murat (1767–1815) gained fame as a cavalry commander in the campaigns of Napoleon, who made him King of Naples.
35. *Tous cela au grâce de vous'*: 'It's all thanks to you.'
36. *'Il a eu ... Simon a eu tort'*: 'He has had a contretemps with the local commander. Simon was in the wrong.'
37. *General Klugenau*: General F. K. Kluki von Klugenau (1791–1851), the Russian commander in Daghestan in the 1840s, had at one time negotiated with Hadji Murat in an attempt to win him to the Russian side.
38. *Prince Tarkhanov*: In 1851 Lieutenant Colonel K. Tarkhanov was military commander of the Shusha district.
39. *Lezghian Line*: A line of Russian forts in the eastern Caucasus along the border of Daghestan and Georgia.
40. *Loris-Melikov*: M. T. Loris-Melikov (1825–88) was of Armenian origin. He subsequently became a general and, in the late 1870s, a prominent political figure, first as head of the Supreme Executive Committee set up to combat revolutionary terrorism and then in 1880–81 as Minister of the Interior.

41. *'. . . the Prince will send it to the Tsar'*: The account of Hadji Murat's life narrated to Loris-Melikov was published in 1881 and was a prime source for the description of their interview given in this chapter and chapter 13. The narrative explains clearly enough the background to Hadji Murat's situation.
42. *Khunzakh*: The seat of the Avar khanate.
43. *... until Kazi-Mullah was killed and Hamzad took his place*: Kazi-Mullah was the Imam who first declared the holy war against the Russians. He was killed fighting in 1832 and was succeeded by Hamzad, who was killed by Hadji Murat and his brother Osman in 1834.
44. *Rosen*: General Baron G. V. von Rosen (1782–1841) was commander-in-chief in the Caucasus, 1831–6.
45. *shaved of their whiskers ... hung to their noses*: These details are included in Hadji Murat's account of events given to Loris-Melikov. In a letter of 1975 to the translator M. B. Khadzhi-Muradov (Hadji Murat's great-grandson) explained that a man was dishonoured by the shaving of his whiskers; appending food to the pierced nostrils was a punishment for greedy or mercenary individuals, though this was not, in his view, a usual practice among the Caucasian mountain tribes.

NOTES

46. *Mansur*: An early leader of resistance to Russia's advance into the Caucasus, who called on the tribes to make common cause against the infidel invaders. He died in Russian captivity in 1794.

47. *giaour*: See *The Cossacks*, note 28.

48. *Chernyshev, the Minister of War*: Prince A. I. Chernyshev (1785–1857) was Minister of War, 1827–52.

49. *Groznaya*: See *The Cossacks*, note 22.

50. *General Zavodovsky*: General N. S. Zavodovsky (1788–1853) was in overall command of the Caucasian Line, 1845–53.

51. *Zakhar Chernyshev*: Z. G. Chernyshev (1796–1862) was a relative of the War Minister. For his involvement in the 'Decembrist' rising in favour of constitutional reform at the time of Nicholas I's accession in 1825 he was exiled and A. I. Chernyshev attempted to acquire his rights of inheritance.

52. *Prince Dolgoruky*: Prince A. I. Dolgoruky (1804–68) was Deputy Minister of War, 1848–53.

53. *'Sa Majeste vient de rentrer'*: 'His Majesty has just returned.'

54. *The Winter Palace . . . fire*: Much of the interior of the Winter Palace had been destroyed by fire in 1837.

55. *Nelidova*: Varvara Arkadevna Nelidova (1814–97) was a lady-in-waiting at the court. Her relationship with the Tsar was common knowledge.

56. *King of Prussia*: Nicholas I's wife Alexandra was the sister of Friedrich-Wilhelm IV.

57. *Grand-duchess Yelena Pavlovna*: Yelena Pavlovna (1806–73), daughter of Prince Paul of Württemburg, was the widow of the Tsar's brother Mikhail. An intelligent and cultured woman, she was well known as a patron of the arts and charitable causes.

58. *1848*: In 1848, 'the year of Revolutions', Friedrich-Wilhelm IV approved a revision of the constitution and the summoning of a Parliament – which he dissolved the same year.

59. *Yermolov and Velyaminov*: General A. P. Yermolov (1772–1861) commanded the Russian army in Georgia from 1816 and initiated the policy described for the subjugation of the northern Caucasus. It was continued by his successor, General A. A. Velyaminov (1785–1838), who became commander of the Caucasian Line in 1831.

60. *Poles*: Nicholas I had brutally suppressed the Polish insurrection against Russian rule in 1830–31.

61. *Bibikov*: General D. G. Bibikov (1788–1870) was Governor-General of the Western Provinces (Kiev, Volynya and Podolia), 1837–52. Much of the population of this area of the western Ukraine belonged to the Uniate Church, which used the

Russian Orthodox liturgy, but recognized the Pope as the head of the Church. Under Nicholas I there was a policy of forced conversion of the Uniates to Orthodoxy.

62. *Volkonsky*: Field Marshal Prince P. M. Volkonsky was Minister of the Court, 1826–52.

63. *Baron Liven*: Baron V. K. Liven (1800–1880) was at the time an *aide-de-camp* to the Tsar.

64. *Count Rzhevussky*: General A. A. Rzhevussky (1801–88), a member of the Tsar's suite.

65. *'La Pologne ... de ces pays' ... 'Oui, oui ... laissé l'embarras'*: 'Poland and the Caucasus are the two running sores of Russia ... We have to keep almost one hundred thousand men in each of these countries.' – 'You say Poland.' – 'Yes, indeed, it was a master stroke on Metternich's part to encumber us with ...' – presumably a reference to Metternich's role at the Congress of Vienna in 1815 when the Congress Kingdom of Poland was allotted to Russia (in fact, a smaller fraction of Polish territory than Russia had hoped to gain).

66. *... sharpshooters in high boots ... crossed their way*: Columns advancing along the stretches of cleared forest were protected on either side by riflemen who had to make their way over the transverse spurs and gullies that lined the cleared route.

67. *Mashka ... Marya Dmitrievna*: The common familiar form of the name Marya is Masha; Mashka takes familiarity a stage further and can be pejorative if applied to a grown-up. The change from Mashka to Marya Dmitrievna here indicates a change in the level of respect with which she was regarded.

68. *Karabakh*: A sturdy breed of horses from the Karabakh Mountains in the southern Caucasus.

69. *Kist girl*: The Kist were a small tribe related to the Avars.

70. *in 1840*: It was in 1840 that the Chechens, previously 'peaceable', made common cause with Shamil against the Russians, who, according to Shamil's propaganda, wished to turn them into peasants and recruit them into the army.

71. *gurda*: A blade of the highest quality made by the Caucasian swordsmith Gurda.

72. *Baryatinsky*: General Prince A. I. Baryatinsky (1815–79) was commander of the Left Flank of the Line, 1851–3. In 1856 he was appointed Viceroy of the Caucasus and ended the conquest of the region by the defeat and capture of Shamil in 1859.

73. *General Argutinsky*: General Prince M. Z. Argutinsky (1797–1855) was the commander of Russian forces in southern Daghestan.

74. *Nukha*: A town on the southern slopes of the Caucasus a hundred miles east of Tiflis.

75. *St George Cross*: A military decoration awarded for gallantry.

76. *Old Believers*: See *The Cossacks*, note 9.

77. *Karganov*: Lieutenant Colonel Karganov was military commander of the Nukha district.

78. *Hadji-Aha*: Hadji-Aha was in Russian service with the rank of captain.

79. *Akhmet-Khan*: Akhmet-Khan served as cornet in a Cossack regiment; for his father, 'Hadji Murat's enemy', see Hadji Murat's narrative to Loris-Melikov, p. 307.